Scotch & Dreams

Scotch Series: Book Two

August Lindsay

August Lindsay

Published by August Lindsay Publishing

First Edition 2025

Book cover design by Ana Arias

Library and Archives Canada Cataloguing in Publication

August Lindsay

Scotch & Shortbread/ August Lindsay.

Contents

Chapter 1

Oh Fuck

SHE HAD ZERO RECOLLECTION of how she got here, how long she'd been here, or even where she was. Deep blue eyes were intense on hers. Concerned. Intimate. Caring. They weren't familiar eyes, but in her haze of confusion, those eyes brought her an unexpected yet solid sense of comfort.

"How are ye feelin'?" The man spoke slowly, gently. His burr was deep, rich, and as warm as honey on her fractured thoughts.

"I-I don't know. My head hurts," she said in a voice that didn't feel like her own as she touched her swelling forehead. She felt strange. Her thinking was muddled. It was odd. She was certain she didn't know the man who was kneeling inches from her, but he felt safe somehow. Not lock-your-doors safe, but fall-into-my-arms-and-I-will-catch-you safe.

Panic was lurking around the outer edges of her mind, ready to choke her, but his touch, his voice, and his presence were helping to pull her from its sticky grip. Strong hands gently but firmly held her shoulders. Deep blue eyes anchored onto hers and wouldn't let her go. Later, she would recall the strange intimacy of it, but at the moment, everything felt off, unfamiliar, fleeting.

"What's yer name, lass?" His voice was a salve on her battered mind.

"Violet Munro." The name tumbled out without any preamble. When she tried to retrieve thoughts, they seemed to flit around like uncatchable fireflies. She was certain of her name, but how or why she was certain of it felt like a complete mystery at this moment. It was just there. Her name was clear and rose to the surface all by itself. A moment's relief seeped into her.

"Verra good." He smiled at her with the warmth of an embrace.

She found him mesmerizing. This stranger. Finding an escape from her jumbled thoughts, she let herself fixate on the details of his features. He was a magnet for her mind, visceral, Technicolor in her haze of grey confusion.

Studying him brought a desperate focus to the heap of disarray in her brain. His white button-down shirt was crisp with dark pinstripes, and there was a sharpness to his navy blazer. The way the golden skin of his neck looked in contrast to the white of his shirt. His straight nose ended in a slight flare to his nostrils. Blue eyes so deep they tugged at her very soul. And his smile with its slight crookedness, perfectly imperfect. She felt a sudden wild urge to press her lips to his to see what it would feel like to be kissed by such a contradictory mouth.

Her senses felt heightened in some ways, so aware yet so out of sorts. Bewildered as she felt, one thing was crystal clear: this man was an angel in the ashes. The kind of man every woman's fairy tale heart yearns for. The strong hero who could love her to the furthest reaches of her soul. He was warmth, comfort, and sexiness. Violet concluded, as she stared into his otherworldly eyes, that she had to be dreaming. Her world was as solid as a puff of smoke but for him.

"Do ye ken where ye are, Violet?"

She made the mistake of breaking eye contact to view her surroundings. A beach, the sea's waves washing gently onto the shore. The air was mild. Long tufts of grass grew at the back side of the sand. She could see a pier all lit up with fairground lights in the distance and a smaller wooden pier directly in front of them. The sun was setting, casting a pinky-purple hue.

Violet looked down beside her and noticed that she was sitting on the long grass. She ran her fingers through the dry blades. Hot tears pricked her eyes. *I'm on a beach*, she thought to herself. *But I don't have the slightest idea how I got here. Oh fuck.*

The dream man gently wiped away a tear that rolled down her cheek. She leaned her face into the palm of his hand. She desperately sought the comfort he so freely gave.

"I-I don't know where I am." She swallowed, trying to hold back the fear that threatened to drown her. "I don't recognize any of it." She looked at his handsome features, searching for something, but she didn't know what. She was lost. "How did I get here?" Quiet tears spilled down her face as she grappled with the understanding that she couldn't remember anything. She shivered, maybe from cold. Maybe from shock? It didn't matter.

"It's going to be okay, lass," he murmured as he slipped off his blazer and wrapped it around her shoulders.

His strong, comforting arms wrapped around her, and she melted against him, still unable to quell the shivering that racked her body.

Chapter 2

Catch of the Day

THIS WASN'T LACHLAN'S USUAL beach, but he knew it well. He lived close by, up the winding hill and along the shore, maybe ten kilometres away. There was a quieter, more idyllic beach closer to his home. He preferred that one over this beach right in the middle of town. It was typically busier here, more touristy.

He came into town this evening for a business meeting with a potential client. Most of the trendy restaurants were along this strip. It was always a perfect location for business dinners. The meeting went well, and he was pleased. He'd worked hard and earned a solid reputation in the industry. Nowadays, securing new clients came rather easily. As he left the restaurant, he was thoughtful about his success. He appreciated how far the business had come.

Lachlan noticed the waterfront was unusually quiet. Surprising as it was a rather warm March day. The salty sea air drew him in as it always had since he was a small boy. He'd lived by the sea all his life, and it never got old. He decided to sit and watch the sunset before heading home.

The beach was virtually deserted, but then *she* came along. A lone jogger with her golden blond hair up in a messy bun, she wore typical running wear, a sleeveless top, calf-length stretch pants, and trainers. Lachlan sat back on the grass and watched her as she slowed her pace and took in the view. It was one of his favourites when it was quiet like this. The old wooden pier stretched out into the breathing sea.

He found himself strangely captivated as she walked onto the pier and out toward the sea. He knew all too well how salubrious it was. You could see the water below you between the cracks of the pier, making you feel almost like you were literally walking on water. The rest of the world, the busy, the stress, all of it could wash away. It was mesmerizing watching her, as if he could feel her reaction to the effect of the gentle waves and the setting sun.

The serenity of the moment came to an abrupt halt. Lachlan watched, horrified, as if in slow motion, but so fast he was powerless to do anything. A familiar, brief fear tangled in his gut as a helpless memory splintered through his mind. *No.*

She must have caught her foot on an old board because the next thing he saw was her body propelling forward. And as she went down, her head caught on one of the long wood benches that stretched down the sides of the pier. Her neck snapped back in an odious fashion that had Lachlan springing to his feet and racing toward her. His worst fears threatened him. By the time he reached her, she'd recovered enough to sit up, and he felt an instant palpable sense of relief.

"Ye okay, lass?" he asked breathlessly, more from panic than the run. He squatted down beside her. She looked up at him with a soft smile, taking him off guard. She was captivating up close.

A light chuckle escaped her. "Oh, yes, thank you. I'm not sure how I ended up here." She looked puzzled as she gingerly stood up.

Lachlan reached out to steady her.

She swayed and grabbed onto his forearms. "Just a little dizzy, I guess." She tried to smile, but her brows pinched together. He couldn't tell if it was from pain or confusion, but it troubled him.

"Can I help ye get somewhere?" He asked, feeling a growing concern for the lass. She was already stepping back toward the beach with a hand to her head. He noticed her unsteady gate with each wobbly step. "Are ye sure ye should be walking? Maybe ye should sit for a minute or two?" He walked alongside her, wishing he knew how to help, his worry deepening as her balance faltered.

She abruptly stopped and looked at him, and this time, there was no doubt. Her expression was one of utter confusion. And in the next instant, she tumbled toward him. He caught her with ease, but his worst fears coursed through him.

"Lass? Hello?" Lachlan tried to get a response, but she was completely limp in his arms and didn't make a sound. "Shite," he bit out, feeling dread coil in his belly.

Without a thought, he scooped her up and carried her off the pier to the grassy reeds at the edge of the beach. He gently laid her down. She was breathing but still out cold. With shaking hands, he pulled out his mobile and called for help.

To his relief, she regained consciousness while he was on the phone. Hanging up with the emergency dispatcher, he focused his attention back to the lass. Not giving a thought to his Armani suit, he knelt in the grassy sand in front of her, and she moved to sit up.

"Easy, lass," he said, gently helping her to sit.

She grasped her bare arms around her bent knees, and her mossy green eyes landed on his. He smiled lightly. The bewilderment he sensed in her broke his heart, but God, the way her eyes clung to him like he was a lighthouse in a storm. It shook him.

Chapter 3
Find a Friend

VIOLET AWOKE TO A nurse putting a blood pressure cuff on her arm. She felt groggy and tired. Her head throbbed. She eyed the dimly lit room and then promptly drifted back into a deep sleep.

When she next awoke, the morning light shone through the drawn-back curtains of the hospital room window. It felt like a slice of heaven streaking its warmth through the sterilization of the room. Violet let her eyes close again as she took a mental inventory of her situation.

A dull ache was still present in her head. Thoughts of the day before peppered her mind. She distinctly remembered *not* remembering. It sent a chill down her spine.

"Oh my God." Her eyes snapped open, her voice a barely audible whisper. Bursts of memory started to go off in her head like a succession of fireworks. In her mind's eye, she could see her Airbnb. Sitting on the edge of the bed. The worn dark green carpet with the small gold diamond patterning. Putting on her blue runners. Going to the bathroom sink. The white tiles and the one with a chip to the left of the sink. Gulping down water.

Events of the day before were percolating in her mind. It was a slow trickle, one memory at a time, but indeed, she was remembering. Relief washed over her, and she couldn't help but try and recall every detail of the day before.

"Good morning, Violet." A clean-cut man with salt-and-pepper hair walked into the room.

Violet looked at him, and with surprisingly little effort, she remembered him.

"You're the doctor," she stated.

"Aye, Dr. Campbell. Yer memory is returning?" he asked, studying her from under bushy dark brows.

"Yes, it all seems to be coming back to me. Am I okay? I mean, will I be okay?"

"Aye, I'd say the prognosis is good." He smiled reassuringly. "You hit your head rather hard, but fortunately, all the scans were normal." He came over to stand beside the bed. "May I?" he asked before lifting her hair away from her forehead. He pressed gently but firmly around her bruised head.

Violet winced, feeling a stab.

"Ye have bruising that will likely get worse before it gets better, but I'm pleased that the swelling has already improved substantially. You're very lucky," he said, stepping back. "Any nausea?"

"No, just a bit of a headache." She gestured to her bruised head.

"And you said your memories are coming back?"

"Yes, in a flurry. It's so odd. It's like they didn't exist at all—but now they're coming back to me, ultra vivid."

The doctor nodded as he scribbled some notes, presumably on her chart. "Ye've suffered a concussion and with it some post-traumatic amnesia."

Violet's eyes went wide.

"Nothin' to worry about," he assured her. "Ye are remembering now, and that is a very good sign. Ye should make a full recovery in no time."

She let out a sigh of relief. "Does that mean I can go home then?" She looked at him hopefully, knotting her fingers in the starchy bedsheet.

"Aye, I think ye are well enough to leave. However, I would like someone to stay with you for the next twenty-four hours. Ye shouldnae be alone."

Not the news Violet wanted to hear. She'd only just arrived in Scotland and didn't know anyone. Who could she get to stay with her? She bit her lip worriedly. "Why do I need someone with me? My memories are coming back, and I feel way better."

"Aye, and that's excellent." Dr. Campbell slid his pen into his chest pocket. "However, with a concussion, complications can sometimes arise a day or two later. It is best if someone is with ye to keep an eye out."

"Well, if something happens, I can just come back here."

He seemed resolute, but Violet wasn't going to give up so easily.

Dr. Campbell smiled kindly at her, his jowls lifting, "It's important, Violet. It is rare, but seizures can occur after a bang to the head like yers. Usually, if they are going to occur, it happens at night. Ye were fine last night, but either ye stay here another night or ye promise me to have someone stay the night to watch ye," he said, with a finality that she couldn't argue with.

With Violet's promise, Dr. Campbell signed her release papers and told her she was free to go but that she should take it easy over the next day or two.

After such an ordeal, Violet couldn't wait to get out of the hospital and into the fresh highland air. She felt weak, and her head ached. But she also felt almost a new lease on life, kind of feel. It certainly fortified her belief to live every moment to the fullest.

Now the only problem was who was she going to get to stay with her. The lady she was renting the Airbnb from was offsite, and they hadn't even met in person. She considered texting her, though. In their interactions to date, she seemed nice and easygoing. Violet crossed her arms over her chest, realizing that she didn't feel comfortable asking her Airbnb lady to come babysit her. Maybe she could find an all-night café or something. She bit her lip. Oh, this was maddening.

When she wasn't racking her brain trying to think of who she could get to stay with her, Violet's memories were still flooding her mind. She walked over to the wardrobe in her room and opened the door. Her black stretch running capris and bright peach tank hung neatly on wire hangers. Her black underwear was draped carefully over a third hanger, and her black sports bra hung on a fourth. Slowly, she recalled the nurse telling her the night before, *Lassie, I've hung your clothes up in the airing cupboard. They're a wee bit damp.*

Violet reached up and touched her bra. Dry. She pulled it down and got dressed, silently thanking the thoughtful nurse. She was so happy she was okay and getting out of the hospital that she didn't even care that she had to put her dried-up, sweaty jogging clothes back on. Getting dressed knocked the stuffing right out of her.

As she pulled her hair up into a messy bun and plonked herself back on the bed, she closed her eyes and took some deep breaths. She needed a few minutes to recover. The knock at the door made her jump, and when she opened her eyes, there he was.

Chapter 4

The Other Woman

WHAT A CRAZY EVENING. Lachlan sat on the edge of his bed, elbows on his knees, fist in fist under his chin, and he just stared blankly with the events of the past couple of hours replaying in his mind. He wondered if he could have done more to help the lass. It all happened so quickly. What could he have done to prevent it? He couldn't have known it would happen, but it still felt like he should've been able to do more. It was not the first time in his life that the what-ifs had haunted him. He ran his hand through his hair, tension still filled him. It was all too similar to a life-changing event of his past. Those memories felt eerily fresh.

When the ambulance arrived tonight, Lachlan told the two medics all he knew, which wasn't much. The pair, one younger woman with tattoos and a lanky middle-aged man, took charge with practiced efficiency. As relieved as Lachlan felt knowing they were taking good care of the lass, he didn't like how quickly he felt as useless as the grass she sat upon. And then, before he knew it, the male medic told him they were taking her, and Lachlan realized that was apparently his cue that he could leave now, too. The ambulance crew had taken over, and he was no longer needed. As they whisked her off to the hospital, Lachlan had stood there for a time, wondering if he should follow them. Everything felt very undone.

Lachlan thought about the way Violet Munro had looked at him. Her deep moss-green eyes were so confused and lost. She looked into his eyes as if he were her only lifeline. It made him think, even now, that he should go to the hospital, be there for her. He felt inexplicably connected to her.

His phone dinged. He glanced down at it and raked his hand through his hair, blowing out a breath before opening the text.

Anna: Still hate France. It is nice to see Liz happy, though. Not so keen on her friends from New York, but I suppose I'll have to suffer through. Only a couple of days, thank God. How was your meeting? Did you land another client?

Lachlan stared blankly at his phone for what seemed like an eternity. He didn't feel like talking with Anna right now, but he supposed he should message her back.

Lachlan: *Maybe it'll get better. Glad Liz is happy. Meeting went well. Client landed. Night x*

Lachlan hit send, feeling exhausted. A moment later, his phone dinged again.

Anna: When I get back, we should go out and celebrate! You should book a reservation at Skye's. We can get dressed up and go all out, champagne, all the courses! Ooh maybe you could rent a limo too, really top off the night.

The last thing Lachlan wanted to think about right now was making arrangements for a limo and a Michelin-starred restaurant. It was not that he was opposed to taking his girlfriend out for a special evening, but his mind was completely preoccupied with things much more important than a night on the town.

Lachlan: We'll sort something out when you're back. Have a lovely time, say hi to Liz. I'm off to bed. Early morning for me x

Lachlan dropped his phone on the bed and strode into the bathroom to wash up. When he came back, his phone was lit up with messages from Anna.

Anna: I think we need that night out. Definitely look into getting it booked for us.

Anna: Skye's has long wait lists, so you need to reserve ASAP.

Anna: A spa day would be great too!

Anna: I'm going to need pampering after this hen weekend. These women are crazy, and I'll need to detox France from my system when I'm back. How people think French is a beautiful language, I'll never know. It's horrible. Can't wait to get back to the UK.

Anna: Biggg kiss, good night xxx

Anna: Ps. hope you are thinking about that thing we talked about ... xxx

Reading Anna's texts made Lachlan feel even more exhausted. He definitely was not thinking about *the thing*. He had no desire to think about it. That morning, Lachlan had driven Anna to the train station—it felt like a lifetime ago now. She was headed to Marseille in France for her best friend's hen do. She'd kissed him in the car before getting out and hinted again about her moving in with him. He'd smiled at her at the time, but he couldn't deny the uneasiness he'd felt.

As soon as he drove away from the train station, a lightness seeped into his mood. He felt free and was content not questioning it. He had been pleased at the prospect of a few days to himself, but he hadn't realized just how good it would feel. All day, he felt energized like the hit of a coffee on a sunny Saturday morning. He had purposely avoided analyzing why and instead soaked in how good he felt. But now, as he sat here reading Anna's texts, it forced him back to a reality he wasn't sure he wanted anymore.

Lachlan rubbed his temples. God, it had been a crazy evening, and he felt exhausted. Now was not the time to start contemplating things with Anna.

Turning off the nightstand light, Lachlan lay back in bed with a groan, feeling his body sink into the mattress. He pulled in a deep breath and released it. His thoughts settled back on Violet Munro.

It bothered him how confused she had been. He couldn't help but think the worst. What if she'd injured her brain? What if her memory didn't return? He rolled over, trying to clear his worrisome thoughts. Fretting about it was not going to help her. Lachlan eventually drifted off to sleep, but the night was restless, with disjointed dreams, tossing, and turning. Dreams of the past intermingled with snippets of the evening. It felt like he'd barely slept, and then it was morning.

Opening his eyes, Lachlan's first thought was of the lass. He rubbed his scratchy eyes with the palms of his hands and sighed. He was not usually a worrier, nor someone who got anxious about things. This was all very new for him and rather uncomfortable. In reflection, he realized the events of the evening before were intense and bore similarities with his sister's riding accident. Perhaps his anxious reaction was a normal one, but it still bothered him. He couldn't seem to stop stewing.

He glanced at his phone and felt relief that there were no more messages from Anna. That was something he *should* be thinking about—his relationship with Anna. She'd more than hinted about taking it to the next level, but Lachlan struggled to think about Anna moving into his home. He'd known Anna, or at least known of her, for many years. The MacDonalds were an influential, wealthy family, and they'd met each other at various events over the years. They had a couple of mutual friends who eventually set them up.

Lachlan had shied away from dating with his life being so busy, but on that first date with Anna, he enjoyed himself and decided maybe he could fit dating into his busy world. In those first few dates, he found himself liking her clever humour although now found it to be often more snarky than clever. Anna MacDonald was a confident, independent woman. Beautiful. Sociable. A man should be so lucky to date her. Never mind live with her. Possibly marry her. Even his mam was not so subtle in encouraging his relationship with Anna, not that she knew her overly well. Lachlan suspected it had more to do with the fact that she was a MacDonald—her family had a good reputation.

Lachlan sighed, staring up at the ceiling, thinking about the boxes she ticked, and wondering why in the hell he wasn't jumping at the chance to have Anna MacDonald move in with him. Pushing thoughts about his relationship with Anna aside, he got up out of bed and padded to the bathroom to brush his teeth.

As he got ready for the day, he found that more often than not, his thoughts turned to Violet and not Anna. A concern for the lass sat heavy in his chest. Not knowing how she faired bothered him. He tried to tell himself that he needn't worry, as she was in the best place possible. Surely, the hospital staff were doing everything they could to take care of her. It was not like he could do anything to help her. Why couldn't he just let it go?

She'd haunted his dreams in the night. It bothered him that his dreams were so disjointed, although he couldn't recall much. There was one part of a dream that was incredibly vivid and real. Not only could he remember every detail, but he couldn't forget it if he tried.

In the dream, Violet was talking to him, her green eyes so intense. They were on the beach. He let his eyes drop to her lips, which smiled teasingly at him. The need to kiss them and taste them was overpowering. It was like he knew that kissing them would unlock another world. The dream was so intense, and the sensations were so real. He desperately wanted to kiss those lips that promised something magical, and as he leaned in, desire like he'd never known singed him. But right before their mouths connected, he'd awoken with a start. His heart was pounding, and his cock was painfully hard.

As the dream replayed in his mind, he wondered what the hell was wrong with him. The content wasn't the worst, but it was how he felt. Crazy intense off the fucking charts arousal. Not that he could control his dreams per se. But Christ, he shouldn't be having dreams like that.

For one, he had a girlfriend. It damn-near felt like cheating, and Lachlan found cheating repugnant. Two, why would the anticipation of a mere kiss make him off-the-charts aroused? And three, the worst reason of all. He was having dirty dreams about a lass who was in the hospital with a head injury. Lachlan groaned, unimpressed with himself. *Very gentlemanly*, he thought sardonically. Thank God it was just a bloody dream.

Lachlan was planning to go to the distillery to do some paperwork for the deal he'd made last night with his new client. His admin, Iona, would take care of most of it after the weekend, but he wanted to get things started. After a quick lifting session in his home gym, he showered and dressed, got into his car, and headed for work. Violet was still very much on his mind, though. Normally, he wasn't the easily distracted type. He was usually very focused, probably one of the traits that had made him so successful. But today, he was mightily distracted.

Accepting that he was not going to get anything done until he knew how the lass faired, he pulled a U-turn. It was apparent he'd never get the lass off his mind until he checked in. He'd get some flowers, go check on her, and then go to work and move on with his life. Then perhaps his mind would be clear enough to figure out what he was going to do about Anna.

Chapter 5
The Hospital

WHEN HE ARRIVED AT the hospital, he went to the information desk. An overly tanned, leathery-looking woman with pointed, fake fluorescent pink nails sitting on the other side of the desk sighed heavily before looking up at him as if it pained her to be interrupted from what she was doing, which appeared to be playing a game on her phone. Her eyes landed on him, and it was like a neon sign on a casino flicking on. Her face lit up as she straightened and leaned forward toward him.

"Can I help ye?" she said breathily as her eyes trailed greedily over him.

Lachlan smiled politely despite feeling like a piece of cake she'd like to devour. "Good morning. I was hoping ye could tell me which room Violet Munro is in?"

"Och, aye, of course. One second, love." She clicked away on her keyboard with surprising efficiency, given the length of her nails. "Are ye family?" she asked.

"Aye," Lachlan lied and cringed inside. He never lied, but he realized he might not be allowed to see the lass if he wasn't family.

The woman looked up at him. Her eyes narrowed. "Husband?"

Lachlan nodded, feeling his neck heat. Christ, for all he knew, her actual husband could be in the room with her now.

The woman glanced at the bouquet in his hand and must have decided that he was being truthful. "Second floor. Ward eight. Room Two B. The elevator is just behind ye love." She grinned up at him.

"Thank ye." He nodded and turned toward the elevator.

"God, some lassies have all the luck," she muttered.

Lachlan smirked to himself, pressing the button for the elevator.

"Gor," she groaned. "I should take a picture of that arse. Claire will be sorry she missed it."

He scrunched his eyes closed, wishing he hadn't heard that part. Clearly, the woman didn't realize how her voice carried in the hollow walls of the hospital. Lachlan was about to go find the stairs when the elevator doors, thankfully, opened, and he was able to make his escape before his arse ended up on the woman's phone.

Ward eight was the neurology department, and a wave of trepidation rolled over Lachlan. He stood outside Violet's hospital room door. His hands were suddenly sweaty. He feared the worst. What if the lass had a brain injury? He swallowed, trying to steady himself. If it was bad, wouldn't she be in the ICU? He tried to think logically. Running a hand through his wavy quiff of short hair, he exhaled deeply and settled into his usual calm demeanour before gently knocking on her door.

Violet had been so busy recalling the events before her fall that she hadn't gotten to what happened after. The memories of after quickly crashed through her mind. This was the man who'd helped her, her knight in shining armour.

She hadn't realized he was so tall, and he was looking at her now with a slight tip of a smile that made her heart skip a beat. For a moment, she closed her eyes as she recalled how badly she had wanted to kiss him last night. She flushed at the memory. Violet, with a clearer mind than last night, opened her eyes, taking in her rescuer with fresh eyes. Well, she hadn't been wrong. He was extremely handsome, in a sort of quiet book smart-looking way.

He was tall and clean-cut, lean, but clearly muscular under his crisp white dress shirt. The sleeves of his neatly tucked shirt were rolled up casually, revealing a sleek black titanium watch on his solid wrist. An expensive looking leather belt wrapped around the trim waist of his dark slim-line pants, and the ensemble was finished with a pair of stylish cognac brown leather lace-up shoes. This man was seriously put together. Sexy and maybe a little bit nerdy like in a Clark Kent sorta way.

"My rescuer." She gave him a friendly grin.

He chuckled. "Aye, I suppose so. I hope it's all right that I've come by to see ye."

Violet nodded. "Of course."

"Yer lookin' a lot brighter than when I last saw ye. How are ye feelin' this morning?"

He held a bouquet of flowers in his hand. She wondered if they were meant for her. "I'm feeling so much better." She sighed, realizing how relieved she was. "I can't thank you enough for helping me. I don't know what would've happened if you hadn't been there." As she thought back to the fall, she realized she couldn't piece together everything that had happened. "Did you see me fall? There are parts that still feel fuzzy," she said, trying hard to will the memories to come back to her.

"Aye, I did." He looked as if he were contemplating on whether or not to say more.

"It looked bad," she stated, trying to read his features that had turned serious.

He nodded.

"I remember walking along the pier just soaking in the beauty of it all, and then I remember my foot caught. And there was nothing I could do to stop from falling, but then it's a blank until I was sitting on the grass with you."

He looked reluctant to speak about it, but she was grateful when he did.

"I got to ye as fast as I could, and by the time I did, ye were trying to stand and walk. But I could tell ye werenae steady, and the next thing I ken, ye passed out on me."

"Sorry about that," Violet interjected, liking that she'd gotten a smile out of him.

"I had to carry ye to the grass. I called for the ambulance, and thankfully, that's when ye came to again."

Violet was surprised that he'd actually carried her. God, he really was her knight in shining armour. She knew it was ridiculous, but she wished she knew with all her might what it had been like to be carried in those strong arms. There was no doubt she'd stew on that little tidbit for a long time to come—thanks, smut books.

"I wish I could huv done more," he said as if he hadn't been an absolute hero.

Violet eyed this stranger who stood before her and wondered what else he could have possibly done. He'd come to her rescue without hesitation. What would have happened if she'd awoken alone? The thought made her shudder.

"You were amazing. I think a lot of people would have turned a blind eye." She tucked her hair behind her ear. "You sat with me and comforted me. I'll never forget that." Her voice quivered slightly, recalling how connected she'd felt with him. She remembered how tender he'd been with her, as if she wasn't a total stranger but someone special to him. Logically, she knew it was ridiculous to think his kindness was anything more than him being a decent human being, but for her, it had felt like so much more. He shifted, and the rustle of the flowers he held brought her back to the present. His expression had turned sheepish, and the effect charmed her.

"Ach, lass. I'm just glad I was there." He looked down at the flowers in his hand as if only just remembering he had them. "I brought these for ye," he said, stepping toward her.

And she found her eyes more drawn to the way his dress shirt tightened around the curve of his thick bicep than the bouquet he held out to her.

“Oh, that’s so sweet. Thank you.” Violet willed herself not to ogle the man and brought the pretty bouquet of white freesias and pale peach and pink tulips to her nose, breathing in their fresh spring scent. "They are beautiful." She eyed him over the bouquet. Her knight in shining armour was a pretty decent guy.

Gesturing a hand toward the hospital green vinyl chair in the corner of the room, he asked, “May I?”

Polite too, Violet thought as she nodded, feeling glad that he didn't seem to be in a hurry to leave. Her knight pulled the chair closer to the bedside where she sat perched, and he leaned toward her, sexy veiny forearms resting on his dark pants. Then his eyes seemed to lock onto hers and hold them like how a couple holds hands, intertwined, firm, and intimate. Butterflies erupted in her empty stomach.

“Yer memory has come back then?” he asked, his deep voice gentle and soothing. Like it had been last night.

She couldn't help but take in his handsome features. His nose was long and narrow but quite proportioned to his face. He was clean-shaven with a strong, defined jawline. His lips sat straight, but she recalled that when he smiled, they tugged to the side. A crooked smile, almost flawed—but definitively not. Despite all of those features, it was his eyes that held her captive. They were a deep, intense cerulean blue. *Who has eyes like that?* And with the way he was looking at her, she felt like he could look into her soul if he so desired. It was oddly comforting and disconcerting all at the same time.

"I remember you," she said, a smile touching her lips.

Those impossibly blue eyes dropped to her lips, and Violet sucked in a breath, unconsciously leaning in closer to him. And then, in an instant, the moment was gone as he stood and stepped to the window.

"Well, that's something," he said as if praising her for recalling anything at all while at the same time glossing over the significance of the recollection. He leaned up against the frame of the frosted window and crossed his muscular arms over his chest, unaware of how it made him look as if he were a model in a GQ spread.

Violet blinked, wondering what had just happened. Had he wanted to kiss her? Well, if he did, he certainly didn't want to now. Not that she could blame him. She'd spent the night in a hospital, and she sat here before him in her own dried-up sweat, never mind her mouth hadn't seen a toothbrush in twenty-four hours. *Gross. Of course, he'd moved away from me.*

"My memories are all coming back this morning. Thank goodness," Violet added brightly, even though she was feeling a bit more self-conscious now.

"Och, I'm so pleased to hear that." Even from across the room, warmth emanated from him. "I confess, I was worried for ye lass."

"Fortunately, it was a temporary little brain scramble," she quipped, liking how he called her lass.

"Aye, well, I'm truly pleased that ye are well. It must huv been quite frightening for ye." He dropped his arms, and his big hands curled casually over the window sill.

"It was such an odd thing," she said, reflecting on how it felt. "It was as if nothing existed prior to that moment. My mind was just totally blank. I literally had zero recollection of anything before the fall."

"I can no' imagine."

"It was so weird," she continued, hugging her knees up as she tried to wrap her brain around it. "It is a *massive* relief that my memories are coming back. Even menial, nothing stuff from yesterday, like what I had for breakfast. I never thought things like that would be happy memories," she joked light heartedly.

"I'm sure." His lips tugged in his side smile that grew sexier every time she saw it.

"Well, I'm genuinely so pleased that yer so much better, lass. It's nice to see ye upbeat and..." His voice trailed off, and he got that sheepish look again.

"And able to hold a conversation?" she supplied with a laugh.

He chuckled and nodded. "Aye. It is nice to huv a proper blether with ye, lass."

Violet was momentarily confused by his Scottish slang, but then she realized that *blether* must mean conversation or something like it. "Thank you," she said genuinely. "It feels good to be myself again."

Putting the flowers on the bed, she stood gingerly, and her knight was across the room in an instant, reaching out an arm to steady her. Sheesh, was this guy for real?

"Is it okay if I give you a hug?" she asked, looking up at him.

"Och, aye, I think we could both use a good *coorie* after everything."

Violet assumed coorie must be another Scottish term. From the way he said it, it sounded cozier than a hug—more like a cuddle. And looking at the broad, handsome man before her, she definitely wasn't opposed.

She was a relatively tall woman at five-foot-eight, but it was still a stretch to reach up and hug him. The man had to be at least six-foot-four. She wrapped her arms around his broad shoulders, and in turn, she felt his strong arms wrap around her waist. There was a rightness to being in his arms that she couldn't explain. Violet settled in, laying her face against his chest, hearing the steady beat of his heart, and feeling his warmth wrap around her like a sun-drenched towel after a cold swim in the sea. He curled down over her, pulling her in closer to him, and a little sigh escaped her.

It seemed such a natural thing to do. They might be strangers, but they'd been through an intense ordeal together. It felt right to hug the man who'd virtually saved her and cared enough to get her help and even come back the next day to check on her.

Her knight was a good guy...with an incredibly broad, firm chest. A new awareness tingled through her as his hand stroked down her back. It was as if time stood still as his deliciously muscled arms snugged her in closer. Her head nestled perfectly into his chest. *Mmm*, and he smelled yummy—clean and fresh with a hint of expensive spiciness. Unfortunately, she remembered her own disheveled state: stale and sweat-laden skin and clothes after a long night's stay in a hospital.

Reluctantly, she untangled herself from their embrace. Aside from her current hygiene-deficient condition, she probably shouldn't be lusting after the man anyway, especially not in her hospital room.

Chapter 6

Popping the Big Question

LACHLAN WAS MUCH RELIEVED to find the lass doing so well and recovering from her ordeal, but what niggled in the back of his mind was the awareness that relief wasn't his primary emotion.

There was something more than concern or common courtesy, but Lachlan couldn't identify exactly what it was. Every time she pinned him with those beautiful eyes, he felt a visceral connection that defied logic. He always made eye contact when speaking with someone, but with Violet Munro, it felt intimate somehow. It wasn't something he could wrap his mind around. Needing to look somewhere else, he made the mistake of dropping his eyes to her mouth, and his dream about their almost-kiss slammed back into his thoughts.

Instantly, he felt like a creep. The last thing in the world he should be thinking about was snogging the lass. It was wrong on so many levels. Just when he thought he'd sorted himself back out, she asked to give him a hug. It was not like he could say no, nor did he want to. Lachlan was a hugger. He hugged many women friends and men friends, too—this shouldn't be any different.

A cuddle between friends. Lachlan was a pro at the friend cuddle. This was certainly the right occasion for it. Christ, he'd been so worried for her, and they'd been through a traumatic event together. A cuddle seemed the most natural thing in the world, right up until she was in his arms, nestled against him. Part of him, the Lachlan part of him, appreciated the moment for what it was: two people who'd gone through an ordeal finding comfort in a warm embrace. But then there was another part of him that seemed to be channeling his brothers' mindsets—Drew and Alex. That part of him was aroused beyond measure.

It was not like him. Not like him at all. This was wild and needy and far too carnal, but ironically, he didn't want it to stop. The poke of her perky breasts against his torso scorched him. The soft sound of her contented feminine sigh was like a stroke on his cock.

In the back of his mind, he knew that he shouldn't pull her closer—knew he shouldn't feel his heart race as he touched the curve of her back. He held Violet Munro tight to him, and when she finally pulled away and stepped back from him, he felt disoriented.

Schooling himself, Lachlan stared down at her, trying to understand why his reaction to her was so visceral. He cleared his throat. "Can I get ye anything?" he offered, cutting the tension that sparked between them as thick as New York cheesecake.

"I—" she hesitated.

He looked at her expectantly, sensing she needed something from him, and, by God right now, he was damn-near willing to do anything she asked.

"Could you stay with me for the next twenty-four hours?" She blurted out in a rush. She wore a vulnerability in her expression that was different from last night but no less compelling. However, that was the last thing he expected to hear, and he had to stop himself from instantly saying, *hell aye.* Thoughts racing, he forced himself to slow down a minute.

"Right, hmm. I was thinking along the lines of a cuppa tea or perhaps a warm blanket," he teased lightly, but he felt bad when she looked down awkwardly. Her cheeks and neck flushed a pretty shade of pink. He hadn't meant to embarrass her.

"It's okay." She sighed, leaning back onto the edge of the bed. Her eyes were cast to the puddle grey, utilitarian floor. "I'm sorry. I don't know what I was thinking," she said, shaking her head.

Lachlan studied her, wondering why she wanted him to stay with her. She must have a good reason for asking. Christ, it was like his horny arse brothers had taken over his mind because suddenly, he conjured the idea that she wanted him as her sex slave for the next twenty-four hours. He felt tension crush between his brows, mortified by the direction of his unbidden salacious thought. What on earth was the matter with him?

Pulling himself together, he went for the straightforward approach. "Tell me, lass, what do you mean? Why do ye want me to stay with ye?"

Shifting herself back onto the bed and neatly pulling her legs up under herself, she sat cross-legged and had the look of a school girl trying to solve a math problem.

"It's just that... Well, I'm permitted to leave the hospital now." She rubbed her forehead and winced when her hand scraped over her bruise.

Lachlan had to stop himself from reaching out to comfort her. Fortunately, she quickly recovered.

"The problem is, the doctor said someone needed to stay with me for the next twenty-four hours. Actually, he made me *promise* that someone would." She sighed, obviously unimpressed with the doctor's orders. "Apparently, I could have a seizure or something," she muttered like it was the stupidest thing she'd ever heard. "I don't know, but I guess, at night, there's more of a risk for it." Her slender shoulders slumped on a sigh.

Even slouching, she had a swan-like grace about her.

"Why dinnae they want to keep ye in the hospital then?" Concern pricked his thoughts.

Violet gave an exaggerated shrug. "Who knows? But to be quite honest, I'd really rather not stay here if I don't have to." Her pert nose wrinkled. "The doctor said the seizure thing is rare but can happen, so apparently, I need a babysitter."

Lachlan's lips twitched in a half-smile at her less-than-thrilled description and the juxtaposition of the irritated frown on her china doll features. "Well, that makes sense. Ye dinnae want to risk something happening if yer alone. But dinnae ye huv somebody who'd be willing to stay with ye?" Surely, the lass must know somebody who'd be more suited to keep watch over her. They didn't even know each other.

"Nope," she muttered, leaning back with her hands on the bed behind her. "I just moved here. Hmm, what is it? Two days ago now. I don't know anyone. Except for you. And you... Well, you've been so nice and helpful, I just thought... Oh, God. Never mind." That alluring pink crawled up her neck and face again.

"Ye moved to Scotland and dinnae huv any family or friends here? No one?" he ventured, attempting to understand the situation.

"No one." She shrugged as if it had never really occurred to her. "It's just me here. All by myself," she said, apparently at ease with her situation.

Lachlan wondered what had brought Violet Munro here to Scotland alone. But he didn't feel it was his business to ask at the moment.

"Och, lass, what a way to start."

"Ha, right?" she muttered.

"I didnae mean to sound insensitive."

"Not at all. You're right. Definitely an unexpected start." She shook her head. "But I supposed life happens no matter where you are, and despite what happened last night, I'm glad to be here." Her lips tugged in a smile.

And Lachlan found himself admiring her positive take on it. He could only imagine that if it was Anna, the complaining would never end. He caught his spiralling thoughts and pushed them aside to focus on the dilemma at hand. Lachlan was more than a little surprised by Violet's request. As odd as it was, he wasn't opposed to it. Being that she was by herself in his country, it made sense now why she'd asked for his help. That, and they'd formed an unlikely connection, he supposed.

With Anna out of town, he'd intended on a quiet weekend to focus and work on some upcoming projects and, of course, get a jump start on the new client file. He was also supposed to be deciding on his current living situation and whether or not his girlfriend was moving in. *Och*, he really didn't want to be thinking about that.

Staying with the lass would put a dent in his plans for the weekend, but it was only for twenty-four hours. And how could he in good conscience say no? Violet needed a friend—a helping hand—and he'd always prided himself on being a good friend and a gentleman.

He'd be remiss, though, if he didn't consider his unexpected reaction to the lass. He had to admit he was attracted to her. The truth was they'd shared in some heightened emotions given Violet's accident. The attraction was likely due to the remnants of those emotions, he reasoned. Now they'd had a *cwtch* between friends, he was sure it would be fine. He was good at being friends.

Then there was Anna. He had to consider her too in this. *Hmm.* She didn't seem the jealous type, but she might not be totally keen on the situation. He tried to be pragmatic. As bad as it sounded to spend the night with another woman, the reality was the circumstances were completely innocent, and truthfully, what kind of arse would he be if he said no to the Violet? She literally had no one else to help her.

"All right then," he said, his mind made up.

"What *all right then*?" she asked as if she'd forgotten what she'd asked him.

"All right, I'll stay with ye," Lachlan confirmed. "Be your watch for the next twenty-four hours."

"Oh." Her eyes grew wide.

"Is that a good, *oh*?" he hedged.

"Yes, yes, of course." She leaned forward with her legs still crossed under her and ran her fingers through her long golden hair, pulling it over one shoulder. "Sorry. I'm just surprised that's all. And grateful. I'm very grateful." She exhaled with a smile.

He felt glad as he watched the tension drop away from her pretty features. "Are ye ready to get oot of here then?"

"Definitely!"

Making sure her phone and earbuds were in her stretch pant pocket, she picked up the bouquet from the bed and stood up. Her chivalrous knight stepped toward the door and held it open, gesturing for her to step through.

"Thank you." She smiled softly up at him as she moved past him. Despite it being a short stay and being grateful for the medical care, Violet was very glad to be getting out of the hospital. It had been a long night.

For a minute there, she was afraid she'd offended the handsome man who'd come to her rescue. When Violet had asked him to stay with her, she almost laughed at the shocked look on his face. She was sure he thought she was nuts. He was her only hope, though. It was him or an all-night café. It was a huge relief that he'd actually agreed. She truly needed his help, but at the same time, she didn't mind in the least that she'd get to enjoy his company for the next twenty-four hours, including that crooked smile that was the perfect combination of adorable-nerdy-shy guy and I-know-I'm-hot sex god.

"Did you tell me your name?" she wondered, not knowing if she'd inadvertently forgotten it from last night.

They walked side by side down the corridor to the elevator.

"I don't think we got as far as that yesterday." A smile tugged the corners of his mouth, and he looked down at her out of the corner of his eye. "Lachlan Mackenzie."

"Lachlan." She sighed lightly. "Do you know my name?" She looked up at him uncertainly.

"I do." There was warmth in the timbre of his voice. "It was one of the first things I asked you."

"Oh yeah," she said exaggeratedly as the memory of it flooded back to her. "I remember your eyes," she said thoughtfully.

They stopped before the elevator, and Lachlan pressed the button, then turned to gaze down at her. "My eyes?"

With his attention full on her, Violet felt timid and almost wished she hadn't said anything. But he looked at her in a way that implored her to tell him. Her voice was quiet and sobering. A wave of emotion hit her out of nowhere, and she looked away from him. Crossing her arms around herself, she absently stared out a nearby window, recalling the intimacy of the connection she'd felt with him.

"I remember your eyes felt like a lifeline. I felt like the confusion would drown me, but something about your eyes holding mine kept me afloat. It's like you were connected to me somehow, willing me to be okay." She ventured a glance back up at his handsome face, worried she'd confessed too much.

He stared down at her with the intensity of fire. His nostrils slightly flared, and she noted the slight tick in his clean-shaven, chiseled jaw. Without a word, strong arms encircled her, pulling her in close to him, and she felt him drop a kiss to the top of her head. She sighed in wonder, feeling so safe and protected with his arms around her. This man she barely knew.

"I'm glad, lass," he murmured into her hair as the door to the elevator opened.

By the time they got out to the parking lot, Violet was feeling exhausted again. It shouldn't have surprised her. Dr. Campbell said it might take a day or two before she got her energy back.

"Ye feeling okay, lass?" Lachlan's hand briefly touched the small of her back.

Violet had to reign in her girlish reaction to it. The man was certainly perceptive. "Yeah, just going to take a bit for my energy to come back, I guess. So silly, such a short walk and it's drained me."

Violet's attention was drawn to the glossy jet-black Maserati that Lachlan was opening the passenger door to. *Wowza*. He gestured for her to get in, and she gingerly slid into the tan leather seat, instantly noting the way it gently held her in all the right places. Lachlan's car seat was literally more comfortable than any bed she'd ever slept in.

A memory from her childhood surfaced. Sitting beside her two little sisters and her dad at the dining table. While her mom, animated with her frosted pink lipstick, told them of another new home-based company she'd signed up for. And how this one was different. This one was going to make them rich. It would take hard work, but she was going to get to diamond status. And if she could reach diamond status within the first six months, the company would give her a brand new sports car. Violet couldn't recall what sports car, but she could still clearly see the sheer thrill in her mother's cool mint green eyes. And the weariness and feigned excitement in her dad's warm hazel ones.

Letting the memory fade, she settled back further into the seat. Guess Lachlan must have achieved diamond status. A sardonic smile quirked her lips.

"I should have picked ye up at the door. I didnae think. I'm sorry, lass," Lachlan said as he slid into the driver's seat beside her, pulling her from her thoughts.

"Oh, no, don't apologize. It was probably good to walk a bit and get some fresh air."

He eyed her meaningfully. "Well, as long as I huvnae worn ye out. I take my responsibilities very seriously, lass." That crooked smile tugged at his lips.

Violet giggled. "Good to know."

The engine made a beautiful purring sound as Lachlan started the car. Violet balked that she'd even noticed such a thing.

"Your car is ridiculous," she stated matter-of-factly, completely changing the subject.

"Sorry?" A confused crease appeared between Lachlan's brows.

"I mean, it's awesome—like ridiculously awesome," she quickly clarified.

He chuckled. "That's good then, aye?"

"Yes, definitely good."

She could barely tear her eyes from his I-know-I'm-hot-as-a-sex-god crooked smile as he pulled out of the parking lot.

"So where to, Violet? Are ye hungry? Do ye want to go fer breakfast? It's only just nine o'clock now."

"Actually, would you mind if we went to my Airbnb first?" she asked sheepishly, not wanting to impose or take advantage of his generosity. "I could use a shower and some clean clothes." She wrinkled her nose as a fresh wave of self-consciousness rolled over her.

"Aye, of course. Which Airbnb is it?"

Chapter 7

Cam and Elizabeth Are Trouble

LACHLAN SAT IN THE only chair in Violet's Airbnb, and it was awkwardly tiny for his tall, broad frame. No matter how he shifted, he couldn't get comfortable. While he waited for Violet to shower and get ready, he looked through some emails on his phone, but there was nothing that required his attention urgently.

Putting his phone away, he eyed the modest room. By the window that overlooked a tidy patch of garden, Lachlan sat in a chair at a small round table. There was a queen-size bed, two mismatched nightstands, and a large white wardrobe. Small, but cozy enough, he supposed. Anna would hate it.

Fed up with the tiny chair and not wanting to entertain thoughts about his girlfriend, he stood. What a whirlwind the past day had been. It wasn't an exaggeration to say he felt an immense sense of relief at Violet's recovery. The worry he'd felt through the night and morning about her had thankfully dissipated. Maybe he'd actually get some sleep tonight. A little voice in his head quipped, *You think you'll sleep with this lass so near?* He quickly squashed the unruly thought. And turned away from the window.

He caught sight of a few books stacked on the nightstand. With nothing else to do while he waited for the lass, he went over to inspect what books she was reading. He picked up the first book, *Atomic Habits* by James Clear. Lachlan smiled to himself, as it was one of his favourite books. Flicking through the pages, he noticed her annotations. He stopped on one highlighted section and couldn't stop himself from reading her neatly printed note: *habit stacking is the baby steps to your goals*. He couldn't agree more. Clever lass. Then he found himself wondering, what were Violet Munro's goals? He literally knew nothing about her, which was ironic since he felt somehow like he knew her well. Like his soul knew her soul. Lachlan snickered out loud. He wasn't one for fanciful thoughts.

Looking back down at the book in his hands, it occurred to him that he shouldn't be reading the lass's annotations. They were her private thoughts, much like a diary. Tempting as that was, he had no right to snoop, so he reluctantly closed that book and glanced down at the one below it and almost laughed out loud. It was the other end of the spectrum from *Atomic Habits.*

On the cover was a half-naked, overly chiseled dude dramatically embracing a voluptuous woman with wind-swept hair. He smirked to himself before curiosity got the better of him. He opened up the book to a random page and read:

Cam hadn't been able to get Elizabeth out of his mind since the moment he'd laid his eyes on her long red locks. She was a fiery temptress. He no longer cared about propriety. No longer cared he couldn't give her more than just lust. He needed her, and he needed her now. The moment their lips touched, it was like a bolt of lightning shooting through him. He'd dreamed of this since the moment he'd met Elizabeth Macduff. She tasted of honey and sin. The sweetest nectar he'd ever known.

Lachlan stifled a laugh, but he kept reading despite himself.

The kiss deepened. Tongues entwined. She softly moaned with his rock-hard column pressed up against her. She wantonly rubbed herself against him. Cam knew she was a vixen deep down, and nothing pleased him more.

Her body was heavy and tingly. Elizabeth didn't know how Cam could turn her molten with only a look. And now he was ravishing her senseless. She couldn't think straight. She could feel something building deep within her. A longing that only he could satiate. She felt his hand reach up into her long tresses. He firmly tugged her hair back, exposing her neck. His hot, wet tongue seared a trail down her neck to her breasts. Her back arched. She shuddered with ecstasy as he licked her pert nipple through her gown.

He reached down and released his manhood from his trews. A shiver ran through her. She would be a maiden no more. He positioned himself between her legs, and she felt him nudge against her. "Cam, I need you," she begged breathlessly. Pleasure seared through her. But then he stopped himself, and she could see in his eyes that his conscious was stopping him. "Please, Cam," she breathed, needing him.

"I cannot take your maidenhead. It will ruin you. You deserve a husband." His voice was strained.

The bathroom door opened, and Lachlan half-jumped out of his skin. He quickly shoved the book back down, as if it was on fire, and stepped back toward the window. That's when he realized he had a hard-on.

Violet scurried out, all wet, with a towel wrapped around her. His mouth went dry, and his cock tightened even harder.

"Sorry," she quipped without even looking up. "I forgot to grab clean clothes." She was back in the bathroom, door closed, and Lachlan let out the breath he'd held. He ran his hands through his hair and then adjusted his pants to relieve some pressure from his awkwardly uncomfortable bulge.

Then he thanked his lucky stars that Violet hadn't looked up. Even if she didn't notice the cock that was straining against his dress pants, he wasn't sure he could hide his guilt over his current hot and bothered state.

Squeezing himself back into the tiny chair, he glanced back over at the reprehensible book. He turned his attention to the greenery out the window, trying hard to extricate the image of Violet wrapped in nothing but a towel from his mind.

What was wrong with him? He shouldn't be thinking of Violet in any other way than platonic. It was probably the damned book making his thoughts go astray. As he sat staring out the window, his thoughts turned back to the book, and he actually found himself curious if Cam and Elizabeth did it or not. And then he wondered if Violet had read that bit yet.

Shite. He needed to get his head out of the gutter immediately. It wasn't like him to have sex on the brain. That was where his brothers' heads lived, not Lachlan's.

He definitely didn't want to be thinking of Violet in a sexual manner. That was just plain wrong. She was a sweet lass who needed his help, needed a friend, not for him to be some lecherous creep. To say nothing of the fact that he was in a relationship. Christ. Lachlan ran his hands over his face with a heavy sigh. *Anna.* Thoughts of their relationship weren't sitting well with him. Until he figured that out, though, he definitely needed to reign in this sudden randiness. It was completely inappropriate. Utterly wrong.

Agreeing to stay with Violet probably wasn't his brightest decision, but he couldn't back out now. He needed to focus. The only purpose he had right now was helping out a woman, a friend, he modified. One who'd been through a traumatizing ordeal. Violet didn't know him, but she trusted him, to some extent, at least. And that meant something to Lachlan. He'd not abuse that trust. Nor Anna's trust.

Sadly, he'd known men, and women for that matter, who couldn't control their sexual urges. Or perhaps it was more that they chose not to control them. Yes, that was the problem: people choosing to act on their urges. Well, Lachlan would never be one of those people. All he had to do was control whatever the hell had gotten into him for the next twenty-four hours. This was not a problem.

Lasses always liked Lachlan because he was the nice guy. Perhaps because he had sisters, he was comfortable and at ease with women. He'd been told more than once that he was a good listener. Lachlan found women much less complicated than most men thought them to be. Kindness and gentlemanliness went a long way. With Violet, he just needed to remember why he was in her company. It was to help. To be a friend. Christ, he wasn't a barbarian. He could enjoy her company and, at the same time, help her—as any friend w ould do.

Chapter 8
Craggy's

"WHERE ARE WE GOING?" Violet asked as she watched, spellbound by the views from the passenger-side window. The mountainous terrain was rugged and wildly beautiful, and it stunned her how the lochs would run parallel to the car.

"I'm taking ye to one of my favourite places to get a proper Scott's breakfast." He glanced at her. "Ye must be starving."

"Yep, pretty sure I could eat one of those highland coo's," she teased, drawing out the *O* to mimic the Scots accent.

They drove past a handful of copper furry cows grazing in a pasture beside the narrow road, which was no wider than a Canadian back alley.

He chuckled. "Well, that's no' exactly the breakfast I had in mind fer us. Hopefully, a little haggis and black pudding will suffice."

"Eew." Violet made a face.

He looked at her, mock offended. “Eew? Did ye just say *eew*? Och, lassie, if yer gonna live in Scotland, ye better get used to a wee bit o’ haggis.”

She laughed. “We’ll see.”

“Have ye ever tried it, then?”

“Haggis?” She raised her brows and then got distracted by a car that passed them so closely that Lachlan could have reached out and high-five'd them.

“Aye, or black pudding?” he said, clearly not the least concerned about how close the cars drove to his.

“Nope, can't say I've tried any of that,” she admitted. “But who would eat something called *black pudding*? I have a feeling it’s not a dark chocolate dessert.”

His rumbling laugh tickled down her spine. “Och, God, no, not even close!”

“Well, what is it then?” She eyed him suspiciously.

He glanced toward her, giving her a flash of his blue eyes. “How about you try it first, and then we’ll chat about what it is?”

“Oh, that sounds promising. Sign me up for mystery pudding.” She intoned, to which Lachlan chuckled again.

They drove in companionable silence. Violet watched the scenery go by, sneaking glances at Lachlan's profile every now and then.

The safe, vanilla Violet she had been before deciding to shake up her mundane existence and move to Scotland would have given her a stern talking-to for going off with a virtual stranger. It was funny that she didn't know anything about Lachlan aside from his impeccable taste in clothes and cars, but she did know that he was a very good man. The kind who helped old ladies cross the road and rescued women and then looked after them, apparently. All that, and he was easy on the eyes. What world had she found herself in? *Not the worst company to have here in Scotland*, she thought, appreciating the pronounced point of his Adam's apple so masculine above his crisp white shirt collar.

Craggy's, aptly named, sat perched on a craggy part of a hillside that overlooked the sea. The ocean stretched itself to the sky where she could barely tell where one met the other. It was so vast that Violet's heart squeezed. In her twenty-nine years on this planet, she'd seen the ocean for the first time just two days ago—from the plane—and now it surrounded her in all it's breathtaking expanse.

The inside of Craggy's was cozy and quaint. Sea-farer paraphernalia from years gone by adorned the white-paneled walls. A large stone fireplace with low, rugged old wood beams added to the charm of the old place. The best part was how delicious it smelled inside, like a breakfast bouquet of pancakes, bacon, toast, and coffee. It gave her hope for the black pudding.

Lachlan led them to one of the plaid-covered booth seats near large windows overlooking the sea. Violet slid into the seat opposite Lachlan. They'd only just sat down when an older, portly man with thick white hair and kind, crinkly eyes put his meaty hand down on Lachlan's shoulder.

"Lachlan, laddie, it's been an age! How's yer mam and da then?"

Lachlan patted his hand. "Aye, they're well. Always fussin' each other, but they're good. Mam, just got back from a trip to Portugal with the ladies."

"Och, aye, aye. Portugal's lovely this time of year."

Violet sat back, thoroughly enjoying their easy banter.

"And who's this lovely lassie then?" The light-hearted man turned his attention to her.

"This is Violet. Violet, meet Robbie, owner of Craggy's and chef extraordinaire."

"Och, aye, owner, no' sure 'bout chef and all that, but I do make the best haggis in all of Argyle. Can I tempt ye, lassie?"

It took Violet a moment to comprehend what Robbie said because his accent was so thick. "Well, I suppose when in Rome..." Violet smiled lightly, a little nervous to try haggis.

"Och, American," Robbie said as more of a statement.

"Canadian," Violet corrected. She'd been asked the same question her first night here when she ordered take-out from a little café near her Airbnb. She supposed it was a common assumption.

"Och, right, right. Canadian. I huv a cousin that lives out in Toronto. I've always meant to go myself, but I cannae seem to get away from this place." He grinned.

Violet sensed he was completely content right where he was.

"Maybe one day." She smiled at him.

"Aye, one day. And just so ye ken, lassie. Yer not even close to Rome."

Violet giggled, and Robbie winked at her.

"Aside from the haggis, what else ken I git the two of ye for yer dining pleasures this fine morning?"

"We'll take two of yer famous Scots breakfasts," Lachlan said.

Violet wondered how often he came here for one of these breakfasts. Craggy's looked to be a favourite spot for the locals. She could hear the din of Scottish accents. There was something that charmed her about the small-town feel here.

"Aye, good choice, laddie." Robbie grinned, and his eyes twinkled as he whipped the drying towel he'd been holding over his shoulder. "We'll huv it out to ye in a wee shake of a lamb's tail. Lovely to meet ye, lassie," he said as he turned to mosey on back to the kitchen.

"Nice to meet you too," Violet called out.

Robbie lifted a hand in acknowledgment. Violet turned back to Lachlan, who was watching her with those cerulean blue eyes, making her pulse kick up a notch.

"So I suppose breakfast includes the dark pudding too?" she asked, reluctantly.

Lachlan chuckled. "It's called black pudding, lassie, and aye, it does."

Violet eyed him skeptically. "Great."

"I can hear the excitement in yer voice," he teased.

"Mmhm," she muttered, leaning her elbow on the table and shoving a hand under her chin.

"I dinnae realize ye were Canadian. I also assumed ye were American. I huvnae been to Canada, but I've always wanted to go."

"You should go." She eyed him thoughtfully. "I grew up in cottage country, north of Toronto."

"That sounds rather idyllic."

"It is very beautiful. It reminds me a bit of here." She nodded toward the window, looking out. "Lots of vast greenery. And lakes. But you also have the ocean right there, and I think you have more sheep." She grinned. Her best friend, Sierra, had told her that there were more sheep in Scotland than stars in the sky, and now, after the thirty-minute drive to Craggy's, Violet thought she might be right.

"Aye." Lachlan's lips lifted into his crooked smile.

Her heart stuttered.

"So what brought ye to Scotland? I assume it wasnae our sheep population."

Violet chuckled and looked up at the ceiling before blowing out a breath. Here she was, in Scotland, and even now, her parent's disapproval nagged at her. Everyone in her life seemed to have an opinion on her dreams. And what she should and shouldn't be doing with her life. The only person who supported her unconditionally was Sierra, who was currently traveling the world. Violet hesitated to talk about i t.

"That's also a long story."

Lachlan's eyes were fixed upon her. "And now ye huv me even more intrigued."

Violet sat back, assessing the handsome man before her. She didn't know much about him, but she knew he was kind-hearted. Something told her that he wouldn't judge her as harshly as everyone else did.

She shrugged. "I think the movie *Braveheart* did it."

Lachlan's eyes lit with humour. "Not *Outlander*?"

"Oh, yeah, of course. That too." She laughed. "Scotland just always seemed like this mythical, magical place. And my favourite drink is scotch, so I figured I should come to the source."

He threw her a raised brow, "Aye, we are known for our mythical legends, but even more for our whisky. But why move here, why not just visit?"

"Right, that." Violet felt a familiar trickle of nerves at explaining her actions. "The truth is, I wanted to prove it to myself that I could do it—that I could move to another country and start a new life. Not that I'm off to the best start." She sighed, imagining what her cynical mother would have to say about it.

He studied her thoughtfully, and her heart fluttered at an unsteady pace. It was the way he seemed to peer into her very soul. She shifted on the seat, worried he'd take the same perspective as her family and think she was impetuous. "I think that is verra admirable," he said finally.

Relief seeped through her.

"A concussion and a hospital stay may no' be an ideal way to start, but do ye ever think..." He stopped, his gaze impossibly intense on her.

"Do I think what?" she was dying to know what he was going to say.

"I, well—"

Unless she was mistaken, strong, confident Lachlan was uncomfortable.

"What?" she nudged.

"Just that things happen for a reason."

"You mean like us meeting?" She smiled, her pulse ticking up a notch.

His lips tugged sideways. "Aye, I suppose, but also ye ken, the expression, 'that which doesnae kill us, makes us stronger?' I mean ye survived probably the worst that Scotland will throw at ye, so the rest should be easy now, no?"

"Oh right, yes, I guess so." Violet sobered, realizing he wasn't referring to their kismet meeting and the connection that buzzed excitedly through her veins—apparently, he was buzz-free. Maybe it was leftover meds in her system, making her pulse kick up like a woodpecker drumming for a mate in spring? She scoffed inwardly, knowing better.

Violet smiled and tucked a strand of hair behind her ear. "I originally intended to move to London. I'm planning to start a personal styling business, helping people with their wardrobes, and I thought London would be the spot. But somehow, Scotland kept calling. I wanted to be by the sea, and although London is a huge mecca, it just didn't feel quite right. It was almost too busy. I wanted somewhere where I could find my own niche, you know?"

Lachlan could relate to that sentiment. He liked London and the larger cities in Scotland, but he much preferred the pace in the Highlands of Scotland. "Aye, that makes sense.

Ye could probably have a monopoly on the styling market all the way out here."

"Exactly." She lit up, excited that he understood.

"I also love being outdoors, hiking, and that sort of thing. I'm not really a big city type girl," she pulled her long blond hair absently over one shoulder. "Scotland feels like to be the right fit.

Lachlan looked at her thoughtfully. "So ye would work with clients on their business attire. That sort of thing."

"Exactly. People who want to find their sense of style or need to build up a workplace wardrobe. I'm also planning to reach out to branding photographers to collaborate. I could style their clients, and they could do branding shoots for me. Well, once I have some, that is."

"That's a clever plan. Were you a personal stylist in Canada too?"

Violet appreciated his vote of confidence. It was nice to be able to share her ideas with him. She'd gotten used to all the nay-saying. Lachlan's reaction was refreshing.

"No," she huffed and picked up a sugar packet that was sitting on the table and fiddled with it between her fingers. "I had a soul-sucking job at a law office for the past four years. I was the assistant to one of the law partners at the firm. He was fine, and the job was fine. And I know I should be grateful to have landed the position, but I honestly hated it." She glanced up at Lachlan, who watched her impassively.

"I knew I needed to make a change, so eight months ago, I began an online styling diploma program. I always loved fashion, so it felt like something I'd enjoy. The plan was to get some credentials and start a new life in London, but then Scotland kept calling, and apparently, I listened." She grinned. "So here I am."

Violet's parents tried to discourage her, not because they wanted her to stay per se, but because they thought she was crazy to try and start a career in a foreign country she'd never even been to. They couldn't understand why she wasn't content to stay at the law firm. Then her mom tried for the umpteenth time to rope Violet into her latest MLM. There was no way she would ever follow in her footsteps with those kind of companies.

Violet loved her family, but she knew that she needed to do this—to at least try to live the life of her dreams. She surprised herself opening up to Lachlan. She wondered if it was because this was probably the first real conversation she'd had since arriving here.

Hearing her reasons for coming to Scotland, would he think she was irresponsible and reckless like her family did? She shouldn't care what he would think of her, but somehow, she did. He'd come to her rescue last night, and now, he was helping her again by staying with her. She didn't want him thinking poorly of her.

"I admire ye, lass, fer following yer dreams. People talk about their dreams, but very few take the steps toward them. It takes courage."

Violet felt her shoulders drop as the tension began to melt away. Again, she was surprised by his response. God, where did this guy come from? Definite relationship material. Not that she was looking, per se. She was in Scotland to follow her dreams—dating wasn't even on her radar."My family would not agree with you, but I appreciate your perspective. Sometimes, I wonder if I'm crazy, but you only live once, right?"

Lachlan stared at her as if her words had struck him. "Ye call it crazy, but I think it's incredible. Most people dinnae ken what they want. Life just happens to them, and I think most of us dinnae even notice the direction it is going in."

Violet had the sneaking suspicion he was referring to himself and not just people in general.

His gaze was drawn out the window at the sea. "Ye make me wonder about my own life. I used to think I ken what I wanted."

"You're not sure?" she asked gently, noting he seemed to be grappling with something.

“I dinnae think I am. No.” He scraped a hand over his jaw, and she let him be with his thoughts. “Ye are givin' me pause, Violet Munro.”

She almost shivered at the sound of her name on his lips. The way he rolled the *R*. Her name had never sounded so good.

“Is that a good thing?” she asked.

He turned back to her and smiled lightly. “Aye, lass, it is. Ye are a dreamer, and ye are reminding me how important it is to dream.”

Violet was taken aback. It made her heart happy to know she might be pushing the needle for her knight. He’d done so much for her. She was glad if she’d inadvertently done something to help him.

Despite having a slight headache, Violet was having such a good time with Lachlan. As they waited for their breakfast, he told her more about the town and surrounding county. His love for his homeland made her all the more happy to be there.

Chapter 9
Saint Lachlan

"I'M JUST GOING TO zip to the washroom before our breakfast arrives," Violet said as she slid out of the booth seat.

"Washroom." Lachlan chuckled. "They are known as toilets here."

Violet crinkled her nose. "Really?"

"Aye." Lachlan smiled. "Down this aisle and to the left at the end."

As she walked away from him, his eyes inadvertently dropped to her butt. He didn't intend to look, but it just happened. She wore a white delicate blouse with a red cable-knit cardigan, slim-fit navy denim cuffed at the ankles, and tan pixie boots. She was so damned attractive, and then there was her arse. Lord help him, he shouldn't have looked down. As she walked, her perfectly formed, heart-shaped arse was like a leash that he was on the end of. He couldn't tear his gaze away. It wasn't until she turned the corner that he discovered he wasn't the only one absorbed by the view.

"Damn," the first comment came from a booth over.

"Feckin' hell," came the next.

Lachlan felt his muscles tense. He was a calm guy, took things in stride, and gave people the benefit of the doubt. He couldn't recall ever wanting to hit anyone. But a very distinct desire to do just that was snaking through his veins. It was a completely unfamiliar sensation. He sat stone still, listening. His fists tightened as he tried to keep control of his reaction. Of course, the lads would notice her. He certainly had.

"Blimey, that's the sweetest sight I've seen in a long time."

"Aye, I'd die a happy mon if I could have a piece of that!" Laughs all around.

"You'd have to save some for the rest of us. We'd all want a turn!"

Lachlan was up and at their table before they uttered another crude word. "That's quite enough, lads." His tone left no room for argument. He was deadly serious.

"Well, if it isn't my big brother, wonders never cease." Lachlan hadn't even noticed his youngest brother among the foursome of men. He was stunned as he took in the sight of him. He'd barely recognized him.

"Drew?" A familiar apprehension replaced Lachlan's tension. "What are ye doin' here?"

"Lovely to see you too, Big Brother." Bitterness laced the younger man's voice. "Still Saint Lachlan, I see." Contempt resonated in the tight curve of his smile. "Goin' to bat for all the helpless lasses." His voice dripped with sarcasm.

Sadly, Lachlan had grown accustomed to Drew's malevolence toward him. It had been almost two years since Lachlan had seen him last, and he'd hardly recognized the scruffy, tired-looking man before him. Time had done nothing to ease the younger man's bitterness. Lachlan wondered if he'd ever see him again. And if he did, would it be any different? And now here they were, the reunion not going well.

"Are ye finally getting some action then, Lachlan? Sweet piece of ass too. How the hell did that happen?" His brother goaded him.

"That is enough." Lachlan's voice was edged with steel. He didn't like any man speaking rudely about a woman, but his brother got under his skin worse than anyone else could.

"Aww, is that a sore spot, Big Brother?" Drew stood face to face with Lachlan, and the pair squared off, ready to do battle as tension bounced between them. In the back of his mind, Lachlan knew he should walk away. But he couldn't.

"Just leave it alone, Drew," Lachlan warned, feeling his fists clench.

"Oh, I think I get it now." Drew grinned lewdly back at his friends, who sat riveted by the interaction before them as if it was all for their entertainment. "Of course. How could I forget? Saint Lachlan doesnae fuck them. He friends them." Drew laughed crudely.

Lachlan's blood boiled even though his brother's offensiveness was nothing new. But then he crossed the line as he turned back to look Lachlan in the eye.

"If she's not sucking yer cock, mind if I give it a go? I should like the feel of that sweet mouth..."

But before he could finish, Lachlan's fist slammed into Drew's smug face, dropping him like a ton of bricks. Lachlan had already turned and was walking away when he heard Drew swearing behind him, and that's when he saw Violet. Her moss-green eyes were wide with apprehension.

"Lachlan, what's happening? Are you okay?"

He turned her toward the door, feeling a surge of protectiveness and wanting to get her out of there as quickly as possible.

"Go get in my car. I'll be out in a minute," he instructed her.

"Okay." Her eyes were filled with uncertainty, but she turned away from him and did as he told her. He didn't have time to feel bad. He just needed her out of there. He couldn't think straight until they were away from his brother.

When Lachlan turned around, Robbie stood behind him, concern etching his wrinkled face.

"Sorry, Robbie," Lachlan muttered awkwardly. Pulling out his wallet, he took out some cash and held it out to him.

"It's okay, lad," Robbie said, pushing his hand away. "Dinnae fash yerself." He grabbed a bag from the counter and handed it to Lachlan. "Two Scots breakfasts, to go." He smiled reassuringly.

Lachlan nodded his thanks and headed out the door without looking back.

Aside from asking Violet if she was feeling okay when he first got into the car, Lachlan hadn't said a word. He just drove like a man on a mission. Violet could feel the anger emanating from him. Should she be scared? His don't-fuck-with-me attitude radiated off him.

Up until this point, Lachlan had been kind, funny, emotionally connected, and gentlemanly, but this side of him was far different. He'd become intense and raw like testosterone was barreling through his veins from the tick in his clean-shaven jaw to the way his biceps seemed to be busting out of his dress shirt as he death-gripped the steering wheel.

Violet didn't know why, but even like this, she trusted him. He was angry for sure, but she was certain that his anger wasn't directed toward her. She had a sneaking suspicion that he was angry at himself.

She didn't know what had happened exactly, but she prudently decided now was not the time to ask questions. Violet had forgotten about her hunger, but the dull throb in her head intensified. She felt tired. She looked out the window as they sped along the rugged coastline. Waves hypnotically rolling against the sandy shores. It was otherworldly. Slowly, she drifted off into a deep sleep.

Chapter 10

In His Bed

VIOLET FELT THE SOFT pillow under her head, and she pulled the crisp, clean duvet tighter around her. She breathed in deeply, feeling sated. Mmm, clean, fresh spiciness filled her senses. And something else. What was that? She crinkled her nose. In her dreamlike state, she felt like she was being watched, and her eyes sprung open.

A wet lick to the face greeted her. Startled, she sat up. A horse lay upon the bed, staring at her expectantly. Okay, maybe not a horse, but definitely an oversized dog—not a normal-sized dog at all. This dog was enormous. And his tail was wagging excitedly. Feeling disoriented, Violet looked around the room.

It was the second time in less than a day that she woke up wondering where she was, but at least this time, she noted her head felt better. She eyed a huge stone wall fireplace on the wall toward the foot of the bed. She looked up at the dark wood posts of the beautiful four-poster bed she lay in.

Nice room, she thought to herself, feeling in awe of her surroundings. The oversized dog beside her inched closer and looked at her with anticipation in his big brown eyes.

"And what is it I can do for you?" She smiled, rubbing the shaggy white-gray beast on his head and giving his soft ears a scratch. He rolled onto his back in appreciation, offering his hairy belly up for a rub. Violet laughed at the move, but then also noted the big hairy creature was a girl dog, not a boy. Almost as quickly as the dog had rolled over, she'd rolled back and jumped off the bed, getting to the door just as it opened.

Lachlan peeked in the narrow opening of the door, and Violet realized he was checking on her. "I'm awake. You can come in," she said sleepily, and the door opened. Violet's heart did a little flip-flop at the sight of him as if she'd forgotten how his very presence seemed to take her breath away.

"Hi." He smiled lightly as he came to sit on the end of the bed. He seemed much more at ease again. That intense, angry energy was gone.

"Hi," she said awkwardly, belatedly realizing she'd been asleep in what she could only assume was his bed.

He ran his hand through tousled locks and looked at her from under his brow. The effect did funny things low in her belly.

"Did ye have a good rest? I think ye must've needed it."

"I slept like the dead." She smiled with a fortifying stretch and wondered if she'd imagined his eyes dropping to her chest for the briefest of moments.

"That's good. I see ye've met Sally." He ruffled her ears and patted her back.

Sally, not the name she would have imagined for this oversized scruffy beast. Although she did seem very sweet. "She's a big lady."

"Yer not scared of dogs, are ye?" he asked with concern etching his handsome features. "She'd never hurt ye. In fact, she hasn't left yer side since the moment I brought ye in."

A little shiver ran down her spine at the thought of him carrying her inside. She couldn't believe she slept through it—again! Although the first time he'd carried her, she wasn't asleep. Still, it would be nice to be conscious the next time he decided to carry her—if there was a next time. *One could only hope.*

"No, no, I love dogs. All animals. I love animals," she rambled, trying to focus on anything other than the fact she was lying in this dreamy guy's bed. Fortunately, he didn't seem to be concerned by it.

"I had a feeling about that. I don't think Sally would've taken to ye if ye weren't a dog lover. She's an excellent judge of those things."

They sat silently for a moment. He raked his hand through his hair again, and she wondered how he could make such a benign gesture look so freaking sexy. It could be the way it tousled up his dark pompadour fade haircut, or it could be the way his bicep bulged when he did it. Either way, she liked it.

"I'm sorry I passed out on you," she said, aware it had happened twice now. Although this time, she'd slept and not blacked out.

He chuckled. "Ye really slept like the dead. Didn't even stir once when I brought ye in. To be honest, part of me worried ye were sleeping too deeply. I stayed here for a time to be sure ye were okay. I didnae want to leave ye, but ye seemed to be sleeping peacefully, so I eventually just left ye to it.

"Thank you."

"Of course. I did come back to check on ye. I didnae forget that I agreed to keep watch."

Violet's heart flip-flopped, liking that this handsome man was taking care of her. He really was like a knight.

He went quiet, and she sensed he was trying to find the words for what he wanted to say. A little piece of her worried that he'd changed his mind and didn't want her to stay here after all.

“About earlier,” he began. He was looking down as if grappling with himself. When he glanced back up at her, his eyes were so piercing and blue.

“I’m sorry,” he said. His gaze never wavered from hers.

A little trickle of relief rippled over her. She assumed he was referring to what had happened at Craggy's. There was a crease between his brows, and she could practically feel the tension emanating off him.

“It’s okay,” she said, hoping to ease his mind.

“No, it’s no’.” His eyes dropped from hers, and he took a deep breath. “‘It's a long story. Safe to say, we were at the wrong place at the wrong time.”

She nodded, still not understanding what had happened, only that Lachlan was a bubbling cauldron when he'd told her to go to the car and when he got in moments later.

Lachlan looked down at the floor, hands rested on his waist, but his broad shoulders looked tense, and she wished she could massage away his tension.

“It’s okay,” she said. “I’ve got time for a long story if you feel up to telling it.”

That slightly crooked smile touched his lips, nearly knocking her back down into his bedsheets.

“Right. How about a wee bit of dinner first?”

“Oh my God, what time is it?” She scanned the room for a clock.

He chuckled. “Dinner time, lass. Come on, I’ve made us some supper. You must be ravenous by now. That doctor will no’ think much of me if ye starve to death.”

Smiling, Violet threw off the soft, cozy duvet, immediately feeling the cool of the room, but she willed herself to get up off the bed. She pulled her sweater a little tighter, crossed her arms around herself, and padded her way to where Lachlan stood by the door.

“Och, lass, ye look as cold as a bug in a snowstorm."

She giggled lightly at his turn of phrase as he wrapped her in his arms and pulled her close. Violet had to hold back a groan. It felt so good to snuggle into his warm broad chest. She could get used to his brawny arms around her. *Mmm, fresh yummy spiciness,* she thought to herself, breathing in his scent. He rubbed his hands on her back to warm her. She unfolded her arms and put them around his waist. She became aware as her breasts pressed against his firm torso, and it sparked a different kind of hunger in her. Pressing a kiss to the top of her head, to her disappointment, he released her.

“Come on, Violet. Dinner awaits.” Lachlan hadn’t thought anything of it when he pulled her in close to warm her, but the feel of her in his arms reminded him he needed to be on his best behaviour. He was much too aware of her every curve and her light vanilla scent. He reminded himself that she was in his home as his guest and as his friend. Nothing more. It didn't help that she'd slept in his bed, though. Despite having a guest bedroom, he still hadn't furnished it. Where else was he supposed to put her to sleep?

When he agreed to stay with Violet, he hadn't exactly thought through the sleeping arrangements. And even now, he wasn't sure what he was intending for the night. He had to keep an eye on her, so it would make sense to stay in the same room at the very least. Shite. Perhaps he could make up a bed on the floor for himself.

"Tell me it's not reheated mystery pudding?" Violet said as she followed Lachlan out of the bedroom.

"Fine idea, lass," he teased.

"Your home is beautiful."

He could hear the awe in her voice, and he felt a sense of pride. He loved this house. "Thank ye. It was my grandparents, but after my grandda passed, my nan moved in with my parents. She was older and frail. This big old house was too much for her."

"That makes sense."

"Aye, she was going to put it on the market, but I couldn't imagine letting this beautiful place go. So I bought it from her."

"I bet she was glad to keep it in the family. It's so beautiful." Lachlan nodded as he looked back at Violet, who was running a hand over the rugged stone wall of the stairwell as if it were treasure.

The curved wall that hugged one side of the stairwell was all made of various shades of stone. In front of them stood a wall of windows with views of the Scottish countryside, and above them was a vaulted ceiling that had heavy wood-hewn beams running the length of it. Lachlan loved the character of this manor house. Most people appreciated the beauty of this home, but for some reason, it warmed Lachlan how taken Violet seemed to be.

"My grandda and his da did a lot of the woodwork ye see. I had some things modernized a few years back, but I'd never touch the woodwork."

"Why would you? It gives it so much character."

Lachlan smiled, glad Violet could see its beauty, too. He could imagine his grandda now, proudly telling her how he'd hand-planed the cedar wood beams himself, readying them. He felt nostalgic thinking about his grandparents. His nan had passed away only a few months after his grandda. His mam insisted that she died of a broken heart. Lachlan couldn't say one way or the other, but he did know that his grandparents had loved each other fiercely, passionately.

He snuck a glance at Violet, who was now looking up at his grandda's beams like she was seeing the stars for the first time. And it struck him—this woman was like his grandparents' love. Fierce and passionate. And fearless—moving to the other side of the world to start a business, not knowing a soul. He'd never met a woman like Violet.

Chapter 11

Stepping Into His World

The table had eight carved chairs around it, but with only two place settings—one across from the other. It was rustic wood with a farmhouse feel to it. The simple black iron chandelier that hung above the table was dimly lit. Two well-used tapered candles burned. Wax drippings caked the sides of the small glass holders.

Lachlan brought two plates, with dinner already laid out, to the table. Violet breathed in the delicious scent. Her mouth watered—she was starving. The plate had a bundle of deep green-coloured beans, sliced steamed beets, buttered baby potatoes and sliced seasoned chicken breast.

"Please," Lachlan gestured politely for her to begin. Violet sipped at the water in front of her and he suddenly jumped up. "I'm so sorry, would ye like a glass of wine? I completely forgot to offer."

She found it amusing and sweet that he was berating himself over wine. "Not right now, thanks though," she smiled, putting a mouthwatering forkful of food into her mouth.

"Mmm," she cooed. "How do you get your chicken so tender?"

"Ah, that's top secret, lass."

Violet hadn't realized how famished she was until she'd plowed through her meal in record time. She put down her knife and fork, feeling satiated.

"Can I get you some more?" Lachlan offered, standing up.

"Oh no, thank you. I don't think I could eat another bite. It was delicious." She couldn't recall the last time she'd managed to eat everything on her plate. Violet was more of a snack type than a full meal type.

"Can I offer ye a whisky? I know ye like it." He eyed her, throwing her his irresistable crooked grin.

"Are you going to have one too?" she asked tentatively.

"Och, aye," he said, his Scots burr rolling thickly, sending a warm tingle down her spine. He stepped over to a nearby side cabinet. Opening the door below, he picked out a dark bottle, pulled the cork and sniffed it. It appeared to be a well-rehearsed ritual. He poured two glasses and then picked up a carafe of water from beside the glasses and carefully poured a drop into each glass. Swishing them both in his hands, he walked back to the table.

Handing Violet a glass, he clinked it with his, and sat down, "Slainte."

"Slainte," Violet smiled back at him, realizing the word, pronounced slanj-uh, must mean something like cheers. Before bringing it to her lips, she breathed in its rich, deep scent. Taking a sip, she closed her eyes. The warm amber liquid danced on her tongue. It was so flavourful, like buttery spicy fruitcake that had warmed in a campfire. She swallowed, and when she opened her eyes, her breath hitched.

Lachlan was watching her with a hunger in his intense gaze. Awareness crept through her as she licked the hint of scotch off her bottom lip. The way he eyed her made her feel like he'd like to do it for her. A heady sensation rippled through her and she shivered.

"Too strong?" His voice had a huskiness she hadn't noticed before.

"No, it's perfect." A smile played on her lips as she tried to calm her kicked-up pulse. She took another sip, despite the tension that suddenly filled the space between them. The heat from the whisky only deepened the flush in her cheeks "Mmm, this is so good." The words slipped out more breathy than she intended, and she forced herself to focus. "I don't know how to describe it."

With her eyes closed, she sat still, half wondering if Lachlan was watching her—while marvelling at the scotch's complexity, the way the flavours mingled on her tongue like an unfolding love story.

Opening her eyes, she was disappointed to find Lachlan's gaze was downcast as he took a longer sip of his whisky. *Spell broken?* she wondered, suddenly unsure if she'd misread the look in his eyes when he'd watched her. Picking up her plate, she stood, intending to help clean up.

"Oh, no ye dinnae," he scolded, stealing her plate from her hand. "Ye go sit yourself in the lounge. I'll take care of this." He shooed her away. "Ye need to take it easy."

"I'm pretty sure I can help with the dishes," she argued.

"Oot with ye, down the end of the hall is the lounge," he nudged her out of the dining room, not allowing her to argue with him.

"Alright, alright," she smiled. "Thank you."

"There's more whisky in there if ye need a refill, help yerself."

"Mmm, it is going down awfully easy. Seriously, I think it's the nicest I've ever tasted," she added.

"Really?" Lachlan asked, "It's one of my own."

"As in you made it?" she asked, dumbfounded.

"Aye" was all he said, with a gleam in his eyes, before taking their dishes to the kitchen.

Violet stood there, contemplating his comment, and then took another sip—as if needing to test it. Still delicious. He'd really made this? She honestly couldn't remember tasting a better Scotch. Not that she was a connoisseur—but still. Every sip seemed to get better than the last—more complex. Was that even possible? And what did he mean, anyway, when he said he made it? Like... in his house? She glanced around, half-expecting to spot a door to a secret whisky-making room. Was this some kind of Scottish pastime? Smirking to herself, she made her way down the hall to find the lounge.

It was really more of a corridor than a hall. The man's home was grand. Like a castle. A room with an open door caught her eye. Curious, she poked her head inside. A heavy-looking wooden desk with drawers sat in front of a large picture window. A tall bookcase lined one wall, filled with books and carefully placed decor. The whole room looked beautifully styled—like something out of a magazi-ne.

Not bad, she thought wryly as she carried on down the hall. For the first time, she wondered what Lachlan did for a living. A Lawyer? Not a chance—she ruled that out immediately, having worked with lawyers before. A doctor? That didn't fit either; he'd been just as rattled as she was by her accident.

Violet strolled through double doors at the end of the hall, and the rolling sea greeted her. "Oh my god," she whispered in awe. Large windows lined one long wall, and through them was a pebbled beach and the sea—this was Lachlan's backyard. The gentling rolling waves sounded so loud and clear. She'd noticed the salubrious sound earlier but had no idea how close the ocean was to Lachlan's home. The sun had set, and dusk painted the evening sky in deep blues and purples with ribbons of orange and pink.

Mesmerized, Violet stood for a moment, simply gazing out the window, reflecting on how lucky she was to be in Scotland, chasing her dreams—and the serendipitous bump in the road that led her to cross paths with Lachlan. Sally lumbered into the room, pulling Violet from her musings. "Hello, big girl," she cooed to the dog, who easily stepped onto the couch and settled in. Flicking on a lamp, Violet took in the room—two deep forest green tufted leather sofas faced each other, flanking another large fireplace. Lachlan must have lit the fire while she slept.

The wood crackled and popped, the flames warming the room. Violet wandered slowly, taking it all in. On the low, oversized coffee table between the two sofas sat the scotch. "Don't mind if I do," she murmured to herself, pouring a small splash in her glass. A carafe of water sat nearby, so she followed Lachlan's lead and added a careful drop.

A cluster of well-used pillar candles sat on the table. She looked around for matches and found some near the hearth. She lit the candles appreciating how their warm glow added to the ambiance. On the wall opposite the fireplace, a gallery wall of framed photographs caught her eye. Scotch in hand, she wandered over to take a peek. The photos spanned decades—family snapshots that clearly went back to Lachlan's childhood. There were pictures of his parents and what she assumed were siblings and friends. A few formal family portraits stood out, and Violet lingered on them.

She quickly discovered that Lachlan had a twin. Identical—or nearly. His brother didn't seem to possess that slightly crooked grin that made her knees increasingly weaker every time it spread across his handsome face. Aside from a twin brother, there appeared to be a younger brother and sister, as well as an older sister. One photo of the five siblings was particularly adorable—Lachlan looked about seven or eight. They stood in front of a Christmas tree, each holding a toy, except for the eldest sister, who was holding a white Scottie dog with a red bow. Every face was lit with a matching ear-to-ear grin—Lachlan's, with its telltale crook.

Another image caught her attention—Lachlan and his older sister, dressed in riding gear, standing in front of two stunning horses. Violet adored horses. Seeing that he had experience with them made her heart skip a beat. He really seemed like the perfect man. Her knight in shining armour, she thought whimsically, and then chuckled to herself as she took a sip of scotch. "Woah there, Violet," she chided.

Chapter 12

Dirty Dishes and Dirty Thoughts

Lachlan washed the dishes and tidied up after their dinner. All the while, his mind replayed the events of the day. He'd been so distracted that he hadn't noticed she'd fallen asleep in the car until they arrived at his home. When he drove into his garage, he considered leaving Violet in the car since she slept so peacefully, but it would defeat the purpose of him watching over her.

Decision made, he carefully opened the passenger side door so as not to disturb her. At six-foot-four, crouching down to maneuver a lass from his car was tricky and made even worse by how soundly she slept. Her slender limbs were dead weight. It was a struggle, but he managed to scoop her out. As he stood, he adjusted her in his arms, and she stirred and looked directly at him with sleepy bedroom eyes, smiled, and promptly fell right back into a deep sleep. To his chagrin, that innocent fleeting look made his cock stir.

"Bloody hell," he cursed under his breath. He wondered why in God's name his dick suddenly had the mind of a horny teenager. It's not that he wasn't a virile man, but it was almost comical how many times his cock had stood at attention in the past twenty-four hours. It was also mildly disturbing. He had no business reacting this way to Violet Munro, and perhaps even more troubling was the lack of this reaction to his girlfriend—during sex, yes, but outside of it, no. Lachlan wasn't the kind of guy to have spontaneous erections. He couldn't recall a time as an adult when his dick had gone so bloody rogue. Christ, this was not good. Not good at all.

Wiping down the counter, his thoughts replayed to when they'd arrived at the house. He tried to focus on the task at hand, carrying Violet into his home, and without knowing where else to lay her, he brought her up to his room. He lay her on the bed, and as he looked down at her, the oddest feeling passed through him. It was like his muscles relaxed, and he had almost a serene sensation wash over him.

Lachlan was accustomed to a baseline of anxiety thrumming through him. It was something he'd accepted as part of being an adult with responsibilities, but as he stood watching Violet with her long sun-kissed blond hair on his pillow, the familiar buzz of anxiety and tension in his muscles was notably and inexplicably absent.

He had known he should make an exit and allow her to rest, but before he turned to leave, his eyes dropped to her booted feet tucked up on his crisp white bedding. Lachlan took after his mother in the cleaning department, and at times, he was perhaps a little bit OCD. He liked things tidy and organized, but he didn't know what had him more distracted. The tan ankle boots on his bed—outdoor footwear on his clean sheets—or the long slender legs curled above them. His eyes had almost bore through those boots, as if he could've distracted his thoughts from the keen awareness that she lay *in his bed*.

He tore his gaze away, turned to walk out the door, and then suddenly doubled back, crouching down to carefully unzip one tan ankle boot at a time. Gently, he slid them from her feet so as not to disturb her. Although, he'd almost bet a herd of elephants could trample through the room and the lass would sleep through it.

Lachlan wasn't a fan of feet. Most feet were pretty gross to him with their gangly toes and weird smells. He knew damn well his feet aversion stemmed from when he was younger and his brothers and even his youngest sister, Orlagh, would tease him mercilessly, shoving their grubby toes on his bare arms or even his face if they were lounging watching a movie, which they did often as kids. His dad hated feet, too. Just one of those weird quirks, he supposed. As he'd gotten older, he didn't hate them like he did as a kid. He'd even grown accustomed to when Anna's feet would touch his legs in bed.

Not that he liked it—he'd never like it— but he'd accepted it. He still drew the line at foot massages, though. No way, no how, would he ever be the giver or receiver. *Rank.*

Before he slid off Violet's boots, as odd as it seemed, he braced himself for ugly feet to accost his senses, despite knowing it wouldn't likely be the case. In the back of his mind, he almost hoped for Violet to have reprehensible, hideous feet so that maybe he could stop bloody lusting after the woman. He needed something to help him lock out the prickles of desire that kept assailing him.

As he carefully slid off one boot and then the other, he almost groaned. Smooth soft-looking skin, delicate ankle bones, perfectly trimmed nails with a soft pink polish, and a natural beauty he didn't think feet could possess. Of course, the woman was the definition of graceful, almost swan-like beauty. And when the boots came off, her toes stretched out then curled in softly as if pleased to be free. Right there and then, it occurred to him that if he were forced to suck on toes, he'd choose those toes right there. Lachlan swallowed and stood, running a hand over his smooth jaw. *Where in the name of fucking Mary had that thought come from?*

Then he pulled up the blanket that lay on the end of the bed, covering the lass, and made a prompt exit. Knowing he'd need to check on her regularly, he went downstairs and grabbed a wee whisky and his laptop before heading back up the stairs. He knew he could've used some space from the lass, but the entire reason she was with him was for him to keep an eye on her—space was not really an option. He'd sat in one of the lounge chairs in front of the bay window niche in the hall near his bedroom, checking on her more than necessary.

After putting the last dish away and hanging the hand towel to dry, Lachlan picked up his whisky glass and rolled its contents. His thoughts still on the woman who'd literally fallen into his world. He couldn't keep the vision of how Violet looked sipping *his* whisky from his thoughts.

Dear God. The way she closed her eyes to savor the dram he'd given her. She'd looked almost aroused. *Had she been aroused*? Then he chided himself for such a ridiculous thought. But when she'd opened her eyes and licked her full, lovely lips, his damn dick had tugged again, and he'd had to force his thoughts to something benign. And heaven help him, the first *benign* thought that popped into his head was Anna. And a new shame had rolled over him.

Lachlan set down his glass again and rubbed his palms over his eyes, trying to ease the strain that sat behind them. Anna was his girlfriend, and he would *not* do anything to disrespect her. It was not like him to be so distracted—by a lass, no less. Lachlan always kept relationships with women platonic. He assured himself he was nothing like his playboy brother Drew. There was a reason Drew called him Saint Lachlan, and the truth was that Lachlan wasn't bothered by the nickname. Even Alex had taken to calling him by it. He wasn't a saint, but he was a man of integrity and morals. And he was certain that was why a part of him wanted to get as far away as possible from Violet Munro. If she was safely away from him, his integrity would not come into question. Another part of him knew damn well that he couldn't abandon the lass—he wouldn't. It was like the universe was having a wee laugh at his expense.

And then there was Anna. They had an okay relationship. They didn't argue, and for the most part, it was easygoing. Lachlan had grown accustomed to her. Despite a short courtship, he supposed moving in together was the natural next step. At least, that was what Anna kept telling him. His mam had said something along the same lines as well. It was not that he thought it was too soon per se, but he just wasn't sure it was what he wanted.

Lachlan gripped the counter, leaning over the sink with his head dropping. He lolled it from side to side, attempting to ease the tension that clenched his neck and shoulders. Try as he might, every time he thought of Anna moving in with him, something nagged at him about it. He didn't want things to change. He was content with the way things were. Or was he?

He raked a hand through his hair. Were the reactions he was having to Violet more about Anna? As if Violet was one last fling before he committed to Anna? *Christ.* Probably not the best way to think about it. But maybe it was like having cold feet before a wedding. Not that anyone had talked about marriage. But that was the next step after moving in together. The thought sent a shudder through him. H e *definitely* wasn't ready for marriage. *But what if Violet was his wife?* He growled, crossing his arms over his chest, alarmed at the direction of his thoughts. Obviously, he was attracted to her, but *for the love of Mary,* he needed to get a grip, or this could be disastrous.

He would *never* have a fling, nor would he give in to any of those lusty feelings that were stumbling haphazardly in his head. It was absurd, though, how difficult it was to control his thoughts and reactions to Violet. His mind incessantly jumped into fantasy, and his body practically thrummed any time he touched the lass. It wasn't in his nature to get so bloody randy. That had always been a Drew trait, and if this morning's encounter with his younger brother was any indication, it still was.

Drew. That was another heavy thought. God, he'd missed him. He would have hoped time had changed things, but clearly, it had not. Drew still hated him. How he wished things were different. They used to be so close. He missed the brother he once knew. Lachlan picked up his whisky and sipped, savoring its familiar burn.

Violet probably thought he'd gotten lost. He should go be with her. The thought both excited him and had him trepidatious. Before heading to the lounge, he chugged back an ice-cold glass of water, hoping to curb his fiery thoughts. Violet was an attractive and intriguing lass, but his only objective was to be her friend and help her. "This is no' a difficult task," Lachlan muttered to himself, adjusting his overly sensitive cock in his pants, silently begging it to behave.

Chapter 13

Sgt. Pepper

LACHLAN DETOURED TO HIS cellar before heading into the lounge. Violet seemed to appreciate Cailleach whisky. The least he could do was be a good host. He brought up a bottle of one of his favourites for her to taste. She seemed to have a discerning pallet. He'd be curious to get her take on one of Cailleach's finest drams. Lachlan felt lighter and more in control as he strode down the hall.

Coming through the double doors of the lounge, he did not anticipate the sight that greeted him. Violet had found his old record player. Music filled the room, and there she was, cardigan discarded, dancing and singing, unabashed and carefree. In his entire thirty years, Lachlan could say with certainty that he'd never been spellbound—until now. She sang along to "Jolene" by Dolly Parton, belting out the chorus like a weekend festival goer, high on life. And God help him, he couldn't stop his eyes from dropping to the thin white blouse that glided and tugged over her perfectly peaked breasts.

A loud pop from wood burning in the fireplace, swiftly brought Lachlan back to his senses. He drew in a breath, reminding himself of his resolve. Violet glanced up, noticing him in the doorway. Her singing trailed off, and she stopped dancing. Her cheeks turned pink as she took in his presence.

"I'm sorry. I totally got carried away," she said, chin tilted down shyly in complete juxtaposition to the bold, carefree woman he'd just witnessed.

"Please dinnae let me stop ye."

But the song ended, and she picked up her cardigan from the back of the settee, slipping it back on. "My parents had a record player when I was growing up. I haven't actually listened to a real record since I was probably twelve years old," she said wistfully. "I'm sorry. I just found it irresistible."

She was irresistible. He quelled the unbidden thought and smiled. "Now I ken ye must be Canadian. Ye've apologized twice in less than a minute."

Her eyes twinkled, and she let out a throaty chuckle.

"Those old records dinnae get played near enough." He was far too aware of her as he strode past her to the record console that once belonged to his nan. He carefully picked up the single forty-five from the player, put it back in its yellowing paper sleeve, slid it alongside the other stack of forty-fives in the cabinet, and scanned the twelve-inch LPs until he found the one he wanted. Setting the record on the turntable, the needle landed, and there was a nostalgic crackle and pop before it found the groove, and "Sgt. Pepper's Lonely Hearts Club Band" began to play.

"Ooh, I love The Beatles!" She crooned as she rhythmically began to sway her slender hips with her arms bending as she let the music move her.

Lachlan pulled his gaze away and absently flipped through the records. It surprised him that she had put on music and danced so freely in his home. He wasn't used to anyone being quite so at ease with him—or with themselves. The people in his life tended to be rather proper and overly polite if not careful around him. He wasn't sure what to make of the lass before him. As if sensing his thoughts, she leaned in close to him.

"I'm sorry. I should have asked if it was okay to snoop through your records."

He stiffened slightly at her nearness. Practically hearing the smile playing her lips, her breath tickled his ear.

"And I just said sorry. Again. God, it really is a Canadian thing." She chuckled that throaty melodic sound, oblivious to its effect on him as she plopped herself onto his settee.

"I willnae hold it against ye," he teased back, stepping to the fireplace to add some logs. The flames crackled and spat as they caught fire. It was mid-March, and the evenings could still get rather cool, especially in this room full of windows.

"God, that felt good." She sighed contentedly.

"Aye, far cry from being held up in a hospital bed," Lachlan said poking the logs in the grate and reminding himself why she was in his home in the first place.

"I think between my extra-long nap and that scrumptious dinner, my energy is making a comeback."

"And the whisky," he teased.

"And the whisky." She raised her glass. "It feels a bit overkill, me being here," she said quietly.

Lachlan was glad the lass didn't seem to have any repercussions from her ordeal, but it seemed prudent to err on the side of caution. "Better to be safe than sorry. And it was the doctor's orders," he reminded her.

"I guess so," she sounded reluctant. "Well, if I haven't said it already, I'm grateful you agreed to take me in."

"I'm happy to have you here," he reassured her, and he meant it. He couldn't remember the last time he enjoyed anyone's company more.

Fire adequately roaring again, he stood up and almost went to sit beside her on the settee when he thought better of it and sat on the one safely across from her instead.

"I brought up one of my favourite whiskys from the cellar. Would ye like a wee dram?" he offered.

"Ooh yes, please, I'd love to try it. I can't imagine it could be as good as this one." She smiled slyly.

Avoiding looking too long into her playful bright eyes, he pulled the cork and poured some amber liquid into her empty glass and poured one for himself as well. "*Slainte Mhath*," he said, clinking glasses with her.

"Cheers." She grinned up at him before taking a sip.

And he couldn't help but study her pretty face, knowing the flavours were drizzling over her tongue.

Her eyes widened delightedly as she looked up at him, swallowing, "Mm, oh. Oh, my," she gushed.

"I thought ye might like it." He smiled, feeling pleased.

"It's stronger. It has more depth to it than the last one. I wouldn't have thought that possible," she said sipping it again. Her pretty golden brow furrowed in concentration.

"It's so rich and rugged. It's like I can taste dark chocolate and sea salt, but with a hint of sweet tangy cherry and vanilla and, like, tobacco." She sipped again as if trying to figure out the puzzle in her mouth.

"Aye, yer right." Lachlan felt equally surprised and impressed at just how accurate her description was. She was picking up on notes that professional whisky tasters missed.

"This dram," he said, holding it up to the light admiringly, "has aged in a variety of casks—oak, bourbon, and sherry. That's part of what adds to the complexity and depth."

"Wow," she breathed. "I've never tasted scotch this good. It's like each sip brings out even more flavours. It's amazing."

Her proclamation had Lachlan's chest puffing with something akin to pride. Perhaps he'd take her down and show her his cellar. Better yet, he should arrange to give her a tour of the distillery. Lachlan took a sip, feeling himself relax as he began to enjoy the easy company of Violet Munro.

She studied him over the rim of her glass like she had something she wanted to say.

"What's on yer mind, lass?" He asked.

"I'm wondering about today," she admitted. "I know you said it was a long story, but what happened at Craggy's?" She sat back and tucked her legs up on his settee.

"Ugh, right." Lachlan sighed reluctantly. He didn't know how to talk about it. It was such a long, heavy story, and with the evening being so pleasant, why go down that path? "Must we discuss this, Miss Munro?"

She raised her brows. "So formal. You did save my life, remember. I think you can call me by my first name."

He smirked. "Aye, of course, Violet." He couldn't help but notice how beautiful she was sitting across from him. The firelight played on her features. "I dinnae think I saved yer life though."

"I beg to differ, and you are avoiding my question." She looked at him pointedly.

He almost laughed at her directness. What a lethal combination, sweet and direct. "I am avoiding yer question."

“Oh, come on. Our bellies are full, we’re enjoying exceptional scotch, and the fire is roaring. It’s the perfect time to spill your guts. Your secrets are safe with me.” She grinned conspiratorially.

His lips quirked. The lass had a very disarming manner, and he found himself mightily tempted. The problem was he didn’t know how to open up about it. Lachlan was never good at speaking about his family matters, especially when it came to his younger brother, Drew. He hadn’t even told Anna the full extent of his relationship with Drew. She only knew that they hadn’t spoken for over two years.

“It’s okay, Lachlan,” Violet said softly, seeming to recognize his struggle to find the words. “You don’t have to tell me everything, but maybe tell me about today. What happened?”

He raked a hand through his hair and exhaled heavily, reluctant.

“I heard raised voices when I was in the ladies’ room, and then when I came out, I saw you hit some guy,” she began for him.

Shite. Lachlan didn't think she'd seen that. Christ, what she must think of him? "Violet, I need ye to ken that is no' me. I'm no' some brute, I dinnae go around punching people." He stood up and walked back toward the fireplace with tension winding through his shoulders as his thoughts weighed heavily on his mind.

"If I thought you were dangerous in any way, I certainly wouldn't have gotten into your car," she stated.

When his eyes met hers, he felt almost overwhelmed by the warmth in them. Perhaps she didn't think the worst of him, though, he wouldn't blame her if she did. He supposed that he could at least try and explain. He owed her that.

"Tell me," she encouraged. Those moss-green eyes were so disarming.

Lachlan cleared his throat. "Ye saw the table of lads beside us, aye?"

She nodded.

"I overheard them talking about ye when ye went to the ladies, and I dinnae like what they were saying." Lachlan felt the tick in his jaw as it tightened, recalling their crude words.

"Oh," Violet said softly.

Looking up at her, he continued, "It wasnae right, so I told them to mind their manners."

Her eyes widened.

Lachlan cupped his hand to the back of his neck, tension pulling tightly on it. "And that's when I noticed one of the men was my brother. Drew."

"Your brother?"

He didn't miss the shock in her voice.

"Aye. I huvnae seen Drew in a long time and—" he paused. "We dinnae see eye to eye on things." Lachlan shook his head. "I shouldnae huv let him goad me this morning. I dinnae normally react like that, but things are complicated with my brother." He was stumbling to explain it.

"So I take it he deserved a good punch to the kisser," Violet summed it up.

Lachlan almost laughed as a bit of tension eased. "Aye, he deserved it. It's been a long time in coming." Lachlan stared blankly as memories flooded his mind.

"He deserved it, but you still feel bad?" she asked.

"Aye, something like that."

"Why did he call you 'Saint Lachlan?'"

"Och, lass, ye ask hard questions." He was silent as he considered the question. "Our parents raised us with strong morals and values. It might sound old-fashioned, but I consider myself to be a gentleman." It was true, despite his wayward thoughts since meeting Violet. He was a man of morals. Talking about his convictions with her was a good reminder.

"I've noticed." She smiled lightly. "It's not old-fashioned. It's refreshing. I think you're a rare breed."

He didn't necessarily agree with her assessment, but he appreciated the sentiment. It made him wonder about the men in her life. Were they not gentlemen? The thought bothered him.

He cleared his throat and attempted to explain things further. "Drew was always a cad." Lachlan was struggling to find the words. "He always had a lass on each arm. I huv never been like that." He shook his head, feeling awkward. "I had plenty of women friends, but it wasnae like Drew." He looked up at Violet to judge her reaction, and fortunately, she was still looking at him warmly. "Dinnae get me wrong, I'm into women," he paused, realizing he was making a right mess of trying to explain himself. "I just... I'm not..."

"A womanizer," she finished for him, summing it up perfectly.

"Aye, exactly. Anyway, Drew gave me a hard time. I had women friends, but I wasnae one to..." He paused, awkwardness creeping back in. "Unlike my younger brother, I didnae huv the need to sleep with every woman who came into my sphere."

"That doesn't sound like a bad thing," she quipped.

"It's no'. But it is where 'Saint Lachlan' came from, I suppose."

"You have had girlfriends, though?"

Her curious tone made it sound like she feared he lived the life of a monk, and he had a very masculine, primal need to dispel her of the notion. He was vaguely aware that now would be a good time to mention that he had a girlfriend.

But the words didn't come out, and instead, he found himself saying, "Och aye. I'm no' really a saint."

"You're sure?" Violet teased, her eyes twinkling mischievously.

He liked it far too much.

"Do ye want me to prove it to ye, lass?" His voice dropped an octave, and the second the words were out of his mouth, he wondered what in the hell he was doing. But God help him, at the same time, perversely, he needed to know he wasn't the only one feeling whatever the hell it was he was feeling.

Those green eyes widened, giving away her surprise. But her teeth caught her bottom lip, causing his chest muscles to tighten and bunch, and an odd flutter banged in his lower abdomen.

Christ, the woman was pure temptation. Never had a lass tempted him like this. Lachlan cleared his throat, aware that the door he'd just cracked open needed to be slammed closed and locked.

"I'm sorry, lass. I shouldnae huv said that." He tore his gaze away from her and took a hearty sip of his whisky.

He could feel her eyes on him, but thankfully, she didn't say another word about it. Instead, she changed the subject as if the air hadn't grown thick with sexual tension, and he felt like he'd barely just dodged a bullet—one that would have killed *Saint Lachlan* with a single shot.

Chapter 14
Feet and Family

"I WAS LOOKING AT your photos," she said, gesturing to the wall behind him. "You look like such a loving family." He looked back over his shoulder at the photos. They were a loving family. *They are a loving family*, he corrected in his mind, despite the troubles they'd all been through. Troubles they were still going through. There was always love.

"Aye," he said wearily.

"You were close growing up?" she hedged.

"We were. Very close. We fought as every sibling does, but there was much love." He smiled nostalgically. It was true. They'd always been close, and despite the estrangement with Drew, he still believed the bond that tied them together as a family remained.

"I realize something must have happened between you and Drew, but what about your sisters? And I see you have a twin brother too. Are you still close with them?"

Lachlan was surprised that this woman he barely knew would ask him such personal questions, and yet, strangely, he didn't mind it. He was generally leery of people trying to dig into his personal matters. Being from a wealthy family, there were people who tried to get close to him for their own personal gain, but this— This was very different. He didn't know what it was about her, but he felt at ease in her presence like he could take off his wealthy businessman's coat of armour and just be himself. Maybe it was because she was unapologetically herself, pure and authentic—an intoxicating combination. In Lachlan's experience, people weren't always so genuine. There was a lot of smoke and mirrors in his world. Something deep in him knew the lass sitting across from him was as pure and real as it got—a rar ity.

Still, he never spoke about his family matters with anyone other than family. It struck him just how tempting it was to talk with Violet Munro. Really talk with her. Maybe it was to do with the events of last eve together, but something made him feel he could speak openly with her without fear of it coming back to haunt him.

Lachlan stood and walked over to the photos, looking at them. *Remembering.* Rolling the amber liquid in his glass, he took a sip.

"My older sister, Helena, she and I were very close growing up. We were very similar and always had a bond." He took in a deep breath, and it lumbered out heavily. It was never easy to talk about. "Helena died. In a riding accident. We were racing, and her horse caught his hoof in some low branches. She was thrown, and her neck broke." His voice wavered, and he stopped to fight back the tears that threatened. Swallowing down the lump in his throat, he added, "It was quick, and thankfully, she didnae suffer."

"Oh, God, Lachlan, I'm so sorry. I can't imagine how hard that must be." The lass wore her heart on her sleeve. She'd gotten up to stand by him. Her nearness was both alarming and comforting to him.

"Aye. It's been thirteen years, but the ache is still there. I miss her." He cleared his throat and stepped away from the photos—and away from the woman whose heat wreaked havoc on his senses even though she hadn't even touched him.

"I'm sure. I don't think you ever stop missing someone you love."

"No, that's true. Ye learn, somehow, to live without them," Lachlan said as he sat back down on the safe-distance-away settee.

Violet had settled herself back on the settee across from him, and he was oddly grateful for the oversized quartz coffee table barrier between them. The sky had turned dark through the windows behind her as day turned to night.

"Drew hasnae forgiven me, though," he said, surprising himself at the confession.

"What?" Her brows knit together in confusion. "Hasn't forgiven you for what?"

Lachlan shrugged. "He blames me for Helena's death." He glanced up to gauge her reaction.

She sat still, listening intently. There was no judgment on her pretty features, only a sadness etched around the corners of her eyes. "He thinks I should huv done something or that I shouldnae huv let her ride that day. I dinnae ken, exactly. I do ken that I'd give anything to huv her back, though."

"I'm sure you'd take her back in a heartbeat, but how could you have done anything to prevent what happened? It's not your fault," Violet said softly.

It was a bold proclamation for a lass that barely knew him, and despite the pain of it, he liked her all the more for it. Lachlan smiled sadly. "Well, according to Drew, it is. I was the one riding with her. It was because of me we were racing. If we hadnae, she would still be here." Those were realities he'd grappled with every day since the accident.

"Oh, Lachlan." She came over to sit beside him and laid her hand on his.

He was far too aware of the warmth of her slender fingers laying across the back of his hand, gently squeezing.

Looking him in the eye, she asked, "Do you believe that?"

He was silent for a moment. Most people tried to comfort him and reassure him that Helena's death was an accident and not his fault. There was always pity in their eyes, but he knew they meant well. Had anyone *ever* asked him what he thought? It shook him to realize that no one ever had. They only ever told him what they thought. A borage of opinions and words. This was the first time he'd been asked what he thought, and it threw him off. But as he sat there, with her hand on his, he knew exactly what he thought even though he'd never spoken it—he knew the truth.

Swallowing hard, he said, "Aye, for a time I did. I blamed myself. Guilt ate at me. The what-ifs gave me nightmares."

Violet sat quietly beside him, listening intently without judgment. He was almost waiting for her to jump in with her pity or well-meaning advice, but the lass just listened. Perhaps that was why he found himself speaking freely.

"I was riding one day a few months after Helena's accident. And it struck me that I was actually enjoying the ride. I wasn't just going through the motions, but the pleasure of riding came back to me. I was so aware, and it was like a peace settled over me. I felt good. For the first time in months, I felt good. And it came to me. I knew my sister, and she loved riding even more than I did. Nothing would have stopped her from riding that day. Nothing. She rode rain or shine. Why would that day huv been any different?"

The more Lachlan spoke his thoughts out loud, the more free he felt, and the words continued in a rush. "It was a freak accident. A terrible, terrible accident. It was horrendous, and God, I wish with everything in me that it hadn't happened. For so long, I wished we hadnae gone riding that day. And yet, I knew— I know," he corrected, "Helena was happy on her horse that day, like every other day. She wanted to be riding. Being on her horse with the wind whipping through her hair made her feel alive. Some people die and never know what it's like to truly feel alive, but my sister knew. And that brings me comfort somehow. I ken nothing could change what happened that day."

Lachlan ran his forearm across his wet eyes. "After that day, I ken in my bones, what had happened wasnae my fault. It was nobody's fault. It was a tragic accident."

Violet's smile was soft on him, and he could see the unshed tears in her eyes as well, making them impossibly green. "Thank you for telling me." Her voice was gentle and soothing like a balm on his soul. "I can't imagine what you've been through, but I'm so glad you found peace. She sounds like she was a free spirit."

"Aye, she was, and I realize how lucky I am to have spent time with her—to huv had her in my life. Even our last ride together. I'm even grateful for that. I feel privileged to have seen her last moments of pure joy on this earth."

A tear slipped down Violet's cheek, and she quickly wiped it away. "That is a beautiful perspective." Her voice was a whisper.

Lachlan let his whisky roll over his tongue. Helena would have liked Violet. From what he'd seen of the lass, she was a free spirit, too. It still surprised him how easy it was to open up to her and lay his deepest thoughts bare. Three months of dating Anna with the tentative plans of moving in together, and he hadn't once spoken about the day Helena died with her. Twenty-four tumultuous hours since meeting Violet Munro, and he was bletherin' away like he was on a daytime talk show with Oprah Winfrey. He would have suspected that talking about his family would be akin to pouring cask-strength whisky on an open wound, but to the contrary, he felt calm, almost like a weight had been lifted. He'd carried his thoughts for so long. It felt good to finally set them free.

Stealing a look at the woman sitting beside him, he again wondered about the strange connection that seemed to flow invisibly between them. That connection must have bloomed due to the circumstances of last night, but still, it was interesting how he felt when he looked at her. Like he wanted her to know everything there was to know about him, and he wanted to unravel every little mystery of her.

“What about your other sister? Are you still close?” Violet pulled him from his reverie.

“Aye, we are, thank God. She’s the baby in the family. Heart of gold, that one, and a little spitfire too. Orlagh. Helena had called her Rolo since she was a baby. And after a while, we all started to call her by it. Before Helena died, she'd roll her eyes at us when we called her that, but since, it's like she wears the name proudly. She was only twelve when Helena died. It was hard-on all of us, but Rolo looked up to Helena so much. We all did, but I think being the only other lass in the family, she idolized Helena. It was really hard to see her so heartbroken.” His sister's pain felt almost worse to him than his own. He remembered wishing he could take the pain for both of them. Like if he could only carry her burden, he would.

“I can’t imagine.” Violet’s eyes glistened with tears.

“Anyway, we got through, I suppose. We are all close,” Lachlan felt a familiar heavy ache settle in his chest, “except for Drew.” He rubbed a hand over his jaw. “In some ways, I think he took Helena’s death the hardest.”

“What makes you think that?”

Lachlan didn’t really have an answer. “Drew was thirteen when the accident happened. I think maybe it was his age. Our poor mam, she thought she’d had a hard time with my twin, Alex—he was a dare devil. My da swears he is the reason for his white hair, but Drew? Drew was a rebel. Always trying everything from smoking to drinking to sex. He was always playing in various bands with his friends—which was sometimes a good thing—but trouble always seemed to find hi m."

Slipping her hand from his and moving to lean back against the arm of the tuxedo sofa. Her knees bent up, and her bare feet settled mere inches from his thigh. If it had been anyone else's feet, he'd throw a pillow over top so he didn't have to look at them, but with Violet's, he had to fight the urge not to pull them onto his lap. And slowly slide his thumb along the hollows of each feminine arch. *Christ Mackenzie*, he chided himself inwardly and lifted his gaze to the darkness outside so he could focus his thoughts.

"Your brother played in music bands?" she asked, blissfully unaware of his unruly musings.

"Aye, there was barely a day that went by when there wasn't a racket in the garage. When Helena died, it was like Drew cut himself off from all of us. He was just with his friends, and a lot of them were absolute shite disturbers."

Violet's chuckle drew his attention. Her apple cheeks were rosy, perhaps from the whisky. "Sorry," she grinned, "didn't mean to interrupt."

"Shite disturbers," she said in a mock serious tone, urging him to continue.

Feeling his lips tug in a smile, he carried on. "Aye, shite disturbers. I dinnae ken. It's like Drew just got swept away into a different world. There were various bandmates over the years, but also he seemed to always hang out with some real arseholes."

"Got it, shit disturbers and arseholes. That can't be good." She bit her lip, clearly trying to stifle a giggle.

Cheeky lass. Christ, he liked her teasing, though. "This is a serious story," he admonished with an arched brow.

"I'm sorry," she said soberingly as she repositioned her long, slim denim-clad legs to sit cross-legged, and he regretted her feet sliding away from him.

"Och, lass, yer showing yer Canadian again," Lachlan teased, and the smile she gave him made his heart stutter. *Damn.*

"Tell me what happened with Drew," she coaxed with her throaty honey voice.

Lachlan stretched his arms over the length of the settee and crooked one arm to take a fortifying sip of his whisky. "Drew had less and less to do with us, and then about two years ago, he just up and left without a word. After a few days, he messaged Orlagh to say he was gone and for us to not bother trying to find him. He'd find us if and when he was ready. Today was the first time I've seen him or spoken to him since."

Surprise flashed in her eyes. "You haven't spoken to him at all since he left?"

Lachlan shook his head. "We didn't even know where he was for the last two years." His brow creased, and his voice grew thick. "The older Drew got, the more he began to drink. He'd lose himself in drink and women. He was always a flirt, our mam said he flirted even when he was a wee babe. I suppose it is his nature, but god, he went through women like they were nothing more than chewing gum. New flavour all the time, chewing them up, and he just spat them out. It's no' that they werenae willing participants, but it just seemed so meaningless. I thought he was trying to numb his pain with women and alcohol, and I made the mistake of telling him so."

"Oh," Violet said with her mouth in a perfectly shaped *O*.

"Aye, it wasnae good."

"I can imagine."

"I called him out on his shite—told him he needed to grow up." Lachlan shook his head, the memory sitting like a lead weight. "I didnae handle it very well. And neither did he. He came out right and told me that he blamed me for Helena's death."

"Oh, wow. That's heavy."

Lachlan nodded.

“I’m so sorry. If I hadn’t been there today, things could've gone so differently,” Violet said, regret marring her beautiful features.

“What? No." He didn't want her thinking that today had anything to do with her. It hadn't. Not really.

“Lachlan, you literally punched your brother defending me,” Violet argued.

“Ach, Lass, I’ve been wanting to punch him fer years. Ye just gave me a good excuse.”

“Really?” she said meekly.

“Aye, the arse deserved it, and it felt so freeing to let it fly.”

Violet snickered, a smile curving her lips.

Lachlan ran a hand through his hair. “The truth is, I love that mon so much, and I’m pissed off that he doesnae get that.”

“Maybe he does, deep down. Anger can blind people.”

“Aye, it’s true.” Lachlan considered it, and then his attention was drawn to where Violet had scooched closer to him. He caught her gaze, the soft lighting of the room glowing warmly on her face, drawing him in like a moth to a flame.

“Thank you for talking to me.” Her fingers slid into the open cup of his hand, and he looked at it, almost afraid to look into her beautiful eyes. He let his thumb lightly stroke over her fingers, feeling like he was toying with danger. Violet

seemed blissfully unaware of the feeling warring inside of him
.

"I can understand not wanting to talk about your family troubles, but I'm glad you told me. "

"I dinnae ken why, but I'm glad I told ye too," he said, not looking up, knowing that if he did, he'd regret what was bound to happen next.

Chapter 15

Not a Date, Date

THIS WAS THE ABSOLUTE farthest thing from her mind when she envisioned following her dreams in Scotland, but she was certainly enjoying the turn of events. This was, hands down, the best non-date, date, she'd ever had. She wondered when was the last time she'd had such deep and meaningful conversation with anyone. She and Sierra were best friends and always could be real, but she'd only just met Lachlan. And yet, he was so open with her.

There was something about him that made her feel so at ease. He possessed a calmness and strength. He was a good guy. *Even if he did punch his brother*, she thought sardonically. In truth, she found it kind of romantic, like he was defending her honour. She'd known from the moment his eyes held hers when she'd felt so utterly lost that there was a connection, but as the hours of the evening slipped away like minutes, she knew that her being here with him was more than just a kind man doing her a favour.

Violet became aware of Lachlan's gaze on her. He studied her as if he were trying to solve a puzzle.

"What?" she asked speculatively under his sudden scrutiny.

"I ken ye said ye were a fashion stylist, but I wondered if ye were also some kind of therapist." He raised a questioning brow.

"Like a massage therapist?" she quipped back.

"Och, are ye?" he asked, beginning to rub his neck as if it were tight, and he hoped she might help him out.

She chuckled."Nope, sorry to disappoint you. I'm not a massage therapist." Although she wouldn't mind giving it a go.

"Too bad." He flashed her his crooked grin, and Violet felt heat tingle at the juncture between her legs. Wholly affected by that grin of his, she pondered how a lopsided smirk could make him look as if he was the gatekeeper of some kind of sexy secret.

"I dinnae recall the last time I was able to speak so freely, lass. I feel like you could be a psychologist or counsellor. You're verra easy to talk to."

She eyed him with a gentle smile tugging her lips as she felt her cheeks flush under his praise. "Maybe you just needed to talk." She shrugged.

"I suspect ye hear yer fair share of stories styling people. Like a bartender, ye could be a shrink."

She laughed at the truth of it. The few clients she'd had definitely seemed to take their time together as an opportunity to unload all kinds of things. "I have heard a few tales."

"I huv no doubt." Lachlan leaned forward, picked up the decanter, and poured another round in each of their glasses. Sitting back again, he ran a hand down the front of his white dress shirt as if to smooth it, then he gave her a sly sideways glance.

"What is yer expert opinion? How am I doing? Do ye think I could use a style makeover?" He held his chin up in profile as if allowing her to assess him.

Violet smiled. "I don't think you're doing too badly, Mr. GQ."

"Och, lassie, the flattery is going to make my head big." His blue eyes twinkled with mischief.

"It's true. You are very stylish," she said matter-of-factly.

"I might have a wee shopping problem." He bit his lip.

Violet grinned. "Me too. I'm surprised, though. Not to stereotype, but most men hate shopping." From what she'd seen of him, the man was a very snappy dresser. From his rolled-sleeved dress shirt and his Patek Philippe watch she'd spied, down to his perfectly tailored trousers and argyle socks, the man was impeccably dressed.

"A good friend of mine owns a luxury men's shop in Glasgow. Obviously, I huv to support him." He threw her an angelic little smirk.

She laughed out loud.

"Ach, fine." He rolled his eyes to the ceiling. "I cannae help myself."

She chuckled. "Me neither. I think you may be my spirit animal."

He laughed, and the low rumble of it tickled her senses. The man was seriously appealing. Violet leaned back against the arm of the couch, and Lachlan sat back against the other arm. One long, strong leg was bent on the couch with his arms casually resting on it. The other was stretched out with his socked heel on the cow hide area rug.

"And what about you? What do you do for a living, Mr. GQ?" she quipped, taking a sip of her scotch, thoroughly enjoying the evening with him. She wouldn't be surprised if he modelled—from his physique to his features, the man was stupidly handsome. It would explain the sporty car and gorgeous house. It was quite plausible that his modelling career made him filthy rich. She almost laughed at the thought.

"I told ye what I did." He looked at her from under a quirked brow.

"What? No, you didn't. Oh my God, did I forget?" Her eyes grew wide, and her body tensed.

"I make whisky," he said and nodded toward her glass.

"You make whisky?" she repeated, looking down at her glass, not really understanding what he meant.

"Aye, yer drinking it. Therapy in a glass."

"You make this for a living?" She held up the glass, still not quite certain.

"Aye, for a living," he confirmed, his lips tipped at the corners in mild amusement. "Cailleach Distillery."

"Oh." Violet was still putting together the pieces in her mind. "You work at *Cay-lee-yak*"—she scrunched her eyes at her butchered pronunciation—"distillery? As in, you actually physically make the whisky?"

"Ach, lass." He chuckled heartily. "I own the distillery, and aye, I do huv a part in the making of it."

"Oh, right." She was trying to absorb this new piece of information. *He owned a distillery?*

Apparently noting her confusion, he leaned back. "What did ye think I meant earlier when I said I make whisky?"

"Ohh," she said exaggeratedly, recalling his comment, and then she giggled. "I don't know why, but when you said you made the scotch, I pictured you like one of those old guys who make terrible wine in their kitchen, straining barley in old lady pantyhose. Like a hobby or something."

He raised his brows. "I cannae say we huv ever used old lady pantyhose in our process."

She laughed despite herself. "I mean, like I thought you made it with a kit or something."

He nodded toward her glass. “Please tell me that doesnae taste like it’s from a kit?”

Violet looked at the contents remaining in her glass and took the final sip, making sure to let it linger over her tongue before she swallowed. “Nope, definitely not boxed scotch.”

“Ye dinnae say.” His crooked grin teased her.

“Modest, aren’t we?” she mocked.

“From time to time,” he jabbed back.

Violet laughed at Lachlan’s dry humour. The perfect host, he picked up the decanter to refill her glass.

“I think I better slow down,” Violet said, feeling the warming effects of the golden liquid.

“Just a drop more,” he hedged.

Maybe against her better judgment, but how could she resist? “Okay, just a drop.”

He smiled as he poured a splash more in each of their glasses.

She took a sip, still marvelling at how good it was and the fact that the man across from her owned the frickin’ distillery. Feeling her head swim a bit, she threw him a sly glance. “Are you trying to get me drunk?” She immediately regretted asking when he looked aghast.

"No, no, of course no'. I'm sorry. Ye dinnae huv to drink it." He leaned forward to take her glass, but she quickly pulled it close to her chest as if protecting its precious contents from him.

"Don't you try to steal it from me. It's mine!"

Lachlan's deep chuckle danced down her spine. "Do we huv a problem here, V?" His voice seemed to have dropped an octave.

"Only if you try to take my drink away," she challenged as she eyed him over the rim of her glass, taking a sip as if demonstrating her ownership over it. She liked that he'd called her V.

Her heart beat a little faster, and she shifted where she sat across from Lachlan as their eyes locked on each other with an electric charge so palpable between them that she swore she could see the sparks fly. The sound of a ringtone shattered the moment. Lachlan's phone lit up on the coffee table, and Violet seemed to be holding her breath as she waited to see what he'd do.

His blue eyes swiped back to hers. "I should take this," he said as he stood taking the phone with him out of the room.

Violet slumped back against the couch as her heartbeat returned to a reasonable pace. Sheesh, she'd known this morning when Lachlan came to the hospital that there was some attraction there. Heck, she'd even known it last night in her memory-void mind!

Slow down, Violet, she thought to herself. She couldn't deny she was very attracted to Lachlan, but she was in his home because she had a concussion. And speaking of which, she looked at the empty glass in her hand and put it on the table. She'd probably had at least three if not four drinks tonight, and although Lachlan didn't over-pour, she'd be wise to cool it. That doctor from the hospital probably wouldn't be too thrilled with her getting buzzed with her head injury.

It did feel better, though. Her headache had subsided. Aside from being a bit tired, she felt pretty good. Maybe the company had something to do with it. Violet smiled to herself. She'd never imagined meeting someone like Lachlan. God, he was literally like a knight in shining armour coming to her rescue. And he was funny. And hot. She bit her lip.

Who knew? Maybe after doing this favour tonight, he'd want to take her on a date or something. Not that she was in Scotland to date. That wasn't her intention, but she never expected to meet her dream man. She laughed out loud at herself. She was being silly. She shouldn't even be thinking about dating when she needed to focus on getting a business up and running. It was not like she had unlimited funds.

She should keep her focus...but if Lachlan asked her out, she couldn't say no.

Mindlessly running her fingers over the burnished brass studs on the back of the sofa, she let her mind wander. Lachlan could maybe show her around the area. That wouldn't hurt. And he already ran a business. She was completely green to business ownership here in Scotland, so perhaps, he'd let her pick his brain. Violet was hyper-aware that she'd likely find any excuse to be in the man's company again.

Maybe it was the trauma of last night, but she had this new lease on life, live-for-the-moment feeling enveloping her. And Lachlan was very much *the moment.* It was like they were meant to cross paths. He was making her feel crazy things she had no business feeling for somebody she barely knew. God, it felt like she did know him, though. They just clicked so effortlessly. Mmm, and all she could think about was what it would be like for his sexy crooked smiling lips to kiss hers. The very thought sent butterflies careening through her belly.

Chapter 16
The Kiss

ONLY A HANDFUL OF people could call Lachlan's phone and get through when it's on silent. When he glanced at the screen, he knew it was Anna calling. For a split second, he actually considered ignoring her call, but then he caught himself. Christ, he needed an excuse to put some much-needed space between him and the lass who was bewitching him with each passing minute.

"Hiya, Anna." He cringed at his forced tone.

"Oh, good. I'm glad I got a hold of ye," she said, seeming not to notice his feigned brightness. "Listen, the girls and I have decided to stay on a little longer. You ken, being it's Liz's last hurrah and all. Ye dinnae mind, do ye?"

"Right. No, of course I dinnae mind. Stay as long as ye like." He scrunched his eyes close, realizing that was probably not the best thing to say. Lachlan was surprised Anna was changing plans last minute. She despised when her schedule was thrown off. He'd talked her off a ledge on more than one occasion when plans had changed unexpectedly. She was not the spontaneous type. He wasn't about to bring that up now, though.

"I thought ye didnae like France?" he said instead, deciding it was a less volatile query.

"Erm, I think it's growing on me," she said lightly, with the sounds of a busy restaurant in the background. "Anyway, I hope ye haven't booked our Michelin dinner yet."

"No, I dinnae get around to it," he said, awkwardly knowing that he hadn't thought about it since she'd mentioned it.

"Okay, good." Her response was bright, which threw Lachlan, but he didn't comment.

"When are ye coming back?"

"Um, I'm not sure yet. I— The girls haven't decided yet. We're just going to run with it. You're okay with that, right?"

"The New York girls? And Liz?" he asked, feeling somewhat perplexed. Anna hadn't even wanted to go on this trip.

She gave a shrill laugh that had him pulling the phone away from his ear. "I suppose I've grown to like them. The New York friends, that is."

"Aye, right good." When she didn't say more, he added, "Keep me posted, then."

"Of course."

"I'm sure France willnae be the same once ye lot huv done with it," he joked.

Anna's laugh sounded forced. "I huv to go. Speak soon. Bye."

The line went dead before Lachlan could say another word. He looked at his phone, considering how odd the conversation had been. Anna didn't like France, didn't like the New York friends, and didn't like last-minute changes to plans, so what was that all about? He didn't mind in the least if she was having a great time and wanted to stay. He certainly wasn't her keeper, but he did find it strange.

Hearing soft footsteps making the hardwood creak lightly behind him, he turned to see Violet. His heart almost stopped in his chest as she smiled shyly at him. Her cheeks were flushed and rosy, and her eyes were half-lidded and sleepy—bedroom eyes. Seeing she was tired, he had to fight the urge to scoop her up into his arms to cradle her against him and carry her to his bed.

Instead, he smiled gently back at her. "I'm sorry about that." It struck him how vastly different he felt talking to Anna and the world it pulled him back into versus the world that he'd been in with Violet tonight. God help him, escaping into a realm with just him and Violet was something he could become addicted to.

"It's okay." She yawned, sliding the back of her hand over her mouth. "I suspect running your own business means you have to take calls at all hours."

That was true, although Lachlan had learned to set boundaries regarding work. There was nothing that was life and death when it came to business. It took years, and even though he did work long hours, he had learned to turn off work and make himself unavailable more regularly. Lachlan could have said it wasn't a work call. He could have said—maybe should have said—that it was his girlfriend on the phone. His girlfriend, whom he thought would be back tomorrow afternoon, was now staying in France for who knew how long. Instead of correcting Violet's assumption that it was a work call, he didn't say anything and just nodded.

With another yawn, she gathered her long blond hair and pulled it over one shoulder, he noticed it was a habit she had. One he liked as it exposed her delicate, kissable neck. Lachlan felt his cock stir and swallowed. Her eyes caught his, and something passed between them.

Lachlan's breathing shallowed as the lass stepped closer to him. She was tall, probably around five-foot-eight, but he still towered over her at six-foot-four. Part of him knew he should move away. The situation felt dangerous, but his body refused to move. Instead it thrummed with anticipation. His eyes focused on the beautiful lass before him.

She reached up, touched his jaw with the open palm of her hand, and allowed her fingers to graze his evening stubble.

He held back a groan. He stood stone still as she touched his face. Her gorgeous eyes looked at him as if he fascinated her, and lord help him, he liked it. He couldn't fathom anything better than being the object of this woman's intrigue.

Her slender fingers slid higher up his jaw, scraping into his hair. He closed his eyes, barely able to breathe as his head followed the hypnotic stroke of her hand. He felt suspended in time, utterly lost to the sensations rocking his body under her simple touch.

And when he opened his eyes again, she was looking up with her desire laid bare in her green eyes. Her lips were slightly parted, ready for him, begging to be kissed, and he knew he'd gladly go to hell for just one taste of those peaked, heart-shaped lips.

When her hand slid to the back of his neck and she raised on her tiptoes simultaneously pulling his mouth to hers while tilting her chin up until their mouths collided, fuck, he was a goner. The second their lips touched, desire like he'd never known tore at him relentlessly. It was torture. He wanted her but warred with himself because he knew he shouldn't.

Those lips that he'd watched sipping and tasting his whisky, tempting him all night. Smoky whisky mingling with the strawberry sweetness on her breath was an aphrodisiac.

Her cupid lips pressed tentatively against his and then greedily snatched around his top lip before her tongue slipped against his bottom lip. A snap of electricity tore straight down to his cock, thickening it to painfully tight proportions in his trousers.

She kissed him thoroughly, and he just let her. Her wet tongue slid across his lips for a second time, effortlessly snuffing out the moral code he'd always lived by. The walls of a gentleman crumbled, and he felt a tumult of emotions.

He wanted to punish her for making him so fucking horny. He wanted to grab that pretty creamy neck and squeeze while he shoved his tongue into every crevice of that sweet, torturous mouth. But instead, he held himself still, allowing the warmth and softness of her fucking glorious mouth to do as it pleased with his.

He didn't kiss her back, but he didn't stop her either. Even in his half haze, he hated himself for not being a better man. When her breasts tentatively poked his chest, he felt pre-come squeeze out of his hungry cock. Christ, it was like he was an untried lad. If he so much as felt her body slide against his dick, there was no doubt in his mind he'd be jizzing fully fucking clothed. He could take her right now in his fucking hallway. He could tear down her jeans, rip off her panties, free his hard cock, and slide right into her.

God, what in the hell was he thinking? No. No. He needed to stop this. But before he found the will to stop the madness, Violet pulled away from him and searched his eyes. Her golden brows were pinched together in concern.

“I-I’m sorry. I shouldn’t have done that," she said, stepping further away.

He knew damn well what she was thinking. He hadn’t kissed her back. Her slender arms crossed self-consciously over her chest, and she looked decidedly uncomfortable.

She thinks I don't want her. God, nothing could be further from the truth. He wanted her in a way that defied logic. Had he ever craved a woman like this before? His need to taste every square inch of Violet Munro bordered on insanity, but he couldn’t tell her that. Instead, he just stood there, shell-shocked by a sweet torturous hunger he’d never known before.

It didn’t matter how intense his need was. Lachlan was in a relationship with Anna. Whether he wished to be or not, he was in it, and nothing could happen with Violet. Fuck, he was the worst kind of arsehole lusting after another and letting her kiss him. It was disrespectful to both women, and he knew it. Yet, still, his cock was stiffer than the starched collar around his neck.

"I— Shoot. I'm an idiot. I'm so sorry. Maybe I should leave. I didn't mean for this— I'm sorry."

She was fumbling her words, and finally, Lachlan's brain kicked in. "Careful, V. Yer Canadian-ness is shining through again," he said, attempting to lighten the situation.

Fortunately, it worked. She looked up at him and laughed that throaty laugh that hit him square in the groin every time. He ran a hand through his hair and smiled. "Ye cannae leave. I have the doctor's orders, and I'll not renege on our arrangement."

She grew serious again. "I understand, though. If you want to," she said softly. "I'm sure I'm fine now. I don't want to be a bother to you."

"V." He took her hands in his, holding them up between them as he gently squeezed them and looked at her over their joined hands. "I want ye to stay. I promise ye, ye are no' a bother." He wanted to tell her she was perfect as she looked up at him, but he held that back. She still didn't look totally convinced as she stifled a yawn. The poor lass was likely exhausted, and as much as she might feel fine, he still felt like it was important to keep an eye on her as per the doctor's orders. He'd rather play it safe. Sally plodded down the hall and sat at Lachlan's feet.

"Must be eleven, " Lachlan said, looking down at Sally, who was quivering with eager anticipation. "Ye go on up and get ready for bed. I left your bag beside the bed. I just have to let Sally out."

"You're sure?" Violet still sounded skeptical.

"Aye, lass, verra sure."

Chapter 17
To Sleep or Not To Sleep

VIOLET STEPPED OUT OF Lachlan's ensuite. She hadn't really thought it through when she'd grabbed her sleep shirt from the B&B. It barely covered her behind, but she wasn't about to sleep in her jeans. What did it matter anyway? She doubted Lachlan would care one way or the other. If she'd hoped there was something more happening between them, she'd clearly misread the situation. *Saint Lachlan*. Perhaps it was an accurate moniker. She looked at the king-size bed with its crisp white bedding, still ruffled from where she'd slept earlier. Did he intend to join her? She turned, hearing the gentle knock on the door.

"Can I come in?"

Her heart skipped a beat, and she quickly slid under the covers. This time, she was very aware of being in his bed and the feel of his sheets on her bare legs. She bit her lip. "You can come in," she called back, trying to calm her sudden nerves.

As Lachlan stood outside his own bedroom door, any reassurances he'd placated himself with that this was nothing more than helping a friend in need all but evaporated. He turned the handle, poking his head around the door. Violet smiled at him from under his covers. *Christ,* what a sight. He smiled back at her, trying very hard to think like a friend—something he'd never had to convince himself to do before. Lachlan had always found it very easy to be friends with women. He'd never had to worry about rogue hard-ons in his adult life. This was new territory, but he was determined to be the friend she needed and remain a gentleman even if inside he was feeling more like a caged lion.

"Ah, good, ye look comfy. Well, I'm just going to do my ablutions." Inwardly, he was berating himself as he strode to the ensuite, not daring to look at her again. Why did he say that like an utter twat when he could have just said brushing his teeth? It's not like he was purifying himself, for the love of Mary. Maybe he should be.

When he came back into the bedroom, Sally was sprawled on his side of the bed. Normally, he'd coax her into her dog bed that lay nearby, but tonight, he decided he'd leave her where she was, feeling like she could help keep an eye on Violet. The lass obviously liked his dog as he'd seen her petting Sally and sneaking her bits of chicken at the dining table. It wouldn't hurt to let Sally sleep on the bed this one time. Lachlan noted the steady movement of Violet's breathing under the duvet. He was relieved she seemed to be doing well. He strode over to the chair in the corner of his bedroom. Fortunately, it was comfy, so hopefully, he wouldn't have the worst sleep. He set his phone to vibrate in ninety minutes so he could check on her and then went to turn off the bedside lamp on the nightstand near her side of the bed.

"You aren't thinking to sleep in that chair, are you?"

He nearly jumped out of his skin. "I thought ye were asleep."

"Not yet," she said, looking up at him. "Are you worried I might accost you in the night?"

Lachlan chuckled at the absurdity of the statement. "Should I be?"

She eyed him with a sly smile playing on her bow lips. It was ironic that a very real part of him would love nothing more than for this woman to have her way with him.

"I'll be good as gold," she cooed, then added more seriously, "I get it, Lachlan. You are helping me out. I didn't mean to make things awkward earlier. I'm going to blame it on a head injury and too much whisky."

Lachlan winced. He clearly wouldn't make a very good nursemaid, plying his patient with whisky. He should assure her that she didn't do anything wrong, but he didn't say anything.

"Anyway, I don't want you to feel you can't sleep in your own bed. I promise to stay on my side." She looked up at him hopefully.

He wondered how anyone could ever say no to the lass. "Right, okay then." He strode back around the other side of the bed and coaxed Sally to her dog bed. "I confess, I wasnae looking forward to sleeping in the chair all night." He slid into the bed and felt far too aware of the lass lying beside him, despite the good pillow width of distance he kept between t hem.

She rolled to face him, hugging the pillow under her head and eyeing him curiously.

"I thought ye were tired," he said, glancing at her.

She smiled coyly. "Second wind."

"I see." He closed his eyes and bent his arm up behind his head. He was trying very hard to focus on anything other than the woman beside whom he could feel her eyes boring into him. "What's on yer mind, V?" he asked, sensing she wasn't going to just go to sleep.

"I don't know. I guess, I'm just curious."

"Curious about what?" His pulse clicked up a notch, thinking she might want to know why he hadn't kissed her back.

"What you do when you're not making whisky?"

A silence stretched between them. He should tell her about Anna.

"Or are you a workaholic? Or worse yet, an alcoholic?" She sounded slightly horrified. "Sorry," she quickly added.

Lachlan cracked an eye and raised a brow.

She laughed.

God, that throaty laugh got him every time. He'd never tire of hearing it. "If I had a pound for every sorry."

"I know, I know. I can't help it. Sorry!" The last one she drew out. "So not an alcoholic then?" she hedged.

He snorted a laugh and then sighed lightly. "Haven't I told ye all my secrets tonight?"

"Not *all* of them."

He chuckled. Although inside, he felt too aware of the secret he was keeping. How was it that nothing seemed off-limits with this woman? He rolled over and faced her. She'd washed off the day's makeup, and her natural beauty took his breath away. Clearing his throat, he answered her, although he still found himself omitting anything about Anna. "I enjoy a wee dram, but considering I run a distillery, I dinnae drink overmuch. And as to the concern of workaholic, I do work a lot. It doesnae seem like work, though—most of the time."

"That's good."

"Aye, but I wouldn't say work is everything. I spend a fair bit of time down at the stables with my horses, and I suppose I see my family often too."

“Wait! Hold up!" Violet sat bolt upright.

Lachlan wondered what he'd said wrong.

"You have *horses*?"

He couldn't mistake the childlike wonder in her voice.

“Aye, down in the stables.” He raised up on one elbow, taking in the look of rapture on her face.

“As in here, or at some faraway stables?” she asked suspiciously.

He laughed. “Here, not fifty yards from the house.”

“Oh my God, and you’re only telling me this now?”

“I wasn’t trying to withhold pertinent information,” he teased.

“Can we go see them?” she pleaded.

And again, he wondered how one could resist her.

“I didn’t realize you had stables right here!”

“Och, aye, it is one of the things I've always loved about this property. It has a stable. I could have my horses near. I can take ye down and give ye the tour in the morning. I think I still huv some left over carrots ye can give them if ye like.”

She sat silently, and he had a feeling they weren't going to sleep just yet.

"Could we go now?" she hedged, throwing him a pleading look that he couldn't fathom resisting.

"Now?"

She was grinning and nodding excitedly. "Please!"

It didn't matter that he didn't want to get back out of bed. She was more convincing than a box full of puppies.

"I thought ye were tired. Dinnae ye think ye should sleep now? It's almost midnight." He didn't know why he was bothering trying to convince her. He was well aware the battle was already lost.

"I can sleep later."

He wasn't sure the last time he'd seen someone jittery with excitement. "It'll be chilly," he warned, in a last-ditch effort.

"You know I'm from Canada, right?" She looked at him from under an arched brow.

He was lost. "Ach, all right then." He chuckled.

She practically flew out of the bed, her excitement boiling over. In her mad haste, Lachlan got a damn fine view of white cotton panties patterned with little cherries, revealing full curved arse cheeks squeezing out the bottoms, and for the first time in his life, he well and truly understood the expression, *buns*. Those ass cheeks—hot out of the oven, rounded smooth plump looking buns—had him longing to fill his palms with them.

Chapter 18

The Wolf and The Horses

VIOLET DIDN'T EVEN THINK as she tore the sheets off and flew out of Lachlan's bed. She turned to thank him, and the words locked in her throat. Lachlan's demeanor had changed, and she felt the air suddenly thick with tension. He was eyeing her like a wolf, and she was his dinner. A shiver ran down her spine, and she self-consciously tugged down her nightshirt. His cerulean blue eyes had darkened from under his brow, and there was a tick in his jaw. His black t-shirt seemed to tighten around his biceps, and she noted the veins on the back of his hand as he clenched tightly to the bed sheets. For such a sweet chivalrous kinda guy, the way he was looking at her now was positively feral, and what was worse was that every tick of his jaw was like a flick to her clit. This Lachlan surprised her, but she wasn't mad about it.

The silence that stretched between them was charged, and when she swallowed, his eyes followed the movement of her neck in rapt fascination. It was awfully tempting to see just how wild he'd be with her, but she didn't want him to backpedal again like after she'd kissed him. That had been confusing and frustrating, especially since it lit her on fire. He hadn't seemed to kiss her back, and yet, she was certain that what she was feeling went both ways. It was like he was holding himself back. She couldn't help thinking about what he'd told her his brother called him: Saint Lachlan. He was far from that now, but his capriciousness left her feeling uncertain.

"Lachlan?" Her voice was unsteady.

He raked a hand through his thick wavy hair as he rolled out of the bed. When he turned to look at her again, he threw her that crooked grin that made her want to groan in pleasure. "Come on then, V. Let's go see some horses."

And just like that, he was charming, easygoing Lachlan again.

Violet had loved horses for as long as she could remember. When she was younger, she used to save her allowance to go riding at stables near her house. It had been years since she'd ridden, but her adoration had not dwindled. It wasn't uncommon for her to pull over on the side of a highway just to steal a few moments for petting and cooing at one of these beautiful creatures. Her childhood dream of owning her own horse was still a little flame that burned in the back of her mind—one day.

As they made their way to the stables, Violet looked up at the sea of stars above them. "Wow, I don't know if I've ever seen so many stars."

"Aye, it's verra beautiful out here, away from the village lights."

They approached the stone stable, and Lachlan slid open the large black barn door.

"Oh my God, I love that smell," Violet crooned.

Lachlan chuckled. "Tell me ye dinnae mean the smell of horse dung?"

"Pretty much. And the hay. It's a beautiful bouquet, don't ya think?"

"I dinnae ken if I've ever met anyone like ye," he said, shaking his head as he gestured for her to step inside the corridor.

"I'll take that as a compliment. Thank you very much."

"Aye, ye should." Lachlan smiled at her.

The soft sound of the horses shifting in their stalls and quietly grunting had Violet's heart fluttering in her chest, and then she thought her heart would burst as one by one horse snouts poked out the front of the stalls.

"Oooh." She swooned and moved to the first stall, where a beautiful white horse eyed her curiously. A pale pink snout sniffed at her. She spoke softly to the gentle giant and was utterly charmed when the horse nuzzled its head against her chest. "Oh, my."

“Her name is Edelweiss.” Lachlan came to stand beside Violet and ran a hand down the horse's neck.

“She’s so sweet.”

“Aye, she is. She was a rescue horse.”

Violet looked back at Lachlan, and she was struck again by what a good man he was.

“When I got her, she was bones, nearly starved to death.”

“Oh my God, that’s awful. Poor thing.” Violet rubbed at the base of her ears, and Edelweiss closed her eyes in appreciation.

“She likes ye," Lachlan said.

"I like her." Violet continued her ministrations, feeling in awe of the beautiful creature.

"It took a long time before she could trust anyone. I never thought she’d let me put a saddle on her, never mind actually get on and ride. But as her physical health came back, so did her spirits. She loves to go for a ride now.”

“Aww, that’s amazing. Sweet girl.” Violet could have just stayed with Edelweiss, but another horse down the way was making himself known. "I'll come back, girl," she said with one final pat and made her way down to the horse who was demanding some attention, too. She could feel Lachlan's eyes on her.

"Do ye ride, V?"

"I used to. It's been a long time. I'd love to again, though."

She stopped in front of a tall chestnut brown horse. "Wow," she breathed. He was stunning.

“Bolt. He was Helena’s”

Violet glanced back at Lachlan and then turned to face Bolt. Lachlan still had his sister’s horse. It was both sad and beautiful. She stroked Bolt’s white snout. “Does he miss her?”

“Aye.” Lachlan smiled sadly. “I’m not sure who loved the other more. Helena adored him, but he adored her back. Even though time has passed, I do no' doubt that he thinks of her daily, much like the rest of us.”

“I bet,” Violet said softly and patted his soft neck. "Animals grieve too."

"I think they feel much more than we even ken," he said, snapping a carrot in half and giving a piece to Violet.

She held out the carrot on her hand, and Bolt's soft fuzzy muzzle lipped at it until he got it in his mouth and happily crunched it up. Lachlan gave him the other half.

“How many horses do you have?” she asked, noting six stalls.

"At the moment, I have three here. I have another stable closer to town where I board more."

"Wow, *two* stables?"

He nodded. "Aye." He strode forward to the end stall, and Violet followed.

"Do you have help with the horses here?"

"Aye. Craig is here full time, and Byron comes 'round a few days a week to help as well. I spend as much time as I can down here, but between here and the town stable and running the distillery, I sometimes dinnae feel like I get much time to ride."

They stopped in front of the last stall, and Violet sucked in a breath. "Oh, wow." The horse inside grunted at her, raising its head high. "You are majestic," she breathed. His coat was a glossy black, and he stood a good two hands taller than the other two.

"Hercules." Lachlan rubbed his neck affectionately.

"He's extraordinary."

"He's a Friesian. Fast, strong, intelligent, but he also listens and feels my cues. He's the most intuitive horse I think I've ever ridden. Right, boy?" Hercules nuzzled his face into Lachlan's broad chest.

"Was Hercules with you that day?" She wondered aloud.

Lachlan looked back at her and nodded. "He got me through then and through many tough times that followed."

They stood quietly as Hercules ate the carrot Lachlan gave Violet for him.

"Perhaps we should go for a ride sometime," he offered casually.

Violet felt pleasantly surprised. "I'd love that."

Did that mean he wanted to see her again? Like a date? Her overzealous mind jumped all over that thought. It was hard not to be attracted to Lachlan. Impossible really. Even now, in a stable, the man was Mr. GQ—tall, broad, dressed in black sweats and impossibly white runners with a black wool overcoat. How he could pull off that look in a flipping stable, she had no idea. And on top of that, he was kind, generous, sweet, and that smile. And... Oh God, and whatever else that was, that sizzling sexy thing when he seemed to be trying to hold himself back. She looked over at an empty stall full of hay, and suddenly, she was imagining hunky Mr. GQ taking full advantage of her.

"Are ye feeling okay, lass? Ye look a bit flushed. We should probably get ye back to bed."

God, yes, take me to bed, Lachlan, her girl bits practically hollered. Violet latched onto Lachlan's arm as they made their way back to the house. She tugged a bit on his arm, and he looked down at her.

"Thank you," she said earnestly.

"It's all right. Nothing like a midnight jaunt to the stable."

She grinned, loving the way he teased her.

Chapter 19
Rise and Shine

THEY MADE THEIR WAY back upstairs to Lachlan's bedroom. Violet had gone into the ensuite to change, and when she came back out, Lachlan was already lying in the bed. A muscular arm was tucked behind his head.

He glanced up at her, and a weary look crossed his features. "Would ye like to borrow some joggers to sleep in? It gets cool at night. I dinnae want ye getting cold."

"I'll be fine." She smiled, crossing over to the other side of the bed. Violet felt certain that he wasn't truly worried she'd be cold. She suspected it had more to do with his earlier reaction to seeing her in her nightshirt. For one thing, she never slept with anything on her legs, so sweatpants, or *joggers* as he called them, were not an option. And for two, there was a part of her mind that relished in knowing he was affected by her in her nightshirt. She highly doubted anything was going to happen between them, at least not tonight, but it didn't prevent her from daydreaming.

"Right," he mumbled, avoiding looking at her.

⁂

Lachlan lay stiff as a board on his back, not trusting himself to move in case he felt her naked legs under the blanket. He was far too aware. He didn't trust himself—not a feeling he was accustomed to. The king-size bed felt absurdly tiny. If he reached out a hand, he could touch her hair. Or if he rolled over slightly, he might smell her soft vanilla scent. Violet seemed to save him some grief as she turned away from him, hiking the covers over the back of her head, cocooning herself in his bedding. He reached up and switched off the bedside lamp.

"Good night, Lachlan. Thanks for everything." Her voice was gentle and quiet with sleepiness in the dark, and instead of making him want to sleep, it just played tricks on him.

"My pleasure, lass. Good night," he managed. He stared up at the ceiling as his eyes adjusted to the darkness. An odd sense of disappointment filled him as he realized Violet was going to sleep now. God help him, it was not like he wanted something to happen between them. Of course, he didn't. And yet...

Violet's breathing steadied. She was asleep. Good for her. He had no idea how he was going to fall asleep. His body was far too aware of her partial nakedness so near to him. He scraped a hand over his jaw and turned to pick up his phone. Flicking on the screen, it showed no new notifications. No good night from Anna.

It was like he needed something to ground him and remind him of his real life and not the fantasy world he seemed to be in with Violet. He needed a solid reminder that he was in a relationship, that he was a gentleman, and that the woman who currently slept beside him wasn't some mythical nymph who could command his every desire.

He put his phone back on the charging station and lay back again with a sigh. Contrary to what he thought he wanted, he actually felt relieved that there was no message from Anna. It struck him that in recent weeks, he'd come to feel—dread was too strong a word—but when his phone dinged, his jaw would clench, and tension would creep through his shoulders. Something wasn't sitting right with him about Anna's reasons for staying in France. It just wasn't adding up. He mulled it over, and after a few minutes, he wondered, could she be having a fling? *Possibly,* he concluded—and he felt surprisingly indifferent.

Violet stirred, and Lachlan went very still, listening in the darkness. She stretched out. A soft little moan escaped her, and her long slender leg touched his. He felt scorched. His heart pounded so loudly in his chest that he thought the sound might wake her. And then she settled again, the soft skin of her shin barely touching him, but touching him nonetheless. He should move away, but there was no way in hell that he could. Their kiss from earlier swam through his mind, instantly making him hard. He groaned in frustration, warring with himself. He rolled onto his side away from her before he did something he'd regret.

Go to sleep, you horny old bastard, he chided. Clenching his eyes closed, he breathed deeply and tried to clear his mind. His sister Orlagh, the health nut of the family, had exuberantly taught them all about box breathing a few weeks back at dinner. She prattled on something about stimulating the parasympathetic nervous system. Bottom line: box breathing was meant to relax a person, and at this point, he was game to try anything.

Lachlan awoke on his back again and relished how rested he felt. It was the feel of a lazy Saturday morning sleep-in, which was rare for him. Letting out a low grunt as he stretched, he pulled Violet in closer to him. Suddenly, his eyes shot open, awareness splashing over him like a bucket of ice water. Her head lay tucked in the crook of his arm. Her slender arm was splayed across his abdomen. A smooth, soft leg lay casually over his. And her body pressed up against his side. *Oh. Sweet. Torture.* And to top it all off, he had some serious morning wood.

He didn't dare move. Lying there, he contemplated what he should do. He glanced at the small round clock on the nightstand. Seven. How had his phone alarm not gone off in the night? He'd intended to check on Violet every ninety minutes to make sure all was well, and instead, he'd slept solidly through the night. Thankfully, the lass slept soundly, but God, what was he to do now? Gently remove her and sneak out of the bed? The thought was hardly appealing. Lord help him, but it felt fan-fucking-tastic to feel her in his arms. The right thing would be to detangle himself. But every fibre in him was refusing to move.

Violet stirred and stretched out her body against his. *Oh, mother of fuckin' Mary.* And then it happened. As she sleepily stretched, her hand inadvertently pressed down against his rock-hard manhood. As if that wasn't enough, she proceeded to palm his cock, exploring its shape through his cotton boxers. It was like she was trying to determine what she was touching. Suddenly, she yanked away her hand as if she'd been scalded. To his dismay, her body completely recoiled from him, her eyes shot open, and locked upon his. They squared off.

"Sorry." She sounded breathless, only heightening his torturous hunger.

He swallowed hard, turning away and swiftly getting out of the bed, needing to calm his desperate cock. This was not cool. What was wrong with him? He feigned looking out the window to shield the relentless hard-on in his pants from her view. He cleared his throat and said over his shoulder, "No worries, lass. Did ye sleep well?"

"I did, actually. Your mattress is so comfortable." She spoke light heartedly as if she hadn't just had her hand on his dick.

"Mmhmm, good, good. Right, well, I'm going to take a shower." And he quickly turned and strode into the ensuite, avoiding eye contact.

Violet sat back against the pillows, trying to make sense of what had just happened. She was half-asleep, but she knew she'd inadvertently felt up his manhood. A shiver ran through her. She shouldn't go there, but the memory of how thick and hard it felt was etched in her brain. She scrunched her eyes closed. God, the man flew off the bed like he'd been double bounced on a trampoline. Clearly, he was not thrilled with her unintended touchy-feely start to the morning. How embarrassing. She felt pretty certain that he knew it was by accident, but still, he was gentlemanly—and she'd obviously ruffled his sensibilities.

Despite the rocky morning, she still felt like there was *something* between them. Maybe he preferred to take things slowly, which, if she wasn't so smitten with him, would probably be a great plan. Although, thinking about it, it seemed like there was more to it than that. She wondered how much truth there was to Saint Lachlan, the man who eternally restrained himself.

There were moments in the last twenty-four hours where she was sure he was about to ravish her senseless. The thought of Lachlan losing his gentlemanly control and having his way with her sent a jolt of excitement through her. She didn't recall a time she'd ever wanted to throw caution to the wind and just go at it, but those few moments Lachlan looked ready to pounce on her, it half scared her and half thrilled her.

But then there were other moments where he seemed completely indifferent to the chemistry that bubbled between them. It left her bemused. Her stomach growled loudly, breaking her reverie. Thankful for a distraction, she pulled on her jeans and the hoody she'd grabbed from the Airbnb and plodded downstairs to see if she could rustle up some breakfast for them.

Chapter 20

Eggs and a Garish Creamer Set

Violet's hunger propelled her to throw caution to the wind and make herself at home in Lachlan's kitchen. After all, she intended to make breakfast for both of them. She yanked open the fridge, scanning for eggs, but it seemed like he had everything but. She pulled open a cheese drawer and almost drooled at the variety of cheeses there. Where she was from, the cheese variety was slim at best.

He also had a package of prosciutto that caught her eye. She settled on a sharp goat cheddar that was already open, the prosciutto, button mushrooms, fresh spinach, and cherry tomatoes. Even without eggs, she could whip up something with these ingredients.

When she pulled open a cabinet door looking for some type of cooking oil, she was surprised to find a six-pack of eggs. *Weird*. She opened the carton and peered in at them, wondering if they were safe to eat, then she checked for a date on the packaging. They were well before the best-before date, but who put eggs in the pantry? Her stomach growled loudly as if telling her to just make the damn omelets already. Decision made. She supposed she'd risk a little salmonella poisoning. She was cooking them, so that should kill anything bad, *right*? Her belly groaned its agreement.

As she let the first omelet cook, she put a couple of slices of bread in the toaster, and soon, the comforting smell of toast permeated the kitchen. She found her thoughts turn to daydreams of idyllic Saturdays with Lachlan, going to the local farmers market, walking hand in hand, and choosing fresh ingredients to cook dinner together.

"Mmm, smells good in here."

Violet jumped as if her whimsical fantasy was visible to the naked eye. As she turned toward him, she got an eyeful of his freshly shaved, sharpened jaw. His dark brown hair was styled as if he just stepped off a photo shoot, and a crisp white button-up shirt with sleeves rolled exposed strong veined forearms that would make an ER nurse weep. His dress shirt was a perfect fit over his sculpted broad shoulders. She could just make out the thick curve of his pecs through it. Her eyes continued their descent as the shirt whispered over his torso, tapered down his trim waist, and tucked neatly into his belted dark, slim-fit pants. *Holy shit.* She almost felt intimidated by the gorgeous specimen of masculinity standing before her, peering into the frying pan with approval.

He looked so suave, cool, calm, and collected. Bond-esque, like he might request a dry martini with breakfast, "shaken, not stirred." Her jean-clad knees knocked together, utterly weak, and she almost groaned at how good he smelled. The perfect combination of fresh, intoxicating, and expensive.

Finally catching herself gaping, she quickly moved to the toaster, buttering the popped-up slices, suddenly far too aware of their uneven fashion playing field, and *she* was the personal stylist! What she needed was a sexy black dress with an ultra-low cut back paired with Louboutin stilettos and her hair in an Audrey Hepburn-style French role. Yes, that was the aesthetic that she could imagine suiting his. Not her current state: oversized hoody, messy haphazard bun—if you could even call it a bun— and without a stitch of makeup. And for the first time in her life, she felt small. No, that wasn't it. She felt *petite* next to Lachlan.

Violet was used to being a member of the tall crowd. This felt quite different. "My stomach made me raid your kitchen. I hope that's okay." She found her voice as she dished up the food she'd made them.

"I'm sorry. I should huv offered ye something more last night."

Their eyes caught, and the double entendre silently whispered between them.

“I didn't realize how ravenous I was until I woke up," she said, unintentionally descending further down the rabbit hole of double entendres.

"Aye, me too." His voice grew husky.

The memory of his hardened member in her hand first thing this morning flashed through her mind, making her flush. He winked at her as if he had read her thoughts, but then he sat down at the small kitchen table like the air hadn’t suddenly become thick with sexual tension.

The wink was so quick she could have imagined it, but it was accompanied by that crooked grin of his—somehow even more sexy on his clean-shaven face, assuring her that it wasn't her imagination. She placed one plate in front of him and sat down across from him with her own, her hunger pangs taking a backseat to the butterflies that now flitted low in her belly.

“I couldn’t find any coffee, so I assumed you were the tea type,” she said, nodding to the steamy mugs and the fussy-looking cream and sugar china set she'd filled and placed in the centre of the table.

“I have gotten into the habit of picking up a brew on the drive. I didnae notice I was out of coffee. Tea is great. Thank ye," he said, pouring a drop of milk into his mug. "Where did ye find this?" he asked with a raised brow, gesturing to the over-the-top floral china set as if he'd never laid eyes on it before.

"It was in front of the mugs in your cabinet. You don't know it?" She wondered when she spied the garishly embellished set displayed in front of the hygge vibe grey cream pottery mugs. She really liked the mugs. She'd even checked the bottom to see where they were made: Cromarty, in the Highlands. She made a mental note to add it to her places-to-visit-in-Scotland list.

Violet saw recognition cross over Lachlan's features, and then he stared at the set like it was going to grow legs and march across the table.

"Lachlan?"

"What? Oh." He shook his head and fiddled with the rolled sleeve of his dress shirt. "I suppose, um, my mam must huv brought them here at some point."

Violet didn't know how or why, but she instinctively knew that was a lie. Mr. GQ looked tense and uncomfortable, like if he had a tie on, he'd be loosening it. Not a terrible image in her mind's eye. *Good lord*, what was with her? The man just lied to her about a china set—of all things—but why?

"I dinnae like them," he said as if the realization surprised him.

She wondered if he was actually talking about the china set or something else. But he was being truthful again.

"I dinnae remember seeing them before, though."

Lie. It became apparent that Lachlan was a terrible liar. He would get an uncomfortable look on his face like he had an itch that he couldn't reach to scratch, and he'd avoid looking at her before, during, and after stating the falsehood. Part of her wanted to laugh at how horribly he lied. Part of her wanted to call him out on it. But she chose to let it be.

"I saw them and assumed it would be okay to use them," she said, feeling like she owed him an apology.

"Aye, of course," he said reassuringly as he cut into his omelet and took a hearty mouthful, moving on from the awkward creamer set conversation. "Mm, mm, this is delicious," he crooned between mouthfuls.

Truth.

They ate in companionable silence as the spring sun lit Lachlan's kitchen in gold.

"Mm," Violet broke the silence, remembering she wanted to ask him something. "I found your eggs in the cabinet with the oil. Did you mean to put them there?" Her fork dangled from her finger and thumb as she eyed him curiously.

"You were expecting them elsewhere?" He leaned back in his chair, still holding a half-eaten piece of toast to which he'd added raspberry jam.

"You don't keep them in the fridge?" she hedged.

"The *fridge*? Ye keep yer eggs in the fridge?" His gaze fixed on her.

"Yes, of course. Everyone does."

"No' here, they dinnae. I suppose ye keep yer butter and jam in the fridge too." He said it like a challenge.

She almost laughed. "You don't?"

He shook his head. "I huv a theory."

She was more intrigued by his playful smirk than by the theory itself. "Do tell."

"I huv crossed the pond a few times in my life, and I dinnae ken why, but ye lot huv enormous fridges, like ye all are expecting at any given time to huv to store a moose in it."

She threw back her head and laughed, and his eyes gleamed.

"Dinnae go laughin'. Ye huvnae heard my theory yet."

She sobered, with her lips twitching as she waited for him to enlighten her. "Right."

He leaned forward with his elbows on the table like he was about to share a secret, so she leaned forward, too. His handsome face was close to hers, and she couldn't help the shiver that ran through her.

"I think ye lot put eggs, and jam, and butter, and probably all your bloody jewels in the fridge too because they are so damn big, ye huv to find things to fill them up."

All she heard was *damn big* and *fill up*. She swallowed hard. And when she didn't laugh, he suddenly sobered too.

His eyes dropped to her mouth. "So ye agree? With my theory?" he said in a hoarse voice.

They just looked at each other from across the table, close but not close enough. She wanted to feel his lips on hers. God, how she wanted him to kiss her, and right now, it definitely felt like he wanted to, too. Instead, they just eyed each other in some kind of hungry, tempting trance, with the table and its gaudy creamer set as the only barrier between them.

Chapter 21
Done

Do you have plans today?" Violet asked.

His cock seemed to think that sexy, throaty voice was meant for him. Anna wasn't coming back today now, so—God, what was he doing? He pulled back from where he was, leaned over the table, and stood, taking their plates to the sink. Never had his cock run his life. That was Drew's style, not his, and here he was, his girlfriend away, and it was all he could do not to haul this lass back up to his bed so they could continue where they left off first thing this morning.

The way he was drawn to Violet defied logic. He was supposed to be watching over her, taking care of her, not bloody thirsting after her. Christ, he felt disgusted with himself. It was a very good thing that their twenty-four hours were up because as much as he was certain he would never ever be a cheater, he felt like he was in a losing battle with himself right now. Anna sure as hell deserved better, and so did Violet.

"Aye, I'm meeting my sister for lunch," he said more abruptly than he intended.

“Oh, right, um, well, I’m going to get my bag. I think your nursing duties are at an end.”

"You're feeling better then?" he said, realizing he had been so bloody distracted he hadn't even bothered to ask how she was doing this morning. He made a shite nurse and a shite boyfriend.

"Good as new," she said brightly.

Too brightly. He felt like he should explain himself, but what could he say? Lachlan knew the smart thing to do was drop her off, and that would be the end of it. He could stop fighting with himself. Go back to normal. *Normal.* He had a strong feeling that there was life before Violet Munro and then after. Whatever *this* was, he already knew she was a game changer, although he didn’t know exactly what that meant at present. All he knew was that Violet was a temptation that he couldn’t have in his life right now. So dropping her off and letting her go was the only option.

They were mostly quiet during the drive back to the B&B. Lachlan pulled up outside the small flat. Violet turned to face him. A shy smile touched the corners of her mouth, and his heart jolted. The past couple of days had been quite the experience, and looking at her now, he hated to think he might not see her again. She broke the silence first.

"Thank you for all you've done for me. It really means so much. I cringe to think what would've happened if you hadn't helped me the other night. And then taking me into your home." She paused, glancing up at him with a soft smile touching her Cupid's bow lips. "You're a good guy, Lachlan."

He didn't feel like a good guy. Lachlan was rarely at a loss for words, but he struggled to know what to say to this woman who'd blown into his life like a tempest, leaving him feeling inside out. The truth was, he enjoyed every minute with her.

He sighed. "It was my pleasure, V," he said in earnest. "You're sure yer all right? I dinnae want to leave ye if yer not feelin' a hundred percent."

"I'm good, I promise," she reassured him. "Not even a headache this morning."

"I'm glad you're recovered, lass."

"Me too."

"I'll get your door," Lachlan said, getting out and striding to her side of the car to open the door for her.

She got out of the car and stood before him looking all adorable in her hoody with her messy blond hair tied up. He pulled her into a hug, despite himself. He held her to him, kissing the top of her head, breathing in her intoxicating vanilla scent and hoping he could commit it to memory.

He watched as she walked to the door and unlocked it. She gave him a quick wave before disappearing inside. Lachlan sighed and got back into the car. *Well, that's it then*, he thought to himself soberingly, starting his engine. As he drove away, he replayed their time together. He felt her absence immediately. It was visceral. He wondered how it was possible that after such a short time of having her around, it could feel so empty without her. It was a little disconcerting. Well, it was done now. He'd done the right thing. He helped the lass. That was the important part. Now, he would get on with his life. No need to worry about her as she was clearly doing just fine now. It was great meeting her and spending some time with her, but that was it now. No complication—well, not really. There was that one kiss and almost how many others. He clenched the steering wheel.

Chapter 22
Lunch with the Clairvoyant

LACHLAN MET ORLAGH AT their favourite artisan sandwich restaurant down in the village, *Piece*.

"Lachlan, over here," she called to him from near the front window. Sunlight caught in her brown hair, turning it gold, and made her already sparkly blue eyes look almost ethereal—like some kind of white witch. Orlagh had an essence about her that was hard to miss, as if she had lived a thousand lives and quietly carried the mystery of the universe in her tiny five foot three frame.

He strode over to the table, leaning down to give his little sister a hug and peck on the cheek. "Did ye order yet?" He sat across from her, noting how busy it was. Every seat was filled, and there was a line at the door. Likely, the sunny weather had people wanting to be out and about.

"Yep, two grilled cheese sandwiches."

"Braw," he said, pleased with that decision. He was surprised how hungry he was after breakfast with Violet this morning. A vision of her jean-clad arse standing at his cooker popped in his mind.

Orlagh eyed him dubiously. “You look different.”

“Ah, yes, well, I had my hair cut last week,” he said, turning profile as if to let her fully assess it.

“That’s not what I meant, and you know it," she scoffed.

He smiled, all innocence. She was still looking at him as if trying to solve a puzzle, and it unsettled him.

“Did ye meet someone?” Her face lit up as the words tumbled out of her mouth.

God, he swore she had a sixth sense, but he played dumb. “Someone? Well, yes, I did, in fact, meet a new distributor from California, Steve. Pleasant man.”

"Lachlan! I mean a lass, ye met a lassie. Tell me I'm wrong." Her face lit with glee.

A skinny young man wearing a black t-shirt and a gray waist apron with the word “Piece” written in white sans serif font approached the table and placed down two glasses and a glass water pitcher as well as two mugs of coffee, and then he was away again as fast as he'd arrived.

Lachlan picked up his mug of coffee and took his first fortifying sip. "You ken what I like about this place?" He didn't wait for an answer. "The mugs are a good size. Not the piddly little ones most restaurants are so fond of using, barely big enough for a wee nymph.”

"What?" Orlagh looked at him like he'd gone mad.

"The mugs?" he said, holding it up by way of explanation.

"Never mind the bloody mugs. Tell me about the lass!"

Lachlan shook his head. "Ye ken I am in a relationship with Anna." He said it as if it was the be-all and end-all of the conversation, despite it feeling almost foreign on his tongue today. Christ, it was hard enough to deal with his own emotions at the moment. He didn't need his little sister muddying the waters further.

"Aye, *Anna*." She drew out her name. "I dinnae like her. She thinks too highly of herself."

"Well, she's an accomplished woman," Lachlan half-heartedly defended her.

"An' she ken's it," Orlagh clapped back.

Lachlan rolled his eyes. He knew very well that his sister wasn't fond of Anna. She'd made her feelings clear from the get-go.

"Never mind Anna, right now. Tell me about the lassie ye met."

Lachlan sometimes wondered if his sister was clairvoyant. She was way too perceptive. Orlagh could make a living as a psychic—wouldn't even need a crystal ball.

Several years back, Lachlan planned a road trip with one of his best friends since primary school, Jacob—whom Orlagh had a crush on. She'd practically begged Lachlan not to go. She claimed she had a "bad feeling" about it. On more than one occasion before the trip, she tried to convince him that something was going to happen and that he'd regret going. She even cornered Jacob and tried to convince him to boycott the trip. Lachlan believed the true reason his sister did not want them to go was because she was worried that it was a boys' trip where they'd be on the prowl which, of course, was the plan. Lachlan ignored her warnings, but she managed to rattle Jacob. He questioned whether they should actually go. Lachlan remembered teasing his friend for giving his little sister any heed. Orlagh was not going to ruin their trip.

Sure enough, Lachlan's car broke down in a remote area of the Highlands. The head gasket blew. He couldn't believe their luck, but it was Jacob who quickly brought up Orlagh's premonitions. The trip never ended up happening. Lachlan and Jacob had to wait through the night trying to sleep in the freezing cold car, and then in the morning, they walked four miles to the first little village.

That was the thing about the remote parts of the Highlands. You could go days without seeing a soul. They were lucky there was a village relatively nearby. It could have been worse, but it still sucked. And it sucked even more when he had to face the "I told you so" from his baby sister.

That was just one of many times that she'd had a feeling about something or predicted an event. He often teased her that back in the day, they would have burned her at the stake for being a witch. To this day, Jacob still thought Orlagh had some kind of psychic powers, and Lachlan, feeling hot under the collar, believed he was right.

"Lachlan Rory Mackenzie, spill it," she demanded.

He couldn't help but smile. He adored his feisty little sister, even if she did stick her nose where it didn't belong.

"I'm waiting, big brother. Who is she?"

"Nobody, it's no' what ye think." He laughed at her prodding.

"We'll see about that. Tell me."

"Ach, ye huvnae even asked how I am, and ye're already grillin' me."

"I can see how you are." She gave him a sly grin. "And I want to ken who's done it to ye." She sucked in a sudden breath. "Did you get laid?"

"Rolo!" he scolded her.

"Wow, so no sex, but ye look good. Like glowy or somethin'. I want details. Come on, Lach, spit it out already. Ye ken, I'll find out anyway."

"Seriously, ye've got it wrong. Nobody's *done* anything to me." And then he added reluctantly, "I did meet a lovely lass, though."

"I ken it." She clapped her hands together triumphantly.

The same lanky server brought two oversized grilled cheese sandwiches to the table with large pickles on the side.

He had barely walked away when Orlagh quipped excitedly, "Go on." She took a bite of her sandwich and watched him like she was snacking on popcorn at a movie.

"Och, dinnae let your witchy mind run away with ye. I met a lass, Violet Munro." He recounted the events of their serendipitous meeting. "It was a nasty tumble, and I was the lone witness. So, as any decent person would do, I went to help. That's it."

"Blimey, was she okay?" she said, munching away.

Lachlan knew trying to keep anything from Orlagh would be futile, so he opened up and told her how she ended up in his charge. He left out a few details. He wasn't prepared to talk about Drew, nor did he want to talk about the deep conversations he'd had with Violet. And he certainly wasn't going to tell his sister about the kiss, nor how much he craved to taste her again. No, some things he would not speak of.

"So did ye snog her, then?" Orlagh asked like a bloody mind reader.

How? How does she do it?

"Ah, ye did." She grinned like a Cheshire cat, not bothering to wait for a response. "Of course, ye did. God, it's so romantic, like some kinda fairy tale." She sighed dreamily.

Lachlan took a large bite of his sandwich, refusing to say any more on the subject of whether or not he kissed the lass, and technically, she kissed him.

“So when are ye seeing her again?” Orlagh asked between chews.

“Why would I see her again? I helped her, I let her come stay with me for her twenty-four-hour window, and now that’s it. Done.”

“Och, dear God.” Orlagh groaned. “Dinnae tell me ye honestly have no intention of seeing her again? I mean, look at ye, just look at ye. Yer like a lovesick fool.” She sat back, crossing her arms.

“Christ, Rolo, I'm in a relationship if ye huvnae noticed. And ye may no' like Anna, but I'm no' in the business of cheating.

"Aye, I'm no' suggesting that, but I'm no' blind, Lachlan. It's plain to see.”

He cut her off, frustrated. "What's plain to see?"

Orlagh's features softened. "Ye feel something fer Violet.”

"Right, how can I not? We went through a pretty dramatic experience together. Of course, there would be some feelings there. But that's it now. She's fine and going off to live her life, and I'm living mine." He wasn't sure who he was trying to convince more, Orlagh or himself.

She let out a disgruntled, "Hmm."

Lachlan wiped his mouth with the napkin and put it on his empty plate before reaching for his wallet in his blazer that hung on the back of the chair. He pulled out a credit card, and their server was at their table in record time with the portable card reader. He wanted to get to the office so he could bury himself in work and think about something other than Violet Munro.

The server walked away almost as quickly as he'd arrived, and Lachlan stood, sliding on his blazer.

"Wait, what about Alex?"

"What about him?" Lachlan asked, straightening the lapels.

"Well, did ye talk to him? About Violet I mean?"

"Why would I?"

"Because ye and him huv that twin thing. He's the only person in this world that probably ken's ye better than me."

"Alex is busy fighting the bad guys. I'm no' gonna bother him to tell him about a lass I'll likely never see again."

Their parents weren't happy when Alex chose a career in policing. They'd assumed Lachlan and Alex would run the distillery together and take over the family business. It made sense to Lachlan, though. Alex loved whisky like the rest of them, but he'd lived for danger since they were kids. His poor mam attributed her early graying to Alex and his knack for finding himself in dangerous situations. And if it wasn't

Alex causing her grief, it was Drew. *Drew.* Shite, that was another conundrum. It surprised him that his keen sister didn't know that Drew was back.

He leaned over and gave his sister a quick peck on the cheek.

"I have to go. I'll see ye next week, okay?"

She nodded silently as if accepting defeat—for now.

Orlagh shook her head as she watched her big brother walk away. Needing to ground herself, she pulled a peppermint oil roller from her bag and applied a swipe to her temples and the back of her neck, the tingling effect immediately rejuvenating her.

She struggled to understand why he wanted to stay with a woman like Anna, especially when she could see the spark in him after meeting this Violet lassie.

Couldn't he see it? Maybe she was grasping at straws, but it was like Lachlan was just blindly bumbling through the motions with Anna. But why?

Anna MacDonald came from an influential family, and she ensured everyone knew it. Outwardly, she was very beautiful, and she was apparently intelligent, having earned a doctorate. But the second she opened her mouth, it was worse than listening to a twelve-year-old learning to play the violin. Lachlan invited her one time—thank God just the once—to their Sunday Sandwich date, and it was all Orlagh could do to not rip open her grilled cheese and throw the gooey bread slices over her ears to try and drown out the sound of Anna's incessant boasting. She didn't know how her brother could stand it. He had looked tuned out most of the time, and she couldn't blame him. As far as she knew, that was the only time Lachlan had brought Anna around any of the family, and as much as he made it sound otherwise, she was certain deep down he knew she just didn't fit in with the Mackenzie clan.

Orlagh was almost meditative in thought when someone sat in the chair across from her.

Chapter 23
The Reckoning

"Hello Rolo. How's my wee sis?"

Orlagh's eyes shot up. A little older and rougher looking than the last she'd seen him, Drew sat before her.

Tears sprang to her eyes. She jumped up and wrapped her arms tightly around him. "Och, Drustan, where have ye been, love?" She held him tightly, afraid to let go, as she muttered about missing him and how it had been so long.

Finally, Orlagh pulled away. And the next moment, she gave him a punch to the chest. He deserved a good wallop for what he'd put them through. She furrowed her brow, concerned as she looked up into his bloodshot blue-green eyes, one sporting a swollen shiner.

"It's okay, Rolo. I'm okay." He answered her unasked question.

"We didn't know what had happened to you. I ken ye were leaving, but ye just dropped off without a word. It was bad enough losing Helena." Her voice broke off, the emotions threatening to overwhelm her.

"C'mon, let's get out of here."

She nodded and headed out the door with him. They walked across the street and down to the waterfront.

"I never meant to hurt ye," Drew finally broke the silence.

"Well, ye did, ye big oaf. Ye hurt us all."

"I know. I couldn't take it. I was so angry. I couldn't see straight. And I had to escape it." He looked out over the rolling sea, storm clouds slowly moving in. "Getting out of here seemed like the only way."

"The only way to what?" she asked him point blank.

He picked up a handful of pebbles as they strode along the shorefront. "I thought I could escape the pain. I thought leaving would make the pain stop somehow."

He skipped one of the stones across the water, and after three jumps, the waves gobbled it up.

"And did it stop? The pain?" Orlagh asked, already knowing the answer.

"Nah." Drew exhaled. "If I thought I was at rock bottom when I left, I was wrong." He threw another stone into the s ea.

"Where did ye go? Nobody ken. Ye put us through hell." The wind had picked up, and she tightened her cardigan around her, trying to protect from its sudden bite.

Drew pulled off his jean jacket and handed it to Orlagh. "Put it on."

She did, not only glad for the extra layer but to see a glimmer of the Drew she once knew. One that cared for his family.

“Spain. I started in Spain.”

“Spain?” Orlagh whipped her head around to look at him.

“Aye. It was far from here, and that’s what I wanted. I wanted to escape this life.”

“And did ye? Escape this life?” She always dreamed of escaping, too. No, not escaping, adventuring.

Drew turned away from her and stared out over the water. Despite his scruffy facial hair and black eye, he was still a handsome one. When Orlagh was a teenager, she didn't understand why on earth the lassies chased her brothers, but she did now. Handsome buggers.

"Aye, I did. I hit rock bottom, Rolo. Tried all kinds of drugs to try and numb the pain. It was a dark place. Waking late one afternoon with my face laying in my own vomit, I realized I hated the shite life I was living. I missed Scotland. I missed making music. And I missed my family." He turned back to her.

She moved in to hug him, tears rolling down her cheeks.

"Losing Helena was too much to take. I had myself convinced that Lachlan could have prevented her death—that he was somehow responsible.”

"Och, Drew."

"I directed all my anger toward Lachlan. He was the scapegoat. All that blame, and I only ended up screwing up my own life."

They began walking again, the beach virtually empty now with storm clouds brewing and the winds picking up. "I saw Lachlan yesterday," Drew said calmly.

"What? Ye did?" Orlagh whipped around to look at him. Why wouldn't Lachlan have said anything to her?

"Aye, unfortunately, I didnae behave very well."

Orlagh saw regret etched in his features and wondered what had happened between them.

"I doubt he'll want to see me again. Seeing him just triggered all those old feelings. It suddenly brought everything back, and it didnae help that when I saw him, I had just run into some old friends. No, not friends, acquaintances. People I should have steered clear of." He shook his head.

She could practically feel the regret rolling off him.

"I suppose old habits die hard."

"Aw, Drew, I'm sure Lachlan wants to see ye again." Despite everything, she knew Lachlan loved Drew and vice versa.

"I doubt that. He clocked me one." Drew gestured to his black eye.

"Lachlan did that?" Orlagh was floored. She could see Alex doing that, but not Lachlan. Lachlan was too reasonable to use his fists. "What did ye do?" She tried to imagine what on earth could provoke Lachlan, of all people, to throw a punch, and by the looks of it, he didn't hold anything back.

"Let's just say I deserved it and leave it at that. To be honest, I think I needed it. I've been thinking long and hard since. I dinnae want to go back to that old way of being. It's no' who I am anymore. I am no' going to see those guys again. I ken they are bad news. I want to be a better man. I dinnae like who I became."

Orlagh wiped the tears that kept coming with the back of her hand. She was so relieved her brother was finally back and wanted to be the good guy she always knew he was deep down. "I'm proud of ye, Drew."

He shook his head as if he didn't think he deserved her praise. "I huv a lot to make up for. I ken that."

Orlagh nodded.

"I plan to connect with the guys from the band. See if they want to jam again. I want to make things right in my life and with my family."

The band had always been a good thing for Drew, despite the racket they used to make. Music was something that always made him truly happy.

Orlagh could see that there was still much unsaid, though. "Drugs?" she asked, fearing she knew the answer.

Drew swallowed hard. "Aye."

"No more drugs?" she asked nervously.

“Nah, I’m clean. I willnae ever go down that path again." His voice was quiet, but she could hear the conviction in his words.

Orlagh smiled lightly. “Ye do seem different. In a good way,” she added. “Are ye back to stay then?”

He chuckled, and it made her heart feel lighter to hear it.

“I dinnae ken, honestly. There are a lot of paths to mend, and some that I’m no’ sure can be. I hope so, though.”

Chapter 24
Shit Hits the Fan

After a few fruitless hours at work, Lachlan drove the quiet, narrow road of the coastline, hoping to clear his head. He knew Orlagh meant well, but she'd struck a nerve. Between his traitorous thoughts and his sister's words beating through his mind, he struggled to think clearly about anything. He cranked The Beatles—a pleasurable torment. The Beatles' music might forever remind him of *that time* he spent a damn-near perfect evening with the most beguiling woman.

It was early evening when he finally unlocked his front door, and Sally greeted him, shimmying so aggressively it defied her size. He bent down and ruffled her ears as he let his forehead rest for a moment on hers. He could always count on Sally—faithful girl. "Come on, Sal. Let's go for a walk."

Lachlan chucked a ball down the deserted stretch of beach, and Sally bolted after it, kicking up sand and water in her wake. The storm that had threatened passed, and the sun peeked out just in time to kiss the sea good night.

Lachlan breathed deeply, the familiar briny sea air helping set him at ease. After Helena died, he spent many hours walking along the beach, trying to come to terms with the loss. As time went on, he realized he'd never get over losing her. None of his family would, but they learned to live with the loss. There was the life they led before Helena died, and the life they led now that was vastly different—and yet so much remained the same. How odd it was to be the same person after a loved one's death and yet be so utterly changed at the same time.

In the beginning, every day was an impossible battle. Lachlan would work or be cooking dinner, and in brief moments, he'd almost forget. Then, suddenly, reality would strike. She was gone, and then the grief would wash over him again as if he'd not yet grieved at all.

As soon as he felt his wounded heart was healing, something would remind him of her, of the life lost, of the hollow left behind, and it was as though his heart was flayed open yet again. But as time marched on, his heart managed to hang onto the healing for longer periods. The lashings to his heart became less frequent, although no less painful. He missed her. What he wouldn't give to talk to her right now.

What would Helena think of Violet? He knew—she would've liked her. Violet was so real and spirited. Helena would've appreciated that about her. He picked up Sally's ball, throwing it far down the beach again and watched her bound after it in the evening twilight.

And what of Anna? Would Helena have liked her? He knew the answer to that, too.

"Come on, girl. Let's get ye some supper," Lachlan called to Sally. As they made their way back to the house, Lachlan made the decision. It was time to end things with Anna. Maybe *past* time.

She'd messaged him before he'd met Orlagh for lunch, saying she was planning to be back tomorrow. Lachlan decided that he would meet with her and end it. He didn't relish the idea of breaking up, and he hoped there would be no hard feelings. But with every step he took, his resolve fortified. *Aye, this was the right decision.*

In the quarter of an hour it took to get back to the house, Lachlan's mind had started to buzz with plans for a side project he'd taken on but hadn't been focused on as of late.

Before Helena had died, she spent much of her time giving riding lessons to kids. She used to talk about wanting to open up a horse sanctuary of sorts for children. A place where they could be around horses and learn to ride. She especially wanted it for the kids who would not otherwise get the chance. She often talked about the effect of the horses on the children. How even the kids with attitudes would warm up and seemed to find a sense of connection, spending time at stables. Helena was right. Horses were therapeutic and not just for kids.

Years back, he'd had the idea to build the sanctuary Helena had dreamed of. He'd been so busy with the distillery that it had just idled in the back of his mind until a few months back.

Orlagh had been babysitting her friend's five-year-old daughter and brought her to see the horses at his house. She was only a wee thing and had been nervous of the big beasts hiding behind Lachlan with the back of his trousers fisted in her little hands. Not that he'd admit it, but the gesture melted him. He scooped her up with reassuring words and watched as the child followed his lead, putting a hand on Edelweiss's snout.

In no time, her little confidence grew, and by the time Orlagh took her home, she was begging to stay with her new *horsey friends*. As he watched the little girl looking longingly out the window from the backseat of Orlagh's car as she pulled away, Lachlan knew it was time to start building Helena's dream. Ideas flooded his mind so steadily that he barely slept for the better part of two weeks. Around that time, he started seeing Anna, and as much as he was still working to get it going on the side, he'd lost his focus.

Stepping up to his side door, he was taking inventory in his head for the next steps when he caught a glimpse of a car in the driveway, and his heart and mood sank: Anna. Walking in the side door to the kitchen, he scooped kibble into Sally's bowl and felt the tension creep into his shoulders and neck as he went to greet his soon-to-be ex-girlfriend.

When he didn't find her on the main floor, he made his way up the curved staircase. "Anna," he called out, but there was no answer. Seeing his bedroom door ajar, he gently knocked on the door before opening it to find her standing in a black sheer chemise with some fluffy fur or something on the bottom of it. It should have tempted him, but it didn't. His only thought was how over-the-top French fashion could be. The hardness of his cock, which he'd almost grown accustomed to during Violet's brief stay with him, was notably absent.

"Ye utter prick!" Anna's words were as sharp as a slap to the face. She held a white piece of paper in her hand. Lachlan could see it had writing on it, and belatedly, it dawned on him—Violet. She must have left it there when she'd gone up to gather her things this morning.

The near overwhelming desire to read it was perhaps normal. The desire to smell it and even touch his tongue to it to see if held any traces of her taste, surely was not. When he drew his gaze back to Anna, she was deftly throwing daggers at him with her eyes. Christ, what could he say? Although he hadn't cheated, he very much felt like he had. He didn't have words of reassurance for her.

"I willnae claim innocence, although I assure ye it's no' what ye think. I'll leave ye to get dressed, and we can talk downstairs."

Apparently, that was not the right thing to say, as the very next moment she flopped down on the bed with her shoulders drooping heavily, an exaggerated pout on her face, and *the note* carelessly discarded. Lachlan struggled to tear his gaze away from where it lay on the floor by the bed.

"Lachlan." Anna's voice calmed, capriciously. Then she dropped back against his pillows, theatrically throwing an arm up across her forehead. "I wasnae the perfect angel in France either," she sighed melodramatically.

Lachlan knew her confession should have at least some effect on him, but he felt unmoved. He should want to know what happened, but he found he didn't want to know at all—and not because it would bother him. It was that he was impassive. He didn't care. He was officially checked out of this relationship and already wondering how he could have possibly ever been checked in.

She sat up straighter and looked at him, holding her hands in her lap like a pupil in school. "It's not surprising, really," she explained. "We are about to take the next step in our relationship. It's only natural we'd have one last fling before settling down."

That sentiment pissed him off. What kind of shite logic was that?

"It makes total sense. We both cracked under the pressure of knowing we were about to commit to each other. It's a big step, after all, moving in together."

She was right. It was a massive step! He struggled to fathom how they'd thought they'd gotten to it. Looking at Anna now, he realized their relationship had been surface-level at best. Did they even know each other at all? He couldn't help but think of Violet. In just over a day, they'd forged a connection that ran deeper than Loch-fucking-ness. It was a stark comparison.

"I think we were testing the waters to be sure we were making the right decision."

Lachlan's focus snapped back to the present. The more she spoke, the more she looked like she was buying into her own pish explanation.

"I ken, with complete certainty now, I only want to be with ye, Lachlan. We make sense together, aye?" She said it rhetorically like she didn't need an answer from him.

"No."

"Oh, dinnae be silly," she cut him off. "If I ken forgive *ye*, I'm sure ye can forgive me too, aye? And as a bonus of this little experiment, I realize just how lucky of a lass I am," she purred and her gaze dropped to his crotch. She stroked the black fluffy stuff on her negligee with a gleam in her eyes that reminded him of Cruella de Vil in *101 Dalmatians*, petting her coat while daydreaming about her nefarious plans. "We are even, Lachlan, and now we can move on from this and find our happily ever after."

Lachlan was too distracted by the note lying discarded on the floor to respond.

"I ken I said I hated France, but I ended up in Paris and fell in love with it. It really is such a romantic city, and ye ken what I was thinking? It's the perfect place for a destination wedding." She swooned. "If I started planning now, we could huv a fall wedding there. Oh, can you imagine? I could even shop for my dress there!"

Lachlan stood back, unable to comprehend how she could be so delusional. The veil had dropped, as it were, and he felt like he was truly seeing her for the first time. Lachlan felt like he'd entered some kind of hellish twilight zone. Suddenly, he understood what it was that Orlagh had seen in Anna. The woman was self-absorbed. One dimensional.

"Stop. Enough." He couldn't listen to another word. "I dinnae want this, Anna. I dinnae want any of it. We are no' good together, and if anything, this past weekend just proves i t."

"We both had a fling. It's nothing. Dinnae let it ruin us." She got off the bed and, as if in one final attempt to convince him, reached out to touch his face, but he caught her wrist between them.

"For the record, I dinnae huv a fling, but it doesnae matter. It's no' about that. We were never good together. No' really." That was painfully clear to him now.

"How can ye say that?" Her features contorted into an ugly sneer, and she bit out, "Was she that good of a lay?"

Lachlan shook his head and almost laughed. He had no doubt that aye, she was that good of a lay, but unfortunately, he didn't have first-hand knowledge. "We are done. Ye can gather yer things. I'll be downstairs," he said, with finality, and he turned, striding out of the room with her cursing from behind him.

Coming down the stairs, anger emanated off her like steam from a rooftop in the cold of winter. She barely spared him a glance as her high heels clacked obnoxiously on the slate floor, and she stormed out the front door.

Lachlan felt completely spent by the time Anna left. He didn't like how tense things had gotten. He'd imagined a more diplomatic finish to the relationship, but he couldn't deny that he was relieved it was over and done with. Exhausted, he fell asleep the moment his head hit the pillow. It wasn't

until the morning that he realized the note from Violet was go
ne.

Chapter 25

He's Just Not That Into You

For the first week after her overnight with Lachlan, Violet jumped every time her phone rang. With every text that came through, she subconsciously held her breath. But each time, a pang of disappointment pinched her heart when she realized it wasn't him. She hadn't expected to hear from Lachlan right away, but she thought he'd message at some point just to say hi or see how she was doing. It surprised her and disappointed her more than she wanted to admit.

Their day and night together had been so good, despite the circumstances. No, not good, epic, definitely epic. As time went on, she wondered if it was only she who had thought it was incredible. After all, horses, scotch, and a castle-like home were his norm. More than likely, he had women lined up for that crooked grin and charm and maybe the deep conversations, too. She had felt like there was something special between them, but maybe she was wrong.

Violet knew she should get past it, move on. But Mr. GQ was present in her thoughts more than she wished. "Ugh, but he's my knight in shining armour," she whined on the phone to her best friend Sierra as she sat on the bed in her Airbnb, trying to put on her makeup using the mirror stand she'd bought that was clearly meant for a solid surface and not a lumpy bed.

"Seriously, I don't care how dreamy he is. *He's just not that into you*, which means he is *not* your knight. Sorry for the tough love, babe, but it's been a month now. If he wanted to see you again, he would have."

"I'm sure I put my number on the note I left." Violet started to second-guess herself, pausing midway through streaking on her eyeliner.

"Of course you did. No one writes a 'thanks for the night before, the morning after' note and forgets to put their phone number on it."

"Right." She bit her lip. "Maybe he lost it?"

"Babes, if he wanted to see you again, he would have found a way. He knows the Airbnb you are staying at."

"True. All right, all right. I get it. He would've connected." She sighed heavily in resignation. "Crap."

"Aww, Vi, forget about him. You went to Scotland with dreams in your heart. Follow them, and forget about the boy."

"I know, you are so right." Violet knew it was true. She'd been far too distracted with fantasies about Lachlan. It was time to move on. "Fine, that's it. I'm done! No more waiting, hoping, pining, daydreaming about Mr. Not-So-Wonderful-After-All. Done. Back to my life and the reason I'm here. I have goals to achieve, dreams to follow, life to live!"

"There ya go. That's right, you do! How's the styling business, anyway?"

"Slow, but there's hope. I landed my first client. She works in advertising and feels like she's not making the best impression with her wardrobe." Violet mimicked the way the woman had said it to her. "She's exactly the type of client I want to work with, I just hope I can get more like he r."

"It's a start, at least. How'd you get that one?"

"Randomly. We met at the coolest little coffee shop, literally a hole in the wall." Violet chuckled. "She gushed over my shoes, and it went from there."

"Jeepers, well, I guess that's one way to snag in potential clients: keep going to charming little dives and luring them in with your killer wardrobe."

The two women laughed.

"Ah, I wish it was always this easy. It's a start, though. In other news, I got a job at a horse sanctuary."

"Sorry, you what?"

Violet could practically see Sierra's confused expression. She had to admit, it did sound strange, even to her.

“Um, it’s just sort of a side thing. I don’t know, I thought I’d try it out to make a little extra money while I get my business going. And you know I adore horses.”

“What are you going to be doing? Like mucking out stables?” Sierra scoffed.

“No, no. Well, I don’t think so. It’s supposed to be a place for kids to go to be around horses, ride them, or groom them. That sort of thing. I'm not sure of much yet, but anything to do with horses, I'm in. I suppose whatever they need.”

“Does it pay well?”

Violet laughed. "What do you think? I mean, considering I don't even really know what I'm doing yet, it is more than minimum wage, so that's good.”

“So you're side hustle is a random job with horses?” Sierra clarified as if she didn’t quite believe it.

“Yeah, sure. Why not?”

“No, that’s fine. I’m just surprised. I thought if you did anything on the side, it might be working in the fashion world. Or at least something that pays well.”

Violet was very aware that her savings would only take her so far, but she was confident it would all work out eventually. “Right, well, I don’t know. It just sounded good at the time. Nobody says I have to stay there. But I need something to do in my spare time, and I get to go riding as often as I wish, which is pretty wicked. I don't even need Mr. GQ's horses. He can keep them. I've found my own!"

Sierra chuckled. "That's right. You don't need his stinkin' horses. I mean, that's probably the only reason you even liked him. He's got no pull on you now you've found your *own* horses."

"Oh my God, Sierra, I frickin' miss you!" She looked in her tilted mirror for a final check and zipped closed her makeup bag.

"Miss you too, lady. How's the head? Everything still good?"

"Yep, it's been good, thank God. I still can't believe how crazy it was that happened."

"Which brings me to my next question. Have you made any friends there yet?" Sierra said it as if Violet might find herself in need again.

"A few. Actually, my friend Fiona was the one who told me about the horse thing. She's going to be doing it too, and she introduced me to her friend Andy. We've hit it off, they've been really great."

"Good, I'm glad you at least have someone out there. And what about a place? Any luck there? Or are you still living at the Airbnb?"

Violet snickered. "I'm still at the Airbnb, and I'm so over it. I've checked out a couple of places. One was perfect, but it came with a not-so-perfect price tag. I checked out this one place that should be condemned! It was disgusting and smelled like rotting vegetables."

"Gross."

"Yep, it was. Actually, I better get going. I'm meeting the agent at another place this afternoon. I'm afraid to hope."

"Aww, well, I will hope for you that this one will be the one. Miss you, my friend. Good luck today, and remember, that dude's *just not that into you*, so forget about him!"

Violet laughed. "Yeah, yeah, I got it. Miss you too. Talk to you soon. Bye."

The cottage was too good to be true! But as Violet unlocked the door to her new place, the reality sunk in. Sun shone through the picture window, casting an inviting glow to the airy room. The old walnut wood floor creaked in welcome as she walked in. She strolled to the bedroom, where a view of the sea in the distance drew her to the window.

Oh, this place was perfect—so perfect. A little farther away from town than she would have preferred, but it was too good to pass up. And the price was right. It took a while to find. But she knew as soon as she saw it that it was the one. Another draw was how close it was to the horse sanctuary, literally a couple minutes' walk down the most perfect little country road and only a fifteen-minute drive to town.

Violet sank into the navy winged-back chair and looked around the room, imagining where she might hang her non-existent artwork—one day. She sighed with contentment. Staring out at the green hills and that little patch of sea beyond them, Violet's thoughts turned to Lachlan.

She had done well to get him off her mind this past month since speaking to Sierra, but somehow, the distant rhythmic sound of the rolling waves took her back to that evening in his lounge. And then the kiss in the hallway—one-sided, and yet not. Either way, it was burned into her soul. A delicious shiver tingled down her spine at the memory. A knock on the ajar front door pulled her from her reverie.

"Hello, anybody home?" Fiona called out.

Aware of the direction her thoughts had taken, Violet was glad for Fiona's cheerful voice at her door.

"Welcome to my humble abode!" She spread her arms wide as she walked out of the bedroom to greet her friend.

"It's simply gorge', love! Let's celebrate!" Fiona held up a bottle of champagne.

Violet whooped. "I'll grab a couple of glasses!"

"Better grab me one too." Andy strode in behind Fiona with more champagne in hand.

"Aww, you guys are the best!"

Fiona and Andy plunked themselves down on the white shabby chic overstuffed couch.

"Pretty great little place, Violet," Andy quipped as he made himself comfy.

Violet walked back into the living room and looked around meaningfully. "It is, isn't it?"

Andy did the honours, popping a bottle open and pouring them each a fizzy glass. They held them up for a toast. "First, apologies that we are having champagne out of coffee mugs. I might need to add champagne flutes to the shopping list!"

"Uh, yeah, ye do." Fiona laughed.

"Thank you guys for everything. I'm so grateful that you interrupted my reading. I'll never forget the deadpan first words out of your mouth and the side eye you threw me: 'is it fuckin' steamy?'"

Fiona grinned widely, her signature bold coloured lipstick on full display. "I'm always looking for new recommendations for my TBR."

"What in God's name is TBR?" Andy eyed them like he wasn't sure he wanted to know the answer.

"To be read," Violet and Fiona responded in unison, then giggled.

"As in the list of books you want to read," Violet added, noting Andy's confused, slightly ruffled brow. "Anyway, I was just so glad someone decided to talk to me." She reflected on how lonely she'd actually been feeling—until Fiona popped into her life.

"Oh, I'm certain I wasn't the first."

"Fair. But you were the first to ask the fun questions. I never expected to find a lifelong friend in such a short amount of time." Violet reached over and gave Fiona's hand a squeeze.

"Hey, what about me then? I suppose I'm just the soggy peas on the side that nobody cares about," Andy said, wallowing in self-pity.

Violet giggled. "And you, Andy! I'm thankful we met, too. I feel like the two of you took me under your wing—thank God. I'm no longer a loner in Scotland, cheers!"

With a laugh, they clanked their glasses. "To no' being a loner!" Fiona concurred and took a healthy sip.

As the sun set, Violet sat in her lovely new cottage, enjoying champagne and the company of her new friends. She felt like she was living her dream life. It was one of the best evenings Violet had had since arriving in Scotland. Only one other could beat it, but she pushed that memory aside.

"So now you have a business client, a job, a place to live, friends, how about a man? Any prospects?" Fiona flashed a sly grin, swept her long dark hair forward over her shoulder, and batted her lashes in a flirty gesture.

Violet guffawed, throwing back the contents of her mug. The champagne made her head spin.

"Nothing?" She looked aghast.

Meanwhile, Andy was kicked back on the couch, intoxicated and laser-focused on balancing his mug atop his rounded belly.

Violet poured herself some more champagne and leaned over to top up Andy's mug and then Fiona's, emptying the contents of the bottle.

"I don't have time for men. What about you, Fiona? Have you met any hunky amazingness as of late?"

"Really, lassies, ye ken I'm still here, aye?" Andy remarked, tuning back into the conversation.

"Ya, ya, Andy." Fiona swatted at his leg, causing his mug to falter, and he jostled with it before saving his champagne from spilling. "Ye may wanna close yer ears." She teased him and then drew her attention back to Violet. "Have ye seen the owner of the sanctuary, Vi?" Her dark brow raised in a playful arch. "He was there yesterday and och."

"I wasn't in yesterday. He's hot?" she asked, intrigued at this turn of events.

"Oh, girl, ye dinnae ken the half of it." Fiona fanned herself like a 1950s actress who was all *hot and bothered*.

"Do tell. I always assumed it was some old rich dude who owned it." Violet leaned against the cushions of the couch, cradling her champagne eagerly anticipating the details. It was good for her to remember there were other men in Scotland, not just Lachlan.

"Hardly! Mmm, mmm, mmm." Fiona drawled. "Definitely easy on the eyes."

"Really. How old is he?" Violet tried to imagine this easy-on-the-eyes enigma.

"Not that old. I would say late twenties to early thirties."

"The owner's son, maybe?" He'd have to have either a lot of money or some solid investors to own a sanctuary like Highland Haven.

"No, we were told he was it, the master behind the plan."

"Hmm."

"Oh my God, and he was so nice," she droned exaggeratedly. "He was talking about his vision for the sanctuary and how grateful he was for all our help and how he wanted it to be a place we could also feel good about." She took a gulp of her champagne as if it were milk, washing down cookies. "Seriously, good-looking, cares about kids, and rich? My ovaries are dancing a fuckin' jig!

Violet laughed, almost spilling her champagne. "That good, eh?"

"Aye, Miss Canada, eh?" Fiona teased. "That good. I think he'd be right up yer alley."

"My alley? What about your alley? I thought your ovaries were jigging?" Violet slogged the last of her champagne and looked around as though disappointed more was not awaiting her. She was more concerned with champagne than her supposedly hot, rich, children-lovin' boss. It was good to know there were other fish in the sea— maybe even other Knights in shining armour. But Violet found herself reluctant to jump into the dating scene in Scotland. After... whatever the heck that was with Lachlan, she realized the last thing she needed was a distraction— especially when what she really wanted was to find her footing here in this country.

"Oh, well, they jigged but more on yer behalf. I think I prefer the bad boys—gruff and rough, that kind of thing. This one is too nice for that." Fiona yawned, stretching her arms up before settling in a cozied-up ball. "Yep, ye should do the boss. Let us all live vicariously," she said sleepily.

"I dinnae wanna live vicariously in that scenario. Thank ye verra much," Andy suddenly piped up.

Violet jumped. She thought he'd fallen asleep. "The only thing I'm gonna *do* is my bed, like right now. You're on your own, peeps. Blankets are in the closet in the hall. I'm out." Violet padded off to her room, leaving her friends to fend for themselves.

Chapter 26

Hangover, Horses, and Him

Violet awoke to the warm sun bathing her face. When she opened her eyes, a dull ache immediately gripped them. "Ugh," she groaned, not feeling her best. Rolling over she looked at her clock through the slits of her eyelids. Eight-thirty a.m. She was supposed to be at the sanctuary for nine. Shit.

She flew out of bed, past her friends who still lay sleeping in her living room, and into the bathroom to take the world's quickest shower. "Shit, shit, shit."

She'd just gotten her long hair wet, and with her headache blaring, she realized she'd left her toiletries, yet to be unpacked, in the bedroom. Guess she wouldn't be washing with soap today. She slurped water in the shower, hoping to ease her massive headache. Tearing back the cute highland cow shower curtain she'd bought, she stepped out, and tossed a towel around her, throwing her wet hair up in a messy bun. No time for full makeup. She put on concealer, mascara, blush, and a new shimmer lip gloss she'd bought, and ran out of the bathroom, towel still wrapped around her.

In her bedroom, she noted the lovely sunlight streaming through as she whipped on her work jeans and a t-shirt—that probably could use a wash—and zipped into the kitchen. 8:59. She grabbed a shiny red apple and bolted out the front door, grabbing her purse as she went.

"See you guys later," she hollered back before slamming the robin's-egg blue front door closed.

Violet hated being late. She got to the sanctuary at 9:11. Nobody else seemed to even notice, but Violet was reprimanding herself for her tardiness while her head hammered scolding her for her late night boozing.

"Hey Effie." She smiled as she walked into the office. She went to her locker, slipped on her rubber boots, and grabbed her gloves.

"Good morning, lassie." Effie smiled as if nothing pleased her more than to see Violet. But then upon further inspection, her features dropped, and her eyebrows knit with worry. "Are ye feelin' quite well?"

"Just a bit of a late night." Violet wasn't about to divulge the fact that she was hungover.

"Och, right," she said. "Yer eyes are all puffed, and yer hair looks like ye've been drug through a hedge backwards."

Effie was the admin at the Highland Haven and was around sixty years old. On the surface, she was like the quintessential grandma, bringing the staff baked goods most days, always watching out for everyone, but one of Violet's favourite traits was her no-nonsense honesty—the call it like you see it, non-filtered manner that is earned with age. Normally, she enjoyed Effie's blunt assessments, but today, she was more in the market for a warm Grandma hug. Effie must have noticed her wince under her appraisal.

"Och, it's all right, lassie. Yer still as bonnie as ever. Ye remind me of those models ye see on the telly. Ye ken the ones. They'd look lovely even wearing a bin bag."

Violet supposed that was meant as a compliment. "Thanks, Effie."

"I made rhubarb muffins if you're peckish."

Violet's stomach seemed to growl on cue. "You are a godsend." She picked up an oversized muffin out of the Tupperware container Effie offered up to her.

"Did you meet Logan?" Effie chirped.

"Uh, no. Is he new?" Violet answered, biting into the muffin and sweeping crumbs from her t-shirt.

"Yes. Well, no, he's not new, but it's the first time we've all met him. He's the owner of Highland Haven," she said proudly as if he was her son. "Och, he's just a lovely, lovely man."

Violet noted a flush creeping up Effie's soft, crinkled cheeks.

"I believe he said he's coming by again today. He says he's keen to meet all the staff and volunteers. Apparently, he's been away, so he hasn't had the chance to get in here sooner. Och, such a lovely man."

Violet almost laughed at how Effie was gushing. This Logan dude must be something.

"Ye'll like him, Violet. He's the kind of person ye can tell is good, right off the bat." Effie's pudgy face had gone as rosy as a spring tulip.

Violet was starting to wonder how this guy could possibly live up to the reputation he was getting. Well, the women seemed to like him, but was he as good a guy as they thought or just a good charmer? She supposed he must be a decent guy if Highland Haven was truly his. She was pretty sure dickheads wouldn't choose a horse sanctuary for kids as their big money-maker.

"Right, well, he sounds...lovely. These muffins are divine," she said, shoving the last bite in her mouth.

"Oh, lassie, glad ye're liking them. Bill cut the rhubarb fer me over the weekend. It's a wee bit tart, but I just added more sugar. Here, take another for later."

Violet did, knowing it was the sugar hit that would likely get her through the day.

"I hope our Logan will like them too. I'm going to save the rest fer him. He's a big man, ye ken." Her eyes widened as if she were spreading some kind of gossip about him.

“Mmhm." Violet didn't want to comment on his size. "I’m sure he will.” Violet gave Effie a reassuring smile and turned to head toward the stables. "See you later. Thanks for the muffins!”

Our Logan, Violet thought to herself with a chuckle as she entered the small door on the stables and headed straight for Beethoven’s stall. She had to admit, all this talk about their new boss left her intrigued. Neighs and grunts greeted her. Hangover or not, this place was still heaven on earth. Beethoven snorted his approval upon eyeing Violet. She’d grown fond of all the horses, but Beethoven held an extra special place in her heart.

“Hey, boy,” she said, patting his shiny, ebony neck. “Shall we have a nice brush down before our ride? I’ll be right back, handsome.” She had the best side hustle in the world. She was responsible for grooming and exercising the horses. There were around fifty horses at the stable, but she was responsible for the care of half of them at the moment. She always started and ended her shift with Beethoven, though.

She walked down to the tack room. Opening the door, she caught sight of someone else in there, and her heart jumped into her throat. She recognized him immediately, even though the view was from behind. Broad shoulders, modern pompadour hair, and a damn fine ass in his dark denim. She was about to sneak back out when he looked her way. Those cerulean blue eyes she'd tried to forget locked on hers. And she instantly remembered how those eyes had been her lifeline only two months ago.

"Violet?" He appeared as surprised as she was.

God, he looked good, painfully good. Brown, perfectly worn leather boots under his dark denim, navy button-up shirt. Even at a stable, the man looked like he stepped right out of a men's magazine, and here she was again, looking casual AF—and not the cute kind of casual—damn it. She was pretty sure there was a stain on her gray t-shirt, and as Effie pointed out, she basically looked like shit. God. Why, why couldn't she have run into him at a coffee shop when she's working on her styling business or preparing to meet a client, and at least wearing clean clothes? She stared at him, still shocked to see him.

"What are you doing here?" she blurted.

That sexy crooked smile spread across his face, and her traitorous heart almost burst. God, how could she have forgotten the effect of that smile? She unconsciously tucked a stray strand of hair behind her ear.

"At the moment, I'm looking at the tack gear."

"Yes, I can see that. I mean, why are you here at Highland Haven? I hope you're not thinking of purchasing one of our horses." It was the first explanation she could think of.

"Would it be a problem if I was?" he challenged her, pulling down one of the leather bridles from the wall as if he owned the place. Who did he think he was?

"They are not for sale," she said, wondering where the heck this Logan dude was now.

"Hmm, I see. And ye ken this for a fact?" He took a step toward her, closing some distance between them.

It ticked her off that a little, excited tingle rippled down her spine.

"I'm quite certain these horses were chosen specifically for this sanctuary. I highly doubt the owner would have any interest in selling them," she said, trying to sound convincing. Lachlan's gaze unnerved her.

"Ye dinnae sound too happy to see me." His voice lowered.

Her stomach did a little flip-flop. "What? I-I," she stuttered. Why should she be happy to see him? "I suppose I'm surprised to see you," she said honestly.

Although, it was more than that. She was pissed at him. Ticked that he'd literally ghosted her. He knew she had no friends here. Even if he didn't want to date her, a friendly text to say hi or see how she was would have been nice. She'd be wise not to get carried away by the man's charm, but frick, it was easier said than done as he towered before her all manly and good-looking.

The silence stretched between them, and she shifted her weight, crossing her arms over her chest. She noticed his thumb run over the leather strap of the bridle in his hands. Big, slightly tanned hands with veins corded over the backs and strong knuckles. What would it feel like to have those hands on her, feeling down her waist or holding her face before he kissed her with that dang crooked smile on his lips? She swallowed hard, horrified at her own treasonous thoughts.

"They said I still had to meet Violet." His voice was husky and deep, and he continued to rub that leather gently with his thumb, driving her to distraction. "Violet, the wonderful lass who's helped everyone here, the lass who cares about this place as though it was her very own."

She didn't know what to say.

"Violet. I wondered if it would be ye."

And that was when the penny dropped. "*You're* the boss." *Plot twist.* Not Logan, but Lachlan. *Ugh.* So many thoughts ran through her mind all at once, including that *he was her boss.*

He laughed humbly. "Aye, I suppose."

Violet had no words. Would he still want her to work here? Did *she* still want to work here?

"Thank ye for ensuring that no one dare try to buy my horses. Our horses," he corrected.

His correction took her aback. *Our horses.* She knew he meant the sanctuary's horses, but all the same, the word *our* had a strange warming effect on her.

His skin tingled just being in her presence, like she wielded some kind of magic over him. The wary expression she wore and the way her arms were crossed over her chest bothered him. She was apprehensive with him. Who could blame her? After the day he'd dropped her at her Airbnb and the night he'd last spoken to Anna, when he'd discovered Violet's note was gone, he realized that perhaps it was for the best. After ending things with Anna, it felt like he needed time.

And he'd also felt that flame in him again, inspiring him to finally bring Highland Haven to fruition. He didn't want to ponder what it was he'd experienced with Violet. That raw guttural desire that damn-near overwhelmed him, especially not on the heels of breaking up with Anna. He wanted to turn the page on the past and focus on the future. But seeing her now, that fated thrum for her in his veins. He'd be willing to bet money that she was his future.

Glancing over her shoulder at the door, she looked ready to bolt. Shite. "How've ye been?" he said, hoping she'd stay and talk with him.

"Great, I've been great." Her words came out in a rush, and then she added, "I just moved into a nearby cottage, and I have a bit of traction with my styling business. And this place..." her voice trailed off.

He knew she loved it here. He could have predicted that after that first night together when she insisted they go down and meet his horses.

"That's really great to hear. I'm happy for ye. Did ye get the little white cottage on the hill just down the lane? It's been up for let for a while now."

"Yeah, that's the one. I was so happy to find it. It's like a hidden gem." She unconsciously tucked a stray hair behind her ear.

His eyes followed the movement, landing on her exposed creamy neck.

He cleared his throat. "I'm really glad ye're doing well, though I'm no' surprised. I could tell when we met that ye would make things happen."

She tucked her hands in her denim pockets under the edge of her t-shirt and rocked back on the heels of her rubber boots. The first hint of a smile touched her cupid bow lips. The effect was like the sun heating your skin after a cold dip in the sea.

"How's yer head?" he asked after a pause.

"Good, all healed up, thank goodness. It's still crazy to me that that's how I started my time here in Scotland."

"I think a lot of people would've let that defeat them. It's good ye stayed and didn't let it deter ye."

She shrugged as if she didn't think it was anything significant. It was, though. Lachlan knew many who would not have persevered after a setback like that. He wondered what he'd been thinking, letting her slip out of his life as fast as she'd come in.

"I'm sorry that I dinnae get in touch." He didn't want to bring up the fact that he never actually got to read her note, but he knew he could have connected with her again, even without her phone number.

"Don't worry about it, Lachlan." She moved past him, looping a halter in her hand and picking a saddle off the wall rack. "I better get to work," she said bluntly as she carried on down the corridor behind him.

He watched as she used her back end to shove open the side door to the stables, without a glance back at him.

Lachlan blew out a breath and leaned an elbow against the wall, scraping a hand through his hair. He supposed that could have gone worse. At least she spoke to him.

Violet. His Violet. No, not yer Violet, he argued against the possessive thought. *No' yet, anyway.* He had no idea that he was the ripped jeans and t-shirt type guy until now. God, she looked good. Loose fit jeans over her slim legs, with a few fashionable frays where creamy tempting skin peeped through, taunting him, tucked into tall olive-coloured Wellington boots. Wisps of blond hair fell out, slipping out from her topknot and whispering against the skin on her slender neck. He had to tear his mind from imagining her skin goose-fleshing as he ran his tongue along the slim cords of her neck.

He blew out a breath, putting the bridle back on its peg. A few staff members had mentioned the name Violet to him. They had nothing but good things to say about the lass who'd started working there in only the last week. He was tempted to ask more about her. Was she a Canadian lass by chance? But he didn't. He waited with veiled anticipation, bathing the tasks and duties of his day in a lightness.

And now, he knew. It was indeed the lass he hoped it would be. When the mere mention of her name sent a jolt through him, he should have known he'd be done for seeing her again. The prospect of seeing her here at the stables on a regular basis had the same effect as telling a ten-year-old they could attend Hogwarts School of Wizardry. He felt positively giddy.

However, currently, he could foresee two issues—scratch that, three issues. One, she didn't seem to share his enthusiasm for their reunion—not that he could blame her. He'd been an arse to not reach out to her. Two, seeing her at work from time to time was not enough. Not by a long shot. Three, for all intents and purposes, he was her boss. Oh, and fucking number four, he was Saint fucking Lachlan.

Chapter 27
Now What

VIOLET SOMEHOW AVOIDED RUNNING into Lachlan for the rest of the day, but she knew that it would be a losing battle as time went on. She came home and opened the front door to her lovely little cottage, smiling, seeing where sunlight from the living room bathed the whitewashed entry walls. She set her new glass jar of succulents on the window sill.

At the end of her shift, she'd opened her locker and discovered the cheerful pop of green. She slid out the card from its white envelope with two chestnut horses grazing in a pasture painted on the cover. Inside were the words *Happy Housewarming* in somebody's scrolled handwriting in larger print and then a smattering of well-wishes and signatures. Her heart warmed, and she smiled, feeling misty-eyed. *How thoughtful.*

She'd suspected Effie was the facilitator, but reading the kind messages, she'd realized she was lucky to have met such a good group of people. Her eyes scanned the signatures a second time in case she'd missed it on the first read-through. But no, Lachlan's signature wasn't among them. And then she'd chided herself for being distracted by the man and headed home.

Violet noted that Fiona and Andy left the place tidy, which she was glad about since all she wanted to do was curl up on the couch and read the book Fiona lent her. A note on the coffee table caught her eye, and she picked it up.

Fab night, enjoy your charming cottage, speak soon! Fiona x and Andy :)

After devouring a bowl of homemade butternut squash soup she'd found at the small grocery shop up the road from her place, she had renewed energy and decided to finish unpacking. Not that she had much, but still, she wanted to put things in order and then make a list of things she still needed to get. Champagne glasses were at the top of the list.

She sat in the navy wingback chair in her bedroom, listening to the soft swooshing of the waves in the distance. She picked up the book from Fiona and read the words, but they didn't register—her mind was too preoccupied with her new boss.

She groaned, closing her book and pinching her lip between her finger and thumb. It annoyed her that he'd turned her insides to Jello today. Why did he have that effect on her? She thought she was over him. Done. Finished. It was maddening. And now, it turned out she'd likely be seeing him regularly. Maybe he wouldn't be there that often. He did have a distillery to run, after all. He couldn't very well run both businesses full on, could he? It was probably why the staff were only just now meeting him in person. Highland Haven was likely just a side thing for him, where he'd work on it from a distance, not in the trenches. And it was also a side thing for her, so maybe they wouldn't run into each other much at all. She needed to talk to Sierra. She tapped her phone and looked at the time. Eleven p.m. Then she calculated in her head what time it was back home. Early morning.

"Hello?" Sierra answered in a groggy voice.

"Hey, it's me. Sorry to wake you."

"You should be." Violet could hear the ruffle of bedding. "Kidding, I'm always happy to hear from you. How's the new place?"

"Amazing. You need to plan a trip. Now I have room, and seriously, it is so awesome here. How are you, my friend?"

"Great, good. I'm meeting Matt for brunch this morning." Violet could practically hear her grin through the phone.

"OOH, still going strong with Matt, eh?" Violet teased.

Sierra laughed. "Yep, still good. He's a sweetheart."

"I'm glad. You deserve that." Violet ran her finger over a little knot in the fabric of her navy chair. "So, I found out who the owner of Highland Haven is today."

"Yeah, who?"

"It's him."

"Him?"

"Lachlan."

"What? No! Shut up!" Violet could imagine her friend's wide expression.

"Yep, I ran into him there today."

"Oh my God, and how was it? Are you okay?"

"Oh God, Sierra. The man is just so damn perfect. Physically, he is unreasonably hot. Worse than that, though, is just that he is honestly just such a good guy. Everybody over there is already singing his praises. It's going to be torture. I wish he could be an asshole so I could hate him."

"He is an asshole. He didn't phone."

"He's not an asshole. He actually apologized for not getting in touch."

"Big whoop. Easy for him to apologize now. He could have connected if he wanted to, and he didn't, plain and simple. So don't you go letting your imagination run away with you. You know he can be a flirt with you, and you also know it doesn't change anything—he is not interested. You *know* that. Don't torture yourself, Vi. Keep that door closed. Move on. He did."

Lachlan definitely had a way of making her knees weak, whether he meant to or not. Thank God for Sierra. She didn't mince words. That was exactly what Violet needed to hear. He didn't deserve her, anyway. He could have at least gotten in touch with her to make sure she was doing well—just something friendly—but not a word. He'd totally ghosted her. It was actually rude. Sierra was right. She would not let him back into her heart and mind.

"What about that Andy guy?" Sierra quipped.

"Andy? What? To date? No, no, he's sweet, but just a friend."

"The best relationships start as friends, just sayin'."

"You make a good point, but not in this case. No, just no." Violet couldn't think of Andy that way. He was one of the girls, and that was that.

"All right. Well, I gotta go get ready, but it's good to hear from you. Stay strong, my friend. Love you."

"Love you too. Thanks. Bye."

"Bye."

Chapter 28
Guinea Pig and Dirtbag Pig

VIOLET WAS GRATEFUL TO have some time to work on her styling business, even if it wasn't with clients per se. She and Fiona spent a full day on "research." They headed down to Glasgow's west end and hit up as many trendy clothing shops as they could. Fiona was Violet's guinea pig as she worked to create different looks for her, and Fiona was pissed at all the clothes she had *no choice* but to buy. Violet couldn't have talked her out of the shopping spree if she'd tried. Fiona couldn't resist the outfits Violet had put together for her.

"Suppose I'm going to be eating canned tuna for the next month," she said, shifting the shopping bags weighing down her arms.

"Well, no canned tuna tonight. Dinner is on me." Violet snagged a couple of bags off Fiona's arm to help her carry them all. "I really appreciate you helping me out today."

"Ye really do huv a knack for this stuff," she said, looking around to get her bearings. "Now, let's go find some scran. I'm pure Hank Marvin!"

Violet stared at her and burst out laughing, but Fiona was already marching down the cobbled street on a mission. Violet jogged to catch up. She still hadn't gotten used to all the Scottish expressions. But it was safe to assume *scran* was *food*, and *Hank Marvin* must mean *starving*. *Starvin'*, she corrected in her mind, wondering if it was like the Scottish version of Cockney slang, where the last word in a phrase rhymes with the real word.

"All right, spill it!" Fiona declared as the server strode away, leaving behind post-dinner martinis on the glossy black and gold cocktail table of the trendy bar they'd found.

"What?" Violet looked at her curiously over the wide rim of her glass.

"Oh, ye ken exactly what."

"I do?" She picked up the stir stick, sliding off the green olive in her teeth.

"Ye and our boss. What is going on? I cannae take it anymore. I ken there's something, and I'm a little pissed ye huvnae filled me in yet." Any pretence was gone.

Violet giggled at her friend's choice of wording. "Don't be pissed. There is nothing going on."

"Do ye think I came up the Clyde in a banana boat?" she snapped.

Violet snorted and almost expelled martini out her nostrils. She was going to need to get a notebook and start writing down all these expressions.

"There is something going on, and we willnae be leaving this bar until ye tell me what it is." She crossed her arms over her chest.

"Are you holding me hostage, then?" Violet quipped, sucking back the last sip from her glass. That martini went down far too easily.

"Aye, if that's what it takes." Fiona caught the eye of their server, indicating another round.

"Well, as long as they keep the drinks coming, then I'm good with that. I'll settle in," she said, dropping the stir stick back in her empty glass.

"Violet."

"Fiona."

They squared off.

"Stop torturing me. Tell me already."

"What makes you think there is anything going on?" The martini was doing good things, warming her belly and softening her mind. Maybe it wouldn't hurt to talk about Lachlan with Fiona, despite the fact she'd tried all day not to let him cross her mind, an impossible feat lately. Every time she saw the men's section in any of the shops they went into, she immediately thought of him. At first, she'd pictured him in her mind's eye, wearing a very snappy black dress shirt she'd seen in a window display. And when Fiona was shuffling around in the change room, Violet's thoughts gave way to what it would be like if she had the chance to style Lachlan. Finally, she had to deliberately ground her imagination to a halt when her daydream became more elaborate—helping him button his shirt over his incredibly muscular chest while feeling his eyes, hungry on her. That daydream was far too visceral. It was the kind reserved for late at night in bed when she could put a hand between her thighs and let her imagination run wild.

"Hmm, how about that every time he enters a room, ye do yer damnedest to leave it. Every time I've seen the two of ye in the same room, there is some kind of invisible fireworks rocketing between ye. He looks at you like he'd like to throw ye on any horizontal surface and shag ye daft."

Violet almost choked on the first sip from her second martini of the evening. "No, he doesn't!" Violet shot down that idea flat out, but she couldn't help the little wave of excitement that it could possibly be true.

"Och, aye, he does," Fiona stated flatly. "Has he made a move? Did he ask you out? Why do ye seem to run away from him? I dinnae get it. He's wealthy, handsome, and even seems like a decent lad. God, woman, what is wrong with ye?"

Violet took a gulp of her drink, nearly emptying her trendy V-shaped glass. The alcohol burned down her throat, but it didn't stop her from finishing the last little sip. She put it down on the table in front of them, her eyes drawing up to Fiona's, who's were trained on her. "It's him, Fiona. The guy who helped me after my accident."

She stared as if Violet had just given her a very complicated math problem to solve.

"Lachlan, is *him*?"

"Yes. Lachlan is him."

"Oh dear, Jesus, Mary, and Joseph." Her brow furrowed worriedly.

Their server, not missing a beat, brought another round of martinis to the table. Violet leisurely fiddled with her stir stick and plucked off the olives while she let Fiona grapple with this new piece of information.

"Has he made a move?" she finally asked. "Like an actual move, no' just longing looks."

Violet held in an eye roll. They were hardly looks of longing. "No. And he probably won't. He's not interested. He made that clear by not getting in touch after the time we spent together." It still stung after more than two m onths.

"Oh, he wants *something* from ye all right. Pig," Fiona quipped, disgusted.

Violet laughed, though she appreciated the mercurial, instant show of support. "Trust me, he does not want *that* either."

"All men want *that.* Why do ye think our boss would be any different?"

She thought back and remembered how steamy that kiss had felt, even without him kissing her back. He didn't stop her. And it felt incredible to her, but apparently, it wasn't the same for him. He was a gentleman about it. Of course, he was. He didn't make her feel bad for her poor judgment, but still, how embarrassing.

"'Cause that night I spent at his place, before he was our boss, like a total loser, I tried to kiss him, and he didn't take the bait. Not even a little."

"I dinnae believe that fer a second. Ye are gorgeous. There is no way he wouldnae huv kissed ye back."

"You are too sweet, but believe me, it was one-sided."

"Unless he had a girlfriend!" Fiona's eyes went wide.

And the thought unsettled Violet. When she thought back, she was quite certain he didn't, but he'd never really said.

"I don't think that's it," Violet said, although there was a seed of doubt in her mind now.

"Well, I dinnae ken about then, but maybe he's changed his mind. Because I'm tellin' ye, that mon smoulders when he looks at ye like he's about to burst into flames."

"I'm thinking you've been reading too many smut novels. He just has those kind of eyes, doesn't he? The deep blue draw-you-in type. Pure sexy eyes, like they probably are always saying let's have sex, let me sweep you off your feet, and make babies with you." Violet sipped her drink, vaguely aware she was getting tipsy.

Fiona looked at her like she'd lost her mind. "I dinnae ken, Vi. I think it maybe ye who's been spending too much time with the smut novels, aye?"

Violet grinned. "You may be right. Maybe I should just get laid, then I can get that man out of my mind." She looked around the crowded bar as if she might find the right candidate for the job.

"He's still under yer skin, is he?"

"Fuck, I confess, I kinda wish he was."

This made Fiona snort with laughter. "Aye, he's an attractive one, but dangerous. A girl could lose her heart with him. What about Andy?"

Violet sobered and gave Fiona a look that could not be misconstrued. "Ah, right, so that's a no, then. Ye ken, I'm sure he'd be keen if ye were. Ye could get it out of your system. Just have a romp."

Violet looked as though she'd smelled a rotting corpse. "I am not going to have a 'romp' or anything else with Andy. We are friends, and that is it." The two women sat quietly, the bar's music thumping in the background amid the din of voices surrounding them. "Oh my God, have you had a 'romp' with Andy?" Violet looked aghast.

"No, no, heavens no! Well, we did come close that one time, but really, we were just pissed out of our minds. Would've been a complete and utter mistake."

"Right, well, thank God for that." On reflection, Andy was definitely not Fiona's type either.

Fiona stirred her olive around her martini absently. "I haven't been laid in ages. I wish someone would look at me the way he looks at ye."

"Who? Andy?"

"Feck, no! Lachlan."

"Oh, right, Lachlan." Violet's thoughts went back to the first time he'd looked at her. She'd always remember that. His reassuring cerulean blue eyes were a beacon in the storm of her mind.

Chapter 29

The Day the Game Changed

Lachlan sat at the small makeshift desk he'd brought to the sanctuary the week prior after realizing he needed a quiet corner to do some work. He'd eventually order himself a proper desk, but it wasn't high on the priority list. There were too many other things occupying his mind. He'd situated it in a small back room with wood-paneled walls and two windows that looked out over the rolling hills. It was cozy and quiet—just how he liked it.

As much as he liked the staff and welcomed their questions sometimes, he found himself caught up in all the chatter and blethering. He preferred to make himself maybe slightly less accessible so he could focus on the many operations of running two businesses. That, and if he was honest, he hadn't figured out what to do about Violet. Seeing her drove him to utter distraction.

Going through the supply list, he barely heard the soft knock on his open door. He glanced up from his laptop. "Violet." He jumped up so abruptly from his desk that he smacked his knees on the underside with a thump, knocking the desk askew.

"Oh."

He could hear the concern in her voice. Her mesmerizing eyes were wide on him.

He straightened up, nudging the desk back into place. "All good." He smiled, ignoring the faint throb on the top of his knees. "Please come in." He picked up a chair that was tucked in the corner and put it closer to his desk, gesturing for her to have a seat. "Is everything going okay?"

In the back of his mind, he was fearful that perhaps Violet was going to give her resignation. In a way that would solve the problem of him being her boss, but at the same time, he wouldn't see her, at least not with any regularity.

He'd barely spoken to her in the week since they'd run into each other here, but he'd found himself watching her far more than was appropriate. Aside from his typical guy reaction to seeing her—the one that was far from typical for Lachlan—it was seeing her interact with the horses and staff that struck him. What was it about her? She lit a room. It was like she left a sprinkle of fairy dust everywhere she went, making the world a better place just by being in it.

William, his main stable hand, was in his early seventies. Lachlan had hired him because the man knew horses better than anyone else. Even if he was as prickly as a cactus, it was worth having him around. Lachlan was sure the old grump was incapable of smiling, and he'd noted that the staff gave him a wide berth. He could hardly blame them. When he overheard William bletherin' away to Violet like she was an old chum, chuckling with a puffed chest, Lachlan had to pick his jaw up off the hay-covered floor.

And it wasn't just William she'd weaved her spells on. It would be a blow if she were to leave the sanctuary—for many reasons. Shifting in the wooden spindle chair, she eyed him a bit sheepishly. Concern pricked his mind. *Please, please don't say you're leaving*, he whispered to himself in silent prayer.

"I wanted to come talk to you."

He swallowed hard, trying to relax the tension already building in his shoulders. Her hands were clasped in front of her, tucked between her denim-clad knees. He didn't allow his gaze to linger on the tear exposing her perfect shapely knee cap—*dear God, he was losing it.*

"I was going through the programs, and I had some ideas that I was hoping to share with you." He was mightily grateful she couldn't read minds. "It's okay if not, though. I don't want to overstep."

He blew out a breath he hadn't realized he'd been holding and ran a hand through his hair. "Ach, lass, ye mean ye aren't planning to leave us?" Sweet relief flooded him.

Her brows knit together. “What? No. I… Did you think I was giving you my resignation?”

“I dinnae ken. I wasnae sure. Ye looked so serious coming in here.”

She appeared to be letting that thought sink in as she looked down at her folded hands.

“I love it here," she said thoughtfully. "I can’t fathom leaving. Truthfully…" Her voice trailed, and her eyes drew to his.

He hung on to that word between them, aching to know, with a tingle low in his belly…. *Truthfully what?*

"When I’m not here, I’m still thinking about this place.”

He leaned back in his chair, letting go of the silly hope that had momentarily gripped him. What had he hoped? That she thought of him? And not just the sanctuary.

“I’m supposed to be working on my styling business. Highland Haven is my side gig, but to be quite honest, it’s completely become the other way around. I've been coming here during my off hours too." She said it as if she were confessing some dark sin.

Lachlan stared at the beautiful woman before him, sitting like an elegant angel in her uniform of denim, black graphic t-shirt, and rubber boots, and she was telling him that she loved the business he'd built so much that she was willing to work on it even on her days off. She didn't just look like an angel. Violet was intelligent and thoughtful, and the fact that she felt so strongly about the sanctuary and the work humbled him. It was like she was taking his dream and making it her own. She got it. She understood. Highland Haven was as much hers as it was his, and he couldn't be happier about that revelation.

"I dinnae even ken what to say, V."

She got sheepish again. "I'm sorry."

"Sorry? Ach, lass, I'm gonna need ye to tell me the extra hours ye've put in so we can get yer pay sorted properly. And then we are going to have to get ye on the benefits plan as a full-time employee, och, and a raise, of course." When she stared at him wide-eyed, he realized he might be overstepping. "I mean, ye dinnae huv to work full time, but I want to make sure ye are properly compensated for the work ye are doing."

"I do want to work here full time," she cut in as if it was an offer that might evaporate if she didn't snatch it up.

Lachlan smiled, feeling things for the woman in front of him that he had no right to feel. Now, he was really in for it. She would be a full-time employee. Christ, now it was definitely not okay to do all the things he wanted to do to her. Like peeling off her jeans down to those damn-near perfect knees and sliding his face right to her beautiful core to taste her and all her fucking magic pixie dust.

"Um, well, I have some ideas I'd like to share with you if you're okay with that." She eyed him tentatively.

He swallowed, stunned at how far off the rails his thoughts just detoured. He never thought he'd have to keep a short leash on his wayward thoughts. *Saint Lachlan*. "Yes, aye, of course, please tell me. I'd love to hear them."

They ended up holed up in his little office for four hours, talking about the programs at the sanctuary, the marketing, the branding. It surprised him how well she understood the many facets of business. She challenged him, made him re-think things, and it was perfect. Her ideas were outside the box. It felt damn good to have fresh keen eyes on his business, and it made him want to talk about the running of the distillery with her too. He'd only ever relied on himself when it came to business, but talking to Violet now, it gave him a sense of what it would be like to have a business partner.

They began to have regular business meetings that turned into a combination of meetings and productive work sessions. Violet began bringing her laptop, and they'd work alongside each other like business partners for many hours each week. And all the while, Lachlan struggled to keep his insatiable hunger for the lass contained. It was tough, though, especially when her slender fingers would casually brush against his when taking a file from him or when he desperately wanted to put a hand on the small of her curved back when they'd leave the office at the end of another productive day.

That initial meeting was a game changer. He found himself eager to share his ideas with her, get her feedback, or talk through an issue they were having. She was a brilliant problem solver. He wished he could pose the problem of a boss being obsessed with his employee and how she would deal with it. On second thought, he'd prefer not to know. She was too sensible and his feelings too reckless.

Chapter 30

Staff Meeting

Weeks had gone by, and Violet had grown accustomed to holding a flame for Lachlan, and she suspected she wasn't the only one at Highland Haven. She had quietly accepted that the man had wrecked her. If she thought she'd crushed on him before, it was nothing compared to now, after seeing the person he was at the sanctuary.

He was extremely likeable and the yummiest kind of eye candy. Not to mention, he commanded respect without actually commanding it. He was the kind of boss that didn't feel like a boss, more like a leader of a group you considered yourself lucky to be a part of. Lachlan's vision for the sanctuary and his commitment to every detail were inspiring. It was obvious to everyone that he truly cared about the Highland Haven, the horses, and his staff.

That first week, after the initial shock, of finding out Lachlan was the innovator behind the sanctuary had worn off—and after briefly considering quitting—she'd been surprised how easy it was to work with him. Aside from trying not to breathe in his expensive cologne and fresh soap scent and not daydreaming when he gave her his crooked smile, it was going rather well.

In an unexpected turn of events, Violet found herself becoming his sounding board and vice versa. Several weeks back, Violet had some ideas on the programs they were planning to run at the sanctuary. Fiona encouraged her to speak up and tell Lachlan her thoughts. Violet was hesitant. She didn't want to overstep, but she summoned her courage and spoke to him. After that, they'd started having almost daily meetings about the future of Highland Haven, its operations, and everything to do with the business. The meetings would sometimes last for hours. It was like they would feed off each other's ideas, and plans would grow.

Violet loved the work and loved the way she and Lachlan worked together. However, these meetings did little to curb her crush on him. He was intelligent and passionate. She felt inspired by the work they were doing together. But heaven help her, she was an absolute sucker for that crooked smile. Every time he'd throw her that lopsided smirk, she'd imagine all the places she'd like those lips to be on her. She knew very well she was falling for a man who, aside from pleasantries, had kept things all business with her. In fact, it was hard to believe she'd ever kissed him at all, months back in his castle-like home—her knight in shining armour.

They had gotten to know each other better, without a doubt. And sometimes, the conversations left her feeling wistful. But Lachlan hadn't made a move, and if she thought on occasion there was something more in the way he eyed her or the inadvertent touch, time quickly proved her wrong.

Lachlan aside, more and more, it felt like she was invested in the running of the sanctuary rather than her styling business, and it had her realizing that maybe what she'd been craving all along was a chance to be involved in the running of a company—one that she believed in wholeheartedly.

It was Friday, and Violet had yet to see Lachlan. The staff had all received an email early that morning asking them to attend a "very important" staff meeting Friday afternoon, but with no indication what it was about.

The gossip and speculation buzzed in every nook and cranny of Highland Haven all morning, and Violet found herself more than a little bit curious as well. She was surprised Lachlan hadn't mentioned it the day before when they'd been going over marketing proposals.

Standing in the makeshift staffroom Friday afternoon, the nervous anticipation was as palpable as a thunderstorm. Lachlan strode into the room where eight staff members were seated, and five, including herself, stood at the back leaning on the wood-panelled walls. The chattering quieted almost immediately. *The man can certainly command a room*, Violet thought, as she eyed him from the back.

Lachlan looked out at everyone with a warm smile on his handsome face. "Thank ye all for being here this afternoon, I willnae keep ye long. We huv come a long way at Highland Haven in a short period of time. We huv exceeded the initial projections for enrolment, and we are already looking at expanding. We will be starting horse therapy at the local seniors centre later this month, and there are more plans in the works."

Everyone clapped, and Violet felt her heart squeeze. A program where they would bring a therapy horse into seniors centres, possibly the hospitals, and even schools had been her idea. One she'd brought to Lachlan that first day. She'd been so nervous, afraid he'd think she was crazy or that there would be too many hoops to jump through in regard to health and safety, but he surprised her. He loved the idea, and they set to work that afternoon on how to implement it. And now, they were about to launch phase one.

"Mostly, I called this meeting to thank ye. Each and every one of ye huv worked incredibly hard to get Highland Haven off the ground. Ye are the foundation of this place, and I'm truly grateful to ye." He put his hand on his white-shirted chest. "The interest in our programs is growing by the day, and I think we've all witnessed the amazing interactions between the kids and the horses. We are ahead of schedule and doing more than I ever dreamed, and I thank ye all for that. None of this would have been possible without ye."

Another round of applause went up with a couple of whistles. Lachlan applauded them right back. When they quieted down, he continued.

"A fundraiser gala is coming up a week from Saturday at my family's distillery. I would love ye all to be there as my honoured guests." This time, the room erupted with enthusiastic whoops and cheers. "Effie will be sending out an email with the details. Ye are welcome to bring yer significant others. It will be a special night, a celebration of all yer hard work and dedication."

Violet joined in the clapping. She'd never been to a gala. She wasn't really sure what it entailed, but it sounded exciting.

"I'm leaving today on a business trip, so I willnae be seeing ye all until the gala night."

Awareness careened through her as his eyes found hers and locked on them—flirtatiously? It was brief but long enough to see and feel the sizzle of that look. Fiona would insist it was *smouldering*, and if her heart banging loudly in her chest was any indication, it was.

"Have an excellent weekend, everybody, and thank ye truly."

Everyone clapped as Lachlan waved and headed on his way, and Violet was left wondering what in the heck that look was about.

“Exciting in’ it? A gala. I dinnae think I’ve ever been to a gala. Och, Vi, ye have to help me with what to wear!” Fiona grabbed her arm, blissfully unaware of her internal tumult.

Violet smiled in an attempt to mask it. “Of course."

"Braw."

Violet had learned that this term was something akin to *great* or *awesome*, definitely a positive response.

"Do you want to head down to the shops on Wednesday? See what we can find? I finish at four, and I think ye do too. I can drive us into town. We could do dinner too.”

“Yes, for sure. That sounds good.” She tried to muster enthusiasm, but all her brain and lady bits were focused on the fact that this time, she hadn’t imagined the fire in his eyes.

The week felt like it dragged by. Violet had hoped to talk with Lachlan after he left the staff meeting, but he was already gone by the time everyone shuffled out of the room. It was like she needed to confirm that they were business as usual and nothing had changed.

For the most part, she’d accepted her feelings as an epic crush and somehow managed to allow them to drive along beside the business relationship and friendship they had formed—like cars on a highway that were not permitted to cross over the divider lines.

She'd known about his business trip to London for a whisky festival. He was going to meet up with some distributors. Violet had allowed herself to feel like his right hand over the past few weeks, so it stung a little that he hadn't considered taking her on the trip.

Lachlan had begun discussing the distillery business with her lately, too. She supposed she wasn't an official employee for Cailleach Distillery, so she really had no right expecting him to want her on business trips.

It was annoying how much she'd wished he'd come to say goodbye to her, though. Instead, all she was left with was that toe curling, panty-soaking look! Where on earth had that come from? And what did it mean?

Chapter 31

Gala's Have Their Ups and Downs

After a very long week, the day of the gala arrived. Fiona came to Violet's place to get ready. They cranked the tunes and set to work on makeup and hair. Violet wore a deep emerald gown. Layers of sheer fabric gathered around her chest, leaving a diamond-shaped peephole in the center below her breasts, where the fabric lightly flowed down. It accentuated her perky bosom, and the emerald hue of the gown was stunning against her fair skin. She wore a diamond necklace and matching stud-encrusted Mary Jane stilettos.

"Jesus, Mary, and Joseph," Fiona exclaimed as Violet came out of her bedroom in her gown. "Ye clean up well."

For the most part, they only ever saw each other in jeans and T-shirts at the stables. It was a far cry from the fashion world she'd imagined herself in. It was fun to have an excuse to get dressed up.

Violet chuckled. "Right back at you. You're gorgeous!" Fiona wore stunning navy satin wide-leg pants paired with crisp red stilettos that matched her lipstick, and a red satin tartan wraparound halter-style top. The ensemble was funky yet formal, suiting her perfectly.

“Right?” Fiona teased. "We are like two fucking Cinderellas going to the ball.”

"Ha! How many prince charmings do you think might be there?" The truth was, she only had one prince charming on her mind.

There was a knock at the door. “Ah, here's one now.” Fiona quipped, pulling open the door.

Andy stood dressed in a red tartan kilt with a formal jacket and vest, as well as a soft fur sporran adorned with metal accents.

“Looking sharp there, Andy.” Violet smiled.

“No' sure sharp enough for ye two stunners! Wow!”

"Psh, off with ye, Andy." Fiona gave him a gentle shove out the door. “C’mon, we better get a move on. We dinnae want to be late to our first gala.”

The trio took a cab to Cailleach Distillery. They drove up the horseshoe drive to the main entrance. It was a beautiful stone building that appeared old but charming. Now, *this* was a castle or at least more so than Lachlan’s home. Strings of simple light bulbs graced the front, creating a warm, inviting ambiance. Once inside, the building was buzzing with people. Everybody was dressed in their finery. Violet almost felt she’d gone back in time. The men looked dashing in their

Prince Charlie Kilt formal wear, and the ladies were stunning with their jewels, gowns, and tartan wraps.

The inside was just as old and charming and full of warmth as the outside. It was late June, and the days had grown long in the Highlands, with the sun setting late in the evening and rising early in the morning. Tonight, it was damp and cooler outside, so the logs burning brightly in the large stone fireplace were a welcome, cozy sight.

"Wow." Fiona exhaled as they made their way further into the main room. There was a stunning buffet of cold meats and pastries, and another table had layers of beautifully presented finger foods, almost too artful to steal from.

As they walked in farther, a wall of windows gave way to a view of a manicured garden with walking paths and, beyond that, the vastness of rolling green hills. The rain clouds darkened the skies while the garden lights did their best to brighten the stunning vista. *This place is like a set of a fairy tale*, Violet thought to herself, accepting a glass of red wine from a tray a finely dressed server held out to her.

Andy and Fiona followed suit.

"Blimey, now this is what I call a party," Fiona said, taking a hearty gulp of her wine.

"Agreed." Violet looked around, trying to take it all in.

"Good Evening, everyone." Lachlan's voice rang out over the crowd, rich and smooth as dark chocolate.

Violet scanned the open ballroom and saw him standing a couple of steps up in a beautiful stone stairwell, and her heart stuttered at the sight of him. She could only see him from his broad shoulders up with the crowds of people, but God, he looked achingly handsome. It was as if she'd forgotten in the week that he was gone just how good-looking he was, and then that look he'd thrown her before he left popped back into her mind. Perhaps tonight she'd find out what that was about. The thought sent a little thrill up her spine.

The crowd quieted down.

"Welcome to Cailleach distillery. I cannae tell ye how pleased I am to huv ye all here for this wonderful event. And what a stunning group ye are!"

Everyone soaked up that comment with cheers and whistles.

"I'm going to keep this short and sweet."

A couple of people cheered their approval at that statement, and Lachlan's lips tipped to the side in a smile that had her holding in a groan like when she bit into delectable chocolate with a gooey caramel centre. A week without that damn smile of his, and she was on the verge of needing to excuse herself to splash her face with cold water!

"A few things I'd like to mention, if ye're interested in a tour of the distillery and a wee tasting—"

More cheers went up.

"We have a couple guides that will be taking groups. Just head over to the left of the stone fireplace in the foyer. Tours will be throughout the evening, so there is no rush. In the grand hall to the right of this stairwell, you will find some incredible items that huv been generously donated for our silent auction. Please do go huv a look and see if something catches your fancy. We thank ye all for joining us tonight for this fundraising gala. As ye ken the Highland Haven is near and dear to my heart and to many that are here tonight. I'm incredibly grateful to all who've been involved and to all who have donated and continue to donate and support us so generously. This sanctuary would no' be possible without the people in this room. So please eat, drink, dance, and enjoy your evening! Thank ye."

The crowd clapped and cheered, and soon, the hum of chatter and music filled the air.

Violet found her gaze following Lachlan. She inched through the crowd, getting closer to him, and tried to convince herself that her eagerness to see him was because she wanted to catch him up on what he missed at the sanctuary while he was away. She felt her heart beat a little faster the closer she got to him. His eyes glittered, and the grin that played his lips made butterflies dance in her belly—he was magnetic.

Then she stopped dead in her tracks. He was giving that smile to a stunning woman who was looking at him under her perfectly arched brow. Violet recognized she'd come upon an intimate moment. She felt her butterflies turn to lead in her gut. She watched as the woman reached up and touched Lachlan's face.

"Let's go check out the auction items." Fiona pulled Violet from her daze.

Violet turned around and linked her arm in Fiona's. "Excellent idea," she said, not wanting to see any more of Lachlan and that woman. She was desperate to get away from what she'd just witnessed. She didn't know why it bothered her so much. It was not like she had any right to be possessive over him. She had hoped that maybe... Maybe there was something after that look he'd given her. It was silly of her to have hoped anything. He was her boss, after all.

She couldn't help wondering about the woman. Had he met her in London on his business trip? No, they seemed too familiar for that to be the case. Maybe he'd been dating her all along. *Oh God.*

Violet was grateful her friends hadn't noticed that she had been watching Lachlan, nor had they seemed to notice her reaction. Small mercies. *Ugh.* She hated how much it killed her to think he was dating someone. Was he in love with that woman? Her mind was spinning out of control, and her heart felt unreasonably squeezed.

"Right, but after this, I wannae do the whisky tour," Andy informed them as he followed along behind.

"Good idea," Violet concurred. The idea of getting plastered suddenly seemed like a good one.

"We'll look at the auction first, and then ye two can do the whisky."

"You aren't going to join us?" Violet eyed Fiona, the self-professed lush.

"Nope, I can't touch the stuff." Fiona's petite nostrils flared as if protesting the very notion.

"What? Really, Fiona? I didn't think any alcohol was off-limits in your world!"

"Let's just say a certain birthday may huv wrecked me for life when it comes to drinking whisky. I cannae bring myself to do it again. It's a bloody miracle I've even stepped foot in this distillery."

Violet couldn't help but smile. She made the mistake of glancing back over her shoulder. She caught sight of Lachlan still with the woman, and her hand was on his chest. The sting of it had her snapping her focus back to the auction table. Lachlan was not hers, and she was a fool to ever think he could be. What had she thought? He'd made it obvious from the night they first spent together that he didn't want anything from her, and all these weeks working together, he never so much as touched a hand on her. And she knew better! She knew not to let her heart fall for him.

She put her empty glass on a nearby table and wondered where the serving dude was now. Violet began to walk slowly around the auction table, looking at all the items, trying her damnedest to focus on anything other than Lachlan and that woman.

A postcard with the distillery crest lay in a basket with a bottle of Cailleach fifteen-year-old scotch. She read the card and was impressed. It was for an overnight stay at the distillery and a private tour. The bid was already at £825, far deeper than her pockets went. The next item was a helicopter ride through the Highlands with a picnic lunch on one of the peaks. Then, there was a weekend stay at Eileen Donan castle. And a full day at the spa for two with dinner at a Michelin-starred restaurant afterward. And on and on. And the bids were anything but low. At least, the sanctuary would benefit.

A stunning navy and green tartan blanket with thin poppy red stitching caught her eye on the table. Violet ran her hand over the beautiful wool. It would look so perfect in her cottage with her navy wingback chair.

Most of the items were well beyond what she could afford, but as she eyed the sheet for the tartan, her heart jumped.

The page only had a few bids and the current one was two hundred pounds. More than she should spend, but she was so tempted. She deserved a little something to make her feel better tonight—shop therapy. Besides, she was making much more money now since she was working full time and had gotten a raise.

She stared at the auction sheet and ran her hand over the tartan, contemplating. *What the heck?* A little jolt of adrenaline made her feel delightfully reckless as she penned her bid—£225. In fairness, the funds were going to a good cause, so she had even less of a reason to feel guilty about spending the money. It was unlikely her bid would be the final one, but just for the moment, it felt possible.

When she'd finished perusing the items, she realized her friends had, at some point, abandoned her. Where had they gotten to? She scanned the room. They'd just been there. She was about to set off to find them and another drink when a petite woman in a stunning raspberry red ball gown stopped her

Chapter 32

Mystery Woman and the Holy Grail

"WHISKY?" THE WOMAN standing before her offered, holding up a cut crystal tumbler-style glass filled with shimmering liquid gold.

Immediately, Violet liked her, and it wasn't just the offer of a good stiff drink. Sometimes, you can just tell when someone is your kind of person. "Definitely," she answered with a broad smile, accepting the offered glass. "Thank you."

"Slainte Mhath." The woman raised her glass to Violet's, and then both ladies took a sip.

"Mmm. This is beautiful," Violet said, letting the flavour roll on her tongue.

"Couldn't agree more." The mystery woman smiled back.

"Have you had a chance to look at the auction items?" Violet asked, making conversation. "There are some amazing things."

"I huv. What would ye huv if ye could choose something?" She gestured toward the auction table where people were milling about, checking their bids. The other woman's smile was infectious. She was probably six inches shorter than Violet, with striking dark hair in an up-do. The woman was so familiar, and yet she couldn't place her.

"Well, the helicopter ride and lunch on the mountain sounds decent." Violet smirked, and the woman nodded and smiled back. "But to be honest, I actually marked down my name for that beautiful tartan blanket. It was probably the only thing on the table I could afford to bid on, to be honest." She surprised herself confessing such a thing, but she sensed the woman before her was not going to judge her. "I genuinely love it. It would look so good on my navy wingback. Pretty sure it needs to come home with me."

The lady in red grinned up at her. "Och, good choice! Aye, well, let's hope the luck is with ye then."

"What about you? What would you choose?" Violet said, taking another sip of the amazing scotch the mystery lady had given her. She wondered where she'd gotten it from as she hadn't seen whisky on any of the trays the servers were going around with.

"Me? I would take the private ghost tour in the vaults." There was a mischief in her blue eyes that made Violet want to be friends with her.

Just then, the lights dimmed. Violet turned back and saw Lachlan leading the beautiful woman he'd been talking to onto the dance floor. And it felt like watching a car accident where you know you should turn away for self-preservation, but you can't help your morbid fascination. The butterflies that had turned to lead were now acid in her throat. She threw back the remainder of what was in her glass.

The woman beside her was gazing in the same direction. "She's beautiful, isn't she?"

Violet silently nodded, unable to tear her eyes from the couple.

"She's a donor. In fact, her family is the biggest donor to the sanctuary. They are one of the wealthiest in Scotland."

Violet turned to look at the woman beside her, wondering how she knew so much, and also uncertain if she wanted to hear anymore.

Then she leaned in conspiratorially. "Anna MacDonald. She has too much money, and she thinks she can buy whatever she wants, including my brother's affections back."

She didn't know which part of that statement surprised her more. *Back?* Did that mean that at some point, this very wealthy, gorgeous woman, Anna, held Lachlan's affections? Had they been a couple? *Ugh,* whatever the case, the information only confirmed what she'd suspected: there was something between Lachlan and the woman. And then the other part of the statement hit her. She was talking to Lachlan's sister!

"I'm Orlagh Mackenzie." She held out her hand as if confirming Violet's thought.

Violet reached out and shook her petite hand, surprised by the strength of her grip. "You're Lachlan's sister?" It made total sense now why she looked familiar.

"Aye, I suppose I am."

"I'm Violet Munro. I work at Highland Haven," she said, by way of explanation as to how she knew Lachlan.

"I ken," Orlagh replied as if it were common knowledge.

"You do?"

Orlagh gave her a sly smile. "Aye. Lachlan talks about ye."

"He does?" The breath suddenly left her body.

"Aye." There was a twinkle in her eye, making Violet want to prod her for every detail that Lachlan had ever spoken about her. Instead, she looked back at the wealthy MacDonald woman and Lachlan dancing, and Violet chose self-preservation. Why should she care what he'd said or thought about her?

And just when she'd tried to take the high road, Orlagh informed her very matter-of-factly, "He is not the least bit interested in her. He never truly was. In fact, I'm pretty sure he's wishing to God that he didnae huv to dance with her and play nice." Orlagh spoke as if she was an authority on the matter.

Violet glanced back to where Lachlan was nodding with a smile as they danced. "They look pretty comfy if you ask me," Violet said, unable to keep the skepticism from her voice.

Orlagh shrugged. "Trust me, his skin is likely crawlin' huvin' to dance with her. Lachlan is being Lachlan, ever the gentleman. I huv no doubt she wrote a big fat donation check, kennin' full well that Lachlan would be obliged to be civil, especially here at the Gala. Her ulterior motives sing louder than her ta ta's popping out over-the-top of her dress."

Violet snorted, and Orlagh grinned back at her as if they were on the same team. She dared to wonder if it was true, and Lachlan was just playing the part tonight with that Anna woman.

"Anyway, never mind about her. Let's talk about Highland Haven. Do ye like working there?"

"I honestly can't imagine working anywhere better." Violet had never felt so fulfilled in a job. Although she realized that she might need to do something about her massive crush on her boss.

"Lachlan is always talking about his team at the sanctuary. He's says that he'd be lost without ye all."

"It is a pretty amazing group of people." Violet reflected on how true that was.

"Aye, I've heard. But Lachlan talks about ye, Violet, as his right hand."

"He does?" Violet felt goosebumps skitter down her spine.

Orlagh set her empty glass on a nearby table. "My brother holds you in very high regard."

Violet couldn't help the feeling of pride swelling up inside her. She knew she'd become important to Lachlan with the business, but knowing he'd talked to his sister about her being his right hand was so gratifying.

"I hold him in very high regard too," she admitted.

"He said you also huv yer own business doing personal styling as well."

Violet was surprised that Lachlan would tell Orlagh about her business. "I do, although I only have a couple of clients now. To be honest, the sanctuary has taken up more of my focus over the past month. I love it there. It's unlike any job I've had before." Violet didn't miss the look of approval in Orlagh's eyes, and oddly enough, she appreciated it. "What about you? What do you do?"

"I'm no' sure yet what my heart desires, but fer now, I'm helping out at the distillery."

The two ladies chatted for a time as the party seemed to be going on full swing around them. Orlagh was one of those people Violet felt an instant kinship with. She was easy to talk with. Violet noticed that Orlagh spoke about Lachlan as if she thought Violet and Lachlan were close. Saying things like, "Oh, ye ken how he is, always needing to seek out a quiet spot."

It surprised Violet that she *did* know. She'd noticed that Lachlan was a people person, and yet, more often than not, she'd find him where there were no people at all, like he'd intentionally sought to be alone. And yet, he never seemed to mind her intrusion.

“Well, I suppose we should both get back to the festivities. It was great meeting you, Violet. I hope we see each other again soon.” Orlagh gave Violet’s hand a squeeze and disappeared into the throngs of people.

Violet stood there reflecting on the entire encounter when Andy sauntered up to her, ruddy-cheeked and grinning like he was having the time of his life. “Shall we?” he said, offering her his arm in a grand gesture.

Violet accepted it and let Andy lead her through the crowd, not quite certain where they were going.

“I thought you and Fiona ditched me.”

“I’ve lost Fi to the mob, but I huv no doubt she’s keeping herself entertained," he said, with a knowing wink.

As they made their way to the stairs, Violet was scanning the crowd for Lachlan, although she was not certain if she wanted to see him or not, especially if he was still in the company of Anna MacDonald. "Dinnae fash, Fiona didnae want to go on the tour anyway."

"Tour?" Violet asked.

Andy looked at her like she'd lost her marbles. "Aye, the whisky tour, remember?"

"Oh, yes, right." Violet had actually forgotten all about it while chatting with Orlagh and being distracted with Lachlan. Always distracted with Lachlan, since the moment their eyes had locked on that fateful evening on the beach.

"The whisky rooms down here are legendary," Andy quipped excitedly.

"Oh?" Violet asked curiously.

"Aye, they say that somewhere down here is a bottle from the original batch, and well, if ye believe the folklore, they say if anyone were find it and huv a wee sip, it's a bit like findin' the Holy Grail."

Violet snorted.

"Dinnae laugh. There are many who believe it has healin' powers," Andy said quietly as if it were too holy to discuss out loud, and then he crossed himself. "There was even a documentary about it on the BBC."

"There was not!" Violet laughed in spite of his serious tone.

"Och, aye, there was."

Violet wondered what Lachlan would have to say about it since it was his family's distillery. Did he think there was a magical bottle down there? She looked down at the stone steps bathed in warm light from candle-style wall sconces.

They stood in a short line, waiting for a couple more people to arrive for the next round of the tour. The guide, who looked to be in his fifties with thick black rimmed glasses and a coarse goatee of copper and white informed them a group of twelve was the magic number, explaining that he'd only have to open one bottle of each of the sample whiskys, which would mean he wouldn't be obliged to take the leftovers home again "so they dinnae go to waste." His broad grin spread his goatee like a beard.

The man was clearly well practiced at giving tours and keeping the guests entertained.

Violet was grateful to have her mind on something other than Lachlan's whereabouts. In fact, she was enjoying the tour. She was amazed at the extensive process for creating that perfect dram.

She fell behind the crowd in the cask room. She was mesmerized by it all. As fun as the group tour was, she was glad to drop behind and have a quiet moment to take it in. It was amazing to think that Lachlan's family had been making whisky for hundreds of years, and they still make one of the original recipes. The man grew more fascinating by the day. Would her heart survive him?

Chapter 33
Distractions

As the party began and people arrived, Lachlan felt a growing anticipation to see Violet. He'd missed not talking to her. After a long week without her keen input, he made the decision to have her help with the distillery business, too—if she was interested. He was eager to talk it over with her.

Business aside though, if he was being honest, he was damn-near desperate to just see her—her pretty face, the curve of her neck, and to hear her husky voice again. Every woman with blond hair caught his eye, and each time he realized it wasn't Violet, a little jolt of disappointment stabbed him.

With hosting duties tonight, he was left with little time for much else. He usually enjoyed mingling with people and socializing, but tonight, he found the only person he really wanted to mingle with was Violet. Every time he thought he could steal away and find her, someone would snag his attention. And unfortunately, more often than not this evening, it had been Anna. First a greeting when she arrived, then a photo op with her handing over a rather large cheque, and then a dance. None of it was terrible per se, but he'd already had more than his fill of Anna MacDonald tonight.

After their breakup, he came to the realization that he'd really dodged a bullet. Since then, he'd not seen her nor heard from her, and he found he felt lighter and more himself. He wondered how they'd stayed together at all. Looking back, it was like he was going through the motions of a relationship without actually truly being invested. His mam had been encouraging of it, and not that he did what his mam always told him, but he counted it as a plus that she was a fan of him dating Anna—especially since Orlagh was n ot.

It hadn't totally surprised Lachlan that Anna had come tonight. She was a regular donor for all kinds of causes. One of her positive traits, he supposed. However, he also knew she was not one to miss any event where she could shine, drink champagne, and ensure anyone and everyone knew how great she was—it was her way.

While attending to his hosting duties, Lachlan had kept an eye out for Violet, and began to worry that maybe she hadn't come. He was wholly unprepared for when he did finally catch sight of her. The room, the buzz, all of it disappeared when he saw her. She was an absolute vision.

She stole his breath away. Lachlan was used to seeing casual Violet with her hair in a messy bun, wearing ripped jeans, a t-shirt, a hoodie, and rubber boots—and he always found her damned sexy. But the sight that greeted his eyes tonight nearly dropped him to his knees. He watched her from a distance realizing she was by far the most beautiful woman he'd ever laid eyes on—elegant, regal, feminine.

There were beautiful women here tonight, and then there was Violet, in a league of her own. A glowing, rare emerald among clusters of run-of-the-mill diamonds. She stood out. Even from a distance, her dress—with its peephole right beneath her perfect breasts—required an actual effort not to stare. The tight bundle of flesh peeking above her dress made his mouth water, and he recalled how good those breasts felt poked against him. It had been a few months, but the memory was still seared in his mind. What he wouldn't give to feel her pressed against him now. He swallowed hard.

Lachlan forced himself to look away to prevent his cock from giving her an appreciative standing ovation. He was beginning to accept that he was turning into the kind of lust-filled teenager that his brothers had always been. Although for him, there was only one woman who set him alight.

Cooling his cock, he was about to make his way to her, when Anna approached him—again. "Dance with me." She looked up at him coyly. It was ironic, this woman who'd once been his girlfriend, now had the effect of a cold bucket of water thrown over him, minus the refreshing part.

"We just danced, I should probably do the rounds." He attempted to diplomatically deter her.

A pout spread across her face. "I'm sure it willnae hurt ye to dance with yer biggest donor more than once." Despite the fact that he'd rather gnaw off his own arm than dance again with her, she'd made her point.

“Of course.” He smiled, gritting his teeth as he put his hand on the small of her back and guided her to the dance floor. How he wished it was Violet he was dancing with.

"I've missed you," Anna said, as they swayed around the dance floor with other couples.

Lachlan tried not to cringe. He didn’t want to be rude, but Christ, he wished the floor would gobble him up. “It’s been a while. It was good of you to come tonight, and your donation is incredibly generous and appreciated," he said, hoping to steer the conversation away from one that would surely make things more uncomfortable.

"Of course, I'd come." She grinned up at him, rubbing a hand over his back.

He stiffened under her unwanted touch.

"The donation is nothing. Ye ken we have plenty of money to share with those who need it."

He couldn't deny that her family's contributions were appreciated.

"I'd never miss a gala, especially one at Cailleach, but I also wanted to come to see you." The song ended, and she'd put her hands on his lapels, looking up at him."

He took both her hands in his, removing them from him and steering her off the dance floor. "Anna—" he began, but she cut him off.

"Lachlan, I ken it wasn't perfect, but we made a good team. I'm sorry about France. I've had time to think, and I really want to make this work with ye and I."

Lachlan caught sight of Violet over Anna's shoulder. She was holding onto another man's arm, grinning at him brightly, and Lachlan momentarily saw red. Jealousy like he'd never known before coiled in him like a serpent. Never would he have thought himself the jealous type. In fact, he wasn't sure if he'd ever felt jealousy before now. But without a doubt, he felt the desperate pang of it as his muscles went rigid, wanting to fight for *his* woman. He had the primal urge to march over and slug the poor bastard.

"Oh, I see," Anna said, following Lachlan's gaze. "Is that her? The one you cheated on me with." Her tone grew sharp.

Lachlan looked back down at her, latently remembering they were talking.

"What?" He was so distracted, her words didn't register. Before she could answer him, he excused himself. "Thank ye again. Enjoy your evening." He gave her a quick smile and strode quickly past her, unfazed by the daggers she was throwing at him with her scowl.

Anna forgotten, Lachlan was wondering who the hell that boyo was with Violet. He wasn't familiar. Did he come with her? Was he a date? Surely not a boyfriend. The thought was a vile one. Lachlan struggled to get a grip, and he wondered when he'd become a possessive neanderthal. He didn't own h er. *Yet,* his lizard brain supplied. He caught sight of them again, heading to the foyer for the whisky tour.

He couldn't help himself as he followed along behind, unable to take his eyes off them. Something the man said made Violet burst out into laughter. God, she was a beautiful lass. But he wanted to be the one making her laugh, among other things. The more he saw, the more his mind began to calm. To his great relief, they didn't appear to be a couple, likely just friends, perhaps a date for the night. The poor sap looked at her with appreciative eyes, but it was unreasonably satisfying that she did not look at him the same way. There were no sparks in her eyes when she looked at him, just a kind lightheartedness. Lachlan felt certain that Violet had no love interest in this guy. The tension eased from his shoulders.

What would he have done if they were together as a couple? It was a thought that genuinely bothered him. For the first time, he realized that he'd lose his mind if Violet started dating another guy. That was not even a possibility he could think about, the very idea made him feel like he might go crazy. Out of control.

He raked a hand through his hair. What had gotten into him? He had decided he would catch up and join the group, but when he noticed Violet drop behind the rest, he couldn't resist the moment to be alone with her. He never intended what was about to happen.

Chapter 34

A Tasting in the Barrel Room

She stood alone in the barrel room, slowly walking and taking in her surroundings.

"I should huv ken I'd find ye here." Lachlan stood leaning casually against a stone wall near the entrance, only a few feet away from her.

"Oh my God, Lachlan, you scared me half to death," she said with a start, and he wondered if the look in her eyes was something more than nerves.

"Sorry, lass, I didnae mean to catch ye off guard." He watched her savouring the sight of her in his cask cellar. Many people had walked these rooms, but none so captivating as Violet Munro.

"I'm surprised you managed to steal away." There was something in the way she said it. He recognized it. Subtle as it was, she sounded jealous. Had she seen him dancing with Anna?

"Aye, it's been a busy evening. And of course, I have hosting duties to attend, whether I wish to or no'." He hoped to make it clear without saying the words that the dance she might have seen was a duty and nothing more. "Ye look beautiful, Violet." Beautiful was the understatement of the decade.

"Thank you," she said quietly, looking down shyly. Didn't she know how gorgeous she was? How tempting?

"How was your trip?" She asked, turning toward the casks casually, as if to inspect them—although he felt certain she was trying to deflect from the chemistry that flickered so readily between them.

"It went well," he said casually. "I could've used your counsel on a few things, though. I missed talking with ye."

"You did?" She turned back to him, their eyes connecting.

"Aye, verra much."

She studied him as if she were trying to decide how much stock to put into his words, but then she turned away from him. "I can't believe you grew up with all this." She waved her arm, gesturing to the casks, and changing the subject. He'd let her—for now.

"I suppose it's not your typical childhood, but it was a good one." He supplied.

"I bet."

"We spent a lot of time here, both in the distillery working and learning, but also out on the land. It's where I mastered my hide-and-seek skills."

She giggled, and it was like music to his ears. "One of the top childhood skills."

"Aye." He chuckled. "Right up there with tag and red rover."

She laughed. He loved to see her so light-hearted. It was the first time since she'd been working at the sanctuary that she had let her guard down enough to speak of something other than business. It seemed like her walls were not so high tonight.

"I learned not only how to make whisky but how to take pleasure in drinking it." He gave her a wink and stepped over to the casks.

She nodded. "I can imagine." A distant roar of laughter sounded from upstairs. "It's pretty packed up there," she said lightly.

Lachlan turned and closed the distance between them, not taking his eyes off hers. "Aye, it is, and of all those people, it was ye I wanted to see tonight."

Her mossy green eyes looked up at him."Really?" There was a sweet little quiver in her voice that awoke his cock.

Her cupid bow lips were slightly parted, and he could feel the chemistry thumping between them, sparking wildly, like atoms bouncing around trying to escape a stopped beaker. A wave of primal satisfaction rolled through him as she looked up at him with desire in her eyes. *Mine*—the word felt like a sacred oath.

"Aye, really."

Violet closed her eyes for a moment, savouring his words. Lachlan had been on her mind when he seemed to appear out of thin air. And heaven help her, he was looking at her much like he had before he'd left on his business trip. Something was happening between them. She could feel it in every cell of her body.

It was the first time she'd seen him in a kilt, and she couldn't help the vision of being ravished by this highlander from skittering through her mind. He looked so tall and handsome in his tux. The kilt was deep navy and green with a pinstripe of red—like the blanket she'd bid on. Was it a family tartan?

Being alone with him now and the way he was looking, it was like she could feel her blood storming through her body, making it ache hungrily.

"Why are ye down here alone, lass?" His voice had grown husky.

"I was just, um, on the whisky tour." She couldn't keep the breathiness from her words as he'd stepped closer to her.

His eyes never left hers, and she swallowed, not knowing what he intended. Too many times, she'd hoped for something that never happened. Despite her every nerve ending firing, she didn't dare let herself believe that he was looking at her like he wanted her.

He stood before her and leaned in so close she could feel the warmth of his breath on her neck. "I think ye may huv lost your tour group, lass."

"So it would seem." She glanced toward the empty doorway, realizing she was very much alone now with Lachlan, and a delicious shiver danced across her skin.

When she turned back to face him. He was watching her intently, his cerulean blue eyes glittering in the dim, warm light. It was almost unnerving. He was standing so close to her—too close for business. Too close for a colleague. Too close for a boss. She could smell his cologne, see his five o'clock shadow. He was filling her senses, and she was getting lost in the heady feeling of it all.

"And have ye had the chance to try the brew?" His voice was as smooth as the whisky he spoke of.

"I think I've gone and missed that part." She pouted, feigning sadness.

"Och, lassie, we cannae huv that," he said, soothingly playing along. "It's a good thing I happened upon ye then." He gave her a sexy wink full of promise and took her hand, leading her past a row of casks and around a corner she hadn't noticed before. They stopped in front of a barrel that looked more weathered and old than the others. All the cask barrels lay on their sides, including this one with its time-worn wood.

"Ye cannae go on a whisky tour and no' sample the whisky," he said, decidedly, as he pulled out a plug from the side of the barrel and dipped in a long copper turkey baster-looking thing into it. "The best way to huv whisky is straight from the cask."

"I'm intrigued," she said, watching him. "What is that?" She nodded to the copper pipe he dipped into the barrel.

"This? This is a whisky thief. We use it to steal a wee taste before it's bottled."

"Oh, wow, I didn't know you could do that." She watched intently. "So, is this part of the tour?"

"When you huv the tour with the owner, aye." He threw her his crooked smile, making her knees go weak—par for the course—and held the tube up, gesturing for her to come sample its contents.

Oh man. Violet felt her carefully built walls crumbling. Not only did he look like he stepped out of a Scottish GQ magazine, but their easy banter also made him hard to resist. She could blame the drinks, the magic of the night, or this place, but the truth was, she had more than a little crush on the man. He looked up at her expectantly, waiting for her to come over. She looked toward the door where the others had long since gone through. Andy was clearly too caught up to notice her absence. What would it hurt?

"Angus, the tour guide, told us these casks held the original recipe whisky," she said as she tentatively stepped toward him. God, what was she doing? She should probably just go catch up to the group. There was danger written all over this situation, and she knew it. But she stood before him with her legs unwilling to walk her out the door. She'd dreamed of him flirting with her, wanting her, but she also fought against it and told herself not to want him.

"Those barrels dinnae, but this one does. This brew has been made in the same manner with the same ingredients for over four hundred years. My grand-da's great-great-nan created this brew and used it at first as a home remedy for illness, but it was so good that everyone who tried it was always wantin' more. Demand grew, and the distillery was born."

"Really? It was a woman who started it all?" Violet asked, surprised.

"Aye." Lachlan's eyes were locked on her.

Her heart skipped a beat. Damn him.

"I dinnae ken why Angus always leaves that part out. It's my favourite bit."

"So is it the holy grail healing power whisky?" she asked, peering into the blackness of the hole in the cask where the cork had been.

His rich chuckle rippled down her spine like a hot shower on a winter's day, melting her bones. "Perhaps ye should test it and see." His eyes glinted with mischief.

He held the whisky thief toward her like it was a spoon with magic medicine she was supposed to sip.

“No glass?”

He shook his head. His grin gave away how much pleasure he took in her uncertainty. “Tilt yer head back and open yer mouth, V.”

“Seriously?”

He cocked his head. His eyes answered in the affirmative. She’d come this far. She wasn’t going to miss out on the four-hundred-year-old scotch recipe just because she didn’t have a glass. She did as he said, tilted her head back, and opened her mouth for him. He held the copper whisky thief above her and let the light amber liquid slowly drip into her mouth. She closed her eyes and revelled in the flavours that slid over her tongue.

Tilting her head back up, she saw his eyes drop to her neck as she swallowed. There was a wild hunger in his eyes, not unlike a tiger eyeing its prey, and god help her, she liked this feral Lachlan.

She dipped her head back slightly and opened her mouth again, and he allowed more scotch to drip in. The last drop hit her lips as she closed her mouth to savour the dram. She licked the smoky sweetness from her lips, all the while watching Lachlan as he watched her. She didn't know which of them was more mesmerized.

He brought the copper above his own mouth, allowing a good mouthful to pour in, and his eyes landed back on her. It felt as if he couldn't bear to look away from her for too long.

"Liquid gold," she said, seeing the pleasure soften his handsome features as he swallowed. "How old is this one?"

"This one," he said, putting a hand on the old barrel, "is sitting currently at thirty years."

"Wow, that's old."

Lachlan chuckled. "My da had it casked when my brother Alex and I were born."

Violet laughed. "Let me clarify, it's old for *scotch.*"

"We have two barrels of a whisky that has been aging in sherry casks for sixty-nine years."

"No way!"

"Aye. We hope to get it to seventy-five years, and we'll see what's left after the angel's share."

"Angel's share?" Violet thought back to Andy talking about the magical healing powers of the hidden whisky.

"It's the whisky that evaporates over time, but we ken 'tis heaven's angels having their fill," he said with a playful wink.

"Aww, I love that. Maybe your great nan and Helena sit together and enjoy a sip or two." Violet smiled up at him, but Lachlan's expression grew serious. She suddenly regretted her words. She hadn't meant to be insensitive. Lachlan's eyes seemed to be penetrating her soul. "I'm sorry. I didn't mean—"

"Ach, my wee Canadian, always apologizing. Dinnae, V. I've never thought of it before. I honestly dinnae ken if I believe in angels, but somehow, I can see those two in my mind's eye cackling over a wee dram, bletherin' away. It's a nice thing to think. Thank ye."

Violet was relieved. She never wanted to upset Lachlan. She definitely had a crush on the man, but she also had grown to care about him. "How old is your oldest bottled whisky?" she asked, now more curious.

He raised his brow. "We have a small batch of bottles from 1888."

"Wow, now that is old. Have you ever opened a bottle?"

"Aye, we did one year. It was the new year before Helena died. It was one of the last times I remember us all being together as a family. It was such a celebration. We all took great pleasure in finally opening one of the bottles and sampling its nectar, and God, it was so pure and delicious. Unlike any I've know before or since."

"That is so special that you were all able to share in that moment together." Violet touched his arm in comfort, but all she could feel was his rock-hard bicep under his tux. The air suddenly seemed thicker. Sexual tension arose between them. His eyes were on her, hunger rippling on their blue surface.

"More lass?" His burr was deep.

She grinned, tilting her head back and opening her mouth, now accustomed to the process, and he let the scotch spill past her lips.

She swallowed and opened for more, savouring the flavours and the heat as it rolled down her throat. Then he closed off the cask and dropped the whisky thief nearby before one of his big hands gently held the back of her neck, and she heard his sharp intake of breath. He searched her eyes. She knew she should stop this, but she couldn't, and she didn't want to.

There was a longing in the way he looked at her that made her desperate to answer his need. Violet was completely immersed in the moment. All thoughts of making an escape evaporated. She wanted whatever was going to happen next. She couldn't deny it or fight it. With his other hand, he held her face. He ran a thumb over her lightly parted lips. She could barely breathe, though her heart raced. She needed his kiss so badly.

"Ye are stunning, V." His voice was thick with desire.

As if seeing and hearing her heart's desire, his lips crooked up to the side in a smile that was her undoing. Her heart skipped a beat as he lowered his lips to hers. The touch of his mouth on hers rocked her world. She was scorched. Even though they'd kissed before and that had been pretty damn amazing, this kiss was mind blowing. Perhaps because now, she really knew the man. Perhaps because there had been a tension between them for so long, or perhaps because this t ime, *he* was kissing her. She hadn't realized until now just how much she desperately wanted him.

His lips lingered on hers, and her heart nearly jumped out of her chest. They'd kissed before, but this was very different. She'd barely known him then. There was so much longing and need built up now. The feel of Lachlan Mackenzie actually kissing her was earth-shattering.

His lips had gently teased against hers before pressing more firmly. Lips tangling with each other. He pulled away briefly to look into her eyes again as if confirming that she wanted this too. And she did—god, she really did.

With a low growl, he took her mouth in his again, sliding his tongue against hers. He kissed her harder, deeper, like kissing her was the only thing keeping him alive. Violet had never been kissed like this. It was all-consuming. She opened her mouth to him, craving more and more, and he plunged his tongue deeper, ferociously tasting her. Her body thrummed for him.

Chapter 35
Close Call

SHE TASTED OF SWEET, fresh honey and peated, aged whisky, a potent combination. He couldn't get enough of her sweetness that seemed made for him. He relished her taste and the way it felt to finally kiss her lovely mouth, those cupid lips that had tempted him almost daily since she'd come to work at the sanctuary. Lachlan backed her up against a nearby stone wall, all the while making love to her mouth with his. He pressed his body against hers, making damn sure she could feel what she was doing to him and his rock-hard cock under his kilt. God, he wanted her. It was a need that had consumed him. One he could no longer deny.

He deepened their kiss. A gentle moan escaped her, and it nearly drove him over the edge. All the longing, the needing, and she was finally pressed against him. Her luscious body that had haunted his dreams was molded to his. It was beyond anything he could've imagined. In one quick move, Lachlan lifted her bare arms above her head and held her slim wrists firmly against the stone wall with one hand, and she arched her back and pressed her perfect breasts against him.

"Christ, V," he growled as desire like he'd never known possessed him.

Lachlan could feel his passion for this woman taking over his mind and body, and any sense of propriety and chivalry had long since evaporated like the angel's share—gone. It didn't matter that they worked together. It didn't matter that he was her boss. All that mattered was the driving hunger that roared between them.

It felt otherworldly how much he wanted her, needed her. There was nothing that was going to stand in his way. She'd haunted his dreams for more than two months, both sleeping and waking. He just needed to taste her, to touch her—God, to be inside her. To consume and be consumed. His longing for her needed quenching. He couldn't think straight anymore—couldn't hold back any longer.

With her arms still pinned above her head, he broke off their kiss. Her lips were swollen, a lusty strawberry red colour. Her mossy green eyes beckoned him for more. It was a heady combination. He kissed her neck hungrily, tasting, licking, and nipping her. He was starved for her. He could feel her pulse beating wildly against his lips. Lachlan was a man possessed. He wanted to taste every inch of his go ddess.

She was breathing hard. He kissed the top of her heaving tits, allowing his tongue to trail along the top of them. He released her wrists, needing to palm them. Her arms fell to his shoulders, and she clung to him. And god, how he wanted to be her strength and weakness all at the same time.

He kissed her mouth again, feeling her sweet, wet tongue against his, touching, teasing, stoking the flames to burn even hotter. He trailed his kisses down her swan-like neck and back down to those tempting little mounds. Through her dress, he found her pert nipple and grazed at it with his teeth, and she whimpered. He wanted the dress out of the way. First, though, he dropped his mouth to that peephole and tasted the flesh there that had taunted him to no end.

As she gripped his shoulders trying to steady herself, he tugged down the fabric of her gown, which barely budged. Desperate need filling him, he yanked a little harder and watched as one pointed pink nipple popped above the fabric. He could have damn-near cried at how perfect that straining nipple was. He crashed his mouth down onto it, swirling its erect tip with his tongue. His cock throbbed with molten need. He grazed it through his teeth, and she whimpered, her ragged breathing only turning him on more.

He pulled his mouth from her perfect breast and trailed kisses up her neck. His jaw scraped against her silky, soft skin. Tracing the shape of her ear with the tip of his tongue, he whispered roughly, “I need ye, V.” He moved to hold her beautiful face in his hands.

Her eyes reflected the desire he felt. “Then take me.”

Lachlan was sure no sweeter words existed. He slammed his mouth against hers. Passion like he’d never known drowned out everything but the woman before him.

Lachlan splayed his hands against her hips as his mouth continued to taste her, and then he let his hands slide to cup her lush rump through her sheer gown. God, she was heaven with curves dreams were made of. He felt his cock jerk tighter with lecherous need.

He started to gather up the sheer layers of her dress. Her back was still pressed against the cool stone wall of the cask room. Finally, his hand reached under the layers to the bare skin of her silky smooth thigh. There was no doubt the touch seared through them both—lust gripping them. He reached his hand in between their bodies, and he felt the tantalizing lace of her panties with his fingers. They were a barrier he wanted gone—now. With one quick, powerful jerk, he tore them off. She let out a feminine squeal of surprise, and he gave her a satisfied grin before taking her mouth in his again. She whimpered breathlessly.

"Tell me ye want this?" He needed to be sure, and yet, god help him, if she'd said no, it would be like trying to blow a freight train to a stop with a single breath.

She nodded, wrapping her hands around the nape of his neck.

"Say it." He leaned his forehead to hers.

"I want this," she whispered against his lips as she kissed them as if to seal her vow.

Lachlan grasped her thighs and lifted her up to spread her wide to him. He used one hand to free his feral cock.

“Please, Lachlan.” She whimpered against his lips.

Christ, never had he heard sweeter words. With one quick motion, he slid his thick cock into her full hilt. She cried out her pleasure as her soft wet sheath hugged tightly around him. Lachlan groaned, unable to comprehend how incredible it was to have her beautiful body greedily take him in. She was so wet and tight. He had to steady himself. It was almost more than he could take. When he looked into her lust-hazed eyes, the connection, the otherworldly thing that existed between them since the first moment he'd looked into her eyes, he knew. *Mine.* It wasn't a thought. It was an ancient, sacred vow. A certainty that existed in a realm beyond thought, beyond words, beyond everything—she was his.

His breath was ragged as he held himself in her. He’d dreamed of this moment too many times in the past couple of months, and now the reality was almost more than he could bear. Lust drenched his every muscle, his very fibre.

Being deep inside this goddess of a woman and feeling her wet, slippery heat left him feeling like he'd died and gone to heaven.

"Violet, Violet, Violet," he whispered as he took her lips in his again and slowly began to slide out of her tightness that gripped him so well the pleasure was almost too much. He slammed back into her with another groan of sheer ecstasy. "God, lass." His voice was a harsh whisper. She met his every thrust as he slammed in and out of her amazing body that surely was made for him.

"Don't stop," Violet begged, ecstasy lacing her voice.

Lachlan pumped into her even harder, crushing her mouth to his. The friction built, gathering strength like a storm cloud ready to unleash its thunder. Their bodies moved in a sensuous rhythm.

"Christ, ye feel so good," Lachlan ground out, on the verge of exploding. It took every ounce of strength he had to hold back. As much as he needed release, he didn't want this incredible feeling to end. He felt like he could fuck this woman until the end of time and still want more.

Violet felt like her body was on the cusp with every thrust. Lachlan had her pinned against the wall, and he held her up as he slid in and out of her with a strength and stamina that she didn't know was possible. And then suddenly, there were voices, laughter, movement. Awareness careened through Violet like a fire alarm going off. She looked at Lachlan wide-eyed. In one fluid motion, he put her down and pulled her through a nearby door into what seemed like a utility closet, although it was too dark and cramped to know for sure. Their breathing was heavy, and although his hard body was still pressed against hers, the energy had completely shifted.

They heard the small crowd enter the room they'd just been having the most crazy, incredible sex in. Violet's heart was racing. She tried to calm it down. Adrenaline was buzzing through her. It seemed to take forever, but the crowd passed by without incident.

Violet let out a breath she'd been holding.

"Holy shit, that was a close call," she whispered against his chest.

He kissed the top of her head like he'd done that first day and night they'd spent together. It brought back an instant comfort. When they were sure the group was out of the room and well past, Lachlan opened the narrow wooden door. The first thing she noticed was her torn black lace thong tossed on the stone tile floor very near to the large corridor the tour had just passed through. Embarrassment burned her cheeks. Lachlan followed her gaze, and then he strode toward them, knelt down, and picked them up.

"I dinnae think anyone noticed, lass. It's okay." He held up her torn panties as if realizing for the first time what he'd done to them. A smile threatened the edges of his lips. "I dinnae suppose ye want these back?" he offered, and before she could answer, he shocked her as he tightened his fist around them, crumpling them up. He held them to his nose and breathed deeply. His eyes closed as if he was inhaling an aphrodisiac.

Violet was both scandalized and aroused in equal measure. Before she could react, he opened his eyes, gave her a devilish *forgive me* crooked grin, and shoved them into the inside pocket of his tux jacket.

For a moment, she thought to demand to have them back so she could dispose of them, but a little wicked part of her liked that he had them now and clearly wanted them. The way he breathed in her scent like a man breathing in his final breath. She wasn't sure if she found it so erotic because it seemed so out of character for him or simply because he was so aroused by her. There was a wildness in Lachlan that she'd glimpsed before, but he seemed to keep that side of himself more caged. It seemed to her that he'd let that wild beast out to play, and she was surprised just how much she liked it. She tried to imagine what he might do with her torn panties. Would he throw them out, or would he keep them as a memento?

It was crazy to her now that the moment had passed, all that they had done. She wasn't a virgin, but she also hadn't had that much sex in her life. She was pretty sure that the proverbial sex bar was just set at an impossible height, and neither of them even came! She was so close, though, and sensed he was too. What was it about Lachlan that he could make her feel like a goddess that he worshipped?

Violet looked thoroughly ravished and unbelievably sexy. Knowing that he was responsible for her current state was incredibly potent. His cock was in pain. Talk about blue balls. She was a drug to him. He wanted nothing more than to pick up where they'd left off. God, he wanted nothing more than to slam back into her and make her come around his cock, to feel her pulsate, to hold her and look into those mossy green eyes as she shattered in pleasure. Unfortunately, reason was returning, and it seemed that this perhaps wasn't the best time nor place. It pained Lachlan, though. He wanted more of this woman.

Much more.

"Are ye okay, lass?" he asked gently.

Violet had grown quiet as she adjusted her gown and hair in an attempt to right them. She looked up and smiled shyly. He wasn't sure how she could pull a shy smile after what they had just been doing, but somehow, she did.

"Do you think we could have another drop of scotch before we head up?"

Oh my God, Lachlan thought to himself, *I might just be in love.*

Chapter 36

Jealousy's Venom

VIOLET DIDN'T STICK AROUND after getting back from her "whisky tour" with Lachlan. When they came back up to the main room, Violet's heart sank when none other than Anna MacDonald stole Lachlan away. Just because they'd had sex, it didn't mean he was suddenly hers, despite her heart yelling to the contrary.

"I was looking for you," the woman crooned, latching onto his arm, not even sparing Violet a glance. It was the first time Violet witnessed Lachlan looking completely uncomfortable. If she didn't feel so vulnerable in the moment, she might have found it comical. Lachlan cleared his throat.

"Anna, this is Violet. She works with me at the sanctuary."

Seriously, they'd just shared the most incredible connection, and that was how he introduced her. Violet didn't have time to be offended as Anna clearly had other plans for Lachlan.

"Violet." The woman's eyes coolly assessed her. "Not a common name."

Before Violet could respond, Anna had already turned her attention back to Lachlan. "The first minister and his wife just arrived. Since they are friends of mine, I thought I could make the introductions," Anna said smoothly.

Violet sensed it was more of a ploy to get Lachlan's attention. She didn't consider herself the jealous type, but something about this woman rubbed her wrong. Not that she had any business being jealous at all, did she? Now they'd come upstairs, she felt so uncertain as to what had just happened between them. What did it mean? Did it mean anything at all?

Lachlan scanned the room. "Aye, I'd appreciate that."

Violet was surprised when Lachlan turned back and stepped close to her. She couldn't help her instant reaction to him being in her space again. Her pulse kicked up with need snaking through her as if her body wanted nothing more than to be wrapped in his.

She swallowed, looking up into his reassuring eyes. He tucked a strand of hair behind her ear that had come loose downstairs.

"I'm sorry, lass. Duty calls." Why did he have to look at her like she was an angel while at the same time rejecting her? Maybe she had no right to wish that he would want her by his side. His right hand, as Orlagh had said, but also something more—her heart hoped.

"It's fine." The words felt like a lie. "I know you have lots of people to talk with." It was true. He was the host of this party, after all, but her heart wished that he wanted to keep her on his arm. Show her off proudly. She almost snickered out loud at her own stupidity. What had she thought, that they'd given into desire and suddenly they'd be a couple? She was his employee! God, she was such an idiot.

He kissed her forehead and gave her hand a squeeze before turning from her and striding toward an eagerly awaiting Anna. Violet watched them get lost in the crowd and wondered how she'd gotten it so wrong—again. For a suspended moment in time, she felt like he was hers completely. Now back upstairs, it was like the magic of that cask room was broken. Hadn't he felt it, too? That indescribable pull, that all-consuming need? Surely, it was not common place between two people.

And then a terrible unbidden thought crossed her mind. Despite knowing that everyone had sex, the thought that he'd probably had sex with Anna not only flashed through her mind, but it had her questioning—had it been like this for them? Was Lachlan just a casanova? She hated that she even questioned it after what just transpired between them.

Ugh. What was she doing even thinking about it? She'd be lying if she denied the sting of how he'd introduced her to his so-called ex after just having earth-shattering sex with her.

An ache settled into her temples. What did she want him to say? That she was his girlfriend now? After all that had just transpired, it felt like nothing had changed. She was still just his employee. A friend.

Violet had made her way to the front foyer to retrieve her wrap and head home when she was approached from the side.

"Going home already?"

Violet looked at the woman, who was a couple of inches shorter than her. Her beautiful face was marred with a smug smile—Anna. Alarm bells went off in her mind.

“I have to work in the morning," Violet responded.

"Oh yes, that's right. You’re a worker at Lachlan's horse place."

"Highland Haven. Yes." Violet got the sense the woman was trying to belittle her in some way, and she was in no mood, with the incessant ache taking up residence in her head. She turned to face her in hopes she would cut to the chase.

"Lachlan is a very important man, a very prestigious man," Anna said as if it were somehow relevant.

"Mmhm. Important, but not pretentious," Violet lobbed back.

"Well, let me frank with ye. It would be a bad look if he were to"—she ran a judgmental gaze over Violet—"dabble with the help." Her beady little eyes were pointed on Violet.

She could not believe the nerve of this woman. Violet had never been made to feel like she was inferior, but this woman was clearly trying to do just that. Violet wanted to give her an earful, but before she could respond, the woman slipped a piece of paper from her gem-encrusted purse, and Violet's heart sank.

She recognized it immediately. It was the note she'd left Lachlan when she'd stayed at his place. How on earth did this woman have it? *Oh God*. The pieces started to fall into place. Lachlan was dating her when she'd stayed at his house. Violet felt like she was going to be sick.

"Ye may want this back," Anna said, a snide smile spreading across her face.

Tears stung Violet's eyes but she'd not give the woman the satisfaction of seeing her cry. Taking the note from her hand, she turned and left as fast as her high heels would carry her. Thankfully, there was a cab waiting outside, and she slipped inside. She pulled out her phone and texted her friends that she had a headache and was heading home, and then she sat back and let the tears come as she re-read the note she'd left Lachlan at what felt like a lifetime ago.

Hi Lachlan,

What a wild weekend! I never expected quite so much excitement when I arrived in your country. I honestly don't know what would have happened if you hadn't come to my rescue on the pier. I'm eternally grateful. And then being willing to let me stay here. You're a pretty great guy, Lachlan Mackenzie. Thank you for being the best nursemaid a girl could ask for. I owe you one, to say the least. If you ever want company when you go riding or someone to hang out with and listen to The Beatles, or you need a whisky taster, haha, let me know!

Yours,

Violet x

0161 569 8991

And for the first time, she wondered if he'd ever seen it. Was that why he didn't contact her? Sierra's words came back to her, *he could have found you if he wanted to.* That was still true. She bit her lip. But did he even know she'd left him a note at all?

Walking into her little cottage, she headed straight for her bedroom and took off her gown. The events of the night played over in her mind. She didn't know how she felt. Thoughts of his hands and mouth all over her and of how good it felt to have him inside her consumed her as she undressed. She climbed into bed and snuggled under the covers.

There was a distinct chill in the air tonight. Immediately, she imagined him in bed with her, warming her up. His ripped body pressed against hers. She shivered. Then she picked up her phone and looked at it. Nothing. No phone calls. No texts.

She rolled over with a sigh. Fortunately, her headache had eased a bit. That Anna woman was a piece of work. She couldn't fathom the Lachlan she'd come to know being with her. She thought back to what Orlagh had said—something about Anna making Lachlan's skin crawl from having to dance with her. Was he just playing nice? Being the dutiful host? But it was clear to Violet now that this woman wanted Lachlan and likely had him at some point if she had come into possession of Violet's note. And Orlagh had said something about the woman trying to win Lachlan's affections *back*.

It made her head hurt again trying to understand it all. God, what a night. She let her mind wonder back to being with Lachlan down in the cask room—without a doubt the most erotic experience of her life. *Mmm, and he felt so good inside her. Geez, what would have happened if they hadn't heard the tour coming?* She cringed at the thought. Thank God, they were able to get out of sight in time. Then she thought about how he'd torn off her panties with such masculine determination. A wave of desire shuddered through her at the memory. She rolled onto her back, throwing her arm across her forehead.

"Shit, shit, shit," she cursed. As incredible as the night was, when it came down to it, she was afraid. Afraid she'd let him in and not just physically. He had her wound in knots. Telling her how he'd wished she'd been there on his trip. But that was for business, she reminded herself.

She was actually thrilled with how he'd come to rely on her with business. She loved it all so much. She'd grown in the past six weeks and could see the potential for her role in the sanctuary. She was so passionate about it all, but it turned out she might actually have quite the knack for business. Even his sister said that he talked about her. Did it mean something? Or was it just all about the business? And then she wondered if what had happened tonight would change things.

Anna's words rang in her ears about it not being a good look dabbling with the help. What a horrendous thing to say, and yet, Violet couldn't help the little seed of doubt that had formed in her mind.

All the walls she had worked so hard to build. Business was one thing. But their chemistry was off the charts. *Och, lass, I've needed to taste your lips for two long months.* His words haunted her now. She had learned not to think about him—to not dream about him. She'd almost taught herself not to want him. Almost. And now it was like all her walls and rules had been scattered like shredded paper to the wind in one wild, unbelievable evening. She was exposed. No walls to protect her heart. Maybe something had changed. Maybe he did want something more with her. Ugh, she was so unsure. She wanted to cry again, but she was so tapped out.

I need ye, V. His words echoed in her mind.

She was so fearful that it was *she* who needed him. For him, perhaps it was just a night of passion, a fling. The ones who got away always tasted sweeter, didn't they? But for her, he was seared on her soul. Branded.

"FUUCKK," she hollered out to the cool quietness of her room.

Chapter 37
All the Gossip

VIOLET AWOKE TO THE sound of the sea crashing in the distance. She opened her eyes to a dimly lit bedroom and glanced out the window on a stormy Sunday morning. Rain was blowing hard against the glass.

Normally, she'd go to the sanctuary on a Sunday, but today, she didn't think she could. The truth was, she was afraid to see him again. Afraid he'd had his fun and was done. Afraid he'd be just her lovely amazing boss. How was she supposed to deal with that? She looked at her phone. Two missed calls from Fiona and still nothing from Lachlan. Her overzealous heart hurt, and she sighed heavily.

There was a knock on her door, and in a flash, her heart popped back to life. *Here we go!* She wanted it to be him. God help her, there it was. *She wanted it to be him*. Throwing her legs over the side of the bed, she stood up, took a quick look in the mirror, and wiped some makeup from under her eyes—not her best look, but no time to fix it now. She reached the door holding in her breath. Pulling it open, she found Fiona on the other side, drenched as a rat holding a tearing wet brown paper bag. A wave of disappointment washed over her. She recovered quickly, though.

"What took ye so long?" Fiona asked, chucking off her boots and barging past Violet, heading straight for her kitchen.

Violet smiled. "Good morning, Fiona."

"Morning? It's half past noon, ye daft lass! Have ye just woken then? I've been trying to ring ye all morning."

Violet looked at the clock, confirming Fiona's claim. Violet couldn't remember the last time she'd slept past ten a.m., never mind noon! She must have been more exhausted than she realized. She had tossed and turned much of the night before falling into a fitful sleep.

"I had no idea the time," Violet said with a yawn, pulling her fluffy yellow bathrobe tighter around her—funny how she'd looked at texts but not the time.

"Clearly. So how was your evening then?" Fiona asked with a conspiratorial look as she brought a plate full of bagels into the living room.

"Mmm, yum. Thanks," Violet said, snatching up a buttered cinnamon raisin bagel.

"I'll put the kettle on. I want the details," she said, walking back to the kitchen.

"What details?" Violet asked from the living room with her mouth full. She hadn't realized how hungry she was.

Fiona came back a few minutes later with two mismatched mugs of tea and sat on the sofa across from her friend. Violet had picked up a few random mugs at a flea market, but there was a certain charm to them that she just adored.

As she picked up her mug from the coffee table, her mind flashed back to Lachlan's sugar and creamer set. The one he'd gotten all weird about. The one that was garish and pompous looking, and suddenly, she understood. It was Anna's. *Ugh. Had they lived together?* Retracing her memories, she wondered if she'd missed any other signs of that woman in Lachlan's home. Interestingly, that was the only thing that screamed Anna MacDonald.

She polished off the first bagel and picked up another, ripping off a small piece and popping it into her mouth.

"Jeez, woman, when did ye eat last?" Fiona said, picking at her own bagel.

"Sorry, I didn't really eat anything at the gala."

"Too busy drinking and schmoozing, I suppose."

"I guess." Violet continued to devour her second bagel.

"Ye left without me and Andy last night," Fiona said like it was a question. "When I couldn't get a hold of ye this morning, I wondered if ye might be somewhere else?" She threw her a conspiratorial smile.

Violet laughed. "No, I was here. I had a headache." She took a sip of tea. "Sorry, I ducked out on you guys. I was exhausted, so I slipped out. I didn't want to cut your evening short." It was partially true.

Fiona was way too perceptive, and Violet wasn't sure she wanted to talk about last night. "How was your night? Did you have fun?"

"Braw!" Fiona beamed.

Violet wondered why her friend had a little twinkle in her eye today.

"Gosh, it was just a dreamy night, wasn't it?" She didn't wait for Violet to respond. "I felt like Cinderella going to the ball! The food, the dancing, the ambiance. Did you dance at all? I kept looking for ye, but ye were nowhere to be found. Andy was useless by the time he came back from the whisky tour. He was three sheets to the wind. I dinnae even think he remembered he'd gone on it with ye down there. Where'd ye get lost to then?" Fiona asked expectantly.

"Oh, I just spent a little more time down on the tour than Andy did, I guess." Violet didn't want to lie, but she wasn't ready to divulge about her night.

"Ah, right, you're into all that stuff then? Whisky making and such." Her voice sounding bored by the very idea.

Violet laughed. "I suppose so."

"Ooh, you'll never guess what happened!" Fiona said, taking a nibble off a piece of her bagel.

"Do tell," Violet said, finally feeling satiated.

"Did ye happen to see the beautiful brunette in the white sequined gown? Anna MacDonald?"

Violet swallowed her tea and felt herself tense. "Yeah, hard to miss," she said, trying to be casual.

"Well, I mean, it's a bit of gossip, and I'm not sure how true it is, but apparently, your boy Lachlan—"

Violet interjected, "He's not my boy."

"Yeah, yeah, dinnae fash. It seems you're not the only one with a crush on our boss."

Violet felt suddenly ill again. Fiona didn't seem to notice, and she continued to animatedly tell her story.

"I huv it on good authority that this wealthy Anna woman was hoping to snag Lachlan's attention, but apparently, Lachlan's sister overheard the woman being a real cunt to someone."

Violet gripped her tea mug a little tighter. Was that someone her? Had Orlagh overheard them?

"The same person told me that he overheard Lachlan telling that Anna woman off. And do you know what he said?" Fiona's eyes were alight.

"He told her that he'd sooner date a slice of fucking stale moldy bread than be in her company and that she could take her money and her bitchy fucking attitude and go back to the hole from which she'd crawled out from."

Violet stared at Fiona and then burst out laughing. She laughed so hard tears formed in her eyes. She didn't believe for a second those words would have come out of Lachlan's mouth, but she enjoyed the story all the same. She wondered if there was any truth to it. Had Orlagh overheard Anna being a C-word?" That wasn't hard to imagine. It didn't necessarily mean she'd overheard their conversation, though. And had Lachlan told Anna off?

"Who told you all this?" she asked when she finally was able to breathe again from laughing so hard.

Fiona looked at Violet square on and grinned from ear to ear. "So I met someone last night."

"Ooh?" Violet took a sip of her tea, eyeing Fiona expectantly. Who was this mystery person who apparently was privy to all the gossip? "Do tell!"

"Right, well, I was standing back just people watching when this drop dead gorgeous man started to walk my way. It was crazy, like he was on a mission. He was staring right at me as he came my way. I didnae ken what to think. My first thought was that someone was behind me. I didnae think he could possibly be coming to me. And then I thought that he was maybe some kind of security and I was getting kicked ou t."

Violet snorted, almost spitting out her tea.

"Dinnae laugh!" Fiona chided. "It wouldnae be the first time."

That was a whole different conversation that Violet would need to have with her, but at the moment, she wanted to know about this mystery guy.

"Sorry, I'm just imagining the situation. I can't believe you actually thought you were getting kicked out." The wind rattled against the windows outside, and Violet tucked her legs a little tighter under her on the couch.

"Aye, well, it crossed my mind. Anyway, he walked right up to me face to face, I thought my heart was going to jump out of my chest."

"And?" Violet urged.

"And he was flipping gorgeous!"

"Yeah, I got that, but what did he say? I'm assuming he didn't lead with the gossip of the evening." Violet was glad to have something to distract her from the memory of her own events from the night before.

"He handed me a glass of champagne, winked at me, and then stood alongside me as if to join me in my people watching. I didnae ken what to think. Hot men dinnae just come and hang out with me. It was most extraordinary."

"Well, he was probably like, 'hot women *dinnae* just stand in the corner alone.'" Violet mimicked Fiona's accent. "So then what?"

Fiona got all serious and moved in closer as if to tell a secret. "He asked me if I wanted to leave with him."

"What?" Violet asked incredulously. "You didn't?"

"I sure as heck did."

"Fiona!" Violet was shocked.

"What? He was hot, and I haven't had a good lay in ages." Violet stared at her friend, unable to close her mouth.

"Why are you so shocked?"

"You left with a complete stranger?"

"Aye, I did." Fiona grinned like the cat who got the cream.

Violet chuckled. "Well, I'm glad it went well, but jeepers, he could have been trouble!"

"Oh, he was trouble, all right."

Violet laughed. "Oh my God. Well, good for you then."

"Brilliant night. To be honest, we didnae actually huv sex. He's hot, but no' really my type, but I will say the man has his talents." She grinned as if recalling the details in her mind's eye.

"So, *one* wild night, or are you going to see him again?"

"I doubt it. Ye ken, kinda a one-and-done type thing. Eased my dry spell." She smiled as if she were speaking of someone fondly from her past and not the guy she'd just seen last night.

Was it one-and-done with Lachlan? She almost winced at the thought stumbling through her head. Violet wanted to be supportive, and the truth was, she was happy for Fiona—but also maybe a little surprised. Violet had a sneaking suspicion that the hot bad boy from last night wasn't her type because Fiona actually batted for the other team. She hadn't said as much, but there were little things. For example, when they were in Glasgow, she'd noticed her eyeing up the women, not the men—but Violet hadn't given it much thought until now. It would also make sense why she hadn't actually had sex with the guy last night. Not that it mattered. She didn't care which team her friend batted for. Fiona seemed happy, and that's all she cared about.

"And it was this guy who told you all that gossip about Anna MacDonald?"

"Aye. When we were leaving, we saw her looking flustered and downright pissed off. She barged ahead of us, nearly knocking into me, and she literally busted a high heel in the process. At the time, I thought it served her right for being so rude cutting us off, and when we got in the cab, Drew told me the story."

"His name is Drew?" Violet swallowed hard. Could it be Lachlan's brother? Violet chided herself—not likely. They were in Scotland. There were likely plenty of Drews. Although, it was a bit ironic that a good-looking guy named Drew was at the Calliach Distillery Gala, and he seemed to know the family gossip.

Chapter 38

No Regrets

LACHLAN STOOD AT HIS kitchen counter, looking out at the stormy white caps smashing in the sea. He raked his fingers through his hair. Last night with Violet played through his mind. Being with her, being intimate with her, was well beyond what his mind had conjured up these past months. He had never experienced such strong desire for someone. In the light of day, it was a bit overwhelming to realize just how intense his feelings had become toward her. He took a sip of his coffee. His hardened cock was a constant reminder of how much he'd wanted her over these past couple of months, but he never imagined that it could be like what it was between them last night.

During the short period of time they'd spent together months ago, he'd fought his physical desire for her. He had no intention of taking advantage of the situation. He prided himself on being a gentleman. That was who he was to the core. Lachlan had always been disciplined and always had self-control. It wasn't really something he thought about.

It was just his character. He wasn't the guy who cheated or took advantage of a woman. Those were things that would never change. But he never would have imagined himself crossing the line with an employee.

The thing was, he didn't think of Violet as an employee—not really. In many ways, he'd come to rely on her as a business partner. Not that crossing *that* line was any better. But here he was the morning after, and regret was definitely not one of the emotions running through him. Violet made him feel alive. She brought out something in him he didn't even know existed. It was something raw and authentic.

It was foreign for Lachlan to feel so many urges he'd never felt before. Sure, he was a guy like any other. Of course, a beautiful, intelligent, sweet woman was tempting. He would have to be dead not to feel some kind of pull. But this felt like the pull of the moon on the ocean's tide—massive.

After that first weekend Lachlan had met Violet, he mistakenly assumed his fires would cool as soon as they'd parted ways. That the part of him she'd cracked open would seal back up and disappear without a trace. He couldn't have been more wrong. Every moment with her, the crack deepened, splitting wide open and somehow setting him free.

Last night, everything had built up. Instead of the Scottish gentleman Lachlan was used to being, he felt like a feral highlander, and god help him, it felt good. Lachlan was already feeling things toward Violet that he'd never imagined. Their business relationship had grown and become one that Lachlan was incredibly grateful for and enjoyed. But when he saw Violet at the gala, she was positively jaw-dropping. Watching her was his complete undoing. He hadn't intended any of what had happened, but this morning, he regretted nothing.

Having sex with Violet had been one of the most intense moments of his life. The only regret he felt was that they got interrupted before he could give her sweet release. He wished he could have done things differently after they'd come up from the barrel room.

After meeting with the first minister and his wife, Orlagh came and told him how she'd overheard Anna talking down to Violet. It utterly incensed him, and when he'd asked Anna about it, she'd tried to downplay it. Her biggest mistake was the moment she tried to imply that Violet was somehow unworthy of him. Lachlan hadn't held back when he told her that Violet had more class in her perfect little pinky finger than Anna would ever dream of having and that she could take her money ram it up her arse.

A few months back, he never would have imagined saying such a thing, but Christ, it felt good. It was freeing not to have to say or do what was expected of him and to stand up for Violet and himself. He'd do anything to protect Violet—anything.

Sally barked excitedly, pulling him from his thoughts. He recognized Orlagh's voice loving up his mutt, and then the two bumbled into the kitchen.

"Put the kettle on then. It's freezin' out there," she ordered through cuddles and kisses with Sally.

"What are ye doin' here so early on a Sunday morn' anyhow?" Lachlan asked while filling up the kettle with water and turning the knob for the gas stove burner. He turned back to his baby sister, who was settling in at his kitchen table.

"The Gala went well," she began.

He nodded. "Yes, very well. I haven't got the final numbers for the silent auction, but I think we raised a lot of funds. Minus the check from Anna, I was sure to give that back to her." Lachlan poured the boiling water into Orlagh's favourite blue argyle mug, stirring in a blob of honey and a splash of milk. He topped up his black coffee and brought the two mugs to the table.

"Wait," Orlagh stopped Lachlan just as he was about to sit. "Do ye huv any bickies?" She looked like a blue-eyed cherub about to fall happily from grace.

He smiled knowingly. "Uh, yes, how could I forget?" he said, walking over to the cupboard.

"Any with chocolate should do," she instructed.

"Right," he replied flatly.

His sister's sweet tooth was rather infamous. Lachlan didn't often eat biscuits and sweets, but he always kept some on hand for when his sister popped 'round. He grabbed a side plate and filled it with plain oat biscuits, a chocolate covered version, and also a cream sandwich style and brought it to the table.

"Ooh, lovely jubbly," Orlagh said, reaching for a cream sandwich one and dipping it into her tea.

"Out with it, Rolo."

She looked at him under her lashes for a moment, munching her biscuit and reaching for another. "Oh, all right."

Lachlan clearly knew her all too well.

"Well, firstly, I'm proud of you for the way you handled that dreadful woman. I'm so glad you came to your senses and dumped her arse."

Lachlan gave her a warning look from under his brow.

"All right, all right. Never mind all that. But I am glad ye put her in her place."

"Aye, right. What else? I can see there is something else going on in that head of yours."

"I had a delightful little chat with Violet last night." She grinned through chomps of biscuit.

Lachlan sat up a little straighter. "Did ye?" he said, trying to stay cool even though the very mention of her name had his pulse galloping like a horse when a gate gets left open.

"I brought ye this. Thought maybe ye would want to give it to her." Orlagh handed him a large, brown paper shopping bag. He peered inside and pulled up a folded soft wool tartan. He looked at his sister, confused.

"Why would I want to give Violet our family tartan exactly?"

Orlagh munched on another biscuit. "Because it was her favourite item at the auction last night. She even bid on it."

"Really?" Lachlan was surprised, but he also felt oddly gratified that Violet liked their clan tartan and wanted the blanket for her home.

"Seriously, Lachlan, she loved it, and it would be a romantic gesture for you to give it to her." She spelled it out for him.

"And why exactly do ye think I need help in the romance department?"

"Oh my God, Lachlan, just give it to her—she'll like it." Orlagh huffed. "Please tell me ye at least talked to her last night?"

What? Aye, aye, of course, I did. Why?"

"Brother, ye huv it bad. Did ye ask her out?"

Lachlan took a sip of his coffee, thinking back to being in the cask room with Violet. “No' exactly.”

“Lachlan, ye need to get on with it already. Lassies like Violet dinnae come around every day, ye ken. Please, please, dinnae get stuck in the friend zone with this one.”

Lachlan almost spat out his coffee. There was no way in hell that was happening. “What are ye implying?” He arched his brow.

Orlagh rolled her eyes at him. “Oh, Lachlan.” She sighed, shaking her head.

“Ye dinnae huv to worry about my love life.” He knew what his sister was thinking—that he’d mess things up—but if his yelling heart was any indication, she needn’t worry.

“Och, did ye just say love, Lachlan Rory Mackenzie?”

It was Lachlan's turn to roll his eyes, although, in fairness, he didn't mind Orlagh's ribbing this morning.

"Ye huvnae stopped thinking about her since ye met her—admit it—and ye sing her praises all the time.”

“Well, she’s amazing with the business. I've told ye she's become my right hand.” He knew damn well what his sister was trying to say, but he wasn't going to give her the satisfaction. It was far too much fun to let her stew.

"God, Lachlan, sometimes, ye're such a numpty. Dinnae ye think ye owe it to yerself to at least see where it could go?”

Lachlan was silent for a moment. Pensive. “Aye."

Orlagh stared at him, bewildered, before she jumped up, clapping her hands together.

"Ye're going to ask her out then? Och, I like her Lachlan, and I huv such a good feeling about the two of ye." She sat back, grinning at him.

Lachlan smiled reluctantly. Orlagh and her *feelings*. “Right, well, ye best let me get on with it then,” he said, getting up from the table and taking their mugs to the sink.

“Oh, right,” she said, jumping up and taking her cue to leave. “Keep me posted.” She grinned as she sauntered out of the kitchen. “And don’t forget to give her the tartan!”

Lachlan chuckled, took a deep breath, and headed upstairs to shower.

Chapter 39

Flowers and Romantic Things

On the drive over, he stopped at a florist and picked out a bouquet of flowers for Violet. If he was doing this, he was going to do this right, though he struggled to choose just the right ones. The florist must have noted his indecision because she offered to make a custom bouquet. Lachlan liked that idea. It seemed fitting to give this one-of-a-kind woman a one-of-a-kind bouquet.

After asking him to describe Violet, the grinning florist helped him choose a selection of cream and mauve blown roses, Scottish thistle, greenery, and a few sprigs of soft white freesias. According to the florist, the roses represented her timeless beauty, the thistle her hardiness, and the freesias her sweetness. It sounded a bit far-fetched to him, but he had to admit, the final bouquet looked good. He hoped she'd like it.

As Lachlan walked up the path to Violet's cottage, he suddenly felt nervous—not a feeling he was familiar with—and began to second-guess himself. He wasn't used to feeling so unnerved, but it seemed that Violet brought about many feelings he was new to.

Ducking under her porch roof to get out of the pelting rain, he knocked on her soft blue front door and felt his heart race as wild as the wind. The door opened, and instead of Violet, another employee from the sanctuary greeted him. An awkwardness replaced his nerves. It took him a moment to remember himself.

"Hi, Fiona." He smiled, trying to regain his footing. He had made sure he knew all his employees' names.

"Hi, Lachlan." She looked understandably puzzled as she waited for him to say something more. Lachlan smiled uncomfortably as Fiona inquisitively eyed him and the oversized bouquet of flowers he held.

"Was Violet supposed to be at the sanctuary this morning?" She smiled at him, feigning ignorance.

He was quite certain they both knew why he was there, and it had nothing to do with Violet missing work.

"What? Och, um, no. I just..." Lachlan was at a loss for words. "Is she here?" he finally managed.

"Aye, she's just popped in the shower. I'm sure she willnae be long. Did ye want to come in? Have a cuppa." Fiona opened the door wider to allow Lachlan to come in, but he stayed where he was.

He smiled, feeling more awkward than when he and his brothers were lads and gave each other wedgies. "No' a worry. I'll just ask ye to pass this on to her if ye dinnae mind, and I leave ye two to yer visit." Lachlan shoved the bouquet and the paper bag with the tartan to Fiona, and turned to walk back down the path with his hands jammed into his pockets.

"Is this from the gala? Did she win it or something?" Fiona called to Lachlan as he was making his way back to his car.

"Uh, aye. From the silent auction," he called back. He didn't want to lie, but he wasn't prepared to tell Fiona why he was bringing gifts to Violet. Things had not gone at all as planned. He hadn't thought about what the staff might think about him dating a fellow employee. Tension crept into Lachlan's shoulders as he pulled away from Violet's cottage, deep in thought.

Violet walked out of the bathroom with her hair wrapped in a towel and saw Fiona, closing the door and smiling broadly.

"Well, that was interesting," she whispered.

"What was interesting?"

"You'll never guess who just showed up at your front door?"

Violet was looking at the flowers in Fiona's hand.

"Our boss!" Fiona blurted it out before she could respond.

Violet's heart slammed in her chest, and she went to the little window by the front door to look out. "He's gone?"

"Aye, but he brought you this. He said it's from the auction." Fiona raised her eyebrows suspiciously as she held out the brown paper bag and bouquet to Violet.

"Oh, wow," Violet breathed. She smelled the beautiful bouquet. She'd once received carnations from a sweet albeit not really her type guy she'd gone on a date with, but never had she received flowers like these. It was, hands down, the most beautiful bouquet she'd ever seen. It was the Scottish thistle mixed in with the delicate, beautiful flowers that made it so stunning. Something about that rugged twist of wild just made the combination so perfect together.

She laid it down on the coffee table so she could look inside the bag. Violet gently lifted out the beautiful rich tartan blanket. "Ohhh," she crooned, holding it to her face to feel its softness. "I wanted this so much!"

She was thrilled, but she couldn't possibly have had the highest bid. Could she? The thought occurred to her that maybe he'd seen she'd wanted it and got it for her. She didn't dare hope that was the case, but, oh, if it was, her heart warmed at the very thought. Violet looked up and saw Fiona eyeing her suspiciously.

"He just dropped this off and left?" Violet asked.

"Aye." Fiona continued to look at Violet with scrutinizing eyes. "What's that man doing coming 'round here bringing you gifts on a Sunday morning? Like it's the morning after the night before." She waggled her eyebrows.

Violet couldn't help but laugh. If only she knew the half of it, but Violet didn't feel ready to divulge. She still didn't know where she and Lachlan stood.

"It's not a *gift*. It's from the auction." Violet asserted.

"And you're telling me that you outbid the rich bastards at that party? Also, I dinnae recall a bouquet like *that* at the auction." Fiona raised an arched brow.

"God, it is incredible." Violet picked the bouquet back up to examine it. "I-I don't really know," she stuttered, not sure what to say or why he had brought it to her.

"Is it the morning after, then?" Fiona asked, clearing her throat.

"Oh, Fiona, don't be ridiculous." Violet tried to shake her friend off. She wasn't prepared to talk about what had happened between her and Lachlan last night. In fact, now that a new day was here, it was hard to believe it actually happened at all. It felt like some kind of erotic dream.

"Hmm, well, I did wonder if it was like maybe a door prize or something, like the chance for us normal folk to have a chance to win," she teased. "Maybe the flowers were an extra 'congrats that ye won and ye're not even rich!'"

Violet chuckled. "Who knows?"

"Interesting that he would come and personally deliver it to you. The flowers seem a definite extra. If ye ask me, I still think he's got a thing for ye." She picked up her coat off the hook at the front door and slipped it on.

"I'm sure he would've stuck around if that were true. The sanctuary is down the road. He was probably just in the neighbourhood. And maybe they had extra flowers from the gala. I'm sure it was just a nice gesture. You know he's thoughtful that way."

"Whatever you say, Vi. Well, I'm going to love ye and leave ye. I've got things to do."

"And people to see?" Violet finished for her, teasing her about maybe seeing that Drew guy again.

"I never say never." She grinned slyly.

Violet waved goodbye from the front door and strode back into her little cottage. Her gaze immediately landed on the stunning tartan that lay on her couch. She smiled and then sighed. *Ugh*, why was it that the man she was crazy about was finally showing her that he might be interested in her, and she couldn't just enjoy it?

Nope, it just made her worry because she still didn't know his intentions with her. She was only guessing. And when it came to Lachlan, she knew two things. He wasn't a sure thing—far from it, and if she admitted she was falling for him, she didn't think she'd recover if he didn't fall back.

She sat down on her couch, picked up her phone, and sighed. She looked up at the flowers and tartan again, biting her lip. She opened her phone to message Lachlan and thank him but hesitated, her fingers hovering over the screen. *Thanks for the flowers, tartan, and incredible sex?* Ugh. Gawd. She threw the phone down on the couch cushion.

It was so hard to get over him the first time, but had she really gotten over him? She never expected she'd be working for him, and she definitely never would have imagined that she'd be working with him so closely day in and day out. She rubbed her temples, the ache settling back over them.

This was more complicated than just her feelings for Lachlan. She also loved the work she was doing. Working at the sanctuary around the horses lifted her spirits, but working on the ins and outs of the business with Lachlan fueled her like nothing else ever had in her life.

Could she do the same kind of work somewhere else? It was something she needed to consider. After all, she couldn't sleep with the boss and hope it wouldn't have repercussions. God, what had she done? The thought of not working at the Highland Haven broke her heart. The thought of not seeing Lachlan again... Oh God, that broke her very soul.

"Shit." A tear slid down her cheek, and she wiped it away. "No," she whispered, refusing to accept what her heart and soul knew.

Gathering up her resolve, she picked up the bouquet of flowers, looked again in awe, then shook her head and marched out the back door of her cottage and into the garden. The rain had eased, and the sun was trying to peep through the clearing clouds. She didn't feel right about throwing away perfectly gorgeous flowers, but she certainly didn't want to look at them all day in her cottage—a constant reminder. She needed to be strong. Violet had to protect her heart.

She put them in a vase on the rickety metal patio table, studied them, and picked them up again. She moved them a few feet away by the ivy-covered stone shed. Stepping back, she stared at them with her arms crossed under her chest. She nibbled her lower lip, anxiety niggling at her. Walking back over to the flowers, she picked them up and walked them around the backside of the shed, setting them on the ground against it.

Stepping back, she realized it looked a bit like flowers set near a gravestone, and then she decided it was the perfect spot. Maybe it was ridiculous, but somehow, it made her feel a small sense of control over her stupid emotions with Lachlan.

She marched confidently back into the house only to see the beautiful blanket. "Arghh," she grumbled. She picked it up and cuddled it into her chest, allowing herself to savour it for a moment. Then she stretched out her arms and held it in front of her, admiring how beautiful it was. "Crap." She sighed as she folded it up and stuffed it back in the bag, and before she could change her mind, she quickly shoved the bag into her bedroom closet. Closing the door, she somehow felt a sense of empowerment. Out of sight, out of mind. She wasn't going to let him in, and that was that. With her head still aching, she decided to go back to bed.

Lachlan left Violet feeling unreasonably disappointed that he hadn't actually had the chance to see her and talk with her. He wasn't totally sure what he was going to say. He supposed he'd ask her out on a date. Try and put the horse back behind the cart, so to speak. The whole thing was complicated, being he was her boss and there were other employees who'd obviously catch wind of things, but as he drove, he decided that they could figure it out—one step at a time.

Lachlan headed to the distillery to do some work there. He thought it might be a good idea to busy himself. He was sure that once Violet had a free moment, she would give him a ring. He was getting annoyed with himself for continually checking his phone.

He found his mind wandering, making excuses for why Violet hadn't called him. Maybe Fiona was still with her, and she hadn't had the chance yet. As the day turned to evening, though, he hadn't heard from her. He decided he'd call her.

For a guy who talked to all kinds of people on a regular basis, it was shocking how nervous he felt as the phone rang. And then it went to her voicemail. He didn't want to speak to her voicemail, but it felt better than just sending a text.

"Hi, V. I'm sorry I missed seeing ye this morning. I hope ye had a good day." He paused. "I'd love to see ye, lass, if ye're not busy. It doesnae huv to be tonight," he added quickly, not wanting to pressure her last minute. "Uh, anyway, give me a ring when ye huv a minute. Right, well. Speak soon then." He hung up, scrunching his eyes closed. God, had he ever been so awkward in his life? Blowing out a breath, he sat back at his desk and tried to focus on this month's batch numbers.

The evening wore on. Lachlan stretched and looked at his watch: ten p.m. He picked up his phone—no messages from Violet, but there was one from Orlagh. He opened it and read?

Orlagh: Sooo??

With a smile, he stood from his mahogany desk and walked over to the small wood marquetry cabinet that had been his grandda's and opened it up, pulling out a bottle. He always attempted to rotate the latest whiskys from the most current bottling.

He poured himself a dram and sat back at his desk. He buried his mind in his work, although more than once, he thought how he'd like to have Violet there to ask her opinion. The next time he looked at his watch, it was after midnight. He glanced down at his phone and sighed, seeing no messages from Violet. He decided it was time to head home. He'd have a chance to see Violet tomorrow at the sanctuary. They could talk then.

Chapter 40

The Loving Husband

THE FOLLOWING MORNING LACHLAN arrived at the sanctuary later than he'd intended. He'd slept through his alarm—something he hadn't done since he was a teen. His usual morning routine included a lifting session in his home gym, but today, he was already behind, and all he had on his mind was seeing Violet.

He tried on one too many ties and actually cut himself shaving. With the way the day started, he should've known it was a sign for how the rest of the day would go.

When he got to the sanctuary, it seemed like everyone needed to speak to him for one thing or another. One of the horses had taken ill over the weekend, and they had the vet in. Lachlan needed to speak to the vet. Fortunately, it seemed like it wasn't too serious, but the horse would need meds administered two times a day for the next week. Then, the admin staff needed to talk to him about the camp numbers. Then the events team wanted to talk to him about an upcoming teen fest they were planning.

At two p.m., Lachlan finally had a moment to search out Violet. He was surprised he hadn't passed by her yet. He went down to the pasture, sure she must be out there as she hadn't been in the stables, but he didn't find her there. He walked through the makeshift office cubicles, noting that he needed to add it to the list of to-do's to have someone design the space properly, but still no Violet. In fairness, he wasn't sure she even had a workspace in the main room. She spent most of the time working in the back room with him, but she hadn't been there today in the brief moments he'd gone to his desk.

Finally, when he didn't see her, he returned to the front reception. "Hello, Effie, how's things up here?

"Och, Lachlan." A grin lit her face, her eyes crinkling in the corners. "Busy as a bee, but it keeps me young."

"Aye." He agreed, and a blush touched her round cheeks. "Huv ye seen Violet around today?"

"Oh, no, she phoned in earlier. She's feeling under the weather, so she decided to stay put today. Poor thing."

"She's sick?" Lachlan felt instantly concerned.

"Aye, well, she didnae go into detail, but she sounded rather rough on the phone. Hopefully, the lassie will feel better soon."

"Aye. Thanks, Effie." Lachlan was deep in thought when someone else came and snagged him with another fire to put out. He was missing Violet today in more ways than one.

As soon as Lachlan could, he snuck out of the sanctuary and zipped home. After taking Sally for a quick jaunt, he grabbed a container of bone broth soup he'd made a few weeks back from the freezer and headed back out the door. Next, he stopped by the pharmacy and stocked up. Who knew what kind of bug she'd come down with, but Lachlan was going prepared. He picked up cold medication, something for fevers, and something for nausea. Then he grabbed a bottle of ginger ale. Finally, he picked up three grapefruits.

As he stood in line to make his purchases, he saw a couple books on display. One had a burly half-naked dude on the cover—*His Hidden Star* by Eliza Rockwood. The other had a couple kissing on the cover—*Her Hidden Valentine* also by Eliza Rockwood. It brought a smile to his face as it reminded him of the book Violet had on her nightstand that morning he'd picked her up from the hospital.

He wondered if she'd read this author's books. It appeared to be a series. As he got to the till, he picked up a copy of each of the books and stacked them with the other items he was buying. The middle-aged cashier scanned it through and looked at him with a sly smile. He smiled back politely as he tapped his cell phone to pay.

She packed everything into a brown paper bag and leaned forward, looking at him like she needed to tell him a secret. Obligingly, he leaned a little in toward her. "Eliza Rockwood is one of my favourite authors. Are they fer yer wife?" She grinned at him like she'd made a new friend.

Lachlan was thrown off by the question but found himself saying, "Aye."

"Lucky lassie. I'm sure she'll love them." The cashier handed him the paper bag.

"Och, right. Good. Thank ye," he said awkwardly, giving her a little nod as he headed back out to his car. His mind lingered on the *wife* comment. It wasn't the first time he'd told a white lie about being married to the lass. The first time being when he'd gone to see her at the hospital. He mindlessly toyed with the idea of Violet being his wife, waking up to her in the mornings, going to bed with her every night. His cock stirred, and he chided himself for the crazy thought. And yet, oddly enough, it didn't feel crazy at all.

It was seven p.m. by the time he pulled up in front of Violet's cottage. All looked quiet. As he knocked on her front door, his heart quickened. He was surprised that even now, his body reacted to the thought of seeing her. It was a weird phenomenon that he seemed to have no control over whatsoever. He knocked a second time and heard some movement inside. The door opened just enough for Violet to show her face. He knew she wasn't well, but he was still surprised when he saw her heavy, red-rimmed eyes squinting at him. Her pert little nose looked as if she'd been standing in the cold all day. Despite being obviously ill, he still found her to be the most beautiful woman he'd ever laid eyes on.

"Lachlan? What are you doing here?" She sounded all stuffed up.

"Och, lass, I heard ye were under the weather. I thought I'd come by and bring some provisions."

Her eyes widened. "Oh," she said, as if she didn't know what to say at all. "I— You... You didn't have to."

"I ken. I wanted to."

Her forehead creased with an uncertainty that he wanted to kiss away. She let the door open further, and Lachlan realized just how unwell she was. Even though she wore a puffy, oversized pale yellow bathrobe, she shivered with cold and looked about ready to collapse.

"Come on, V. Let's get ye back to bed." For a moment, he thought she was going to turn him away.

Her hand gripped the door, but then she let it go. He closed the door behind him, and Violet was already padding toward the bedroom.

"Sorry, I think I do need to lie back down," she called, with a scratchy voice.

Lachlan followed closely behind. Violet gingerly got onto her bed, as if everything hurt, and then maneuvered carefully under the covers. Her eyes were closed, and she was still shivering. He reached over and laid the back of his hand on her forehead. It was hot, too hot.

"Did ye take any medicine, lass?"

"I don't have any. I'll have to pick something up tomorrow maybe," she croaked.

"Where's the tartan I left for ye? That wool will help to warm ye better than your duvet." He looked around the room.

"Uh, it's in the closet there."

Lachlan found it still in the bag in her closet, which seemed odd, but now was not the time to question her. He retrieved it and lay it over her.

"Thanks, by the way. For the tartan and the flowers." She took a laboured breath. "They're lovely," she said weakly, eyes still closed.

"It's no worry, lass." He didn't care about any of that right now. He was more concerned about Violet. Lachlan headed to the kitchen, found a glass, filled it up with water, and brought it back to the bedroom with a tablet to help bring down her fever. "Here, love, take this," he said.

Violet cracked open one eye and cooed. "You brought me drugs." She sighed as if he were an angel, and he almost laughed. She seemed more excited for the meds than the flowers and tartan he'd given her. She took the pill and swallowed it with a sip of water and lay back down. Her breathing was laboured, but she appeared to be resting.

Lachlan hoped the medicine would kick in soon. He swept a strand of hair off her forehead and stood watching her, wishing he could do more to help her feel better. He looked around the room. Piles of tissues lay on the floor beside the bed and a few on the bed. He found a rubbish bin and put them all in it. *Poor lass.*

He went back to the kitchen to put the broth in the fridge. He pulled the other medicine and grapefruits out of the bag and put them neatly on the counter. He also pulled out the books and smiled to himself. She could maybe enjoy reading them later. He walked back to the bedroom where Violet now slept soundly. He put his hand on her forehead and ran it down gently over her face. She already seemed to have cooled a bit, and he felt some tension let go in his shoulders.

Striding to the nearby chair by the window, he looked out. Quite lovely, the view of the rolling green hills and sea in the distance. He could see why she chose this cottage.

Lachlan dropped down into the chair, settling in as he stretched his long legs out in front of him and crossed them at the ankles. Not exactly how he imagined being in her bedroom would be. Nonetheless, he was glad to be here with her. Glad he *could* be here for her. Not that he wanted Violet sick, but he took great comfort in taking care of her. Protecting her.

He recalled that primal oath that had come to him when he'd made love to her. *Mine*. As silly as it seemed by the light of day, the truth was, he felt it in the marrow of his bones. He'd do anything for this lass. She slept soundly now, and he felt a peace come over him. Lachlan watched her for a time and then opened the book in his hand. *Why not?* He thought to himself and began reading.

Chapter 41

The Light of Day

VIOLET AWOKE STILL RATHER ill, but it felt like she'd turned the corner. Thankfully, her fever had broken. The room was dark. She wanted to get another pill to help her feel better and get back to sleep. She flicked on her night light and saw a glass of water and another pill sitting beside it. She smiled—*Lachlan*. Feeling a bit warm, she slid off her fuzzy robe and discarded it to the end of the bed, then she popped a pill with a sip of water and switched the light back off. When she awoke next, her bedroom was dimly lit. *Must be a cloudy day*, she thought to herself.

The sound of wind and rain confirmed her suspicions as she lay there on her back. Then she tensed, realizing she could hear something else. She got very still and strained to listen. It sounded like heavy breathing. Panic rippled through her.

Slowly, so as not to make a sound, she peered over the covers and scanned her room. She blew out a breath she'd been holding when she saw it was Lachlan. She lay back down and relaxed right before her heart skidded in her chest. *Lachlan.* He was sleeping in her bedroom? *Oh my God*, he must have stayed all night.

She peered back over her blankets. His head was back against the chair, and his arms were loosely folded across his broad chest. He looked good but uncomfortable. She couldn't help but also notice the sexy stubble on his perfect jaw that sent a little tingle through her girl bits. Wow. She must be feeling better. Why did he have to have this effect on her? And why did he have to be so frickin' sweet? Bringing her drugs. Staying the night. How was a girl supposed to resist all of it?

She looked over at the clock. Six a.m. Her head throbbed a little as she sat up, but it wasn't as bad as yesterday. She took a deep breath and gingerly snuck out of the bedroom to the bathroom. By the time she got back to her room, she was freezing. In her haste to leave the room, she hadn't grabbed her robe. Her little cotton PJ shorts and tank top did nothing to keep her warm, and all she wanted to do was plow herself right under her warm blankets. Lachlan stirred as she pulled the covers up around her chin with a shiver.

Rolling his head from side to side and stretching his arms above his head with a groan, he settled back and looked at her. "Good morning." His burr was husky with sleep, and it sent little tingles down her spine.

"Good morning," she said, still stuffed up.

"Ye seem a wee bit better. How are ye feeling?" he asked, moving to sit on the edge of the bed.

She swore he was capable of bringing her fever back on as she felt heat rush to her cheeks at his nearness.

"I think the worst of it has passed." She paused. "Thank you for coming last night and bringing me drugs."

He smiled lightly. "Anytime, lass."

She was still eyeing him from under the blankets. He eyed her back. His crooked smile touched his lips. Her mind went back to the other night, and she wondered if his mind was there, too. She rolled away, hunkering further down in her covers, unable to deal with the sexual tension that was starting to accumulate thick as the morning fog.

She stretched and let out a tension-releasing little growl, and then she looked back at him. "You slept in my chair all night?"

He ran his hands through his hair. The effect was incredibly sexy, and he looked back at the chair as if it had personally offended him. "Aye."

Violet was thoughtful. She couldn't believe that he'd come here to bring her medicine and then stayed the night with her. He truly was such a good man. She was grateful, too. When he'd got to her place the night before, she'd felt so awful. It was comforting to know he'd been there for her. She thought back to the pill he'd left for her on the nightstand. Playing nursemaid for her, again, but she sure did appreciate it. She wondered if she'd ever felt so taken care of.

He stood from the bed and walked toward the door.

"Wait, where are you going?" she called. She didn't want him to leave.

"I'll be right back. Just rest, love."

Lachlan walked out of the room. Did he just call her *love*? Violet settled back in on her pillows, and before she could think on it too much, she drifted off to sleep.

When she woke up, Lachlan was asleep in the chair again. She caught sight of something on her bedside table. Pink juice. She picked it up and tried to smell it. Her nose was still plugged, but she thought she could make out the faint scent of grapefruit. She had a sip, and even though she couldn't really taste it, its tart sweetness was satisfying.

Lachlan hadn't really been asleep, just resting his eyes. He heard her stir and saw her sip the juice he'd put out for her. "My ma always gave us freshly squeezed grapefruit juice whenever we were sick as kids. She swore it would make us well again." Lachlan was watching her from the chair.

"And did it?" she asked, taking another sip.

He contemplated for a moment. "Well, let's just say I still make it anytime I get sick."

She smiled at him. "Thank you. It's good."

Lachlan picked up his phone to check the time. "I should get going."

He stood up and stretched, and as he did, Violet pulled off her covers, got out of the bed, and stood before him. And in an instant, his cock thickened. She no longer wore the thick robe that she'd looked so cute in, sick and all. Instead, she wore some skimpy shorts and a thin tank top that left very little to the imagination, and how he'd imagined—over and over again. God help him, now was not the time to be picturing slamming his cock into her perfect slender body that he knew was made for him.

Barely able to keep control of his aroused cock, her arms wrapped around his waist, and she leaned into him. Those perfectly pointed nipples pinned him. *Christ.* He reminded himself that she wasn't well. Ravishing her senseless was *not* an option this morning. She sighed into him, and he wrapped his arms around her, registering just how right it felt to hold her to him. He pulled her in closer and kissed the top of her head. Despite the arousal that threatened to drown him, he realized he could happily stay like this for hours, just holding her in his arms. It was like two pieces of a puzzle fitting together perfectly.

"I'll let Effie ken that ye willnae be in at the sanctuary today," Lachlan finally said.

"I'll try and come this afternoon."

"Och, lass, just stay put." He dropped a kiss on her forehead, grateful it was not scorching hot like it had been last night. "Besides, no one wants yer germs."

She gave him a little shove. "Hey!"

He chuckled, wrapping his arms around her shoulders, hugging her to him. He didn't want to let her go, but he knew he needed to head out. Reluctantly releasing her, he started toward the door. "I left some bone broth in the fridge. It's another thing my mam used to give us kids." He winked at her.

"Thanks, Lachlan," she said, and she padded back to her bed as he slipped out her bedroom door.

Lachlan was somewhat relieved to make his exit from Violet's. He was on the verge of being completely ungentlemanly. Seemed to be becoming a bit of an issue when he was around her. When she hopped out of bed in her skimpy bed clothes and pressed herself against him, it was all he could do to not peel away her clothes right there and then, sick or not. It didn't help that he'd read that bloody book before falling asleep. It was a love story, but the sex scenes were like reading porn. He actually found that he didn't want to put it down.

It surprised him how much it drew him in. Certainly not his usual reading.

Driving back to his place, he stretched his neck trying to get a kink out. He didn't sleep well in that chair, but there was no way he was going to leave Violet. He had awoken a few times and checked on her. It was awfully tempting to hop into the bed beside her, but he didn't think it was right to assume he'd be welcome there.

He didn't bring up anything about the other night. It didn't seem like the right time to talk about it or about them. It did strike him as odd that he hadn't noticed the flowers he'd gotten her, and the tartan had been in the back of her closet. At some point, when she was feeling better, they would have a chance to talk.

Sally greeted Lachlan as he walked through his back door, and he grabbed her leash to take her for a walk before heading to the distillery. When they got back to the house, his cell phone rang, and he pulled it from his pocket, hoping it was Violet. It wasn't. And in the span of a few moments, his world was thrown into hell.

Chapter 42

Radio Silence...Again.

VIOLET RELUCTANTLY TOOK LACHLAN'S advice and stayed home. She slept almost all day and through the following night. Her body must have needed it.

The following day she dragged her butt out of bed. She was not 100 percent, but definitely better. She showered, had a bite of breakfast, and headed to the sanctuary for her shift. She hoped she'd see Lachlan, but he wasn't there. She hadn't heard from him since he'd left the morning before, aside from a quick text response to one she'd sent him thanking him again.

The week went by, and she still hadn't heard anything from Lachlan, nor had she seen him. She had texted him a couple of times but got nothing back. She didn't want it to sting, but it did. She wondered if he had maybe gone on a business trip, but even so, why wouldn't he just message her?

Violet headed home Friday from a styling appointment. She'd had an awesome day working on a new wardrobe for one of the few clients she'd kept on.

Once she was home, she decided scotch was in order for her Friday night. It wasn't as good as the scotch Lachlan had given her at his house and the distillery, but it would suffice.

She went and sat in her quaint back yard. It was late on a mild summer's night. A thousand stars pricked tiny holes in the clear, dark sky. She sipped her scotch and looked off into the distance at the rolling hills and seaside. God, it was heaven here. She wrapped her lovely new tartan blanket a little tighter around her shoulders. She was glad he'd brought it out for her the other night. She'd maybe been a bit hasty when she'd stashed it away.

Lachlan was on her mind, as per usual. He was a mystery to her. She struggled to know what he wanted with her, if anything at all. In some ways, she felt sure he must be into her and want to see her, but then at the same time, he always seemed careful and reserved. The one night he let loose and gave in to passion seemed like a lifetime ago, almost as if she'd imagined it. Perhaps it was just the excitement of the night, the scotch—the magic in the air.

As much as she was trying to guard her heart from him, he kept breaking down her walls, whether he was trying to or not. She tried to take everything at face value and not read into anything, tried to harden her heart. But he was in it, far more than she felt comfortable with.

She eyed the flowers he'd brought her. Were they meant to say, *Thanks for the quickie sex—that was cut woefully short—now let's just be friends?* Oh, what a crazy, passionate night it had been. She had no intention of making out with him, but it was like she was under a spell that night. Who knew? Maybe it was just the magic of the night. She felt aroused just thinking about it. Curse him.

Then less than a week ago, he'd come to her rescue, bringing her medicine and freaking homemade broth and freshly squeezed juice. He'd even stayed the night. She'd felt so taken care of, so safe. He must care for her. But then he dropped off and went quiet, disappearing from her world.

Way too familiar of a scenario. Last time, he'd taken care of her too and then dropped off the face of the earth. Was the same thing happening again? The thought annoyed her. What was his deal? She felt so confused and fed up. But her heart wasn't ready to give up just yet.

Chapter 43
Guilt and Blame

Nothing could have prepared him for the phone call he received that morning. It was his mam. He barely recognized the quiet, agonized voice on the other end. There had been an accident, and Orlagh was in the hospital. His mom could barely speak. He knew it was bad. He was already back out to his car before hanging up with her.

Lachlan headed straight for the hospital. Fear gripped him like cold, hard steel. It was more than he could take. He couldn't lose another sister. He wouldn't lose her. It brought back memories and pain that he tried so hard to keep at bay.

When he arrived at the hospital, the first person he saw was Drew. Lachlan was taken aback. He didn't expect to see his delinquent brother there. He stood with his back leaning against the pale green hospital wall, his arms crossed, arrogant and serious.

Lachlan was already reeling. He didn't know how to face Drew on top of everything else. He couldn't handle his brother's anger, his judgment.

Drew noted Lachlan's arrival. They eyed each other without saying a word. Alex stood beside Drew, a near carbon copy stance—leaning against the wall, arms crossed over his chest. Although, unlike Drew, he was staring down at the floor as if he wished it would open up and take him away.

Their mam and da stood from waiting room chairs when they saw Lachlan. His mam ran up to him and wrapped her arms around him in a sob.

"Och, Lachlan," she cried into his shirt.

He held her close, with his heart breaking. His da patted him on the back. His whole demeanour was racked with pain.

"What's going on? What's happening?" Lachlan's voice was choked.

Drew's voice was calm and even. "She's in surgery right now." He took a deep breath, avoiding Lachlan's eyes. "She stepped off the curb, and a lorrie came charging around the bend." His voice caught, and he looked up to the ceiling as if that would stop the tears from falling from his eyes.

"I'm gonna lock that fucker up and throw away the key," Alex growled from the corner of the room.

"Language, Alex," his mother scolded him, the habit so misplaced at a time like this.

"Ye were there?" Lachlan stated, looking back at Drew as realization dawned.

"Aye," he said with a deadly calm, but he couldn't hide the anguish on his face.

Lachlan was stunned.

"There was nothing Drew could huv done, Lachlan," his mother interjected, like she felt the need to defend him. "It all happened so quickly."

Lachlan felt hollow, and at the same time, iron squeezed his ribs from the inside. He struggled to think straight. He just wanted to know that his sister was going to be okay.

"What are her injuries? Is she going to be all right?" Lachlan asked, doing his best to keep his composure.

"We dinnae ken all the details yet," his da answered. "All we ken is that she was bleeding internally." His voice cracked, and Lachlan's chest hollowed deeper. "They are trying to help her, lad."

Lachlan put an arm around his da, wishing he could comfort him.

They sat agonizing in silence as time crept by. Pacing. Waiting. Silence. Fear. Denial. Hope. It was terrible. Memories of another tragedy the family had already suffered through washed anew. Lachlan didn't want to think about Helena, but his mind paralleled then and now like a two-lane treacherous race track.

It was more than memories. It felt as if the emotions, the experience, the pain were all being relived. The guilt that never fully went away surfaced again. It clawed at Lachlan now like a beast that had awoken. Reminding himself he wasn't to blame for Helena's death didn't help.

He glanced over at his brother. Pain and worry etched Drew's features. He could blame Drew for what they were all going through now. But that was not what Lachlan felt toward his brother. As he looked at Drew, he vividly recalled the years of blame that he had endured. Drew had been so angry and had held a grudge against Lachlan ever since Helena's death. He hurled all his fury at Lachlan and then finally silence and distance. He was back now, and although they had a run-in with each other, Lachlan didn't truly know what his brother felt for him now—if anything.

What Lachlan realized, though, was that he didn't blame Drew, and that surprised him. Lachlan knew that Drew couldn't have done anything. He knew exactly what Drew was feeling. He'd felt it like a molten knife in his gut all those years ago. Guilt. The what-ifs. They could make you go insane. He could see it on his brother's face, in the hunch of his shoulders. No, Lachlan didn't blame Drew. He empathized w ith him.

Lachlan realized as clear as day. If Drew could have changed the situation, prevented what happened, there was no doubt he would have. If he had any power, any chance of saving Orlagh from a horrible fate, he wouldn't have hesitated. They might not see eye to eye, but Lachlan knew without a shadow of a doubt that Drew loved his family, despite everything.

The truth was, what had happened was out of his control. He couldn't have done anything, or he would have, plain and simple. Accidents happened. Shit happened. And Lachlan knew his family had had their fair share of shit happening, but here they were, helpless to change it.

Lachlan took a fortifying breath and, for the first time, felt a little lighter. All the words people had tried to reassure him with, comfort him with, over the years, fell on deaf ears. But this? Suddenly, Lachlan got it. He understood the truth. He couldn't have saved Helena either, because if he could have, he would have a thousand times over. But there was nothing he could have done. It was beyond him, out of his control.

It was like something finally clicked into place. Lachlan might have felt a sense of relief, but the current situation left no room for such emotions. Right now, he was afraid and feeling a desperate begging hope.

"Mr. and Mrs. Mackenzie?" A women's voice broke the silence. "I'm Doctor Chalmers."

Lachlan's da stood up, his hand on his mam's shoulder to support himself as much as to give her comfort.

"Orlagh is out of surgery. She was in pretty rough shape, but fortunately, we were able to stop the bleeding. She's resting now. It's probably best if ye try and get some rest as well.

"Is she going to be okay?" his da asked. His voice was tight with pent-up emotion and fear.

"Well, as I said, we've stopped the bleeding, so that is good. But it is early yet. We will be monitoring her closely. We've done all we can for now. Now it's up to her to fight."

The reality of the situation felt like a dull ache in Lachlan's chest and mind. He desperately wanted to hear that Orlagh would heal and be well again—that she was going to bounce back. The somber air was thick and heavy.

Chapter 44
Good Fucking Riddance

THE NEXT FEW DAYS were long and painful, and yet time seemed to stand still. It was like the Mackenzies were stuck in some kind of time warp. Lachlan went to the hospital each day, as did his family. Orlagh was holding steady but hadn't shown any signs of improvement. It was so hard to see her this way. Lachlan would sit in her room holding her hand, willing her to open her eyes and chatter away to him. Six long days had gone by without any real change. Orlagh hadn't gained consciousness yet.

Thankfully, the doctors said her vitals were strong. That was what they clung to.

Lachlan's phone buzzed in his pocket. He looked at it and saw it was Violet. She'd texted and called a couple of times. Part of him wanted to talk to her, see her. But he was in such a horrible head space. Too much was going on. He didn't think he could deal with the complete juxtaposition of emotions he felt for her as compared to the pain he was in over his sister. He knew he should answer her, but he just couldn't right now.

He pressed the off button and stuck his phone back in his pocket. He looked back at his sister's pale face. Her features were relaxed, peaceful. He stroked her cheek. He could imagine Orlagh giving him heck for not taking Violet's call. Yep, Orlagh would be giving him hell right now if she were awake. Telling him he should reach out to Violet.

Lachlan sat back in the hospital chair. Maybe she was right. Maybe he should. He ran a hand through his hair. He missed Violet. He wasn't sure he could handle her wonderfulness, though. She was like a happy drug for him, and right now, he didn't think he could do happy. *Do happy?* He could see Orlagh rolling her eyes at the sentiment. Orlagh liked Violet. "Ack Rolo, I need your advice, wake up love." But Olragh laid still, not reacting. Her peaceful state was unchanging. Lachlan sighed heavily. "See ye tomorrow then." He kissed her forehead and left her room.

Lachlan headed to the beach to try and clear his head. He noticed someone jogging along the shoreline. The sun was setting. He couldn't help but be reminded of that fateful night he'd met Violet. What a crazy experience that was.

God, but there was something about her that drew him in from the moment he saw her. She was magnetic. She had a way of making him feel fulfilled and happy just by being in her presence.

A hint of a smile touched his lips. The first in days. It struck him. It wasn't just about seeing Violet. He needed her. She made his world a better place, and he was in sore need of that now. Lachlan decided he'd call her when he got back home.

At first, he didn't notice her sitting on the steps out front when he pulled up his gravel drive. Lachlan closed his car door, thinking about Violet, when the very voice of his dreams startled him.

"Hey."

"Violet, what are ye doing here?" He was so taken aback at seeing her, he realized belatedly that it was the wrong thing to say.

"Checking if you're alive, which clearly you are," she snapped. "You can take back your blanket and flowers." She shoved them toward him. He took them uneasily. She was clearly ticked at him. *Shite.* Not that he could blame her exactly, but he hadn't seen this side of Violet. She was always so amiable and sweet.

"Consider this my notice."

Tearing his gaze away from her perfect ass that swung back and forth as she marched away from him, his brain caught up with what she meant, and he realized he needed to fix things. Now.

"V, wait," he called out to her, knowing he'd royally fucked up. When she didn't respond, he started after her. "Wait, please dinnae leave."

She turned around abruptly with her arms crossed tightly under her perky boobs. "What?" Her voice was clipped.

He'd never her seen her so feisty, and he inwardly chided himself for liking it.

"Where are ye going?" he asked, still not sure what to say. This was not like him in the least, he always knew what to say.

An unimpressed smile touched her mouth. "Home," she said tightly. And suddenly, he feared that *home* meant back to Canada.

"You're mad at me?" he said softly.

"I'm confused by you. You treat me like an equal with business, but with everything else, you are all over the map. I don't like games, Lachlan. And it seems to me that *you* do. One minute, you're hot and heavy. The next, you're bringing me soup, and then the next, you ghost me. I'm out. Done. No more games. It's exhausting. I brought you back the flowers and tartan because I don't want them. I don't want the games. Not interested. And as much as I love it at Highland Haven, I can't stay. I just can't." She turned on her heel and started to walk away again.

"Violet, ye dinnae understand." His anger suddenly pricked, the emotional exhaustion of the past few days catching up to him. She had it all wrong, damn it. "I'm no' playing games," he called out to her, his own tone more short than he intended.

"Call it what you want, Lachlan. I'm done," she snapped, dismissively.

Lachlan felt her jilt. Damn her for looking sexy as hell as she walked away from him. Her black jeans hugged her shapely thighs, and there was nothing more hot than a woman who could stomp away in high heels. Didn't she understand what she did to him? Didn't she understand how much he needed her? Hungered for her like some kind of pent-up tiger who hadn't eaten in a week.

"Violet," he called again, gruffly knowing there was no way on God's green earth he could let her just walk out of his life.

"What?" she said, clearly frustrated as she whipped around. "What, Lachlan? What do you want from me?

'Cause from where I stand, it doesn't seem like much. I'm not going to be strung along." She raged at him, and it only served to heighten his own raw emotions.

Lachlan was usually a very patient person, but with all that had been going on, he felt frayed. His blood began to simmer. A wicked combination of ragged emotion and pent-up desire. He spoke slowly as he tried to wrangle in his frustration.

"Could ye please come in so we can talk?"

She was a good ten paces away and not taking any warning from his tone because she stubbornly called back to him. "Nope. No, Lachlan. You know what? I'm done with talking," she snapped.

As am I, he thought to himself. And without another thought, he discarded the flowers and tartan he'd been holding, and he closed the distance between them in three determined strides.

"Bloody stubborn lass!" he growled as he scooped her up and unceremoniously threw her over his shoulder.

She squealed in outrage. "What are you doing? You neanderthal!" she hollered, squirming against him, which was not helping her cause in the least.

Lachlan felt like a feral beast, and he didn't care. Something had snapped in him. *Saint Lachlan* had been thrown over the proverbial cliff. *Good fucking riddance.* He held firmly around her waist, carrying her like a whisky barrel on his shoulder. The more she wriggled, the tighter he held her.

Chapter 45
No More Games

"PUT ME DOWN, YOU brute." She squirmed again.

He spanked her ass.

"Lachlan!" she raged, furiously. "Put me down!"

Violet didn't know what she was more angry about, the fact he'd hauled her over his shoulder and smacked her ass or the fact she liked it! It was like something snapped, and the reserved, keep it calm, cool, and collected Lachlan got shoved aside by roaring, raw Lachlan. If it wasn't Lachlan, she might have been scared, but she knew from the very start that Lachlan would only ever protect her. He'd never hurt her. Good, maybe he'd fucking realize that he cared for her!

Taking her up his front steps, he put her down as unceremoniously as he'd picked her up. Her feet barely touched the ground, and she regained her balance before he leaned in close to her, causing her pounding heart to stall. Her back touched against the cool wood of the large front door.

Lachlan put his arms on either side of her shoulders and pressed his hands against the door, trapping her. She shoved against his chest, pushing him, but he didn't budge an inch. Despite the shiver that ran down her spine, she lifted her chin in defiance.

His recklessly handsome face was close to hers, and his blue eyes glittered wildly. She swallowed hard, wanting to bite and kiss him in equal measure, but instead, she just glared up at him, unable to calm her racing pulse.

"Ye dinnae want to talk?" His voice was edged with something she couldn't quite put her finger on, but danger was the word coming to mind.

"I—" Before she could answer, he pressed his rock-solid body against hers, and then he moved against her, ensuring she felt the rod that was thick between them. Her breath hitched, and her body betrayed her, again, tingling hungrily at the feel of him.

He dipped his face to her neck. His late-day stubble dragged deliciously against her as he breathed her in. A soft sigh of pleasure escaped her lips.

She whispered his name, "Lachlan." She wanted to tell him no, to be strong to his charms, but she was losing the battle. His sexy smell was intoxicating, the heat of his hard body slammed against hers, and the hunger in his touch, his breathing—she was melting. Her knees felt ready to give out. She pressed her hands against the cool wood door behind her to try and gather her senses, to ground herself. She shouldn't go down this slippery slope with him. She needed more from him but was so afraid he'd never give her what she truly wanted—something more than just sex. But as much as her mind tried to warn her, her body silenced it.

He spoke near her ear, his warm breath caressing against her skin as he did. "Let's no' talk then." His burr was rich and deep and penetrated her. His lips trailed softly down her bare neck, and she sensed reserved, strained hunger with every touch of his mouth. Her body felt heavy and weightless all at the same time. She tingled with anticipation. Suspended.

The tension sizzled between them, unlike anything she'd ever experienced. He pulled away to look at her, that same searching look he'd given her in the cask room as if making sure she wanted this.

This time, she answered his unspoken question with words. "Make love to me, Lachlan."

"Och, Christ, V," he breathed raggedly, his voice strained with emotion. "Aye."

Not wasting another moment, he claimed her mouth with a growl that had her whimpering. He kissed her mouth with carnal need, and she wrapped her arms around his neck, not wanting him to stop.

Hungrily, he kissed her. His hands grabbed her butt, hoisting her easily up to him, and she wrapped her thighs around his waist. With one arm wrapped around her waist, holding her strongly, he fumbled with his key and unlocked the door. He carried her in, slamming the door shut behind them.

She tore her mouth away from his. "No more games, Lachlan," she said breathlessly but determinedly. She couldn't forget why she'd come here. Initially, she'd hoped to talk things through with him. But as she sat waiting, she'd changed her mind. Fed up with being strung along, she had talked herself out of figuring things out. Enough was enough.

Shit. And now here she was, bravado all but gone. If he couldn't at least give her some reassurance, then she needed to walk away once and for all. Given the fact that every cell in her body ached desperately for him, she didn't know how she would accomplish that feat, so she just hoped to God that her gut was right about him and that he'd agree to her terms—*No more games.*

He still held her up, and she could feel the thick head of his dick pressed against her sensitive core, taunting her cruelly, as they looked at each other eye to eye. Those cerulean blue eyes that were her lifeline could still reach into her soul like nothing else ever could.

"No games, V. I promise," he said, and maybe it was crazy, but she believed him.

She almost whimpered in relief. For now, that was all she needed. His lips touched hers in a slow, delicious kiss—a seal of the promise made. His tongue expertly teased and tasted hers. Sighing into him, she wrapped her legs tighter around his waist and put her hand on his strong chiseled jaw, and she could feel his sexy crooked smile against her lips, making her desperate to have him inside her.

As if hearing her silent plea, the head of his cock bluntly rubbed against her in her jeans. He knew just how to move against her, despite the layers of fabric between them.

Violet wanted this man. She needed satisfaction. Her body needed him. Her mind needed him. She hoped to God his promise was enough, but she'd find a way to pick up the pieces after if need be. Right now, she wanted him with every fiber of her being, every ounce of her soul.

Lachlan let her down, and she felt bereft, but only for a moment. He turned her around so her back was against the inside of the door. His eyes were fervent on hers as he dropped to his knees in front of her.

"Lachlan, I don't know if we should..." She didn't even know what she was going to say, but her words were cut short.

"Aye, lass, we should." His voice was determined, and his Scottish burr sealed the deal. His hands held on either side of her denim-clad hips, and then he ran them down the length of her legs as if committing their feel to memory.

Those big, strong hands on her curves made her feel so feminine. He ran them back up to her hips, and then he went for the button on her jeans. Methodically, he unbuttoned them and pulled down the zipper, exposing the front of her pink polka dot cotton panties. She hadn't anticipated the evening veering in this direction. She scrunched her eyes closed, realizing they weren't the most sexy of underwear, but if Lachlan's reaction were any indication, they might as well have been crotchless lace.

"Och god, lass." He pressed his face against her cotton-panty-clad crotch and breathed her in like he hadn't eaten in a week and she was a fresh-out-of-the-oven loaf of bread.

Violet could have laughed, but she was too busy trembling with need as he peeled her jeans off her hips and ass and then down her thighs. He stopped there. Lachlan tugged her cotton panties to the side and then looked up at her before dipping his head between her legs. She felt his warm, wet tongue run the length of her, and she had to fight to keep her knees from buckling.

Violet was breathless. She felt almost drugged. He swiped his tongue over her again, and then, to her disappointment, he stopped. She opened her eyes and looked down at him. His blue eyes were almost black when his eyes locked with hers as he put his fingers in the sides of her panties. He slowly, agonizingly pulled them down, leaving her hungry core fully exposed to him where he was kneeling in front of her. Violet ran her hands through his dark hair, barely able to take the need building within her.

Chapter 46
Revelation

Lachlan's cock jolted with sweet torment. He was rock-hard, but he needed to taste more of her first. He licked slowly at her wetness, and it nearly drove him over the edge. He'd never felt such white hot lust. He groaned as he opened her folds with his tongue and licked the deepest part of her like he'd uncovered treasure. He found her sensitive nub and mercilessly tasted and devoured her, savouring the feel of that tiny pulsing pearl on his tongue. He could feel her desire building. God, he wanted her to come against his tongue. He wanted to drink her pleasure.

"Lachlan," she breathed, her hands fisting his hair. "I need you inside of me."

How could he deny her anything she wanted with a voice and body of an angel? Nothing was going to stop him from fulfilling her every desire.

He pulled off one of her blue stitched denim high-heeled shoes and then the other, tossing them aside. Then he peeled off each pant leg and cast her jeans aside as well. She stood before him with her innocuous polka dot panties pulled tight around her thighs and still in her leather bomber jacket. Sexy didn't even begin to describe her.

He stood up, sliding off his jacket before starting on the buttons of his shirt. She took off her bomber, revealing a sleeveless white blouse beneath that she lifted over her head, discarding it beside her jacket.

His breath hitched as he took in the sight of her perky tits straining against the thin fabric of her bra."Och, V, ye are too beautiful for words, lass."

She smiled up at him. Stepping forward, she took over unbuttoning his dress shirt, and all he could do was watch, utterly mesmerized. Once she'd undone the last button, those magic hands of hers slid over the fiery skin of his chest, causing his muscles to flex under her touch. He could barely breathe as her fingers skimmed down his abs and began to unbuckle his belt. He put his hands on hers and took over, needing the deed done.

They stood before each other, appreciating each other's assets. Violet pulled down her panties from her curvy thighs, letting them drop down, and she stepped out of them.

Lachlan watched her every move with intense fascination. His cock was throbbing, desperate for friction. It was sweet torture. Violet reached behind her and undid her bra. Her blush nipples protruded proudly. He'd never seen such perfect breasts before. Her bra slipped from her fingers, and Lachlan's mouth watered at the sight of her completely naked before him.

"My god, lass, I want to taste every square inch of ye."

Lachlan stepped toward her, raking his hand up into her long blond hair and pulling her lips to his, searing them in a feral kiss. Her breasts crushed against his chest, causing his already hard cock to thicken even more. Then he gripped a handful of her hair at the base of her head and tugged back to expose her creamy neck. He kissed his way down to one pink nipple and sucked it hard into his mouth, causing her to bestow upon him a cock teasing feminine groan. God, she was so intoxicating.

As he suckled and licked her glorious breasts, her hand reached between them, and she began to tug down his boxer briefs. It was satisfying knowing that she wanted him. Breaking their kiss, he quickly pealed them off, freeing his hungry cock. Violet's eyes were glued to his manhood, taking in the sight of him, and it made him feel like a God. He knew he was well endowed, but never had it mattered as much as it did right now. He would make sure to pleasure her well and good with this hammer of his.

"Can I—" She stared at his dick, and her tongue darted out, licking her cupid lips, and as if on cue, pre-come slid out of him, making her eyes widen with intrigue. God, if he wasn't careful, he'd come too soon, but there was no way he'd deny her unspoken request.

"Aye," he croaked.

Violet, as graceful as a ballerina, dropped to her knees before him. She put her hand around him, and he clenched his bloody ass cheeks trying to keep it together. He looked down right as her red tongue slipped out and licked the wet tip of his cock. He groaned, his head rolling back. And next, he felt her lips, and then her entire hot, warm mouth wrap around him, and he trembled, holding on by a thread. She slid his cock into her mouth, and his balls tightened. He gripped her hair, pulling—painfully pulling her sweet torturous mouth from him. She looked up at him, her eyes questioning.

"Did I do it wrong?" she asked.

Lachlan wondered if he'd heard her correctly.

"I've never— I've never done this before."

He wondered how in the hell he'd gotten so lucky. Obviously, she wasn't a virgin—that was clear from the night of the gala—but to know that he was the first man she'd taken into that sweet, sweet mouth. *The only man*, he corrected. To know he was sharing something with her that no one else had meant so much to him. "Believe me, lass. Ye did it verra right."

Before he could stop himself, he had to know. He took her hands and pulled her back up to stand before him. He clasped her chin in his hand and looked into her beautiful green eyes. "And how about the other way around?"

He took her hand in his and guided it between their naked bodies, sliding the tips of her fingers over her glossy wet nub. She whimpered and leaned into him, her nipples grazing his abdomen. He held her hand, coaxing two of her fingers up into her tight channel— he loved that she let him.

"Has anyone ever tasted ye before me?" He couldn't keep the huskiness from his voice as he brought her glistening fingers back up between them and slid them into his mouth, sucking off her honey sweet taste with a groan.

She shook her head. "You are the first." Her voice was soft, and his heart thudded in satisfaction.

It pleased him more than it should. Lachlan wanted her. *Now.* He effortlessly scooped her up into his arms, and she let out a surprised little squeal. He kissed her mouth and winked at her, carrying her up the stairs.

He lay her naked body on his bed. God, how he'd dreamed of this. He climbed over her. The thick head of his cock nudged against the juncture between her thighs, and their eyes locked. He struggled not to just slam into her. Reaching up, he ran his palm lightly over her breast, marvelling at the sensation. He was feral with need for this woman. He squeezed the tip of her nipple between his thumb and forefinger, and she arched against him. He ducked his head to taste and suckle her.

"Lachlan, please," she whimpered. Her hands gripped his shoulders.

His desire overwhelmed him. He rubbed his cock against her wetness and then drew back and pushed himself into her warm wet tightness, throwing his head back and groaning.

And then, he began to move, pulling in and out of her, slowly at first, and he caught her moan in his mouth. He drove into her over and over, and she met his rhythm. He pulled back to his knees and hiked her up on top of him, pumping her up and down on his thick length, feeling her juices run down his balls and loving how damn wet she was for him.

"Don't stop." She bit into his shoulder.

He held her waist, burying his cock deep inside her and then lifting her up before sliding her back down on him—over and over—mesmerized by the ecstasy on her beautiful face. Then he reached a hand into her hair, pulling those swollen red lips to his and tasting her arousal. She arched and groaned into his mouth, shaking, and he felt her hot sheath quiver and clamp around his cock making his own release explode from him in a roar. He pulled her down hard on his spurting cock one more time before laying her back on the bed where he collapsed down on her.

He was breathing heavy, still coming down from the most epic orgasm of his life, when he realized he might be squishing Violet beneath him. He lifted himself to his forearms, still buried deep inside her, and looked down at her flushed face. She smiled at him with her cheeks all flushed and hair mussed from their lovemaking. It was the best smile he'd ever seen. He stroked a stray piece of hair away from her pretty face and kissed the tip of her nose.

The way he looked at her now tugged her heart wide open. She was afraid to hope that this was more than just the most incredibly amazing sex of all time. Even if this ended up being a huge mistake, she would have no regrets. What she just shared with Lachlan went beyond anything she'd ever imagined. She'd had sex before, but it was nothing like this, not by a long shot. This was something completely different. It felt like they had gone to a different world together. Lost in a perfect dream.

As they lay there, she registered for the first time that his stubble was a bit more than his evening five o'clock shadow. In all the time she'd known Lachlan, he was always clean-shaven, and it was only in the evening that he'd have that sexy bit of stubble. She found the extra facial hair sexy.

It fit the rugged wild man who'd carried her in here and spanked her butt. She smiled thinking about it.

"What's that smile about?" he asked, his crooked grin lifting the corner of his mouth.

"Nothing," she said, still smiling up at him.

"No?" He moved in her, and she felt his hardness filling her up again as he slowly ground his hips into hers. "You ken what I'm thinking about?"

She felt breathless as he continued to slowly move in and out of her, gently making love to her. "Mm-mm." She gently shook her head, lifting her legs to take him in more fully.

"I'm thinking I may never let ye leave this bed." He rolled his hips into her again, making her breath catch as the thick head of his cock jammed against her g-spot.

"I see," she managed to say as he started trailing kisses over her jaw and down her neck. "And what about my job?" she asked breathlessly, feeling a building tingle of pleasure.

"I thought you resigned." He looked down at her, still slowly sliding in and out of her body. She wrapped her ankles around his calves, loving the feel of his big muscular body on hers.

"Maybe I changed my mind," she said, nipping his lips. "Do you think my boss will have me back?"

"Aye, I suspect he could be convinced. Ye may huv to make it up to him, though." He leaned to the side on his elbow, pulling her body to face his so he could still make love to her, but he brought his other hand to her breast, his fingers toying with her nipple. And it felt like a button that lead straight to her throbbing clit.

"Mmhmm," she half whimpered. "And what could I do to make it up to him?"

He ducked his head, taking her achy nipple into his mouth. His tongue expertly stoked her desires like he knew her body better than she did. She arched into him, lost in the feeling of Lachlan's mouth on her.

"Ride him." Without warning, he rolled on his back and lifted her on top of him, their bodies still joined.

Violet let out a squeal, but then Lachlan slammed into her from where she now straddled him, hitting her g-spot with glorious precision. She grabbed his hard chest to steady herself and looked down into his eyes that were filled with desire, and then she did what he said and rode him hard until her orgasm rocked her and his chased on the heels of hers.

Chapter 47
A New Day

VIOLET AWOKE AND QUICKLY became aware of Lachlan beside her. His breathing was deep and steady. The room was dark aside from the silvery light from the moon outside that cast a ghostly glow in his bedroom. She shivered and carefully slid out of the bed, trying not to disturb him.

Violet tiptoed to the bathroom. She was so sleepy. She made it quick. She felt chilled as she got back into the bed, and she quickly nuzzled under the covers. Strong, warm arms wrapped around her. Lachlan pulled her body in close to his. It was heaven. She felt so secure and safe in his arms. It felt so right.

She couldn't help the little seed of doubt, though. Everything felt so perfect. The night had been beyond her wildest dreams, but had anything changed? She still didn't know why Lachlan had basically ghosted her, and he hadn't given her any indication that he intended for whatever this was to be more than just a night, more than just a fling. It felt like so much more, but was it? Violet was falling desperately in love, whether she wanted to admit it or not.

Deep in thought, she felt his lips on the back of her neck, and she melted against him. God help her. She rolled over and faced him in the cool darkness of the moonlight, but she could see his eyes intense on hers as he entered her again. Lachlan's eyes didn't leave hers as he slowly made sweet love to her. In no time, they both climaxed before drifting off to sleep again in a tangle of limbs.

Sunlight poured into Lachlan's bedroom. Violet opened her eyes and stretched out like a cat who'd got the cream. She was sore but satiated. The door to the bathroom clicked open, and Lachlan walked into the bedroom. He was cleanly shaven and wore slim-legged blue dress pants with a crisp white button-up shirt and tie. Mr. GQ.

"Good morning, love." He gave her one of his devastatingly handsome crooked smiles, with his fresh aftershave scent filling her senses.

Mmm, the man was so yummy.

"Good morning." She pulled the bedding up over her chest and scanned the room for her clothes and then recalled they were all downstairs. Memories of last night trickled through her mind and gave her a delicious shiver.

Lachlan sat on the edge of the bed and tugged the bedding back down off her breasts, dipping his head kissing one nipple and then the other. She threw her head back in a giggle.

"Do ye ken how perfect these are?" he said, gripping one in each hand and sampling both again with his mouth. "Mm, god, I dinnae want to leave."

"Then don't," she said, tugging on his tie and pulling his mouth to hers. Violet could drown in his kiss.

“Unfortunately, I huv to go," he said, his lips still kissing her.

She reached her hand into his lap and wrapped it around the hard length of him in his dress pants.

"I think you should stay." She let her tongue sweep against his.

He pulled away, panting. "Believe me, if I could, I would. Ye stay, though." He looked at her and stroked her hair from her face. "Make yerself at home. Sally will be glad fer the company."

Violet adored Lachlan's dog, but she'd prefer him as company.

“No, no, I should go too.” She sobered.

“Ye really dinnae have to.” He tried to convince her, but it felt odd to just stay at his house.

And what was he going to do that was so important? It was Saturday. Was he working? God, why didn't she feel like she could just ask him? But there it was. Somehow, even after the epic night together, there was still some kind of barrier between them.

"I have some things I want to get done today." She smiled lightly.

“Aye, of course.” He seemed to understand that it would be odd for her to just stay at his house and wait for him. "Can I see ye later on, though?”

She nodded, mixed emotions warring in her. On the one hand, she was glad he wanted to see her again, but on the other, she could sense that something was going on that he wasn't telling her. It felt like there was so much they needed to talk about, and yet it felt like he was shutting her out somehow.

Lachlan wanted to talk with Violet, but he wanted to wait until they had time and wouldn’t feel rushed. Unfortunately, this morning wasn’t that time, despite him wishing it was.

There was so much he needed to tell her. About Orlagh. About his feelings. The truth was he was crazy about Violet, and last night just solidified it. He had so much he wanted to say. But right now, he had a quick business meeting—one he considered skipping, but it was a new buyer from the States who had agreed to squeeze this meeting into his brief jaunt in the UK, and then he was going straight to the hospital to see how his sister faired. He'd had a text this morning from Alex, saying that she seemed to stir a bit last night, and they thought she might wake today. He was afraid to hope.

It was hard to leave the lass who was still lying naked in his bed, but he had to. For now. God, he couldn't wait to get back to her.

Violet was biting her Cupid's bow lip, looking pensive. He couldn't leave her without putting a smile back on her face.

"Ye are beautiful, lass," he said as he kissed her lips. He held the kiss, and then he took her head in his hands and planted sweet kisses on her cheeks and eyes and chin in a fun, playful way until she giggled, that throaty, beautiful sound. *That's better,* he thought to himself.

She sank further into the blankets, trying to evade his excessive kisses. He wasn't letting her get away, though. He climbed on top of her, the blankets between them.

He wrestled her, trying to kiss her everywhere. "I told ye I wanted to kiss ye everywhere, did I no'?"

Violet laughed. "I thought you had to go."

He was pulling the blanket off her as she tried to hold on to it.

"I do, " he said, kissing her bare shoulder as she playfully tried to shove him off.

They were laughing and tousling about. Finally, she pulled herself out from under him and rolled him onto his back, sitting astride him.

"Ha," she said, triumphantly. As she leaned over him, pinning his wrists down, her long blond hair fell about her. She was a goddess.

"Guess ye got me then," he said, realizing that she really had. There was no way he was going out the door without making love to her at least once more.

He ran his hands up her bare thighs, marveling at their silky softness. She inched down, unbuckled his belt, and opened his pants. He helped her to tug down his pants and briefs enough to free the his dick, which had taken on the identity of a steel pipe.

She lifted herself over him and straddled down on his thick shaft. How did he even consider walking out the door without doing this again? Then she rode him hard and wild, using him to get her fill, and he loved every sweet second of it. He'd happily let her use his body to pleasure herself any time she wanted.

"That's it, love. Ride me. Let me feel ye come."

He flipped Violet on her back and lifted one of her legs onto his shoulder. He pounded into her like a man possessed until she cried out, and he felt her pleasure throb around his cock, milking him until he exploded in one final thrust. He felt drunk with lust as he collapsed down on her, satiated beyond measure. He had no intention of taking her again this morning, but he couldn't help himself. He craved her like a man craved water after walking through the desert. It was wild, unlike anything he'd ever known. Violet was the elixir of life. He opened his eyes, and in his passion-filled fog, he caught sight of the clock on the dresser.

"Bollocks, I have to go! But I want to take ye to dinner tonight. " He gave Violet a quick peck and hastily headed to the bathroom to clean up.

Violet lay there, still feeling the ebbs of her orgasm. She'd lost track of how many she'd had in the last ten hours. That man was her undoing. He wanted to take her to dinner...like a real date? The thought excited her. Maybe this really was something more for him too.

The bathroom door crashed open, and Lachlan strode out the bedroom door, throwing her one of his panty-wetting crooked grins as he went.

"Have a great day," Violet called.

"I'll see ye later, love." He zipped back to her and quickly stole one more sweet kiss before rushing out of the room.

Love, the word hung in the air. Violet rolled over and pulled the blankets tighter around herself. Taking a deep breath, she smelled his fresh cologne in the sheets. It was intoxicating. She thought about their lovemaking. It had been the most incredible night of her life. One she would always treasure, no matter what their future held.

Chapter 48

Everything Changes

LACHLAN HEADED TO HIS business meeting. He was running late. Lachlan was never late. Tension crept into his shoulders. He was meeting with the senior vice president of a liquor store chain out of America. They wanted to specialize in Cailleach Distillery whiskys and carry the whole line. If the deal went through, it could up the profits of the distillery to a level they had never seen, plus having it at this particular liquor store would amp up their presence in the marketplace.

It was definitely a deal Lachlan wanted for his family's distillery. Busk and Shell liquor stores were a very well-respected franchise that Cailleach Distillery would be happy to align with.

Lachlan couldn't believe he was actually late for a meeting this important. Although the reason for his tardiness was well worth it. God, when Violet rolled on top of him with her sexy naked body and actually tried to pin him down...

Giving his head a shake, he walked into his meeting, ready to a make a deal.

Thirty minutes later, Lachlan walked Tom Harris down to the beautiful stone front foyer. Deal made. Details agreed upon. Tom had rightly guessed the reason for his tardiness with a good-natured wink and playful jibe, though he suspected Tom was merely teasing and unaware how accurate his assumption really was. It was a relief that his lateness didn't leave Tom with a bad impression. Lachlan was pleased about the deal, and he was surprised how well he and Tom had hit it off. They were of the same age and mind about their respective businesses—the deal-making came easy. He'd have Iona draw up the paperwork for signing.

After walking Tom out, Lachlan pulled out his phone, and his heart dropped. There were several missed calls from his mam, a missed call from an unknown number, and there was a text.

Drew: Get to the hospital. Drew.

Lachlan ran out to his car and tore out of the parking lot. Fear gripped him. He couldn't think. He just needed to get to the hospital. He prayed, begging a God he wasn't sure he believed in that his baby sister was okay.

He arrived at the hospital feeling frantic. His phone dinged.

Alex: Where are you?

Lachlan's hands were shaking, but he texted back.

Lachlan: Here now.

Lachlan was in such a rush to get there, but now he paused, terrified of the news. He wasn't sure if he could handle what awaited him.

He swallowed hard and somehow made it down the corridor to his sister's room. His legs felt like lead. Arriving at her door, he felt sick to his stomach, and tension gripped his neck and shoulders. He never felt more afraid in his life, not knowing what awaited him on the other side of the door. Tears stung his eyes.

Unexpectedly, the door opened, and Alex stood before him in his police uniform. "Get in here, ye numpty." Lachlan's twin threw an arm around him and pulled him into the room.

Drew was standing over Orlagh's bed, and he looked back at him with a big fat grin on his face. Behind Drew, he saw Orlagh sitting up and smiling brightly. Lachlan felt his knees buckle.

Alex held him up. "Steady on there, mate."

Relief flooded through him, and as he approached her bedside, he practically collapsed into Orlagh, hugging her with all his might. "Jesus Christ. For the love of Mary, Rolo, ye scared the shite out of us."

"Ach, Lachlan." She patted his back. "I just come to, and yer gonna squish the life oot of me!" she teased. Her voice sounded a bit weak, but she was awake and her sense of humour seemed intact. She was going to be okay.

Lachlan took a fortifying breath. Relief flooded through him. He hadn't realized the tension he held until this moment. "Holy Christ, Rolo." He held her to him, unable to stop the few tears that burst free. It felt like everything had suddenly caught up with him.

"C'mon, mon. Pull yer shite together," Drew quipped, giving his shoulder a squeeze.

Lachlan looked back at Drew and found himself looking into the eyes of the loving brother he knew growing up which only grew the damn lump in his throat. "Ye coulda mentioned that it was good news in yer text."

"Aye, Drew." Alex grinned as if he enjoyed seeing his brother get scolded.

"Ye're no better." Lachlan threw Alex a pointed look, and he raised his hands in a truce.

Their mother shot both her sons disapproving looks. "Ye both let Lachlan think the worst? Shame on ye two. How could ye?"

Alex tried to put an appeasing arm around his mom, but she batted it away.

Drew had his hands up. “I swear I didnae even think about it. I just told him to get his fuckin’ arse down here.”

"Language, Drew," Mam scolded.

Lachlan held back a grin. His poor mam, it was a losing battle with his uncouth brothers. As he looked at Drew, though, all Lachlan could see was the kid brother he once knew. He stood up from Orlagh's bed and walked over to him, pulling him into an embrace.

“I still love ye, ye arse,” Lachlan said.

“I love ye too, Saint.” Now it was Drew who was choked up.

"Ach, Christ, damn ye both," Alex said, putting his arms around them and yanking their heads in. The brothers embraced in shared relief over their sister.

“I’m sorry, guys, especially to ye, Lachlan,” Drew croaked.

“Aye, ye bastard,” Lachlan quipped, still embracing both of his brothers.

Drew’s laugh was a hearty one. Lachlan knew that it was an apology for the years that had gone by. For the pain, the distance, the blame. None of that seemed to matter now.

“Right, are we sure I’m alive then? I didn’t expect to see this reunion in my lifetime,” Orlagh teased, although she was wiping away a stray tear too.

"Och, my babies," their mam cried, squeezing herself into the group hug while their da stood back watching on with a quirk of a smile.

"Oh, brother," Orlagh groaned, and even though Lachlan wasn't looking at her, he was certain she was rolling her eyes. "All right, all right, oot with ye all. I need a nap." She shoo'd them.

The relief and joy in the room were palpable. They stayed for a few more minutes and then left Orlagh to rest.

Outside her room, Lachlan talked with his parents and brothers to get the official update on her condition. She had awoken in the morning. Drew had been there and immediately called his parents to come before texting Alex and Lachlan. Alex had just gotten off a night shift and wasn't far from the hospital when he got the text. Whereas Lachlan had been in his meeting.

The doctor had since examined her and was pleased with Orlagh's progress, noting that the prognosis looked good. It would still take some time for her incision to heal, but it was expected she would make a full recovery. Not only that, but as long as she continued to do well, they hoped to release her from the hospital before the week was out. The family's relief was palpable.

The sun was shining as Lachlan walked out of the hospital with his family, and his thoughts turned to Violet. So much had happened today since he'd seen her just a few short hours ago, and he found himself eager to see her.

"Right then, I'm headed home for a kip," Alex said, yawning as he hugged his mam and gave each of the men a pat on the back. "Glad ye're back home, Drew," he added and strode across the parking lot to his car.

"See ye lads later," their da said as he and their mam went to their car. "And stay outta trouble, aye," he added, leaving Lachlan and Drew standing there.

"Shall we go huv a wee drink then?" Drew asked. His lips were tugged in a smirk.

Hearing his brother actually wanting to spend time and hang out with him felt surreal. He wanted to see Violet, but she mentioned having plans for the day anyway.

"Aye," Lachlan replied with a grin.

Chapter 49

The Lads

LACHLAN AND DREW HEADED to one of their old favourite pubs near town, The Coo's House. It was a larger pub out in the country. It was rustic casual, like a good ol' family barn party, but it had a certain urban trendiness that was more typical of the gastro pubs in Glasgow.

When the pair walked in the door, their friend Kian hollered out, "Nooo, it cannae be! Tell me I'm not seein' things!"

"Ye better open the good stuff, Kian. We've got some celebrating to do!" Drew hollered back.

Lachlan and Drew spent the rest of the afternoon catching up and reminiscing over good memories and laughing over some of the bad ones. It was like the wall that had been built up over the last few years came crumbling down. As soon as the one piece of brick fell loose, the rest easily tumbled down. It was so good to reconnect with Drew. Lachlan had forgotten how good it was to talk with his brother and to share a good dram. He'd missed him more than he'd realized. When Helena died, it was like Lachlan and Drew's relationship died, too.

It sounded as if Drew had really turned his life around. He had quit doing drugs and quit hanging around with the crowd that had helped him in his downward spiral. Drew had come back wanting to start back up with the band he'd once played in. The day he'd arrived home, he'd run into the old crowd at Craggy's—and things instantly went awry. He told Lachlan how much he'd regretted the way he'd acted that day.

That wasn't the life he wanted. He didn't want to be that guy anymore. He wasn't that guy anymore. The way he treated Lachlan and his friend that day felt all wrong. He was showing off for the old crowd. Even as he spat crude words, he'd already felt the regret and almost welcomed the punch Lachlan threw. He didn't want it that way. It didn't feel right. It wasn't right.

Lachlan listened to his brother intently and felt so much relief. He apologized for that day, too.

Drew laughed. "Dinnae apologize. I ken I deserved that punch."

"Aye, ye did, ye numpty."

The two men laughed and clanked their glasses before taking a slug.

"I was impressed ye actually hit me, though. I didnae think ye had it in ye."

Lachlan knew exactly the reason he'd let it fly with his brother that day, and her name was Violet Munro. Even then, he'd have done anything to protect her, even from his own brother. Lachlan looked at his phone. Six p.m. already. He should text Violet. He really wanted to talk to her. There was so much to say, and he'd promised her di nner.

"So who was the lovely lass anyway?" Drew asked, waving to their friend Kian to bring another round.

Lachlan smiled, just thinking about her.

"What lovely lass?" Alex strode up.

"Alex, where the hell did ye come from?" Drew stole the words from Lachlan's mouth.

"Och, I ken I'd find ye two here huvin' a dram. Looks like I need to catch up," he said, gesturing to the empty glasses on the bar top in front of them.

"Oi, Kian," Alex called to him over the bar, where he stood with a bottle in each hand, pouring whisky into a row of a dozen or more glasses. He finished his pour, bringing four full glasses over.

"Wonders never cease. I huvnae seen the Mackenzie clan here in years. Welcome back, lads," he said, raising a glass with a wide grin spread over his face.

After sharing a dram with Kian, Alex turned back to Lachlan. "So who's the *lovely* lass, then? Tell me ye arnae talkin' about that MacDonald woman—the one has always wanted to get her nasty claws into ye."

Lachlan wondered how he'd been so blind to Anna when his family obviously couldn't stand her. How had he not seen it sooner? His mam was the only one who had encouraged the relationship, but thinking on it, he realized his mam never actually knew Anna, only her family.

"Fuck no. He dumped her arse and then gave her a right telling off at his gala event. It was brilliant," Drew quipped.

Lachlan didn't relish having to do that, but there was no way in hell he'd let her speak badly about Violet and get away with it.

"Aye?" Alex raised a brow to Lachlan as though he couldn't quite believe it.

"He was defending the '*lovely*' lass," Drew explained.

Alex was still looking at him in disbelief. He knew what he was thinking. Lachlan was always the gentleman, the diplomat. He didn't ruffle feathers. Which was true, but at the same time, he'd fucking tear the devil a new one to defend his woman.

"Aye," Lachlan said, taking a hearty sip of his whisky.

Realizing Lachlan wasn't going to say any more about it, Alex asked again, "So who is the 'lovely' lass then?" He looked between the two men.

"Och, she's a bonnie one," Drew said as if he were an authority.

And Lachlan gave him a warning look.

Alex laughed. "Lachlan, ye look like ye might like to kill the lad. What gives?" He slapped Lachlan on the back.

For the first time in his life, he actually understood his brothers and their love of the lasses, although there was only one lass that he loved. *Love.* He was caught off guard by his own thoughts.

"I think she must be someone special, aye?" Drew said more seriously.

"Aye, she is. Verra special."

"Sounds serious." Alex eyed him. Lachlan rolled the whisky in his glass and took a sip. The concept of being in love was taking up residence in his mind.

"Aye." He felt his lips tug in an almost smile while both his brothers stared at him as if they'd seen a ghost.

A wide grin cracked on Drew's face. "I ken it. I ken it that day! I've never seen ye so fired up about a lass. For the record, I am truly sorry for what I said that day. I ken I was an absolute shite."

"What did ye say?" Alex asked, brow arched. He nodded to Kian to bring them another round.

Lachlan interjected before Drew said something that would make Lachlan have to deck him again. "He was a crude arsehole, and I punched him fer it."

Alex's eyes widened as his glass paused midway to his mouth. "Aye?" he asked as though he'd never heard anything more outlandish in his thirty years on this earth.

"Aye, I was," Drew admitted. "And he did."

"Well, the crude arsehole part doesnae surprise me, but ye punched him, Lachlan?" There was also a twinkle of pride in his eyes when he looked at his twin.

"He did. It was a good one too—knocked me out." Drew boasted, proudly.

"Impressive, Saint." Alex grinned, slapping him on the back—apparently proud of him too. "She must really be something."

"Christ, ye two," Lachlan snapped. "Ye ken I'm no' really a bloody saint."

"She is so bonnie, though," Drew added as if it needed to be said.

Lachlan glared at him and then took another sip of his whisky. "Aye, she is verra beautiful. Fucking perfect if ye really must ken. And ye both better keep yer traps shut if ye ken what's good fer ye."

His brothers stared at him as if he'd grown highland cow horns.

"Right, well, I am glad that ye arenae dating the MacDonald woman anymore. Am I allowed to say that?" Drew ribbed him.

"Aye, I agree. I never liked that one," Alex said, scanning the bar that had suddenly become crowded. Not a surprise on a Saturday night. Lachlan only nodded. He still wondered how he'd been so blind as to date Anna at all.

"I'm proud of ye, too, for telling her where to shove her damn money," Drew added knocking back the rest of his whisky.

"And just how do you ken about that anyway?" Lachlan shot him a look.

"Rolo told me. At the gala."

"Ye were at the gala?" Lachlan eyed Drew, who'd gotten distracted by a group of lasses at a nearby table.

"Aye, I only popped in briefly. I wanted to find a date for the night." He winked. "Speaking of which, I'll be right back." He stood and swaggered over to the table of lasses—the master of flirting.

"Same old Drew," Alex echoed Lachlan's thoughts.

Always the flirt. Lasses on the brain non-stop. Although he did seem different. He'd grown up a lot. That chip on his shoulder was no longer there.

"So it would seem. But I confess, I like him better now. He's not that angry kid anymore."

"Aye, thank God."

They sat in companionable silence before Alex asked, "Did ye really tell off Anna MacDonald?"

"Perhaps not my proudest moment, but she had it coming."

"That's no' like ye, Lachlan." Alex eyed him.

It was true. Lachlan was usually easygoing and let things roll off him. This time was different, though, and he didn't regret it for a moment. "Rolo overheard Anna talking down to Violet, trying to make her feel bad. I think she was just jealous, though. Violet is everything Anna is not."

"Violet? The 'fucking perfect' one?" Alex arched a brow, mimicking his brother's words.

"Aye, the fucking perfect one."

"Ye are protective over the lass."

"Aye," Lachlan admitted.

Drew shoved himself back on the stool beside Lachlan, leaning his elbows on the bar behind him, facing out to the crowded room.

"Christ, it's good to be home." He grinned.

"Got a phone number?" Alex asked nonchalantly.

"Two." Drew winked.

"What are ye boys bletherin' about?"

"Violet." Alex grinned.

"Och, right, Violet. The one we are no' allowed to talk about," Drew teased and turned to Lachlan, who was less than impressed with his brothers' ribbing. "Ye love her?" Drew asked, with Alex standing nearby, listening intently.

Lachlan rolled the amber liquid in his glass, not needing to contemplate the question. "Aye, I do."

"Aye?" Drew laughed heartily, slapping his brother on the back, and Alex smiled like he found the whole thing amusing. "Bloody hell! Another round, Kian," he smacked his hand on the bar top.

Chapter 50

The Truth Comes Out

VIOLET GOT HOME, SHOWERED, and took the two-kilometer scenic walk to the local farmers market. It had become her usual on a Saturday. There was nothing better than fresh little strawberries from the market, and she always loved to check out all the vendors' wares. She rushed through today, though, wanting to get back so she'd have plenty of time to get ready to meet up with Lachlan.

She walked back in her front door shortly before five p.m. and felt a familiar tinge of disappointment that Lachlan hadn't messaged her at all yet. Refusing to get in her head about it, she texted him.

Violet: Thinking about you. Let me know what time you're planning for dinner. Hope you've had a good day. <3

She looked at her message and hit send before she could change her mind. Her phone dinged in her hand, and her heart skipped a beat. It wasn't Lachlan, though. It was Fiona asking her about her night. Violet hadn't mentioned her plans to go see Lachlan and confront him, so she assumed it was just a generic, "Hey how was your Friday." Part of her wanted to gush about how epic her night was, but it all still felt so tentative and surreal. It was like she didn't want to jinx it, so she typed back a non-descript response.

Violet: Good and yours?

The truth was she hadn't stopped thinking about last night and this morning. She had no idea sex could be like that, but it was so much more. She felt so cherished and safe somehow when she was with Lachlan. When they were together, it couldn't be more perfect. She sighed. It was the in-between that left her confused.

As amazing as last night was, she still wished they had talked more. Violet picked up one of the romance books Lachlan had bought for her. She was halfway through the second book. She still loved that he'd thought to get her a book. Definitely a top-notch gift in her eyes. And he'd chosen surprisingly well. She hadn't read any of Eliza Rockwood's books, but after plowing through the first one Lachlan bought, she'd already gone online to order more.

She'd finished the second book from Lachlan and was just finishing another of the Hideaway Valley series she'd ordered when her doorbell rang. She glanced at the clock, it was seven forty-five p.m. *Lachlan*. She almost tripped jumping up from her navy wingback chair. She flung open the door, her heart delighting that it was Lachlan. Maybe he'd meant a late dinner.

Indeed, late dinner, but not with Lachlan. Fiona stood on the other side of her door, hands full with takeout food bags, and Violet's stomach growled on cue. Apparently, she didn't do a good job of disguising her disappointment that it wasn't Lachlan.

"Expecting someone else?" Fiona said, holding up the bags. "I brought sustenance."

Violet felt her eyes sting with tears.

"Oh. Oh, Vi, what is it?" Fiona put the bags of food down on the little bench at the front door and wrapped Violet in a warm embrace, and that's when the floodgates opened.

Violet sobbed on her shoulder. "

What happened?" Fiona said gently, pulling back to look at Violet.

When Violet finally caught her breath, she whispered, "It's a long story."

She watched numbly as Fiona filled up two plates with some unidentified vegan food she'd picked up from a fancy new takeout place in town. Then she poured two large glass-es of white wine, filling them to the brim. She handed Violet a glass and carefully clanked her glass.

Violet took a large gulp of the wine and then topped up her glass before accepting the plate of food Fiona handed her, and the two sat at the tiny bistro table near the back door. Violet fiddled with some beige ball-looking thing with her fork.

"Eat. It's good. And then I want ye to start from the beginning, tell me everything.

Violet didn't feel like eating. But Fiona could be a mother hen, so Violet did as she was told. The food was better than she thought it would be. When she finally set her fork down, Fiona was looking at her expectantly, cradling her glass of wine. Violet knew she needed to get it off her chest. Violet hesitated, though, knowing that Fiona also worked for Lachlan. Even now, she didn't want this to bite Lachlan in the ass. Even if he did deserve it. *Ugh.*

"You have to keep this between us, though, okay? No telling Andy or Drew." Violet still suspected that the Drew Fiona met the night of the gala was Lachlan's brother, and she certainly didn't want to cause more family drama with any of this getting back to Lachlan.

"I willnae say anything. Ye huv my word on it."

Violet took another good gulp of wine and opened up about what had happened the night of the gala.

Fiona stared in disbelief. "Right there in the barrel room? Where they were doing the tours?" Her eyebrows nearly rose to her hairline.

Violet nodded, feeling a bit embarrassed by the confession.

“Blimey!”

Violet told her about Lachlan staying the night with her when she was sick and how he took care of her, bringing her smut books and drugs and making her grapefruit juice and broth—which was so delicious, considering it was just clear broth.

“Och, he’s got it bad for ye, Violet.”

“No, that’s just it. I don’t think he actually does.”

“What? Of course, he does. No man does all this for a little piece of action.”

“There’s more.” Violet laid her elbow on the table and held her forehead in her hand.

Violet continued to tell Fiona how he’d gone MIA right after.

"Och, right. Come to think of it, I didnae see him at the sanctuary either. Maybe he had to go on another business trip?" she offered.

Violet had wondered that herself, but it didn't explain why he hadn't called her or messaged her at least. "Right, but why didn't he message me?”

Fiona shook her head. "Maybe he was doing that three-day rule thing guys do, ye ken?”

Violet didn't buy it. Especially not when she'd messaged him. He could have at least messaged something back. She was annoyed all over again that she hadn't gotten around to getting any answers last night.

"What on God's green earth? How did ye not talk about it then? That's why ye were there!" Fiona snapped when Violet had explained she'd gone to his house for answers but ended up leaving without any.

Violet looked up at Fiona sheepishly and could pinpoint the moment when Fiona understood.

"Nooo! Ye mean to tell me ye had sex but didnae talk?"

"Ugh, I know! I don't know how it happened." Violet got up from the little table and flopped down on the couch, tucking her legs beneath her.

Fiona joined her. "How long were ye there fer?" she hedged.

Violet put a hand over her eyes, unable to believe her own weakness when it came to this man. "All night."

"Jesus, Mary, and Joseph! And in a whole night, ye didn't come up fer air then?"

"Not really. And then he had to go."

"Well, what did he say when he left?"

"He said he wanted to take me to dinner tonight." Violet blew out a breath, realizing that dinner was definitely not happening tonight, but it was more than that. This was Lachlan ghosting her. Again.

Fiona looked at the clock. "And ye havnae heard from him?"

Violet shook her head.

"Och, Vi, no wonder yer a wreck."

Violet finished off her wine in her glass and got up to clear their dishes. She couldn't just sit there anymore.

"Ye need to talk to him. Actually talk. Stop having sex every time ye lay eyes on the lad."

Violet laughed, despite feeling so sad inside. "I think I need to leave," she said, suddenly turning to Fiona.

"Leave? Where do ye wantae go then?"

"Away from Scotland." That was as far as her mind had gotten with the idea.

"Och, no. Dinnae say that. Ye need to talk to him. Dinnae be hasty."

But the moment Violet had said it, she knew she *needed* to go. The uncertainty with Lachlan was too much to take.

"If he actually wanted me, don't you think he would have texted or called by now? This is his pattern. He gets close, and then he ghosts me. I'm not surprised that it is almost nine p.m. and I haven't heard from him. I knew I wouldn't. I wanted to hope that I would, but I knew it. I can't keep doing this. Honestly, Fiona, my time here is done. I'm packing my bags."

Fiona's phone dinged, interrupting their conversation. Violet took the opportunity to go to the kitchen and bring back the bottle of wine. She sat back down on the couch with a full glass, putting the remainder of the bottle on the coffee table for Fiona.

"It's Drew. He wants me to come out." Fiona's expression was unreadable.

"You should go. Really. I'm not much fun tonight, anyways. Go see your beau. One of us should have a good night."

"Och, no, not my beau at all." She looked thoughtful, and Violet wondered what was on her mind. "Ye ken we didnae ever end up having sex, right? Although I will confess, he was stellar in one particular department." She added, nodding to her crotch.

Violet laughed, nearly choking on her wine.

"But when we kissed, it was the oddest thing." She paused, her brows knit like she was trying to solve a puzzle. "Ye ken when it's like kissing yer brother?"

Violet's brow shot up,."Not exactly."

Fiona scoffed. "I dinnae ken either Vi. Dinnae be weird. I mean, we just dinnae huv that kind of chemistry. We hit it off well enough, but more as friends. Good friends, really. Actually, he helped me in a way."

"How so?" Violet eyed her, curious as to where this was going.

"Um, after he, ye know," she nodded to her crotch again. "We ended up having a surprisingly deep conversation. And—well—I guess he encouraged me to be myself."

"Right, well that's good."

Fiona eyed her. "Yes, it is." She drew in a deep breath. "Vi, I'm gay—I like women." She said it confidently, and Violet almost sighed with relief—not because her hunch had been right, but because she was proud of her friend for embracing her truth.

"Are ye surprised?" Fiona asked.

Violet shook her head. "I kind of had a feeling that might be the case and honestly, I'm so happy for you—it must feel good to be free to be yourself.

"Och, aye, it really is." She grinned, leaning back, and taking a sip of her wine.

"I am surprised, though, that you let him...you know." Now she was the one nodding toward Fiona's crotch.

"Aye, right that. Well, to be totally honest, I closed my eyes and imagined it was someone else entirely—I'm terrible, I ken. I did confess to him after I fluffed his feathers about how talented he is with his mouth, of course."

"You *told* him you were imagining someone else?" Violet was floored.

"Aye, and he asked me to describe her in detail." Fiona scoffed. "He's into women almost more than I am!"

Violet laughed at the craziness of it all, grateful for the distraction from her own problems. Her happiness for Fiona lightened her heavy mood. Then Fiona's phone dinged again.

"You should go." Violet said. "Sounds like Drew might make a good wingman." She grinned and stood. "I'm going to start packing."

"Och, stop with yer packing business. Ye cannae leave me. I willnae allow it," Fiona stated flatly as if the alternative were absurd.

Violet couldn't help smiling. She would miss Fiona and the life she'd made here in Scotland.

"Why dinnae we both go? Drew said it's some fancy pub near in the countryside that his friend runs. Come on, it'll be fun. We can get dressed up and just go have a fun night. I think ye need a break from all this gloom and doom."

Violet looked up at her friend. Going out might help her to take her mind off things, and then tomorrow, she could make plans for leaving Scotland. "Maybe," she conceded.

"Yess!"

"If I'm going out tonight, I'm doin' it right! Let's go find something fabulous to wear!" Violet announced, discarding their dinner plates in the kitchen sink and heading for her bedroom.

Chapter 51
The Coo's House

Violet wore a black tank top with a cute red tartan skirt and adorable Mary Jane high-heeled shoes, and she felt sexy. She felt like she needed to prove to herself that she could feel appealing and beautiful without Lachlan—or maybe in spite of him. She was determined to have one last great night in Scotland, and then tomorrow, she'd figure out her plans for moving. The thought was a heavy one, but she pushed it aside.

The two ladies walked into The Coo's House. It was a large room with high ceilings and a bar in the middle. The decor was dark and rustic but with a modern twist. It didn't look old-fashioned despite having old wood barn boards and vintage-style paintings. It was packed with people laughing, drinking, and apparently having a great time. The wine they'd drunk earlier was wearing off quickly, and Violet was ready for a *proper* drink.

"Drew said he's near the stage off the far side of the bar," Fiona said over the din of the crowd. She grabbed Violet's hand and led the way through the throngs of people.

Violet was surprised when Drew scooped Fiona up and planted a very-happy-to-see-you kiss on her. But she just laughed and batted him off like it was no big deal. And that was when it hit her. It *was* the Drew that was Lachlan's brother, although he was clean-shaven now as compared to the scruffy beard he'd had when she'd seen him at the breakfast place. Violet felt a little shock of nerves remembering what Lachlan had told her. He'd punched his brother in her defence.

"This is my friend, Violet," Fiona introduced them. Drew's blue-green eyes landed on her, and she suddenly realized how stupid it was for her to have come out tonight. What had she been thinking? Maybe he wouldn't remember her from that day.

Sheesh, he was a handsome one—the family resemblance was strong. Though, no man could compare to Lachlan. Her heart clenched. Drew's eyes widened in surprise. He recognized her. *Shit.*

"Violet." A sly grin spread over his chiseled features. He looked like he was about to plant the same type of kiss on her as he did on Fiona, but then seemed to think better of it. Instead, he awkwardly shook her hand.

"Nice to meet you," she said, trying to determine the quickest way to the exit.

“Violet!” he said again with excitement, and suddenly, his hands gripped her shoulders in a squeeze. "One sec, dinnae go anywhere," he told her and then inched past her, leaving her feeling uneasy.

“Well, that was weird,” Fiona said, leaning over the bar trying to catch the bartender's attention.

“Look who’s here!” Drew said from behind her.

Violet turned around as Lachlan was shoved in her direction. Her heart hammered in her chest. He looked just as stunned to see her as she was to see him.

“V, you’re here!” There was an ease about him, and she realized he was probably a bit drunk as his handsome crooked smile spread across his face. “Did I tell ye I was here?” A confused, annoyingly adorable expression appeared on his handsome face.

Yep, definitely a bit drunk. This was more important than seeing her? Talking to her? Any of it? *Nice.*

“Nope, you didn't tell me anything. Not a thing,” she snapped, remembering she was supposed to be mad at him despite his easy charm.

"Uh-oh," she heard another voice.

She glanced over her shoulder and looked up. Holy shit. It was Lachlan but *not* Lachlan. Violet couldn't help but stare at the man who was equally as big and gorgeous as Lachlan.

"Oi, fuck off, Alex."

She turned back to Lachlan. *Right. Alex. His twin.* If she wasn't so mad at Lachlan, she would have laughed at the jealous look in his drunken blue eyes. Was he jealous that she'd looked at his brother? The man was hard not to notice. The three of them stood well over six feet tall, muscled, and too good-looking for words.

But her heart ached looking at Lachlan. He was the only man who could set her on fire. Her body was already reacting to his nearness. It was like she yearned for him in a way that defied reality. She was helpless to her feelings for him . *No*, she told herself, hanging on to her conviction by a thread.

She looked at Fiona, who appeared just as surprised by the Mackenzie men as she was. "I have to go," Violet said, realizing escape was her only option. She quickly slipped past Lachlan to make her way through the crowd to the door. With every step she took, the lump in her throat grew, nearly choking her. She didn't want to cry.

Lachlan grabbed her arm right before she reached the door.

"Please, dinnae go," he pleaded.

She turned to face him. Her eyes were burning with unshed tears.

"Dinnae leave. I huv so much to tell ye." He was still wearing the same dress shirt and pants from this morning, but now, he had a five o'clock shadow on his square jaw line.

"If you wanted to talk, why are you here and not with me?" She gestured with her hand. "You said you wanted to see me tonight, Lachlan. Take me to dinner. If you wanted to go out and get drunk instead, why didn't you just say so?" All her anger was bursting out of her.

"Och, I'm sorry. I ken, I'm a numpty."

If she wasn't so furious and hurt, she might have laughed. Damn him, this big gorgeous man looked so cute drunk and grovelling.

"I should huv called ye and no' just texted. That was very inconsiderate lass. I ken it."

"You didn't text me, Lachlan." She leaned against the wall behind her a few feet away from the front door where another group of people were piling in.

Lachlan looked at her from under an arched brow as he stepped toward her, laying his hands on the wall on either side of her head. She was certain he was using the wall for support, but she was wholly affected by the move. She could smell the whisky on his breath and his cologne, and she just wanted to breathe him in and kiss his stupid face.

He leaned forward, their faces inches apart, and he studied her in a way that made her traitorous vagina throb. He picked up a loose strand of her hair, running it between his thumb and finger. "Aye, love. I did. I texted ye ."

"Maybe you thought you did, but you didn't, Lachlan. There was no message, no phone call. No nothing. Once again, you just ghosted me." She was going to hold her ground damn it. Her vagina and heart could just shut up already. He pulled his hands from the wall, and she felt strangely bereft.

He still looked at her, though, as he pulled his phone from his pocket. She gave him all the time he needed to find the so-called text. His lips lifted in his crooked smile, and he held his phone up for her to read it.

Lachlan: Hello my gorgeous lass, I apologize, but I am not going to be able to see you tonight after all. I should have messaged earlier. It is a long story. Let me make you brunch tomorrow, and I'll explain everything. I promise to make it up to you... all day and all night if you let me xxxxxxx

"See?" he said when she looked back up, triumph in his sexy, drunken gaze.

She crossed her arms over her chest. Her pulse tapped rapidly, reading his words.

"You didn't hit send."

His brow crinkled, and he flicked his phone back, examining the screen.

"Och, right, shite," he said.

She could tell he knew he'd fucked up, and then he hit send as if it would rectify things. Her phone dinged, and his eyes landed on hers, his lips quirking into a hopeful grin, and she couldn't stop the twitch of her own lips.

"I texted you, though. I'm assuming you didn't see it." She held her ground. Barely.

He looked down at his phone and ran a hand over his stubbled jaw. Clearly, he'd seen it now as a guilty look passed over his features.

"I am sorry, love. I'm doing a right job of messing things up, aye?"

A grinning Drew appeared over Lachlan's shoulder, draping a muscular arm over him.

"Ye two all right, then?" he asked, his eyes darting between them like a ping-pong ball.

Neither answered. "Och, Saint, did ye tell her ye defended her honor with the nasty MacDonald besom?" Drew supplied as if he thought it would help Lachlan's cause.

Violet found it kind of endearing—both the way he called him Saint and that he was making an argument on his brother's behalf. So it was true—Lachlan had told that woman off. There were still many unanswered questions, though. She still wanted to know what their relationship had been and, more importantly, *when*.

"Ye arnae helping, Drew," Lachlan said, though his blue eyes were still glued to Violet like she was the only person who existed in that crowded pub.

"She doesnae look happy," Drew said to Lachlan as if she wasn't standing right in front of both of them, hearing every word.

She looked at him with his flirty-looking, devil-may-care, wide grin and almost laughed. He was exactly the kind of sibling she could imagine would drive Lachlan crazy. Then she thought of Orlagh, the petite powerhouse of a woman she'd met. How did she manage growing up with these men for brothers? As if on cue, Alex strode up to them, standing on the other side of Lachlan. The three big, broad, handsome Mackenzie brothers surrounded her. And all the while, Lachlan's eyes didn't leave her.

"What's happening here, then?" Alex asked, looking between them.

"As far as I can tell, Lachlan's gone and fucked something up," Drew supplied. "I think he should just tell her he loves her already, aye?"

Violet's heart jumped into her throat.

"Aye," Alex concurred as if they were discussing whether or not the sun would come out tomorrow. "Right, well, are we drinking? Kian's mam Mary just pulled out a bottle of the good stuff. An eighteen-year-old Macallan."

"Good ol' Mary, bless that woman." Drew laid a dramatic hand on his heart.

Lachlan continued to look at Violet while his brothers nattered around them. The corners of his mouth were tilted in a heart-stopping smile. Her head was spinning.

"He's not wrong ye ken," he said, as if it were only her and him, and then he dipped his head to give her a swift fleeting kiss that still had the power to set off fireworks low in her belly. Lord, help her. She was as changeable as the wind because right now, with every fiber of her being, all she wanted was the man towering over her with a sexy twinkle in his eyes, looking at her like she was a slice of artisan cheesecake on a jailbird's lunch tray.

Chapter 52

Drunken Haze and The Light of Day

LACHLAN COULDN'T HAVE BEEN happier that Violet was there at The Coo's House. They still hadn't had much chance to talk. When they got back to the bar, Fiona was there waiting, and she and Violet chatted for a bit before Fiona went off with some other friends who'd arrived. He couldn't take his eyes off Violet. She was so beautiful, and seeing her interact with her brothers made him feel a sense of pride. She was intelligent and engaging, and her brothers seemed to enjoy her company and vice versa. Not that it surprised him, but he liked that she fit in so easily.

Drew had been chatting with her for the past ten minutes or so, and as Lachlan watched, it occurred to him he might not have decked Drew hard enough the first time. He overheard him asking Violet where she'd gotten her gorgeous blond locks. That was something *he* should be asking her, not his damn flirty brother.

And when he touched the ends of her hair, Lachlan's fists clenched. Before he could go over there and pound the shite out of Drew, Alex threw an arm around his bunched shoulders. "Dinnae fash, Brother. Ye ken Drew is always the flirt. It doesnae mean anything. It’s his nature. Besides, ye can see she is no' falling prey to his charms. It's obvious she only has eyes for ye."

"Easy for ye to say. It's no' yer woman he's flirting with." Lachlan was still pissed at Drew. Although he had noticed Violet looked his way often, and it pleased him.

Alex arched a brow at him. "I dinnae think I'd ever see the day where Saint Lachlan was possessive over a lass.”

It was true. Before Violet found her way into his heart, he hadn’t had a possessive, jealous bone in his body, but some primordial part of him told him she belonged to him—plain and simple. Drew had leaned in and whispered something in Violet's ear, and she threw her head back and laughed.

"Och, that does it." Lachlan chucked back the remainder of his drink and stepped in front of Drew, shooting him a warning glare as he did, and then he scooped up Violet into his arms before sitting back down on the stool she'd been on, with her now securely on his lap—where she belonged.

She was laughing breathlessly. The sound danced over his skin, making him hunger for her. He nuzzled against her ear, breathing in her sweet vanilla scent, savouring the feel of her on his lap. This was much better.

"What was my brother whispering to ye?" he asked, feeling calmer now that she was in his arms.

She looked at him, taking his face in her hands, and a grin spread across her beautiful face.

"He told me you were thinking about ways to kill him and that I should laugh at what he was saying and watch how you reacted."

Lachlan shot his eyes back to his little brother, who gave him the cheekiest grin and lifted his glass in salute.

"Bawbag," Lachlan muttered.

Drew laughed good-naturedly, turning back to talk with Alex.

Violet's finger slipped through the unbuttoned top of his shirt and stroked gently against his chest, and he brought his gaze back to hers. She looked serious despite her soft stroking that both calmed and aroused him.

"What is it, V?" he asked.

"I know this might not be the right time or place, but I just need some answers, Lachlan."

"Aye, of course. Ask me anything. I'm an open book for ye lass."

She looked as if she were trying to formulate the right words, and Lachlan decided it might be better to just start at the beginning and explain what he could about why he'd been so off. "After I left ye the other morning, I had a message from my mam. Orlagh was in the hospital." The words were stuck in his throat even now.

"Oh my God." Violet tensed in his arms, her eyes searching his, concern etched on her beautiful features.

"She's okay," he quickly assured her. "But she hadn't been that day." Lachlan managed to explain to Violet about the hellish week with Orlagh.

"I would have been there for you, you know. I could have helped with taking care of Sally or listening or anything really," Violet said, and he loved her for it.

"I should huv talked to ye. I thought about it so many times last week. I wanted to tell ye, let ye in, but at the same time, it's like I didnae want anything to put a damper on the beautiful thing between us. I felt so helpless last week. I didn't even ken how to tell ye about i t."

"I suppose I can understand that. I can't imagine what you all went through. But just so you know, you can tell me anything, Lachlan. I will be here for you."

He looked up into her mossy green eyes, and his heart felt cracked wide open. God, how he adored her. His hand found the nape of her neck, and he pulled her mouth to his, needing to taste the whisky off her lips. And as soon as he did, she opened her mouth to him, and he swept his tongue against hers, tightening his grip on her in his lap.

"Oi, ye two."

Lachlan cracked an eye open and saw Drew's grinning face, far too close to his and Violet's for Lachlan's liking.

"Time to get a room, aye?"

Violet snorted, hiding her face in Lachlan's shoulder.

A short time later, they'd said their goodbyes, gotten in an Uber, and arrived at Lachlan's. After letting Sally out, he slid his fingers through hers, holding her hand in his and led her upstairs to his bedroom. It was hard to believe it was only this morning she'd kissed him goodbye in this very room and then some. They both washed up and got into bed. They lay side by side, looking at each other in the darkness.

Violet's head was spinning a bit from the cask-strength whisky she'd drunk, and she could tell she wasn't the only one feeling its effects. It was a comfy, lazy sort of buzzed state they found themselves in.

"Do ye ken how glad I am ye are here with me, lass?" Lachlan said.

And it felt good when she realized that she did. There wasn't a doubt in her fuzzy, drunken mind. She leaned in and kissed his lips in the darkness, and he sighed against them and then laid his head with his nose against her neck, and he breathed her in. That was the last thing she recalled before falling into a deep, dreamless sleep.

Violet awoke to the sun streaking across her face through Lachlan's bedroom window. She felt a touch of a headache, but it was better than she imagined. She glanced over and grabbed the water she only now remembered Lachlan had put on the nightstand for her—he was always taking care of her. She gulped it back and then lay back down, stretching with a smile on her face as she looked over at the thoughtful, handsome man sleeping beside her.

Tucking her hands together beneath her pillow, she studied his face. Morning stubble graced his strong jaw, and his Adam's apple bobbed slightly with his steady breathing. His nose was strong and straight with slightly flared nostrils. His lashes fanned out against his skin. She loved to see his dark brows quirk in an arch, and his lips? Oh, those lips of his... She wanted them on her.

As if hearing her thoughts, he stirred. His cerulean blue eyes opened, and his lips lifted into his crooked smile. "Good morning."

"Good morning," she said back as they lay watching each other in what felt like some kind of warm love bubble.

There was no denying it. She loved him with every ounce of her being, and she was certain that he had strong feelings for her, too. Perhaps love, like Drew had said, but in the light of day, was it true? Did Lachlan love her? Maybe. She was going to try not to get hung up on it. She felt so much better knowing why he had gone MIA last week, and she didn't blame him. She couldn't imagine the trauma of what he and his family had endured. It was a relief that his sister Orlagh was going to be okay.

Violet still had one thing niggling her, though.

Chapter 53

Whispers in the Bedroom

"WHAT IS IT, LOVE? Ye look a thousand miles away."

She felt petty bringing it up, but if they were going to move forward, she needed to know. "How did Anna get my note?"

A slight tick in his jaw made her almost wish she hadn't brought it up. "I'm sorry. I don't want to make you angry, but if there is going to be an 'us,' I need to know.

A lazy grin spread across his face. "Always apologizing, my little Canadian, with absolutely nothing to be apologizing for."

She couldn't help but smile. He laid his big hand over hers, warm and comforting. "I promise ye, lass, I will never intentionally keep anything from ye, and I want ye to ken that ye can ask me anything. I want ye to ken my soul."

Violet nodded, overwhelmed and so relieved by his response.

"Anna and I dated for about three months. That night of your accident, when ye and I met, we were still a couple."

Violet suspected as much, but it still made her gut churn.

"Anna was in France that weekend."

"Why didn't you just tell me then?" She thought back to that day and night they'd spent together. "You had every opportunity to tell me you were in a relationship. God, Lachlan, I even kissed you."

"I ken, and Christ, how I wanted to kiss ye back," he said.

She stared at him as he utterly missed the point. She rolled on her back, and he propped his head in his hand and used his other hand to lift her chin to look at him.

"I ken it was wrong of me not to tell ye about Anna. And I struggled that night with my own morals. It was not a situation I'd ever found myself in before. I was already realizing that I didn't want a relationship with her anymore. And then ye fell into my world, and it was like a piece of me I didn't ken existed came alive. I dinnae how to explain it. It's like I'd been living my life in a steady hum drum state of black and white, and then ye pulled back the curtain and revealed the most vibrant, beautiful colours. Ye showed me a world I didnae ken existed."

Violet's eyes felt misty as she listened to Lachlan finally talk openly with her.

"Anyway, the day ye left, I made the decision to end it with Anna. I didnae expect her back so soon from France, but she showed up unannounced and apparently came up here to surprise me, but she must have seen your note. When I got to the room, she basically accused me of cheating, which physically I had not, but I ken that my heart had."

He stroked his fingers over her collarbone, and Violet could barely breathe, never mind speak. It was a lot to take in. There was something gratifying in knowing she hadn't been wrong—he'd felt something that first night together too..

"There was a part of me, though, that also understood that Anna never had my heart in the first place. I realized that what we shared was surface level—there was no depth to it. Anyway—either way—I should huv been honest with ye that night and told ye about her."

Violet wondered what that night would have been like if she had known about Anna. Would it have changed the connection she'd felt with Lachlan? "You should have told me," she said.

"Aye," he agreed.

"But.."

His eyes snapped to hers. "But?" he coaxed her to continue.

"I understand why you didn't and—this may be wrong—but a little piece of me is... glad I didn't know." Violet squeezed her eyes shut, a wave of guilt washing over her at her confession.

She felt Lachlan trace her lips with his finger and she opened her eyes to see his gaze fixed on her mouth. "I doonae think ye would huv put these lips on mine if ye'd known, and that, V, would huv been tragic."

Violet warmed at his words. "So you approved of that kiss? The one where you didn't kiss me back?"

"Och Christ lass, that kiss..." His voice trailed off, and he closed his eyes as if replaying it in his mind's eye. "That kiss is burned on my soul for all eternity. Not Kissing ye back was probably the hardest thing I've ever done."

"I'm actually kind of impressed that you didn't," she chuckled. "At least you tried to do the right thing—sort of."

"Och, I fought against myself, believe me. I ken I shouldnae huv wanted ye so badly, but I did. I felt things fer ye I had no business feeling, but I couldnae help it—ye bewitched me."

Violet giggled. "Cast my spell, eh?" She nipped his finger playfully.

"Aye, ye did." He stroked her cheek, then after a moment, continued telling her what had happened with Anna.

"She assumed I'd been unfaithful, and in a sense, I felt like I had." He sighed. "She took the opportunity to confess that she'd cheated on me while she was in France."

"Nooo." Violet was shocked. "That's awful."

"Ye'd think so, but the irony of it was that I really didnae care. When I look back, I dinnae even ken how we had a relationship at all. It was just a parade of restaurants and dinner parties. She didnae ken me at all, and I didnae ken her. It was like we were just going through the motions of being a couple. There was no substance."

Violet had had a couple of boyfriends, although nothing serious, but she could understand the sentiment of what Lachlan was saying. She'd never felt anything toward those men that even came remotely close to what she felt for Lachlan.

"Anyway, Anna somehow considered us to be even and decided that we should move forward and 'take our relationship to the next level.' I'm tellin' ye, V, it was unfathomable to me. I thought she was half crazy. Anyway, it didnae go well. I waited downstairs for her to come down and leave."

"And that's when she took my note," Violet finished.

"Aye, she must huv. I should huv contacted her to get it back, but—"

"I wouldn't have either," Violet cut him off. "When you close a door like that, you don't want to crack it open again for anything."

He smiled down at her. "Aye. But I confess, I wondered many times what ye wrote me."

She grinned. "Nothing all that exciting, but I did leave you my number. I hoped that I would see you again." She sighed and bit her bottom lip. "Why didn't you try to connect with me again? Especially since you'd broken it off with Anna. I know you didn't have my number, but you knew where I was staying."

Lachlan ran his finger slowly along her chin, looking down at her lips like they might provide an answer. "It is a fair question. I did think about it. The thing is, ye literally rocked my world. Ye changed it. I felt alive again, inspired again. It was why I got things moving with opening Highland Haven. It's like I was finding myself again. And then there ye were again, back in my world. Ye found me."

"I did, didn't I?" She grinned up at him.

He kissed the tip of her nose.

Then she recalled one more thing that she'd been wondering about.

"On the night of the gala, I saw you dancing with Anna."

Lachlan sighed and rolled onto his back, pulling Violet in against his side. She nestled there, knowing full well, that no matter the past, he was hers.

"Trust me, I dinnae want to."

Violet smiled. "Orlagh said as much."

"Aye, Orlagh has a very keen sense of things. Anyway, ye are aware the MacDonalds have generously donated to Highland Haven."

"Everybody knows." She quipped.

"Aye, well, Anna gave us a cheque at the gala for a rather large sum. To be honest, given that we hadn't spoken since breaking up, I didnae expect she would show up at all. Maybe I shouldnae huv been surprised. She was never one to miss an event, especially where her generosity could be put on full display for everyone to fuss over her."

"I gather she likes attention?"

"Aye, she does. Anyway, when she sought me out and asked me to dance with her the first time, I thought it was perhaps a peace offering, and then, given the circumstances of being the host and her being a donor, I didnae think I could huv gotten around it. It seemed easier to agree. Thinking we could be adults and leave the past in the past, I danced with her."

"The *first* time?" Violet eyed him, wondering just how much time he'd spent dancing with his attention-seeking ex.

"Aye, I got stuck dancing with her twice. Believe me, I didnae want to.

"It looked cozy," Violet hedged, remembering their smiles.

Lachlan looked at her like she'd sprouted the horns of a highland cow. "I assure ye, it wasnae *cozy*. I suppose if ye saw the first dance, it was more *amiable* than the second, but definitely no' *cozy*."

"What happened during the second dance?" Violet was almost afraid to know, but at the same time—she needed to.

"Good question. I truly didnae want to dance with her again. In fact, I'd just spotted ye and was intending to come whisper in yer ear what a tempting goddess ye are—when Anna approached me."

Violet laughed, "Damn her!" She joked, but his words sent a little shiver of delight down her spine. She snuggled in closer to Lachlan's warm muscled body, savouring the feel of being there with him.

"So what happened with Anna then?"

"Well, I tried to keep it pleasant, but then she went down the weird rabbit hole of wanting to get back together or something like that—I dinnae really ken—I was too busy watching ye with some guy," he said pointedly looking down at her.

She furrowed her brow raising up onto an elbow. "What guy?"

"He was wearing a kilt and jacket."

Violet laughed. "You just described every guy at the gala."

"Fair point," he conceded. "I saw ye go to wait for the whisky tour with him."

"Oh, Andy." It dawned on her who he was talking about. "Andy is just a friend."

"That's good to ken." Lachlan stoked her arm that lay over his chest as she settled back against him. "I suspected as much. Ye didnae look at him like ye look at me," he said rolling her onto her back and gazing down at her. He leaned in, brushing a soft kiss over one eyelid, then the other. She sighed, relishing in his affection.

"So ye forgive me for not connecting with ye after we first met?" he asked.

"Well, in fairness, I wouldn't have wanted to be your rebound girl."

"Trust me, lass, ye would huv never been that." He slid the sheet away from her breasts and glided his hand between them, making her breath catch.

"I almost became the one who got away," she confessed, taking his big hand in both of hers and pressing it against her heart.

Lachlan cocked a questioning brow.

"I was so mad at you yesterday before we met up at the bar—I had planned to leave." She toyed with his fingers as she thought back to how angry she'd been the night before—it felt like a lifetime ago now.

"As in the sanctuary?" He straightened up, and concern marred his handsome features as he looked down at her.

"As in Scotland," she said soberingly. So much had changed since then—she couldn't fathom leaving now.

"Och, God, lass." He scooped his big arm under her neck, so she rested against his bicep. He wrapped the other arm around her waist and pulled her body to him like if he clung on tight enough, the idea of her leaving would cease to exist. "Dinnae leave. Dinnae ever leave."

She laughed against his big warm chest. "Okay, okay," she said, as he squeezed her to him. "I won't go anywhere."

"Promise me, V." He squeezed her again, causing her to let out another squealing laugh.

"I promise. I promise."

He pulled back. His eyes twinkled, and then he dropped his sexy mouth to hers, capturing it in a kiss that felt heaven-sent. He moved on top of her and then broke the kiss. "Good," he said against her lips. Then he lifted his face from hers. "Now then. We have some business to discuss." He kissed her lips again, just long enough to leave her breathless and wanting more.

"I'm going to make love to ye all day and likely all night. Aye?"

"Aye," she agreed, leaning up to slide her tongue over his lips.

"Mm, lass, I'm no' done yet," he said, pulling his mouth away from hers.

She lifted a hand to his hair, gently twisting her fingers through it, and his eyes rolled back in bliss.

"I'm listening," Violet purred, knowing she was driving him to distraction.

"Right." His eyes opened on hers. "Well, firstly, effective immediately, ye are no longer an employee at Highland Haven."

Violet's hand dropped, and she stared at him. She loved working at the sanctuary. Oh God, she understood. It would look very bad for him to date his employee, and as they'd already clarified, she knew Lachlan was a good man. An ethical man. If they were going to be a couple, then of course, he couldn't let her continue to work for him.

"You're firing me?" she asked, her voice shaky.

"What?" A crease appeared between Lachlan's dark brows. "No, no, of course no'. I'm promoting you. I want you to be my business partner. And not just at the sanctuary—at Cailleach too."

"You do?" She blinked.

"Aye, I do," he said a little softer. "Do ye ken how many business coaches I've hired, how many assistants? Too many, and I ken from that very first day ye walked into the back office wanting to tell me yer ideas that ye were the business partner I'd always wanted. Yer ideas and the way ye understood things, V... Ye challenge me but make me so much better with business. I've always loved my work, but with ye involved, it is a thousandfold better, and it's no' just my opinion. The accountant has been beside himself excited at the last quarter's numbers."

Violet could hardly believe what Lachlan was saying. Her heart felt ready to burst. "I bet those numbers would have been amazing anyway," she said humbly.

Lachlan shook his head. "Trust me, love. Ye had much to do with it. Right, now where was I?"

"Business partner," Violets supplied, grinning from ear to ear.

"Aye, Effie and Iona are working together to draw up the papers so we can make it official."

"Really?" Violet was floored.

"Really." He stroked a strand of hair away from her forehead and bent to kiss her lips softly.

It was crazy how instantly his lips could melt her senses.

"There is one more thing." His voice had gone ragged, and she could feel the thick column of him pressed against her core, making little heated tingles fire off low in her belly. "I love you, Violet Munro."

His blue eyes looked into her soul, and she knew her world was forever changed.

"I know." Her voice cracked. "I love you, too. I felt it the first moment you looked in my eyes. You were my lifeline."

"Aye, and ye were mine."

Epilogue

Seven weeks later, Lachlan and Violet sat at Lachlan's parents' dining table in a room with a wall of windows that looked out to a calm, sunny sea. Spotted white seals frolicked on shallowed islands, basking in the warm summer's sun. Alex and Drew sat across from Orlagh, Violet, and Lachlan. His parents sat at the ends of the table. They'd just finished brunch. It had become a regular thing on Sundays, and usually, they were all present. Alex had missed a couple of times as he was on the special forces with the police and couldn't always get away.

According to the doctors, Orlagh had made a miraculous recovery. She'd come out of the hospital a couple of days after she'd awoken from her coma and improved quickly. Thankfully, she had no ill effects after her ordeal. Instead, it seemed to be the impetus to live life to the fullest. She was planning to go back to university in the hopes of getting her master's and then perhaps even a doctorate in psychology.

Violet loved the sentiment as she very much believed that life was short, and you had to make the most of it.

"Right, well, I believe V and I did the clean up last time, so ye all are on yer own," Lachlan said as he stood from the table, taking Violet's hand in his.

His siblings groaned behind them.

Lachlan led them out the back garden door and down the path a little way to an old wood bench that overlooked the small harbour behind his parents' home. It had become one of Violet's favourite spots over the past few weeks. They sat in companionable silence, and Violet closed her eyes, letting the sun warm her face as seagulls' calls filled the warm, salty sea air. She never dreamed that her life could be so perfect.

Ever since that first drunken night together, Violet had stayed over at Lachlan's. A couple weeks back, she'd given her notice to her landlord that she was moving from her cottage. She adored the little place, but she was barely there anymore. She and Lachlan agreed it was silly to hang onto it. Sally put her head in Violet's lap. They always brought Sally for brunch at his parents' since they also had a couple of Irish wolfhounds. The three dogs would run and play together.

"She doesnae seem to want to leave your side lately," Lachlan commented as Violet stroked Sally's head.

"Animals are very intuitive," she said.

Lachlan raised a brow, and Violet took a fortifying breath, her heart beating nervously. She had to tell him—the time had come. "I suspect Sally knows that there's a baby growing in my belly." Lachlan's brow furrowed, and she struggled to gauge his reaction. "I'm pregnant," she whispered.

His eyes grew wide as understanding dawned, and then his warm laugh rippled through her as he dropped to his knees in front of her, putting his hands on her still flat belly. She had noticed that her pants felt a little tighter as of late. She found herself popping the top button of her jeans more often than not, but she wasn't officially showing yet. Violet ran a hand through Lachlan's hair. How she adored him. Nothing made her happier than knowing their baby was growing inside her—and that the man before her seemed over the moon.

"Och, we're going to huv a wee one?" he said as if he could hardly believe it possible.

"Mmhmm." She nodded.

"Does anyone else ken? Aside from Sally." He ruffled her ears.

"Well, Orlagh guessed it last week. I didn't even know then, though. Your sister is freakishly intuitive." She smiled.

Lachlan nodded in agreement. "Aye, I ken it. Now I ken why she kept giving ye those doughy-eyed looks during brunch today. I wondered what the secret was."

"I wanted you to be the first to know, but Orlagh had me pegged. Are you happy about it?" Violet asked, biting her lip and suddenly feeling a bit nervous. Everything was happening quickly, they hadn't even talked about marriage, never mind having kids.

"Aye, I'm ecstatic, maybe a little shocked. But I'm so damn in love with ye, I cannae imagine anything better than huving a baby with ye. Our baby."

Violet felt a tear slide down her cheek as a breeze rustled the long blades of grass around them. When she looked at Lachlan again, still on his knee in front of her, he was holding out a diamond ring to her, and her eyes jumped to his as her pulse quickened.

"I suppose it's good timing. Will ye marry me, V?" He threw her an imperfectly perfect, impossible-to-resist, crooked smile.

"I— How did you know?" Violet had planned on telling Lachlan about being pregnant today, but he hadn't known, had he? "Did Orlagh tell you?"

Lachlan chuckled. "No, I didnae ken. I ken I wanted to ask ye, and when they phoned me yesterday from the jewellers to say the ring had arrived from Edinburgh, I decided to ask ye here. I ken ye love this spot."

"I do love this spot." She touched his face.

"My knee is getting wet down here, love. Tell me yer going to marry me."

Violet nodded. "Nothing in this world would make me happier than to be your wife. Yes, of course, I'll marry you!"

Lachlan scooped her up in his arms and gave her a very thorough, seal-the-deal kiss. She grew breathless as his tongue swiped against hers hungrily. She'd never tire of his kisses.

"Christ, leave those two alone for a minute, and they're going at it like rabbits in the springtime."

"Drew, dinnae be rude." Lachlan's mam scolded her youngest son.

Violet pulled her lips from Lachlan's, realizing they had an audience.

She didn't think she'd ever seen a sight that warmed her heart more. The entire Mackenzie Clan stood there watching them with grins on their faces.

"Did ye tell him about the baby?" Orlagh said excitedly.

"Baby?" Alex, Drew, and Lachlan's Dad, Allan, said in unison.

"I thought they were jus' gettin' engaged," Lachlan's dad added, looking confused.

Diane elbowed him, a silent indication to zip it, and she came over with open arms as the first to congratulate them.

Lachlan felt unreasonably nervous as he stood scanning the familiar faces seated watching him from where he stood in the beautiful, manicured gardens of the distillery. It was coming up to fall now, and the gardens were lush with blooms. It pleased him that Violet's family could be here for the wedding. He could see how happy she was to have them, especially her younger sisters.

It had been five weeks since they'd gotten engaged and he'd found out about their baby. He loved seeing Violet with a little growing bump in her belly. He'd never really thought about becoming a dad, but now that their baby was growing in its momma's belly, making her glow even more beautiful than before, it was all he could think about. He couldn't wait to hold their little one in his arms, to watch him or her grow. They loved their families, but they were both excited to start their own little family.

Lachlan's heart thudded in his chest when he caught sight of his bride at the end of the isle. Her gown was white lace, and she wore her hair up with loose tendrils falling against the smooth skin of her neck. She looked every bit the angel he knew that she was. She had to be an angel because she'd changed his life so profoundly. She truly made everything better, and he couldn't wait to spend the rest of his life with her. Everything felt perfect—beyond perfect.

The ceremony ended, and he thoroughly kissed his new wife so she wouldn't soon forget that she was his. There were hoots and hollers, cheers and whoops from their guests, but Lachlan didn't care. All he cared about was the woman in his arms. When he finally managed to tear his mouth from hers, she looked at him with hazy, lust-filled, mossy green eyes.

"I think I might need a private tour of the cask cellar before the reception starts," she whispered.

"Aye." He grinned.

Also by August Lindsay

The Scotch Series

Book 1: Scotch & Shortbread

Quinn West is a feisty chatterbox with big, innocent eyes and a sinfully tempting mouth, who doesn't know danger-- even when it towers at six foot four in front of her...

Book 2: Scotch & Dreams

If Alex Mackenzie, the brooding hot cop from *Scotch & Shortbread*, stole your heart, it's time to get acquainted with his knight-in-shining-armour brother, Lachlan. Ever the perfect gentleman—or is he?

Coming soon!

Book 3: Scotch & Stones

With a voice that's pure gravel and flirty charm that is as effortless as breathing, lead singer Drew Mackenzie melts lasses faster than honey in whisky—and that's exactly how he likes it. Or so he thinks, until Nova Thea Ellery shows up. She's logical, guarded, and impossible to impress—and she challenges everything he thinks he knows about women...and himself.

Co-Author with Eliza Rockwood: Insta-Love Novellas

The One Night Valentine

A steamy, whirlwind Valentine's Day hookup that might just turn into forever.

Grave Intentions

When sparks fly in a graveyard, love gets a little dark, a little dirty... and a lot unexpected.

About August Lindsay

August Lindsay grew up in Edmonton, just a few hours' drive from the Rocky Mountains, the backdrop for her debut novel Scotch & Shortbread. When she's not writing steamy slow burn romance novels, she can usually be found in nature-- hiking, horseback riding and taking the occasional cold plunge! She is equally happy to be curled up in a cozy chair, candles lit, reading or writing. Travelling is high on her list of life priorities, with Scotland being one of her favourite destinations. Her love for Scotland began in 2007 during her first road trip through the Highlands, sparking the inspiration for her Scotch Series. Above all, she treasure's time spent with her friends and family.

Connect with August Lindsay on Instagram, Facebook, and Tiktok. You can also sign up on her website for her newsletter, The August Files, to keep up with all the latest news!

Made in the USA
Las Vegas, NV
20 June 2025